HIS IMPROPER LADY

His Improper Lady

Candace Camp

THORNDIKE PRESS
A part of Gale, a Cengage Company

LIBRARY OF CONGRESS CIP DATA ON FILE.
CATALOGUING IN PUBLICATION FOR THIS BOOK
IS AVAILABLE FROM THE LIBRARY OF CONGRESS.

ISBN-13: 978-1-4328-9127-5 (hardcover alk. paper)

Published in 2021 by arrangement with Harlequin Books S.A.

Printed in Mexico
Print Number: 01   Print Year: 2022

For Kat.
I could never thank you enough
for all you do.
You are the best!

CHAPTER ONE

There was a screech somewhere in the building below him. It wasn't loud, but it was enough to awaken Tom in his flat on the top floor. He was a light sleeper, a habit ingrained in him from a childhood in which not letting down your guard was what kept you alive. He lay still for a moment, listening. He knew this building in and out. He'd lived here for a year, ever since Con married, and he'd spent his days in the agency office downstairs for almost fifteen years. He knew each creak or pop; normal noises wouldn't have brought him out of his sleep.

More than that, he knew how the empty silence of the building at night felt. And right now something felt wrong. He swung out of bed and pulled on his trousers, grabbing the shirt from the back of the chair as he crossed the room to the door. He eased it open and listened. Was that a thump? It wouldn't be unheard of for someone to try to break into one of the shops on the ground floor, and while it wasn't part of the bargain for the top-floor flat, he felt an obligation to protect the building. It was, after all, the closest thing Tom had ever had to a home.

He unhooked the ring of keys to the building, curling his hand around them to prevent their clinking together, and moved noiselessly to the staircase. He started down just as quietly, sidestepping the board that creaked. Stealth, too, came naturally to him.

There. Now, *that* was a thump; he was sure of it. He took the rest of the flight of stairs in a rush and emerged next to Alex's office. It was dark and silent, and he turned to look down the dark hallway.

He'd expected any intruder to be on the floor below, where the chemist and watchmaker had their shops, but it was the office at the other end of this corridor where a faint light crept out beneath the door. The office of Moreland & Quick. *His* office. He took off at a run. The doorknob wouldn't turn, the door still locked, and he ate up precious seconds fitting the key into the slot.

By the time he opened the door, the light had been doused, and a dark figure was climbing out the window. With something like a growl, Tom tore across the room and grabbed the intruder's arm with both hands, yanking him back inside. They toppled backward and landed on the floor. The thief jumped up more quickly than he, but Tom wrapped an arm around the man's calves and jerked, and the intruder crashed back to the floor on his knees.

They rose together, wrestling, but his opponent was both smaller and less strong, and Tom was able to wrap his arms around him, pinning the man's arms to his sides. Surprisingly, a tantalizing perfume clung to the intruder. Even stranger, the man was wearing not trousers and shirt, but some odd sort of clothes that clung to every curve. And there were definitely curves. Soft, inviting curves.

The thief was a woman.

Shocked, Tom loosened his hold, and the thief took advantage of it. Stamping on his bare foot, she shoved her elbow into his stomach, then twisted away. She was out the window in an instant. Tom hurled himself forward, reaching out the window for her, but his hand grasped only air.

The small dark figure was hurrying away from him along the narrow ledge of stone that ran beneath the windows. Her path was no wider than a man's hand, but she crossed it with quick assurance, one hand steadying her against the brick wall. What the devil was she going to do when she reached the end?

His question was answered when she jumped off the ledge and grabbed the iron bar that held the sign above the shops. The force of her movement made her swing, and incredibly, she seemed to be pumping with her legs to increase the momentum as she worked her way a little farther out on the bar.

After another couple of hard swings, she simply launched herself out into space. Tom's heart went into his throat as she flew through the air and landed with a roll on the metal awning of the building that abutted his own. There the woman slid down the angled awning, turning as she went. She clung to its frame for an instant to break her speed, then dropped lightly to the ground.

Grabbing a bundle that lay neatly folded beside the building, she darted up the street. The bundle, it seemed, was a cloak, for she shook it out and flung it around her shoulders while she ran. Tom watched in stunned amazement as she disappeared into the night.

CHAPTER TWO

Tom didn't move for a long moment, just continued to stare in bemusement at the spot where the woman had vanished into the dark and fog. The swirl of her cloak as she disappeared made the whole scene even more unreal, like the end of a magic act. Mysterious, even sinister . . . and utterly enthralling.

"Blimey," he whispered inadequately and shook his head, as if that would settle the thoughts and questions running around in his brain like mad things.

It had been no magic act. It had been a planned and well-executed escape. She'd even folded her cloak into a neat pile where she could pick it up as she left. God knows, she would need something to cover what she was wearing. What the devil had those clothes been?

The material had been soft beneath his hands, and it had lain as close to her skin as a stocking. The attire had covered her from neck to ankle, including her arms, but it was scarcely modest, leaving nothing to the imagination. Or, perhaps, leaving too much to the imagination, leading to all sorts of distracting thoughts. There had been an exceedingly short skirt, ending a few inches down her thighs, more enticement than concealment.

That wasn't why she had worn it, of course; obviously, it enabled her to climb a building and make those astonishing acrobatic moves. Of course! That was it. Her clothes had been the sort circus performers wore. Theirs were white and adorned with sparkling beads and sequins and such, but they were essentially the same. She was an acrobat, one of those women who flew through the air and trusted some man hanging upside down from a trapeze to catch them.

He wondered if she performed in a circus or at a music hall and broke into buildings to make extra coin. Or perhaps she'd traded in her spangles to devote herself to thievery full-time. Such skills would certainly be useful for a thief. And her skills were impressive.

Tom made a disgusted noise. What was he doing standing about admiring the thief's abilities or thinking about the feel of her breast beneath his fingers and the way her perfume had curled right through him? He needed to work out what was going on. He turned on the gaslights, brightening the room, then surveyed the damage. There wasn't much.

She was obviously a professional, her work quick and tidy. He might not even have noticed that someone had searched the place if he hadn't been awakened. He suspected the noise had come from opening the cabinet behind Con's desk; it had developed a nerve-shredding screech — he'd been intending to oil the hinges, but perhaps he should leave it alone.

Drawers here and there were a little too far out, the objects on his desk not quite in the same place. A book had fallen off a pile — no doubt that had been the thud he'd heard as he went down the stairs. But identifying the noises didn't help him figure out what she had been after. She hadn't left with whatever it was; he was certain of that. There had been nothing tucked away anywhere in that costume, and her hands had been empty. That was all to the good, but it left him not knowing what needed guarding.

Tom supposed she might have been after

money, but there was no reason to keep anything more than petty cash here. Their profits were put in a bank, and it wasn't as if they were paid huge chunks of money. No, if one wanted money, the watchmaker's or the apothecary's shop downstairs had much more valuable items. And both would have had more cash in the till from daily sales.

In all likelihood she'd been after a certain item that had some value other than a monetary one. And since professional thieves were usually interested only in money, it seemed likely that she had been hired to find this desired object. But what was it? Who had hired her? And why?

The logical answer would be that it was something to do with one of the agency's cases, so he ran over them in his mind while he went around the room straightening the little things that had been put awry by the thief. Moreland & Quick was well-known for finding and restoring missing people and lost or stolen items. Sometimes the objects were valuable, and they might store them in the office safe until they could return them to the owners, but there were none in the safe now. They had only one case regarding a stolen item, but they had yet to find it.

That left only information. Which would

explain opening the drawers and cabinets instead of going for the safe. The agency had only a few open cases. There was a woman who suspected her husband of having an affair. Another one who was certain a servant was pilfering various objects, and she wanted to identify the thief. A missing persons case that had sat in their files for months now and was for all purposes dead. Tom hadn't turned up a clue, and even Alex's and Con's special abilities had come up short.

Clearly, they had no useful information on the missing persons case. As for the wayward husband, Tom had trailed the man several times and had notes of his whereabouts. Since it appeared to him that the man not only had a mistress but also now and then visited a certain married woman, the husband, if he had learned about the investigation, might take steps to thwart it. But the information was secure in Tom's head; he didn't really need his notes. In any case, as long as the man kept up his activities, Tom would only have to follow him again.

The same thing applied to the thieving servant — the interesting thing there was that Tom had come to suspect, not one of the servants, but one of the woman's friends, but again, all he had were notes of interviews with the servants, and that information was easily obtained again, as well as being in his head.

There wasn't even one of Con's peculiar cases. Now that Con's wife, Lilah, was expecting, Con had become far less interested in eerie phenomenon and visited the office infrequently, preferring to stay at home and fuss over Lilah instead. Tom smiled faintly at that thought. Tom and Alex had a small wager over when Lilah would crack under Con's over-solicitous care and threaten him with bodily harm.

One of their old cases, then? He couldn't imagine why anyone would grab one of the old files. He went to his desk and pulled out his chair. There was still a trace of that scent in the air here, where they had struggled. It wasn't quite like any perfume he'd smelled before — exotic and lush — and it affected him as no other perfume ever had — instantly, viscerally.

Even this trace of it teased at him. Shrugging it off, Tom started to sit down. A metallic glint caught his eye, just under his desk, hidden until now by the chair. Reaching down, he picked up a delicate chain and a silver disc.

He remembered at one point feeling the

rasp of a chain across his fingers as he struggled with the thief. This must have been her necklace, and the narrow chain had broken and fallen to the floor during the struggle. Certainly, it did not belong to him and had not been beneath his desk this evening when he left the office.

Tom held it up and studied it. The disc was oblong in shape, and someone had created a small hole in one end, no doubt to put the chain through. The chain looked far more expensive than the medallion, which was probably made of tin and stamped rather than engraved. But it had a stylish look to it, and the lettering across it was in a flowing, elegant script: *The Farrington Club.*

Tom closed his fist around the token and smiled grimly. "Well, it looks like you left me a calling card."

Desiree Malone jumped out of the hackney and ran up the steps into the house, her black cloak fluttering out behind her. Hopeful that no one was awake, she slipped through the front door and started toward the stairs, her flexible, thin-soled shoes soundless on the Persian carpet.

"Desiree?"

Blast it. Of course Brock *would* be right there in the parlor. She turned toward him,

17

pasting on a smile. "What are you doing still up?"

"Wondering where you were" was her brother's dry reply. Brock Malone stood in the wide doorway of the front parlor, still dressed in his elegant evening attire, arms crossed and face frowning. "I got back from the club half an hour ago and you weren't here."

"I'm a grown woman, Brock." Desiree bristled. "I don't have to report to you."

"I am well aware of that," Brock replied. "But I saw you leave the club two hours ago, and no one knew where you were."

"We were just worried, Dez." Her twin joined Brock in the doorway. Wells was a leaner version of their older brother, though his coloring, like Desiree's, was lighter than Brock's black hair and storm-gray eyes. He had a lazy way of standing, often leaning against things or lounging in a chair, the picture of vaguely amused ennui. People who took him at face value often regretted doing so.

"Why didn't you take the carriage?" Brock's eyes went down to the front of her cloak. The pugnacious stance she had taken had pushed apart the sides of the concealing garment, revealing a large slice of her costume. "Well, you've just answered my

18

question. You've been breaking in some-where." Her brother sighed and rubbed his hands over his face. "Desiree . . . what are you doing?"

Not waiting for an answer, he waved the other two inside the parlor and closed the door. Brock walked across the room, his limp more pronounced, as it often was by the end of the day, and stood beside the fireplace, crossing his arms and leaning against the mantel to take the weight off his bad leg. Wells slouched in his favorite chair, legs stretched out in front of him, ankles crossed. He didn't scowl at her as Brock did, but Desiree could see the intense inter-est in his eyes, the alertness masked by his lazy posture.

"Now, what have you got yourself into?" Brock asked, his voice now more resigned than stern.

"I haven't 'got myself' into anything," she retorted, but, seeing the worry in her older brother's eyes, the lines that bracketed his mouth, she couldn't help but feel guilty. With a sigh, she took off her cloak, draped it over the back of the sofa and sat down. "I'm sorry for worrying you. But I had something I had to do tonight, and I couldn't tell the coachman about it."

"You could have told me," Wells pointed

out. "Why didn't you ask me to help?"

"Wonderful," Brock said sarcastically. "So both of you could get caught."

Wells turned a cool gaze on his brother. "I don't get caught."

Brock shot Wells a sardonic look and turned back to Desiree. "Going back to that old way of life, even for a night, is dangerous, Desiree. Surely you must see that."

Desiree glared. "I knew I was safe. Sensing danger is what I do, if you'll remember." She decided it was best to skirt the fact that she *had* been caught.

"Yes, we're all aware that you can recognize dangers that ordinary people cannot, but even you can't be right every time," Brock retorted. "And why would you want to go back to breaking into houses? You have no need for money. Don't I provide for you?" He made a sweeping gesture around the elegantly furnished room. "What do you lack? You know I'd —"

"I don't lack for anything. You are unfailingly generous. I didn't do it for money. I did it because Falk told me —"

"Falk!" Brock gaped at her in astonishment.

Wells jumped to his feet, his usually calm face blazing. "You were working for Falk? Good God, Desiree, what possessed you to

20

take up with that scoundrel again? Have you forgotten all the times he —"

"I've forgotten nothing," Desiree retorted shortly. "I despise the man as much as both of you do."

"Yet you stole for him." Brock came forward. "Why? What the devil —"

"I'll tell you if you would both stop scolding me and listen!" Desiree stood up. "And stop looming over me." She sent a hard look at each of her brothers, and they subsided, Wells flopping back into his chair and Brock sitting down for the first time. "Thank you. Falk asked me to break into the office of Moreland & Quick."

"Who?" Brock asked. "Why?"

"Moreland of the Duke of Broughton's Moreland?" Wells's eyebrows shot up.

"Yes, I think so. I'm not sure what the office has to do with the Morelands, but the sign says it's a detective agency."

"Oh, even better." Brock sighed.

She made a face at him. "They won't know it was me."

"I still don't understand why you did something for Falk."

"That was what he wanted from me in return for telling me who our father is."

"*That's* why you risked jail?" Brock surged to his feet again. "I can tell you who your

21

father is. He is a weak, selfish man who was unfaithful to his wife and uncaring about his children. He was a man who couldn't face up to his duty to his legal wife and who abandoned you and Wells. He fled his marriage but he didn't want to have to do it alone, so he took our mother, his mistress, with him, leaving us to starve. Why would you want to find out his name?"

"I didn't say I *liked* him. I know our parents abandoned us like a pair of old shoes. I just want to know who he was!"

"What good will that do you?" Brock asked.

"I don't know. Don't you ever wonder who *your* father was? Whose blood runs in your veins?"

"No. Never. The man is nothing to me. And the blood that runs in my veins is mine." Brock paused, his eyes dark. "Wells and I are your family. Is that not enough?"

"Of course you're enough." Desiree knew her brother well enough to see the pain that lurked beneath his stern face, and guilt swept her. She jumped up and hugged him, saying fiercely, "You and Wells *are* my family. The only family I need. The only family I want." She stepped back, looking intently into his eyes so he would see the truth there. "You've been the best brother one could have. You've always taken care of us, even when you were so young someone should have been taking care of you. You came back for us, just as you said would, and freed us from Falk. You've built this whole lovely life for us."

A smile twitched at the corner of Brock's lips and he raised his hands. "Enough, enough. You've convinced me. I am a paragon of a man." He took her hand and squeezed it, then said, "I cannot think Falk would be a reliable source of information. What did he tell you?"

"Nothing. I haven't seen him yet. I came straight home. I doubt he'll tell me anything because I couldn't find what he wanted. But . . ." Her eyes took on a sparkle. "As it turns out, I don't think I'll need him. Our father was a Moreland."

CHAPTER THREE

If she had hoped to shock her brothers, she certainly achieved her goal. Both men stared at her blankly. Finally, Brock dropped back into his chair. "What makes you think that?"

"I found something when I was in the office. I opened a desk drawer, and there was a ring inside. A ring exactly like the one you have. The one our father gave you."

"Are you certain?" Wells asked skeptically. "I mean, there must have been little light."

"I held it up to my lantern. I could see it clearly. It was just like Brock's ring. A plain gold ring with that crest engraved on it."

"A number of coats of arms look very similar," Brock pointed out.

"It was the same."

"Even so, that doesn't necessarily mean that it is the duke's crest," Wells mused.

"And you don't know that the desk where you found it belongs to a Moreland. I realize the name is on the door, but I doubt a

Moreland actually works there. He probably financed it, and the other chap does the work. What was the other name?"

"Quick."

Brock frowned. "That name sounds faintly familiar."

"You mean you remember it? Was that our father's name?" Desiree asked.

Brock shook his head. "I don't know. I don't remember your father's name. It wasn't something they would have bandied about."

"Quick doesn't sound like a patronym that would have a coat of arms," Wells pointed out.

"I can see that you two are determined not to believe me," Desiree said.

"It's not that we don't believe you," Brock protested. "I'm sure you found the ring. I'm just not sure it means what you think it does."

"I am going to find out and prove it to you," Desiree retorted.

"Are you going to break in again?" Brock asked, his eyebrows winging up in alarm.

"No. I don't like working for Falk any more than you do, and, as you said, I have no reason to believe that Falk would tell me the truth . . . or even know it."

Wells snorted. "Falk wouldn't know the

truth if it walked up and spit in his eye."

"Which is what I recommend you do if he approaches you again," Brock told Desiree. "And on that note, children," he said as he rose from his chair, "I am going to retire, though I'll doubtless have nightmares about Desiree getting hauled off to jail." He started toward the door, then turned back around. "Don't do anything foolish, Dez. Promise me that."

"I won't."

He looked at her doubtfully. "Somehow, I think that your idea of foolish differs from mine."

With a nod, he left the room. Desiree watched Brock leave, then sighed and went over to her twin. Unceremoniously pushing his feet off the stool, she sat down on it and turned to him. "I'm afraid I hurt him. I didn't mean to."

"I know." Wells nodded. "He feels guilty because he was gone for all those years, couldn't keep us from Falk."

"Brock was just thirteen, little more than a child himself. What else could he have done? And he came back for us, just as he said he would."

"I know that. Even he knows that. But I think he feels that he must have failed or you wouldn't want to find our father."

"That isn't it at all. It has nothing to do with Brock."

"Well, that's part of the problem for him, isn't it? The man's not Brock's father, just ours."

"I know." Desiree sighed and leaned her shoulder against his chair. "More than that, he despises our father."

"Well, we were only babies when our parents ran off, but Brock was six. He doesn't remember much about the man, but he was old enough to understand that he abandoned us. It's not the sort of thing that brings up tender feelings."

"No," Desiree said sadly. "He feels the same about our mother. He never calls her 'Mum' or 'Mother.' Just Stella, as if she were merely an acquaintance, not his mother."

"Yes, he has a way of keeping his distance."

They were silent for a moment, then Desiree asked, "Does it ever bother you that you don't know who our father is? Do you never wonder who he was? What he was like?"

"I have some curiosity. I wouldn't mind knowing. But I don't think it matters as much to me as it does to you." Wells shrugged. "I suppose I felt as if Bruna and Sid were our parents." The couple who had raised them after they were abandoned had always cared for them well.

"I did, too, in a way, and of course Brock was always there. The one I could go to when I needed help. But still . . . I've always wondered, is there this whole other family out there that we belong to? What are they like? Do they look like us? Know about us? I used to daydream sometimes that they would find us. That it had all been a mistake, and our mother hadn't really left us. That she had been searching for us for all those years. And she'd take us away, and our father would welcome us. We'd have cousins and aunts and uncles and . . ." She shrugged. "Stupid, I know."

"Not stupid," he told her. "I suspect all of us wished we had parents and families. That someone would whisk us away from Falk, and we'd have lots of food and a soft bed and clean clothes." They sat in silence for a moment, then Wells asked quietly, "Why didn't you tell me you were bargaining with Falk?"

Desiree shrugged. "I didn't see any reason for you to have to deal with Falk again. And if we were caught, the people you work for wouldn't like it. All I would have to face was Brock. Besides, it didn't require two people. It was just a second-floor job, easy to get in and out." She scowled. "Or at least it would have been if that man hadn't come charging in."

"What?" Wells stiffened. "You were caught?"

She waved a dismissive hand. "I knew I wasn't in any real jeopardy."

"Desiree . . ." Wells let out an exasperated sigh. "I know that you can see whether a wall is stable or what is the safest route to take, but people are different. Getting the feeling that someone is lying isn't the same as *seeing* a danger."

"But it *is* the same," Desiree protested. "You understand my physical skills better than the mental ones, because they are more like yours, but the things I can do are all part of one ability, like different currents in the same ocean." It was frustrating that as close as Wells was to her, as much as they had in common, Desiree had never been able to make him fully understand the way her talent worked. "I can see the integrity or corruption in people as clearly as I can see a crack in the wall or a drainpipe that won't carry my weight. And I can sense danger even when I haven't seen it yet. You know *that* better than anyone."

"I do," Wells agreed. "God knows, you've saved my life many a time. But I am also

29

aware that these peculiar skills we possess have limits. You have to focus your ability to read a situation just as I do, and you can't operate with your inner eye open all the time. You miss things — I know because *I* miss things. That's why we worked better together. You should have taken me with you."

"You wouldn't have been able to avoid him any better than I did. He grabbed me from behind. I couldn't see his face. I think he's probably a watchman. He must sleep there — his shirt was unbuttoned." She remembered the feel of her fingers on his bare chest — and the way his hand slid over her body, accidentally touching her breast. She'd been as startled as he was. Her fingertips tingled again just at the memory. "I'm rusty, though. I assumed there was no one there, and I was impatient. I rushed in instead of taking the time to read the place. And when he grabbed me, it took me longer to get out than it should have."

"Good thing we're not making a living off it anymore, then."

"Yes." Desiree was silent for a moment, thinking. "Do you ever miss it?"

"What? Stealing things?"

She nodded. "The excitement. The thrill of getting away. The challenge of getting in.

The anticipation."

"Sometimes," her twin admitted.

"But I guess you have that, doing whatever it is you do."

"It's a bit more comfortable when you're doing it for the government."

"Do you suppose they'd like to have a woman working for them in the shadows?"

He chuckled. "I can see old Pomeroy's face if I suggested that. Are you bored, Dizzy?"

"I hope you know that you are the only person who can get away with calling me that."

"I remember you going after Willie Sparks when he tried to. He got a grand black eye from it, as I remember."

"Lost a tooth, as well. The dolt. Everyone knew I was faster than him and didn't punch like a girl."

"But what about my question — are you bored with your life?" Wells pressed her.

"I suppose . . . a little. Not like I was when Brock sent me to that school for young ladies so I could learn to speak and act correctly."

"Mm. School was a misery."

"At least the boys at your school liked you. I could hardly get anyone to talk to me." Desiree grimaced at the memory of those

31

two lonely years.

"I was shunned at first, until they found out I could ride better and run faster than any of them. And could climb up to tie the proctor's underpants to the steeple — I was very useful for pulling off pranks."

"Yes, well, I can tell you that being able to blacken someone's eye doesn't attract many friends at a young ladies' finishing school."

"I'd guess not." He paused. "I thought after you convinced Brock to let you help at the casino, you'd be more . . . satisfied."

"I am. I enjoy my work. It's never boring, and there's ample excitement in the turn of the cards. I get to use my talent." Her lips curved up a little as she remembered that night at Brock's club a few years ago when she had swept in and proved to him how good she was at cards and how much business her presence attracted. Her protective older brother had finally had to admit that his attempts to give her the life of a lady were not working. "I must sound like a terrible ingrate. I'm not, truly. I very much appreciate everything Brock has done for me — these clothes, this house, freedom, safety. I'd probably be dead or in jail by now if he hadn't come back to rescue us. I wouldn't go back to that old life for anything."

"I sense a 'but' in there."

"But I don't really belong anywhere. I can talk like a lady, walk like one, act like one. But I'm *not* a lady. To the people we grew up with, I'm now a snob. But a gentle-woman knows at once I'm not one of them. One can't simply buy a social circle, and I don't have old friends from school as you do. Even if I did, they'd not want to be seen with a woman who spends her evenings gambling in a club. Anyway, I'd die of boredom doing nothing but paying calls and doing . . . whatever it is that ladies do. I'm not like anyone else."

"You're unique. Nothing wrong with that." Wells paused. "Desiree . . . what are you going to do if you find out our father was one of the Moreland family?"

"I don't know," she answered honestly.

"Brock is right. They had ample op-portunities over the years to see us if they chose. I don't want you to get hurt."

She looked up at him. His dark blue eyes were filled with concern. "I'm not naive, Wells. I realize that they won't look with favor on being connected to a family who owns a gambling club, much less one that used to be circus performers and thieves. I don't expect them to welcome me with open arms. I just want to know who they are."

"I know you won't rest until you do." Wells

33

stood up, reaching down to pull her up with him. Putting his hands on her shoulders, he looked into her eyes. "If you need help, call on me. You know I'll always help you. Don't worry about damaging my position with my employers." The corner of his mouth lifted. "I'm quite capable of doing that all on my own."

Desiree had to laugh. "I know. I will. I promise."

"Good girl." He released her and stepped back. "I have something I need to attend to."

"More 'shadowy' business?"

Wells just grinned and walked out of the room. She didn't hear him leave the house — he'd always been as silent as the grave — but she knew the instant he was gone. Wells left a certain emptiness behind him. Desiree went up the stairs to her room. The evening had held so many reminders of her past that she stopped inside her door and looked around the spacious room.

When they were with Falk, all the children who worked for him slept in a room smaller than this. She could still remember the smell of it, the wariness that only her twin's presence had calmed. She would never take this luxury for granted, and she would never be kin to anyone the way she was connected to Brock and Wells.

But none of that would stop her from uncovering the secrets of her past. And she was certain she was on the correct path. She had seen the faint glow of truth in the ring, felt the rightness of it in her palm. Her mind had buzzed with the implications.

That was why she'd been distracted in her search, why she'd made those mistakes — she'd never before been so clumsy as to knock a book off a desk, and it had taken her too long to hear the man's footsteps. She'd managed to get away, leaving only her lantern behind, and no one could trace a common lantern back to her. But the ineptitude was galling.

Desiree yawned, and suddenly weariness swept over her like a tide. She began to undress, undoing the buttons at the neck of her costume in the back and pulling the fitted garment off over her head. She glanced in the mirror as she folded the costume. Her heart began to pound, her body recognizing what was wrong a second before her mind identified it. Her necklace wasn't lying around her throat.

Her hand flew to her chest and she moved closer to the mirror. The lucky piece she always wore around her neck, the first gambling token she'd won at Brock's club, was gone, chain and all. Icy fear pierced her. She wasn't just rusty; she'd committed a ruinous mistake. She'd left something of herself behind.

CHAPTER FOUR

Tom Quick trotted up the steps to the entrance of Broughton House. The first time he'd seen the stately mansion, he'd been eight years old, hungry and dirty. The place was so imposing that at first he'd thought that Reed Moreland had brought him to the bobbies' headquarters. After all, it would have been the normal thing to happen after the well-dressed man caught Tom picking his pocket.

Instead, Reed had taken him into what was obviously a house, though far grander than anything Tom had ever been inside, and there he'd been fed (to his astounded delight) and bathed (over his strenuous objections) and given a clean set of clothes that had once belonged to Reed himself. Tom had never felt anything as soft as those garments. By that time, Tom had become convinced that he'd been kidnapped by a band of lunatics. He'd told his benefactor that, expecting a blow but needing to maintain his cocky image. All Reed had done was laugh and say Tom was probably right.

Over the years, Tom had become accustomed to the enormity of the duke's house and grounds in the crowded city, at least enough so that it didn't make him pause anymore when he turned up the walkway to the house. He'd also managed to train himself to knock at the front door. When he'd started working for Reed, then Olivia, he had headed instinctively to the servants' door on the side, but finally the family's badgering had pulled him into line with their determined egalitarian attitude. It was difficult to go against the tide of the Morelands.

A footman opened the door, doing his best to maintain an expression of dignity despite the puppy currently tugging on his trouser leg and growling ferociously. "Mr. Quick. Good day. If you're looking for Lord Constantine, I believe that he is still in the breakfast room. This way, sir."

The servant started to escort Tom to the room, trying to unobtrusively shake the determined puppy loose as he did so, with no success. Tom managed to suppress a laugh and said, "That's all right. I know the way."

Tom started toward the back hall just as the Duke of Broughton rounded the corner into the entryway. The older man was tall, though his shoulders had a bit of a scholar's stoop to them, and his hair was almost entirely white save for a small mingling of strands of his original black at the back of his head. Bits of packing straw clung here and there to his well-tailored suit. A magnifying glass hung on a cord around his neck, and a pair of spectacles stuck out of one of his pockets. In one hand he held a large knife. His other arm was courteously given to the woman beside him.

The woman carried herself proudly, her back straight and her head high. What Tom could see of her hair beneath her hat was an iron gray, not a strand out of place. Even though she was too squarely built to achieve the sort of elegance that the duchess displayed, her clothes were expensive and fashionable, if somewhat conservative. She might have been attractive if not for the sour expression on her face.

The duke was saying, "Sorry I couldn't help you, Tabitha. But I promise I will look into it."

"If you remember," the woman replied tartly.

"Certainly, certainly. I'll tell Smeggars. That'll do the trick." The duke looked up and saw Tom. "Why, hullo, Tom." He smiled at Tom in his usual benign way. "Nice to see you."

"It's good to see you, too, sir. How are you?"

"Quite well, thank you. I've been unpacking a new crate. It had an excellent Cretan knife." He held out the knife for Tom to examine. "A very nice terra-cotta head, as well — only a bit of the chin knocked off."

"Very nice, sir." The knife looked like nothing but a battered old knife to Tom, but the duke was always so pleased about his acquisitions that Tom would never say anything to disappoint him.

"Really, Henry," said his companion, who clearly did not have the same qualms about disappointing the duke that Tom did. "All this puttering about with old pots and tools is so undignified."

"Mm, yes, I suppose it is," Henry replied affably. "Never paid much attention to dignity."

"Obviously," his companion said, her gaze turning to the harassed footman, who had finally freed his trousers from the puppy's mouth and was now trying to catch the pudgy little thing. The puppy, finding it a

40

fine game, darted around, jumping and barking merrily.

"I beg your pardon, I haven't introduced you to Mr. Quick," Henry said, oblivious to the noise behind them. "Tabitha, this —"

"For pity's sake, Henry." Lady Moreland's eyes swept over Tom dismissively. "I am not accustomed to being introduced to servants."

The duke looked taken aback. "Oh, but Tom's not a servant." His brow furrowed. "How do you know their names, then?"

She heaved a sigh. "Goodbye, Henry." She gave him a short nod, adding, "Don't forget."

"Yes, of course." The duke watched her walk away. When the door closed behind her, he turned back to Tom. "Sorry about that. She's a bit . . ."

"Haughty?" Tom suggested.

"Precisely." The duke's eyes twinkled. "Well, one can't choose one's relatives, more's the pity." He shrugged. "Ah, well. Are you here to see Con? I believe he's back there." He gestured vaguely down the hall. "I must get back to my crate. Good to see you."

"You, too, sir." Tom nodded to him, and the duke strode eagerly back down the hallway. Tom turned the other way, heading toward the babble of laughter and voices. There was no telling how many of them were in there; three Morelands could manage to sound like an army of people.

In fact, when he stopped in the doorway, he could see that it was only a few of them — the twins Con and Alex and their wives, along with Megan, holding her youngest daughter, Brigid, while Alex played some sort of hand-slapping game with Brigid's slightly older sister, Athena.

"Quick! Quick!" Brigid crowed when she saw him, reaching out to him. For some reason, the two moppets seemed to have a particular fondness for him. Tom suspected it was because of his name; *quick* was a word perfectly suited to Theo and Megan's little girls.

Tom took the child and rubbed noses with her in their customary greeting. Athena ran over to throw her arms around his legs in a hard hug, then abandoned him to return to her game. Tom shifted Brigid to his hip. "I see you have a new puppy."

That statement was a mistake, for Brigid's face clouded and her chin began to tremble. "Rufus went to heaven."

The aging dog had passed on six months ago, but clearly Brigid was not yet over it. Tom felt a moment's panic at what to say.

"Um, yes, I'm very sorry. I'm sure Rufus is looking down on you, and he's glad that you have a new puppy to love. What's the little dog's name?"

"Rufus Two-fus," Brigid replied, brightening. "Where's Two-fus?" She looked around and wriggled down from his arm.

"Let's find Rufus!" Athena joined her sister, and the two tore out of the room.

"I better go save the poor puppy," Megan said and started after her girls. "Nice to see you, Tom."

Aside from the Greats, Megan was the Moreland with whom Tom felt most at ease. She was from the States, and, like other Americans, lacked a proper understanding of class distinctions. Moreover, she had grown up in a rough-and-tumble neighborhood of New York City, more akin to Tom's own background.

"Likewise," Tom said as Megan walked out the door. He turned back to the four people left in the room. The black-haired, green-eyed twins, Constantine and Alexander — given the appellation of the Greats because of their names — were almost like younger brothers to Tom. It was hard to be in awe of someone when you'd taught him how to pick locks.

"Sit down," Alex said, sweeping a hand at

the empty chairs. "Want some breakfast? It should still be warm."

"No, thanks. I already ate." In fact, the roll he'd grabbed from the bakery hadn't erased his hunger, but Tom had long been reluctant to accept the food the Morelands frequently offered. It was foolish pride, he supposed, but he hated to appear that he was using the family in any way.

"Could I get you some coffee, then? Or tea?" Lilah, whose plumper face and rounded stomach were finally beginning to show her pregnancy, started to rise from her seat.

"No, no, I'll get it." Con patted her arm and jumped up.

Lilah rolled her eyes. "Con, I'm not an invalid."

But Con was already at the sideboard, pouring a cup of coffee and handing it to Tom. "What brings you here this morning?"

"Well, I wanted —" Tom was interrupted by the entrance of a servant, cradling a blanket-wrapped baby in her arms.

"I think Miss Marjorie has decided it's time to eat," the nanny said, and Sabrina, Alex's wife, rose with alacrity to take the child from her.

"Tom, you must see the baby. You won't believe how much she's grown." Alex, beaming, went to stand with his wife and gaze down with delight at the baby. "How long has it been since you've seen her?"

"A fortnight, I expect," Tom answered, going dutifully over to look at the baby. Tom was of the opinion that the baby was prettier than most infants even though her tiny head was bald as a billiard ball, but he always found it hard to see the changes in growth that the proud father proclaimed. It was easier and kinder, however, to agree. "Ah, yes, she has grown. She's a beauty."

He held out a finger, which one wildly flailing hand latched onto and tried to drag to her mouth before realizing that it wasn't food, at which point she screwed up her face and began to howl.

The nurse and Sabrina quickly left the room, but Alex dropped back into his chair. "I'm of utterly no use there."

"I believe she's louder than even Athena," Con said with something like pride.

"Just wait. Yours will be louder still," Alex retorted. "It's only fitting."

"I was not a loud child," Con protested, to everyone's amusement.

"Boys," Lilah said. "Let Tom tell us what he came to say."

"Yes, Mum," Con replied, taking her hand and smiling at her in a besotted way before turning back to Tom.

"Someone broke into the office last night."

"Moreland & Quick?" Con's brows shot up.

"Yes, the agency." He glanced over at Alex. "No one got into yours. I don't know if I caught her before she could make her way down to it or —"

"Her?" Lilah interrupted. "The intruder was a woman?"

"Yes. Though she didn't fight like one. We wrestled a bit, and she stamped on my foot and punched me in the stomach. Then she went out the window and walked across the ledge like a cat."

"What ledge?" Alex asked.

"Exactly." Tom nodded toward him. "The stone that's below the windowsill runs all the way across. Couldn't be wider than six inches. Then she swung across to the awning next door and slid down it and was off like a rabbit."

The other three stared at him. Con said, "I don't know whether I'm more surprised that someone broke into our office or that she exited like that. Did she take anything?"

"Not that I could tell. You'd have to come down and look to make sure she didn't get something from your desk, but there was nothing gone from mine, and I couldn't see that any files were missing. I'm positive she wasn't carrying anything when she left."

"Why would anyone break into our office?" Con mused. "Something about a case, you think?"

"I don't know what else. It's not like we have any cash or valuables there. She didn't break into the safe, but I don't know if that's because she wasn't interested in it or she just hadn't reached it yet."

"Do we have a case that would warrant that? I haven't been paying much attention lately, I know, but nothing I can think of would make anyone want to steal anything from us, even information."

"I wouldn't think there would be too many thieves who can move like that," Alex pointed out.

"No, she obviously has acrobatic skills. I'm going to ask some people I know." He didn't need to finish the thought. Everyone knew that Tom kept in contact with people in the criminal world. "But I have another clue." He reached into his pocket and pulled out the gambling chip. "This came off in the struggle."

The other three leaned closer. "The Farrington Club," Lilah read. "What's that?"

"It's a fashionable gambling parlor," Alex explained. "A casino. It's very exclusive. You must be a member or come with someone who is. Or have an invitation."

"I don't know what I can learn from this place, but obviously this gambling chip has special meaning to our thief. She wore it on a chain around her neck, and the chain broke."

"My guess is it's a good luck charm," Con said. "Gamblers are notorious for believing certain rituals or objects can bring them luck at the tables."

"Want me to see if I can get anything from it?" Alex offered.

His words didn't surprise Tom. He was well used to Alex's unusual ability to draw information from inanimate objects. They'd used it many times at the detective agency to help them find a lost object or missing person.

He handed Alex the charm, and the other man closed his hand around it. He shut his eyes as well, as it was easier to focus on the object that way. After a moment, Alex said, "Lilah?" She reached out to lay her hand atop his. For reasons none of them understood, Lilah was able to increase the Moreland twins' odd abilities, though it worked better with Con than with Alex.

"Yes, that's better. But I still can't get much that would help you find her. It belongs to a woman, but I get no picture of her. There's a sense of happiness with it, but there's more — triumph, perhaps? I'd guess she's had it for years, and there's a great deal of affection for some other person attached to it, as well." Alex sighed and handed the charm back to Tom. "I can see a large indoor room, ornate, smoky and full of people and tables. It looks like an expensive casino, but it could be that I'm seeing it because I already know what sort of location it is. No faces. That sort of thing is always more difficult to discern. I'm sorry."

"Yes, I'll have to go there to find out anything," Tom responded.

"But would a thief belong to an expensive club?" Lilah questioned. "And do women frequent such places?"

"A few women, but not many. And I think she'd stand out."

"But how are you going to get inside if one has to be a member or hold an invitation?" Lilah asked.

"I have an invitation," Con said. He glanced at his wife. "I've never used it, you understand. But they've sent me one more than once."

"And you've never offered to take me there?" Lilah said indignantly.

"Well, um, I presumed you wouldn't care

to be seen in such a place."

She laughed. "Darling, when I married you, I tossed aside all thought of adhering to society's rules." Lilah gave Con a playful push on the arm. "Go on. Get that invitation for Tom and go to the agency. I know you want to investigate."

"Are you certain?" Con asked doubtfully. "You felt ill yesterday."

"Feeling ill is a solitary occupation, my love. And since I just ate a trencherman's breakfast, you can see that I am not ill today. If I have an emergency, I am surrounded by servants and a good number of your family. And if you stay here, asking me how I feel or if you can fetch my needlework for me, I shall wind up throwing something at you."

"You know, there are a number of women who would appreciate their husband's concern," Con told her with an offended air.

"Perhaps you should have married one of them," Lilah retorted sweetly.

"Don't be silly," he told her, grinning. "Then whom would I have to annoy?"

"Con. Go." She leveled a firm gaze at him, but her smile when Con bent to kiss her cheek belied any irritation.

The three men went to the office, invitation in hand. Tom paused outside the front door to show the others the thief's escape route. Alex whistled in admiration, and Con walked about a bit, going to the awning next door and back. Like his twin, Con possessed a particular ability. He had an innate sense of true north and could often pick up a person's trail. Con walked slowly up the street to the next intersection, head down, then returned to Tom and Alex.

"It's hopeless," Con said in disgust. "I've been working on tracking specific people, but I still have difficulty unless it's someone close to me. I can see which way you went this morning, Tom, and there are lots of traces of all three of us around here. But in public places like this, where so many people have walked, it's hard to distinguish one trail from another. I think I picked up her track, but it soon vanished completely."

Upstairs, Con looked through his desk and files and found nothing missing. Alex was able to pick up some emotions of excitement and fear, but the place was too much fixed with the presence of Con and Tom for him to acquire any information about the thief. Alex soon went down the hall to his architectural office, and Con sat down to go through the stack of mail on his desk before starting on a more thorough search of their files. Tom went looking for information from his various contacts who lived in the shadowy world of petty criminals.

Though in his childhood Tom was part of that world, few of his acquaintances from that time were still around. Most had died or were in prison; a few had moved into more legitimate pursuits. But over the years at the agency, he had cultivated several criminal contacts who were willing to sell information.

Unfortunately, none of them knew of a female housebreaker. Even his most reliable informer in the world of thievery, a pickpocket named Pike, looked at him skeptically. "A girl? Doing upper-story work? Nah . . . there ain't many of that sort to begin with — too hard. Easier to jump," he said, referring to the practice of breaking into a building through a ground-floor window. "And women?" He snorted. "There's plenty of judies that swipe a bloke's wallet and run. Or take something from a shop, like. But climb like a cat?" He shook his head.

"What about the Farrington Club?" Tom asked.

"That fancy club? Above my touch, lad."

"Any pickpockets working it or thieves

finding marks there?"

"Maybe some swell magsman," Pike said doubtfully. Tom knew he was talking about the sort of well-dressed swindlers who duped their victims into giving them money. "But that place is particular. Takes more'n a few quid to get you inside."

"What about robbing them when they come out?"

"Most of that lot get in their carriage or a hack, don't they? The cabs are lined up outside the door. Two guards outside, too, dressed up like footmen. They keep it clear all around the place. No point in it — easier to wait at some boozer to catch a drunk. 'Sides, more'n yer life's worth to try it. 'E warned us all when he opened it, din't 'e? Don't touch 'is customers if you value your 'ealth."

"He? Who is he?"

"Bloke that owns it, 'oo do you think? Name's Malone. Blew in from Australia ten or twelve years back. Learned pretty quick not to go up against 'im. 'E's a bruiser, and 'is men, too."

"Do you think he's cheating his customers?"

Pike shrugged. "Nobody wins but the house — everybody knows that 'cept a fool. But I never heard nothing about it being

53

any worse than others. But then, I don't know the sort wot goes there."

"Do you think he uses the place to find marks?" Even as Tom said it, he knew that was unlikely. Malone would be making too much legitimately to risk losing customers if word got around that thieves were targeting his customers.

Tom handed Pike a few bills and left. It was clear he wasn't going to find out a great deal more here. He needed to see the place for himself. If he was lucky, his quarry was a regular at the club and might turn up in person.

That was probably wishful thinking; anyone who was high enough on the social ladder to get into the exclusive club would be unlikely to spend her spare time breaking into businesses. It was just as possible that it had been in a pile of loot she had stolen or that she'd found it on the street. Maybe she was a charwoman at the club and had swept it up for the dustbin — though he had some trouble envisioning a woman that daring working at anything so mundane. And if that were the case, why make the chip into a necklace?

No amount of reason could completely suppress his hopes, though, and Tom set out that evening for the Farrington Club in high anticipation. His stomach was a little knotted with nerves; walking into a nest of criminals would cause him less anxiety than trying to pass himself off as someone who belonged in an elegant club. He would have felt more at ease had Con accompanied him, but Con hadn't wanted to spend the evening away from Lilah.

Tom had been careful to dress for the occasion, wearing the same silk waistcoat and tailored suit that he'd worn to Con's and Alex's weddings. His prized possession, the gold pocket watch Reed had given him when he finished his education, hung on a chain, tucked into his waistcoat pocket. He felt a bit foolish with the top hat on his head, but it finished the picture of a gentleman out for an evening of pleasure. He'd been around the Morelands long enough to realize that simplicity gave one more an air of entitlement than flashy rings or jeweled tie pins.

But the proper clothes could not give him the air, the carriage, the underlying surety of one's high place in the world that graced a man raised in the genteel world. He had worked on his accent; he didn't sound like someone from a rookery. Still, he couldn't quite emulate the sound of someone who was born to it.

Tom had never been one to show his fear, though; indeed, he'd been told time and again that he was too cocky for his own good. He'd brazen it through; confidence was what swayed people. He stepped down from the Morelands' town carriage — he had agreed with Con that it was the perfect touch to make anyone believe his status as a gentleman.

As it turned out, the doormen sent him through with a mere glance at his invitation. Inside he managed to glance around with casual interest, not gawking at the ornate chandeliers that lit the large room or the textured wallpaper or the intricate plaster moldings on the ceiling and the heavy red velvet curtains. The place exuded wealth to such an extent that it seemed almost a jest, a playful parody of pretension. Tables were all around, surrounded by men and a few women.

Tom strolled around the room, maneuvering to get a glimpse at each woman — was this one too tall, that one too curvaceous, or another too fragile — as he inspected the games and the participants. There weren't many women, and none fit the description. He saw terror in eyes that were riveted to the roulette wheel and the wild avidity in another face as a man rolled the dice.

Servants passed with trays of champagne; two of the black-and-white clad servers were women. It occurred to Tom that this sort of occupation would be better suited to the intruder. He could see nothing suspicious about them as they smiled and offered drinks to the patrons, but then he doubted that his thief would be obvious. Like him, she would keep her inspections casual.

Smaller rooms branched off here and there, and in these were fewer tables, just one or two, and they were devoted entirely to cards. He paused in the doorway of the third secluded room, and his heart picked up its beat. There was a lone table in the room, though a number of other men crowded around behind the players, looking on.

The reason for the onlookers' attention was clear: at one end of the table sat a woman in a cherry-red gown, the neckline wide enough to reveal her creamy white shoulders. Little puffs of sleeves left most of her arms as bare as her shoulders. A ruby teardrop dangled at the end of a silver chain around her neck.

In the soft golden light of the chandelier, her hair was the color of caramel, and it was done up in a puffy pompadour roll, soft wisps escaping at her temples to drift temptingly beside her face. The top half of her face was hidden by a mask of white and silver, a long white feather curling back over her hair. Below the mask, one could see a straight nose, firm mouth and rather determined chin. Her eyes inside the mask were light in color. She might not be beautiful, but she was utterly arresting. Tom could not look away.

She raised her head and looked across the room at him, and her eyes pierced him. Almost unconsciously, Tom edged around the others watching the game, moving closer to her. She did not look at him again as she continued with the game, keeping up a light chatter and smiling.

Tom maneuvered his way to a spot barely a foot away from her. Perfume drifted up lightly, a haunting, unusual fragrance that made him think of midnight and sultry heat and exotic flowers opening on a twisted vine.

He had found his thief.

CHAPTER FIVE

Desiree noticed the man the moment he entered the room. It wasn't usually something she did; she kept her full focus on the men at the table and the cards. Those who liked to hang about watching were as much background as the walls or the noise from the main room.

But tonight her eyes flicked up at the movement in the wide doorway, and her brain seemed to stutter, her concentration falling. She wasn't sure what it was about him that caught her attention. Like many other men in the room, he was well dressed, but nothing flashy. His hair was blond and his eyes light colored, blue, she thought, or maybe gray. He was neither tall nor short. A man, in other words, who should blend in. But there was something about him that made him . . . different.

She pulled her eyes back to the game. Yet still Desiree was tinglingly aware of him.

She felt more than saw him as he moved around the table toward her. It was fortunate that she held a strong hand, for she had glanced away just as the man next to her called her bid and thus she had missed her chance to watch him as he bid.

There was little to see now in her opponent's cool demeanor. The next man, Herbert Collins, who returned to her games so frequently that she now knew his name, folded. That didn't surprise her: Collins was dreadful at the game of brag; his emotions were so easily readable that she always knew whether he had drawn a good or bad hand, without even using her talent. The third man had already dropped out of the game, and the next one joined him and Collins.

Desiree suspected she could increase her probable winnings by going another round and concentrating on reading the other players with her inner eye, but she was confident of her three-card hand, and she was suddenly eager to end the game. So she smiled and doubled the bet, calling to see the cards. As she had expected, her pair royal easily topped her opponent's jack.

She filed away the man's action for the next time she played him; he was a man who thought he could win by bluffing. Not as easy to defeat as poor Mr. Collins, but not likely to win over the course of time. One needed more skills than just the ability to lie, including a healthy respect for the odds.

"Gentlemen, I believe it's time to take a rest for a few minutes before we start a new game, don't you?" She gave them a dazzling smile and rose without waiting for any response from her fellow players.

As she turned away from the table, there was the man she had noticed, holding out a glass of champagne to her. Desiree rarely drank while she played, but she found herself taking the glass from him. Her fingers grazed his; his skin was a little rougher than most gentlemen's, and the feel of it against her own skin made her tingle.

Excitement quivered in her stomach. It wasn't danger exactly, or at least not wholly that, for she could feel the simple *rightness* of him. It was more the way she felt right before she stepped out onto the tightrope — a little scared, but filled with eagerness. To cover the unaccustomed nerves suddenly dancing in her stomach, she took a sip as she regarded him over the top of her glass.

Up close she could see that his eyes were blue, though marked with crystalline striations radiating outward that gave his eyes a bright, penetrating quality. There was a small curved scar beside his mouth that intrigued her — indeed, his whole mouth intrigued her. He wasn't handsome, exactly; his face was too puckish for that. He was . . . different. Interesting. And she wanted to keep on looking at him. For a long moment, she did exactly that.

"I don't believe we've met," she said, wanting to know his name, wanting to hear his voice.

"No, this is the first time I've come here. But now I'm very glad I did." He grinned, and a dimple popped into his cheek. Desiree's pulse leaped in response.

"I hope you are enjoying your visit." Her words were mundane but infused with meaning.

"Very much." Like her, the look in his eyes said much more. "I wish I had come here before."

"Perhaps you'd like to sit in on the next hand?" she offered. His presence would be far too distracting, but she wanted him to stay.

"No, I'm not much of a gambler. But I enjoy watching." The glint in his eye made it clear that it was not the game that he wanted to see.

"Really? I would have guessed you were more a man who likes to participate," Desiree replied archly.

There was no dimple this time, but a slow and rather wolfish smile, his eyes darkening a little. "I do . . . when the reward is worth the gamble."

"So you must be sure that there's no risk?" Unconsciously, she edged closer.

"No, sometimes the risk is the heart of the pleasure." His eyes went to her lips, and he moved a degree nearer, bending a little toward her.

"Desiree?" Brock said, and she started, the moment broken. She turned to her brother and was surprised to find him standing only a yard away. She hadn't noticed that he'd come into the room. Indeed, she had not noticed much of anything. "I think your table is getting a trifle restless."

Brock was looking not at her but at the man she'd been flirting with, his hard gaze sizing him up. He'd picked the worst time to display his protective brotherly instinct. "Oh, yes, of course." She took Brock's arm, turning him and urging him toward the table with her. She cast a farewell smile over her shoulder at the man whose name she still didn't know, much to her annoyance. She leaned toward Brock and said in a low voice, "Don't you dare embarrass me."

"Me? How would I embarrass you?" He

gazed at her in a puzzlement she recognized as feigned.

"I'm not sure. But you were looking distinctly antagonistic toward him."

"Who is that man? You could have at least introduced us."

"I don't know," she admitted. "And don't you interrogate him, either. I *like* him, and I'm not going to have you scaring him off."

"If you don't even know his name, somebody ought to find out who he is." He started to turn to look back, and Desiree gave his arm a jerk, stopping him.

"Not *you*." She fixed him with a stern gaze. "*I* will talk to him, and I will find out who he is and what sort of person he is. And if you go over there and harass him, I will not speak to you."

"Yes, ma'am." Brock grinned. "I will thoroughly ignore him. So long as you promise not to do anything reckless."

"Me?" Desiree looked up at him in faux innocence, batting her eyelashes. "Reckless?"

"Yes, you." Brock grinned but left her at the table and walked out of the room.

Desiree sat down and picked up the stack of cards and began to deal, casting a discreet glance toward the spot where they had been standing earlier. Her mystery man was still there, leaning against the wall, arms crossed, watching her, just as he'd said. She wondered if he'd purposely not told her his name.

It could have just been a slip, something pushed aside in their flirting. On the other hand, she had given him the opportunity to introduce himself, a bold move, she knew, in the genteel world in which he lived. So why hadn't he taken her up on it? Most of the clientele here would have jumped at the chance. It was part of her mystique to stay aloof, just as her flamboyant masks were, and men frequently attempted to engage her in conversation, to introduce themselves and learn her name in return. Yet he had not. It made him even more intriguing.

Desiree turned her attention to the cards, determined not to be distracted into making a mistake. But now and then, between hands, she glanced over and saw him still there. He changed locations a few times, but for the next hour, he remained in the room.

However, when she called the game to a halt sometime later and stood up to leave, her mystery man had disappeared. She took a stroll through the main room, glancing around in what she hoped was a casual way. She retrieved her stole from the cloakroom and turned to cast another long look around the club before she walked out the door. There was no escaping it: the man was gone.

Tom sat in the carriage, curtain drawn back a sliver so he could watch the front door of the club. He'd wanted to stay and talk to her again. But that was a foolish impulse, one he should not have made the first time. It would be impossible to have another conversation with her without telling her his name. And as soon as he did that, she'd know who he was and why he was there, and he would lose all chance of figuring out who had hired her to break in.

He hadn't intended to talk to her. Well, the truth was he hadn't expected to find her so easily. But if he should be so lucky, his plan had been to follow her — see where she went, to whom she talked. But when he saw her closing the table for a moment, he'd grabbed a glass from one of the waiters and intercepted her. Even then, he hadn't thought she would actually start a conversation with him. He had just wanted to see her up close, to measure her height against his to make sure she matched the thief, to try to make out what she looked like without the mask.

Tom had thought she would brush aside

his advance; she must be approached every night by a bevy of men. Instead, she had taken the glass and struck up a conversation with him. He thought now about their interaction — the challenge in her smile, the flirtation in her eyes, the sensual undertones beneath their words. There was no denying his response to her, the way his blood had heated, the enjoyment he'd taken in their banter, the temptation he'd felt. The urge to move closer, to touch her, to kiss her.

He hadn't been thinking at all, and it wasn't until the other man interrupted — sending an unaccustomed stab of jealousy through him — that Tom had come to his senses. He wasn't going to get anything from her this way. She wasn't going to toss the information he sought into the midst of a flirtation.

However much that subtle scent teased at his senses, however tempted he was to kiss her, that was never going to happen. They were on opposite sides. His task was to find out what she'd been trying to find when she searched their office. And why.

Tom had continued to watch her play. She won the majority of the games, and when she didn't win, she nearly always folded quickly, losing little money. Her stack of chips grew steadily. Tom thought she must be cheating, but he couldn't figure out how.

Tom knew sleight of hand and deception. He'd seen it and engaged in it often enough when he was a child. He'd been almost solely a pickpocket, but he knew enough of the ways to cheat at cards to be able to pick up the signs.

He watched from several different angles. But he could see no indication she was hiding cards — where the devil would she put them, anyway, with her arms as bare as they were? The cards didn't appear to be marked. He saw no signaling to her from any of the men standing behind the other players, nor could he find any mirrors on the walls or ceiling to reflect their hands.

Whatever she was doing, she was clever about it. And that, too, roused his interest in the woman. He'd been sorely tempted to remain and talk to her again. He could, after all, use a false name, but for some reason he found himself reluctant to lie to her. And there was really no benefit in a conversation. So after an hour or so, he made himself leave the casino and return to the carriage to wait.

And think.

Desiree, the man had called her. The name suited her. Exotic. Evocative. Like the

68

scent that clung to her. Tom murmured the name; he liked the way it felt on his tongue.

Who was the man who had interrupted their conversation? Obviously he was someone close enough to her that he addressed her by her first name. But what exactly was he to her? Husband? Lover? Tom's chest tightened at that thought.

Perhaps he was her employer. Perhaps he was the Australian "bruiser" Pike had said owned the club. Though he walked with a bit of a limp, he certainly looked well able to take care of himself in a brawl. Employers often used the first names of their employees. It could have been not closeness but status. Perhaps he hadn't liked her wasting time rather than disliking her talking to another man.

Tom liked that idea better — though obviously that was even more foolish than talking to her had been. Desiree was the thief; she had to be. Standing next to him, she was the right height, the right size. And it went far beyond coincidence to have two women who were connected to the Farrington Club and also wore the same distinctive perfume. She was his quarry, nothing more.

And his quarry had just appeared.

Tom straightened, every sense on the

alert. Desiree paused just outside the doorway, casting her gaze around. Tom waited, hand on the door, ready to slip out and follow her as soon as she walked away. But she didn't leave, simply chatted with the two outside guards.

A carriage pulled out of the line of waiting hackneys and town carriages and rolled up to the entrance. One of the doormen jumped to open the door of the carriage and give Desiree a hand up into the vehicle. He closed the door after her, and the carriage rattled off.

"Follow them, Jenkins," Tom told the driver on high seat in front of him. "Not too closely."

"Aye, sir." Jenkins was used to the peculiar actions of the Morelands and didn't question Tom's instructions.

As they rolled through the night, a discreet distance behind Desiree's carriage, Tom mulled over the implications. The carriage was an elegant equipage, with an equally fine matched pair pulling it. Obviously a private vehicle, not to mention an expensive one, which indicated that the owner was wealthy.

If it was hers, she must be raking in quite a bit from her thieving and card playing. At least enough to hire a carriage to pick her up every night from work. Or perhaps her employer provided the safety and comfort of such a ride for a valuable employee? Certainly Desiree was enough of a draw to the business that it would be reasonable for him to not let her walk home through the dark city streets.

Even more likely was the possibility that it was provided by a husband or lover. Who could very well be the owner of the Farrington Club, as well. Tom's hope was that it was none of these things but instead belonged to whoever had hired Desiree to search the office and that it would now take her to that person.

Her trail led into an area of elegant homes. Not as imposing as the Moreland neighborhood, of course, but still, the houses were large and attractive, with small green areas scattered throughout and the streets lit by ample streetlamps.

Her carriage pulled to a stop in front of a redbrick house, and Jenkins stopped, as well, pulling over close to the curb some distance away. As Tom watched, Desiree exited the carriage, looked up to say a few words to the driver, then went straight into the home without knocking.

Obviously she lived here. It made the wealthy husband far more likely; it was rather a large place for a mistress. Either that or she actually belonged to the social class of the Farrington's patrons, which was ridiculous. Even the Morelands, as free and eccentric as they were, would not let a daughter go running about alone in the middle of the night, playing cards at a casino. Equally unlikely was the idea that the place belonged to whoever had hired her to thieve for him; she wouldn't have just walked into his home without knocking.

"Shall we wait, sir?" Jenkins's voice came through the filigreed screen between them.

"Yes, for a bit. It's odd that the carriage is still sitting in front of the house."

"That it is. Someone's going to be leaving the place soon."

"Let's see who leaves and where they go. Sorry to keep you up so late."

The coachman let out a brief laugh. "I don't mind. It's always interesting working for the Morelands."

Tom settled back to once again take up watch through the sliver of window not hidden by the curtain. His suspicion was that the man at the casino was also an occupant of the house — who else would be so permissive about her visiting the casino alone? But then why was the carriage waiting instead of turning around and heading back to the Farrington Club to bring the owner home after the club closed?

He didn't have to wait long before the front door opened again and Desiree emerged. She was no longer wearing the stylish red evening gown but a plain dark dress of the sort the duchess usually wore when she went out to one of her protests. Sensible dress, she called it, or practical dress, something like that. Rational dress — that was it.

So, clearly Desiree didn't wish to be encumbered by numerous petticoats, corset, and the ludicrously puffed sleeves that were coming into style. But she wasn't wearing the costume she had on last night, so it seemed unlikely she was going back to burgle someplace — perhaps his office again. It raised his hopes that she was about to lead him to the man who wanted something in the agency's office.

"Follow her," he told Jenkins. "Very carefully."

Jenkins waited until the carriage was some distance ahead, then pulled out into the street and rumbled off after it. The quarry left the pleasant neighborhood behind, and the surroundings grew progressively seedier as they went, until it seemed they were heading into the sort of area that Tom had been so fortunate to get out of.

Dark cramped buildings huddled together and the streets grew ever more narrow until they were little more than paths, twisting and confusing to any outsider. Streetlights were few and far between, all too likely to have been smashed, leaving large areas of dark shadows.

What the devil was the matter with the woman? This place was dangerous, even if one was in a carriage. She was nimble and as fast as a rabbit, not to mention capable of landing a few hard blows of her own, but she would be easily overcome by a man bent on robbery, or worse.

It was becoming harder to follow her vehicle without being noticed, for there was very little traffic here and it was easy to lose sight on the twisting lanes. Ahead of them, the carriage slowed, then came to a stop, and Jenkins pulled up short, as well. The door opened, and Desiree jumped down and walked purposefully away.

"I'll follow her on foot," Tom told Jenkins, slipping out the door. "Go home. I'll manage on my own."

The carriage they had followed had driven off, leaving an empty and quiet street. Tom didn't like being out and about in these clothes. His blond hair was too noticeable, but he'd be damned if he'd stroll around here wearing a top hat.

He rounded the corner, keeping his steps quiet. He spotted her in the distance as she passed under a streetlight. Tom trailed after her. She turned the corner at a tavern, and Tom used the noise of the place to pick up his pace without her hearing him.

Tom turned where she had and came to a halt. She had disappeared. He hurried forward, thinking she must have turned again at the next available lane. Had she spotted him? Just as he reached that corner, he heard a thump behind him. Before he could turn around, he felt the barrel of a pistol jammed into his ribs.

CHAPTER SIX

Tom froze in place.

"Raise your hands." It was *her* voice.

He did as she commanded, torn between relief that it was Desiree, irritation that she had spotted him and a reluctance for her to see who he was.

"Turn around." With a sigh, he obeyed. Her eyes widened. "You?" She recovered quickly. "Who are you? Why are you following me?"

He didn't bother to deny it. Instead, he said, "How in the blazes did you get behind me?"

The corner of her mouth quirked up, her eyes sparkling in amusement. "Like most people, you never think to look up."

"Damn," he said more in admiration than annoyance. She hadn't run around the corner. She'd clambered up a building and followed him, dropping down to ambush him from behind. "I've never met anyone who could do the things you do."

"You never will," she retorted. "Now, answer my questions. Who are you? What do you want?"

"I want to ask you a few questions," he replied. "My name is Tom Quick."

He saw recognition hit her eyes, but she said only, "Is that supposed to mean something to me?"

"Why did you break into my office last night? What were you after?"

"I don't know what you're talking about," Desiree said airily.

"No? Then I guess you're not interested in what the thief left behind." He reached into the pocket of his waistcoat, noting that she hadn't even warned him not to pull out a weapon. She might be a superlative burglar, but she wasn't all that good at holding a gun on someone.

Tom held up the token he'd found under his desk. Her eyes lit, and she grabbed for the charm. He let her take it, instead reaching out and wresting her gun away from her. "Now. Let's have a conversation."

"I'm not saying anything to you." Desiree clenched the token in her fist. "You going to shoot me?" She whipped around and started to walk away.

Tom reached out and gripped her wrist,

whirling her back around to face him. "No, but I'm going to bloody well find out what you're up to."

Her eyes went past his shoulder, and to his surprise, she began to scream. "Help! Help me!"

He jerked his head around and saw a policeman running toward them, baton in hand. Desiree seized the opportunity to jerk her hand away, and she took off running, leaving Tom with the gun and the bobby.

"Bloody hell," he muttered as a beefy hand closed on his shoulder. She had outwitted him again.

Desiree darted back the way she'd come, anger fueling her feet. The wretched man had lied to her!

A drunk lurched out of the tavern as she passed it. He reached for her, but Desiree avoided him easily. The companion right behind him let out a hoot and started after her, obviously less drunk than his friend. Desiree increased her speed. Frankly, she was in the mood for a chase tonight.

As she ran, she cast her mind out around her, and the faint outlines of buildings unfolded in her head. Ahead of her on the right was a wall, but its match in her head was only a thick smudge of darkness, warning her away.

But across the next intersection, light glimmered. And though the area was shadowed and murky, in her mind light spread across the side of the building, illuminating the empty cart beside it. The men following her laughed as she sprinted straight toward the wall. Desiree pulled up her skirts as she ran and tucked the ends into her belt, freeing her legs. She took a running leap into the cart, continuing to the higher end without pause and springing up from it to grab the sign above the shop. From there, she scrambled up to the top of the sign and climbed the wall, her feet and hands finding the holes and misaligned bricks.

Grinning at the roar from the men far beneath her, she reached the top of the building and pulled herself up and over onto the roof.

She climbed up the slant of the roof to the top and stood up, looping her arm around the chimney and looking all around her, orienting herself and giving her a moment to catch her breath. Clearly, she was no longer accustomed to running this much. Indeed, she wasn't as good in any way as she had been at fourteen. She'd been caught twice by Quick. And then she hadn't even sensed that his intentions toward her were bad. It was galling.

Knowing she had lost the gambling chip, she ought to have stayed home for a few days. She shouldn't have taken the chance that she'd lost it on the street instead of inside the office. Perhaps Wells was right; she should have taken her brother with her. Wells had always been the more careful of the two of them.

The two men, thwarted of their prize, walked away, complaining. Desiree could have climbed back down to the street, but she did not. This was her territory, and she loved moving across the rooftops, as familiar to her as the streets below. She turned and walked along the center beam of the roof to the other end.

The building behind this one was flush against it, and it was a short drop down to the roof below, which shone like a beacon, calling her. She swung down and made her way across the buildings crowded up against one another. Her mind was still attuned to her extra sense for guidance; it had been years, after all, since she'd used these routes, and things deteriorated. Darkness bloomed along the edge of the one roof and over a patched spot on another, so she avoided both. She came to a gap of a few feet between buildings. A sparkling line stretched out in front of her across the span, and she took a running jump to land lithely on the other side.

Desiree came to a stop when she reached her favorite place, and she sat down on the ledge edging the roof. The street below was blanketed by fog, and it was as if she were sitting on a cloud. There had always been peace and solitude here. Freedom.

During the day, one could see the dome of Saint Paul's from here, poking up through the haze, as well as the steeples of other churches and the tops of the Houses of Parliament. But now the view was only fog and darkness, everything hidden and still. It was the perfect place to think. She thought about what she'd found at the office of Moreland & Quick and what she was going to do about it. She thought about her mistakes. And she thought about Tom Quick.

That smoldering gaze, the faintly suggestive banter, the whole pretense of liking her had been an act. And she had fallen for it, lured by a pair of bright blue eyes and a charming smile. It was galling. *He* had deceived *her.* She'd been as gullible as any mark.

How could her instincts have been so wrong? She hadn't felt the danger in him, hadn't sensed the lack of integrity in his motives; she'd felt only her own excitement. Maybe Wells was right, and she was too quick to assume a moment's perception was reliable. She knew a practiced flirt often glossed over a corrupt intention, yet she hadn't tried to look deeper. Maybe she hadn't wanted to find it in Tom. Clearly she should have focused her talent, sought out his intentions, been more suspicious of his interest in her. Instead, she had let herself be led astray by the sizzle of attraction.

Not only that, she hadn't even noticed that he was shadowing her. It had been the coachman who had alerted her to that fact. Quick must have been behind her since she'd left the club. He'd followed her home and had sat there, waiting. He'd followed her into the East End. And she hadn't seen it, hadn't even looked. She'd been too occupied wondering why he left the club early.

It was some compensation that she had outwitted him tonight. Desiree smiled to herself at the memory of his irritated face. No doubt he'd been equally frustrated when she left him to explain to the peeler why he'd been holding a gun on a woman.

Tom Quick would still come after her, of course. Well, she welcomed the chance to go head-to-head against him. She could hold her own. She wouldn't be stunned at seeing his face, as she had been tonight, and she would deny his charges. There was nothing he could prove. He'd get nowhere with the police.

She was no longer a street urchin. She was now a genteel woman, a woman who could look and sound the part and the sister of a man who was wealthy and not without power. Brock would never be accepted by society any more than Desiree herself, but he had more than one member of the police in his pay, as well as a couple of aristocrats who were in his debt.

On that pleasant thought, she left her perch on the ledge and made her way to the next roof, where she could climb down the drainpipe and cross the street to Falk's place. Falk had moved on from being a kidsman. After his success with Desiree and Wells breaking into houses, the man had gradually transformed his business into the more lucrative field of burglary, as well as adding a bit of extortion to round things out. Street urchins required too much effort and expense — after all, he had to go out and watch the little pickpockets and beggars to make sure they were doing their jobs, as well as give them a bit of food and a floor to sleep on.

Desiree was glad. She would never have come here if she'd had to face children suffering the same life she once had. It gave her a degree of pleasure knowing that the Malones had over the years made sure that Falk's operation running children became more and more difficult.

She went up the stairs, and one of Falk's men let her through to his office. Falk was bent over a ledger on his desk, and he looked up at the sound of her entrance. His clothes and his place were a bit nicer than of old, his hair liberally streaked with gray and his girth more fat than muscle now, but he was still the same Falk — same dark flat gaze and bitter slash of a mouth. So full of lies that she barely had to tap her power to see all the black outlines overlying Falk again and again. As if she was looking at his image in a refracting prism.

"Desiree!" he said in a false tone of good cheer, his lips twisting into a smile. "Ready to come back yet? Lots of money to be made."

"By you," Desiree retorted.

"I'd give you a better cut now, of course."

"Better than nothing? Impressive."

"Now, I always let you have some of the baubles," he said in a wheedling tone.

Desiree snorted. "Enough to buy more

84

food than the gruel you gave us." Sad to say, Desiree knew she and Wells had been treated better than some of the others. At least he had refrained from beating them, since sore bruises and broken bones would interfere with their work. "That doesn't mean you weren't scum. You still are."

Falk scowled, slamming his palm down on his desk. "I rescued you. You'd have starved if I hadn't taken you in."

"You took Brock from us! You knocked him over the head and threw him on a boat to Australia!"

He opened his hands and swept them out, palms up. "And look where it got him."

"You're saying you did him a favor?" Desiree wanted to jump across the desk at Falk and take him by the throat. But there was nothing to be gained by railing at him. The man had no conscience; he would never feel guilt over what he had done. She pushed down her anger and said tightly, "I'm not coming back, Falk."

He grimaced, but he dropped the subject. "Did you get the letter?"

"No. Quick came in on me, and I barely got away. Why didn't you warn me that he watched the place at night?"

"I didn't know. You can't expect me to do

your work for you," Falk retorted. "Go back."

"I searched most of it, and I don't think the envelope is there. The only things I didn't check were some old files."

"If it's not there, go to the Morelands' house. I know they have it."

"Well, you'll have to find someone else to get it for you. I quit."

"You can't quit." Falk glared at her in the way that had always struck fear in her heart when she was a child, his eyes piercing and cruel, his lips drawing back, like a dog about to attack. "I'm not giving you your father's name until you bring me that envelope."

"That look doesn't scare me anymore, Falk." Desiree was pleased to realize that her words weren't a lie. The scrawny little girl had trembled before him, but the present Desiree felt nothing but contempt. "And your bribe won't work, either. I already know my father was a Moreland."

Falk's eyebrows shot up, confirming her theory, but he covered his surprise quickly. "Ah . . . but which one?"

"That's what I'm going to find out."

CHAPTER SEVEN

Tom managed to extricate himself from the clutches of the bobby. Fortunately, he was dressed like a gentleman tonight, which made the policeman more inclined to believe his story that he was struggling with a woman who'd tried to steal his wallet. But by the time he did so, Desiree was long gone, and there was no hope of finding her, so he returned to the office.

Tom didn't think even someone as brash as Desiree would attempt to break in again tonight, but he slept in the office, just in case. He'd slept in places a lot less comfortable. Still, he had trouble going to sleep. He kept thinking about the events of the evening. About Desiree.

He found that she was on his mind when he woke up the next morning, as well. He was torn between chagrin at losing her — again — and a sneaking admiration for her cleverness. Tom was not a man to take defeat well, but somehow her outwitting him made his attraction to her all the more compelling.

She was a challenge. She was a mystery. He had lived much of his life around the women of the Moreland family — intelligent, independent women who frequently broke the rules. They had, he supposed, formed his image of an ideal woman. It seemed cruelly ironic that when he finally stumbled upon a woman who was as fascinating and unique, as unconventional, even outrageous, she would turn out to be his adversary.

Unfortunately, that adversary currently had the upper hand. She knew about him now, and she would be very careful not to let him follow her again. In fact, if he was able to follow her, it was all too likely to mean that she was leading him into a trap. But he couldn't think of a way to draw her out, to get her to come to him. He had no idea what it was she was after.

He knew where she lived. He could confront her, but he had no idea how he could make her tell him what he wanted to know. There was, however, a possibility that he could negotiate with her. He was positive she was working for hire. Desiree was professional enough to realize that she was unlikely to be able to filch anything from the office now that Tom was on guard.

If she couldn't produce what the employer wanted, she was unlikely to get paid. So if Tom offered her money to reveal who had hired her and what that person wanted, she might be willing to do it. Of course, it was just as likely, if not more so, that she might not.

Still, it would be worth a try. Of course, he'd have to get her to talk to him long enough to hear his offer. That could be a problem.

As he pondered the matter, he heard someone climbing the stairs. It was a heavy tread, unlike the way Con or Alex usually trotted up, and that roused his interest. There was only one other office on this floor besides this agency and Alex's business, and it was empty. He and Con were considering expanding into it.

The footsteps passed Alex's office, and Tom looked toward the open door, curious about the possibility of a new client. The visitor stopped in the doorway, and Tom's jaw dropped. The man was the last person he would have expected to see.

"Falk!" Tom jumped to his feet, a turbulent mix of emotions flooding him — anger, resentment, wariness, and even a faint echo

89

of the years-old trepidation. "What the devil are you doing here?"

Tom couldn't remember his life before this man. Falk had always been there; the cramped room he shared with the other children the only home he'd known until he was eight years old. Falk had been a kidsman, and Tom had been one of the lads he used to pick pockets or beg for coins. Tom hated him as he hated no one else.

"Now, is that any way to greet the man who raised you?" Falk strolled into the room and sat down uninvited in the client chair beside Tom's desk. "Sit down, lad, and let's talk." He glanced around the office. "You've done pretty well for yourself, haven't you?"

"Get out of my office." Tom remained standing, unwilling to give any indication that he accepted Falk in this place.

"Now, lad, is that any way to talk? After all I did for you?"

"The only good thing you ever did for me was tell me to steal Reed Moreland's wallet."

Falk's eyes flashed, his lip curling, but he said nothing.

"I'm surprised you'd risk coming here without a guard," Tom went on. "I understand you keep a punisher with you nowadays." He crossed his arms and regarded the older man. It had been over twenty years since Tom had last seen Falk; his nemesis had grown flabby and gray. He'd always had an ingrained fear of the man; the last vestiges of that fell away. Tom let out a sigh and sat down. "What do you want, Falk?"

Falk gave him a poor imitation of a smile. "I came here to make you a proposition, lad."

"You can't be serious. Why would you think I would be willing to do anything for you? You couldn't offer me enough money."

"How about information about your mother?" The sly smile on Falk's face was more natural.

Tom's heart began to pound, but there was no way he'd let the man see how much he wanted what Falk offered. He kept his voice level. "I wouldn't believe anything you told me."

"No? Who do you think gave you to me? I didn't pick you up on someone's doorstep."

Tom hated to give Falk the satisfaction, but he couldn't keep from asking, "And what is it you want me to do for you in return?"

"Just a small thing. Hardly anything, really. The Morelands will never miss it."

"You want me to steal something from the Morelands?" Tom was so astonished that for a moment he didn't even feel angry. Then rage came flooding in, turning his eyes to blue flames, and he stood up, planted his hands on the desk and leaned forward, looming over Falk. "You think I'd do anything to harm the duke? To harm any of them?"

"It's no harm. Nothing that'll hurt the duke. He'll never even know it's gone. Not anything to do with him, really."

"It was you!" The realization burst into Tom's head. "You're the one who sent her here to rob us. You're the one who hired her!" If he had been capable of more rational thought, Tom might have wondered why the idea that Desiree worked for his old enemy enraged him so much, but he was far too consumed with anger to analyze it.

"Desiree? So you figured that out?" Falk's mouth twitched in irritation. "She really has lost her touch."

Cursing, Tom grabbed the other man by the lapels of his jacket and jerked him out of the chair. "What the hell do you want with the Morelands?"

Falk let out a scornful laugh. "You think I'm going to tell you?"

"Who is she? What do you want?"

The other man sneered. "I don't give

anything away for free. You ought to know that."

"Tell me, dammit." Tom shook him. "What are you after?"

"You want answers? Do the job for me, and I'll give them to you."

Blood pounded in Tom's brain, and he wanted to slam his fist into the other man's face. But he knew he would get nothing from Falk now. Any answer Falk gave him was more likely to be a lie than the truth. Tom cursed himself for refusing the man's offer so quickly and fiercely. He'd let his anger overcome his good sense. He should have pretended to be interested in the job long enough to find out what Falk was after.

Tom flung Falk back down in the chair in disgust and stepped back. "Stay away from the Morelands. You hurt any of them, and I'll make you regret it for the rest of your short, miserable life. Now get out of my office."

Falk stood up, ostentatiously straightening the jacket Tom had twisted, and Tom roared, "Now!"

The other man gave up his attempt at dignity and whirled around to hurry from the office. Tom stood for a moment, fists knotted, then grabbed his jacket and shot out the door.

He didn't need Falk. There was another person who knew the answer to his question.

Desiree had finished her breakfast — the household always had a late-morning meal, given their late-night schedules — and was climbing the stairs to her room when there was a thunderous pounding at the front door.

Behind her, Templeton opened the door. "Sir! What do you —"

"Where is she? I want to see her."

Desiree stopped. She knew that voice. Her pulse began to race, and she turned to look down at the entry.

Tom Quick had pushed his way past the butler, swinging the door shut behind him. Desiree gripped the banister and leaned down to see him better. Was he really as intriguing as he'd appeared last night? She decided he looked even better in the daylight. His blue eyes were bright, his hair attractively tousled.

Why was he here? A treacherous hope leaped in her chest, even though she knew it was untrue.

"Really, sir!" The butler huffed, clearly putting on his most imperious air. "I have no idea who you are or what you're talking about, but you cannot simply —"

"Desiree!" Quick snapped. "Get Desiree. *Now.*"

No. He was definitely not here to make amends. Desiree started back down the stairs. "I'm here. I don't know what you think you're about, but there's no need to bully Templeton."

"Miss Malone, I'm so sorry." Templeton turned to her, his face flushed. "I don't know who this man is, but there's no need for you to worry. I'll send him on his way."

Tom snorted. "You think you're going to toss me out?"

Templeton turned almost purple, and Desiree hurried forward. "It's all right, Templeton. I know this very rude man. I'll talk to him."

"Miss, I don't think it's safe to be alone with him."

"It's fine," she assured the older man, alarmed that he might actually try to restrain Quick and get himself hurt. "I can handle it, I assure you."

The butler stepped back, looking uneasy, and Tom walked past him, his attention focused on Desiree. "You belong to Falk!"

Desiree's brows shot up, her own temper rising. "I don't belong to Falk or anyone else. If you'll lower your tone and act like a civilized person, we can go into the parlor to speak. Templeton, some tea, perhaps?"

"I don't want any bloody tea," Tom barked, but he turned toward the door she indicated and strode before her into the parlor.

Desiree nodded reassuringly at the butler and followed him. She was certain Quick, for all his anger, wasn't about to get violent with her.

Tom swung toward her, his eyes still flashing with fury. "I just talked to Falk. He wanted me to do the job since you'd failed at it."

She quirked a brow, a little stung by his description of her break-in. "I haven't 'failed' at anything. That was merely a first effort."

"There won't be another one." He strode forward, looming over her. "I'm not letting you or Falk or anyone else steal anything from the Morelands."

Desiree crossed her arms and gazed back at him coolly. "And you think you're going to stop me? You haven't exactly done a good job of that so far."

"You try it again, and this time I'll put you in jail. I know who you are, Miss Malone." He said her name as if it were an insult. "I know where you live. I'll have the

96

peelers here in five minutes. How do you think all those toffs that come to Farrington Club are going to feel about losing their money to a known thief?"

"Your threats don't frighten me."

"Falk is scum. How the devil can you work for him?" Quick asked, his voice calmer now. He sounded almost disappointed.

"I agree, he is. And I don't work for him. I haven't for fourteen years."

Quick's face changed subtly. "You were one of his 'kids,' too?"

"*Too?* You worked for Falk, as well?" Desiree looked at him doubtfully. "I don't remember you."

"I left him years before you were there, I'm sure." He stepped back and hardened his voice. "That doesn't mean I'm your friend."

"Clearly."

"You're still working for him. I don't believe it was coincidence that you broke into our office two days before Falk shows up, wanting me to steal something from the Morelands for him."

"It's not. But I told you the truth. I don't work for him. This was a one-time job. He said he'd tell me who my father was."

"That seems to be a common theme with him."

"But I'm not doing anything more for him. I'm not going to pursue it. I don't need to." She hesitated, then took the plunge. "I found out my father's name — Moreland."

Tom couldn't have looked more dumbfounded if she'd told him her father was Prince Edward. "The duke?" He let out a short, scornful laugh. "If that's your tale, you'd better rethink it. No one is going to believe that the duke was unfaithful to his duchess."

Desiree could feel herself flush at his laughter. But she was not going to be deterred by ridicule, even if it did sting more than his laughter. "There's more than one Moreland. I don't know his first name."

"The Moreland men are notorious for falling hard and staying that way. They aren't the sort to stray."

"I don't know whether you're naive or lying," she retorted.

"Neither. I just know the Morelands. Whatever scheme you have in your head is not going to work."

"I have proof." When Tom raised a disbelieving eyebrow, Desiree rushed on, "My brother has a Moreland ring."

"A what?"

"A ring like the one in the upper desk drawer in your office. It has their coat of arms on it."

"That's your proof? A ring? Anyone could have a similar ring."

"I didn't say similar. It's the same. I'll show it to the duke, and —"

"Don't!" His eyes blazed. "Don't you dare bother the duke. Stay away from his house and stay away from my office."

"You can't stop me!" Desiree shot back, clenching her fists and taking a step forward.

"The hell I can't!"

"What the devil is all this?" Brock barked from the open doorway. "Who the hell are you? How dare you yell at my sister?"

"I'll tell you who I am." Tom swung toward her brother. "I'm the man who's going to blow up your little swindle."

"Swindle!" Brock's eyebrows rushed together. "What the —"

"You —" Quick jabbed a finger at Brock, then at Desiree "— and your sister, peddle your scheme somewhere else. Leave the Morelands alone."

Brock glared at Tom, lowering his head in a way that reminded Desiree of a bull about to charge. Tom faced him, his fists clenched and his eyes bright, looking as though he'd welcome a brawl. Desiree stepped between them, holding out a hand to her brother. "Brock, don't . . ."

"Don't worry, Dez, I won't break up your furniture. He's not worth it." Brock turned a contemptuous look on Tom. "Get out of my house."

"Gladly." With a last dark glance at Desiree, Tom stalked out the door.

CHAPTER EIGHT

After Quick stormed out of their house, Brock turned to Desiree. "Care to explain what that was all about? Wasn't that the fellow you were talking to last night?"

"Yes." Desiree let out an angry huff of air. "His name's Tom Quick."

"Of Moreland & Quick." Brock studied her. "Is he pressing charges? Do I need to call my solicitor?"

"No. He's not going to do anything to me. He's angry because he found out Falk hired me. I told him about the ring and my father. He knows that trying to do anything to me will mean a scandal for his precious Morelands." Her voice was bitter; she could deal with the man's anger, but the contempt in Quick's eyes burned her.

"Will it?" Brock asked. "Mean a scandal?"

"No! How could you ask that? I don't have any desire to *do* anything to the Morelands."

"What is it you do want, Dez?"

"I don't know," she replied candidly. "I just . . . I don't know anything. About them. About him. I never knew him, never knew my mother."

"You were only a baby when they left."

"I don't even know what she looked like. I mean, Bruna told me when I asked her, but you know how Bruna was — it was 'blond hair, blue eyes' and a shrug."

His mouth twitched up on one side. "Bruna was never one for words."

"Tell me about our mother, Brock. You knew her. You can remember. What was she like?"

Brock sighed. "Let's go to my study."

They walked down the hall to Brock's study, and Desiree sat down in one of the wingback chairs grouped before the fireplace. Brock went over to a cabinet and poured himself a glass of whiskey.

"Bit early for that, isn't it?" Desiree teased. "It's not quite noon."

"Somehow I think this conversation deserves it." Brock sat down with her and took a sip. "Very well. Our mother — I don't remember a lot. I was only six when Stella left. She was blonde and blue eyed, as Bruna said. Her hair was lighter than yours, more the color you and Wells had when you

102

were little, almost golden. She was very pretty, but when she smiled, she was absolutely stunning. That was her nature, too — bright, sunny. She was . . . fun.

"I remember her teaching me to tumble — not the very first lessons, because I must have started when I was two or so, but later, around the time when she put me in her act." He glanced at his sister, explaining, "I did the same sort of thing you and Wells did at first — Stella dressed me up as a cherub with a little harp. My halo happened to fall off, and I chased it as it rolled across the stage. The audience roared, so she incorporated it into the act. I don't really remember that. She told me about it so many times, though, it seems as if I knew it."

"I remember doing that act," Desiree told him. "Wells would pull my hair or untie my sash, and I'd chase him about trying to hit him, and we'd do flips and cartwheels and all that." Desiree stopped abruptly, remembering the young Brock, sitting apart, watching them, no longer a part of the act. "I'm sorry. I — maybe you'd rather not talk about the act."

He shook his head. "It doesn't bother me. That was long ago. And accidents happen."

"But it didn't have to," she said hotly. "They should have checked that rope. You wouldn't have fallen. If we had been in London, they could have found a better doctor. He could have set your leg straighter."

"And we should have listened to you. It was just that you were so young and no one knew about your gift. But I think you feel worse about it than I do." Brock smiled faintly. "It wasn't the end of the world. I was able to do other things around the circus. A little limp has never stopped me from doing what I wanted. The acrobatics didn't mean that much to me. I was never as good at it as you and Wells. Besides, I would have grown out of acrobatics. Sooner or later, I'd have been too big. Now, as I remember, you wanted to talk about Stella . . ."

"Yes. Go on." Desiree wasn't sure how much she believed her brother's denial, but it would serve no purpose to pursue the issue. "You were telling me about her teaching you to tumble."

"Stella was patient, a good teacher — not as good as Bruna was. Stella was too easygoing. She let mistakes slip by without saying anything. But we laughed a lot in my lessons, and afterward, we'd have milk and biscuits. And she sang. I remember her singing me lullabies at night. She had a lovely voice. We had this little one-room place — I only vaguely remember it — but it was cozy. Then she met your father, and everything changed."

"What do you remember about him?"

"Even less. He was tall and slender. He looked a bit like Wells, now that I think about it. Not his coloring. His hair was dark. I don't remember the color of his eyes — something light, I think. But his face, his body had something of Wells in them."

"Do you remember anything else? Anything about him?"

"I'm sorry. I know how much you want to know about your father. But it was so very long ago, and I was a child. Children look at things differently. Mostly what I recall is that everything was different after that. We moved into a bigger house, where I had my own bedroom. There was all this space. I remember liking to run up and down the stairs. But suddenly everything revolved around *him*. Stella was with him or she was thinking about him. Buying his preferred wine, keeping the humidor filled with his favorite cigars, preparing the dishes he liked. And crying when he didn't come for dinner as he'd said he would."

"She was unhappy?"

"More often than she had been before he

came along. She was giddy with happiness when he was there, when she was getting ready for his visit, but he was only there sometimes. A few hours here or there. No doubt he had a wife and another family. Legitimate children. I think she cried as much as she laughed. She was besotted with him. It shouldn't have been any surprise when she ran away with him."

"You disliked him."

"Yes." He sighed. "I don't know. I'm not sure how much of my opinion of the man was colored by the fact that he took Stella away from us, that he left us behind like old luggage. There was no reason for him to care about me, but you and Wells were *his* children. So, it's hard for me to remember exactly how I felt before that happened. I'm not sure if I *dis*liked him. But I didn't like him, either."

"Was he mean to you?"

"No, not at all. Whatever else I think about him, he was obviously mad for Stella. He wouldn't have done anything that would make her unhappy. He tried to win me over. That's why he gave me that ring you set such store by. He was trying to please Stella. I knew it was only a bribe."

"You kept it all these years," she pointed out. "Through everything that's happened."

"I kept it for Wells. It's his heritage."

"Yet you've never given the ring to Wells."

He glanced at her sharply, but he didn't speak, only stood up and went to pour himself another drink.

"Did I hear someone take my name in vain?"

Desiree and Brock turned to see Wells standing in the doorway. His tone was light and unemotional, but Desiree noticed that his hair was uncharacteristically mussed and his color high, his posture not as languid as usual. She wondered what he'd been up to, but she knew she'd never find out.

"Dez thinks I should have given you your ring," Brock told him, pouring his brother a drink.

"My ring? That's your ring, old chum . . . although it seems that our Dizzy has quite an interest in it, too. Well, you two will have to sort it out. I have no interest in it. I don't fancy jewelry."

"Mm," Brock said noncommittally and handed Wells the glass. "At least nothing that's identifiable."

Wells crooked an eyebrow at him, but said only, "Now . . . why are you discussing this ring?"

"Brock was telling me what he remembers about our parents."

107

"Which is damned little," Brock added.

"I take you're still intent on finding out who sired us," Wells said to Desiree.

"Yes." She turned to Brock. "What did people call him? Surely someone must have said his name."

"My lord — that's what the servants called him. Stella . . ." Brock looked off into space. "She called him 'my love' and 'darling.' She'd say to me, 'His lordship is here, and he has a headache, so you must be quiet, love.' "

"Wasn't anyone else ever there? A friend?"

"There was a man." Brock frowned. "I don't recall his name. He visited sometimes. He seemed to be his friend, but . . . he'd visited us before then, too."

"You mean, he was an admirer of Stella's, too?" Wells asked.

"I don't know — I wouldn't think a former admirer would still visit after your father had set Stella up as his mistress, would you? And your father was quite friendly with him, as I remember. Perhaps he was merely a friend of both. He was a jolly sort of fellow. I liked him better than 'his lordship.' He used to give me candies."

"Was he — Do you think he might have been *your* father?" Desiree asked.

"Anything is possible." Brock shrugged.

"But no one ever said anything like that. Stella told me my father was a hero, a commander in the navy who was lost at sea. Obviously that was a fantasy, but I've no clue who the man really was. I don't really care."

Desiree sighed. "I've no idea how to find out any more about him. I could go to the duke, I suppose."

"And get shown the door immediately," Brock said. "Probably by the butler. I don't think dukes are easy to meet."

"What about Sid Upton?" Wells asked. "He was Bruna's husband. Even if she wouldn't tell us, she might have told him."

"No. I've asked him before," Desiree said. "He doesn't know anything."

"But you have something now that you didn't have before — a name. If you asked him if he'd ever heard of a Moreland in connection with our mother, it might jog his memory."

"Old people love to talk about the past," Brock put in, interested despite his resistance. "And now that he's retired, he has plenty of time to think and remember. If nothing else, he'd enjoy a visit from you."

"Did you ever show Sid that ring?" Wells asked.

"No," Desiree admitted. "I didn't know

that it was important."

"That's it," Wells told her. "You have to know what to ask when you're questioning someone. Show him the ring. Give him the name. Tell him about this chap that Brock remembers. He might know who that friend was."

"You're right." Hope began to rise in her. "All I ever asked him was what Bruna had told him about our father."

"They all worked in the same music halls even though they were in separate acts," Wells pointed out. "He could have seen your father waiting for Stella outside the stage door. Or he could know some other performer or friend. And surely they came to visit her at the house after Stella stopped working. After all, they were good enough friends to our mother that they took in her children after Stella left. One doesn't take on a six-year-old and a pair of infants for a casual acquaintance."

"Not many would have done that even for a close friend," Brock said. "They were kind people."

"Yes, they were," Wells agreed. "They were our parents, really."

"It was a good life," Desiree agreed. "I enjoyed it — the tricks, the traveling."

"Bruna the Italian Angel and the Magnificent Malones!" Brock raised his glass in a toast, smiling in reminiscence. "It was grand rolling into town in the wagons. All the people turning out, following us to the edge of town."

"The horses with the plumes on their heads, the harnesses shined, the wagons all decorated," Desiree added.

"You remember you and Wells sitting on the lead horses?" Brock said. "And they'd have me dressed like the ringmaster in the driver's seat, holding the reins. It made everyone laugh."

"And gasp when you pretended to fall out the side, then scrambled back in." Desiree laughed. "Wells loved the parades."

"I did," he agreed with a smile. "I loved everything to do with the horses. You, as I remember, were scared of them."

"I was. I had no desire to learn the riding tricks with you."

"Wells has always been a bit mad," Brock said. "My heart used to be in my throat, watching you ride around the ring, Wells, standing on the horse's back. You were so little up there. And absolutely fearless."

"Oh, I had plenty of fear. I'd fallen off enough times — once the horse almost kicked me in the head when I tumbled off."

"The best trick was when you'd jump off

the horse onto the platform and somersault off, then run around and back up the steps and jump onto Bonnie's back again as she ran by."

"More like trotted by," Wells told her. "The timing was everything there. But it wasn't that dangerous. Not like you walking across the tightrope."

"I always had a net." Desiree leaned her head back against the chair, remembering. She could almost smell the sawdust and feel the rope beneath her feet. The gasps of the audience as she flew through the air from her trapeze into Sid's hands, the breathless silence as she walked across the rope, the thunderous applause. "It was fun."

"Most of the time," Brock agreed. "Of course, there was also the time when the circus disbanded in the Cotswolds and we had to make our way back to London on our own."

"True. As I remember, Sid kept to the city and the music halls after that," Wells said.

"The Royal Aquarium. The Golden Palace. I thought they were so glamorous."

"And we could nab food from the vendors." Wells grinned.

Brock let out a little huff of a laugh. "True. It was a good life." His face darkened. "Until the fire."

Wells nodded. "Until Falk."

The conversation died after that, and Desiree left her brothers, going up to her room. Her anger at Tom Quick hadn't died, just simmered beneath the surface during her talk with her brothers, and she could feel it bubbling up again as she climbed the stairs.

She didn't fault him for being upset that she had broken into his office; it was a violation — even though one would think it might have counted for something that she hadn't stolen anything and had taken care not to damage the place in her search. Annoyance, even anger, was understandable, especially given the fact that she'd slipped out of his grasp twice.

But last night he had seemed more frustrated and chagrined at being bested than anything else. Today, it had been fury that shone from his eyes. Obviously, he hated Falk; that was understandable, too. But why had he lit up like a Roman candle when she'd said she was a Moreland?

Desiree remembered the way he'd looked at her, the utter contempt in his eyes. *She,* obviously, was a nobody, someone who would stain the entire family just by existing. As if she was the one who had done something wrong, not the man who'd indiscriminately spread his seed around. A Moreland, apparently, could do no wrong in Tom Quick's eyes.

She snorted, thinking of his claim that all the Morelands were utterly faithful to their wives. You'd think they were a family of saints, the way he talked. He couldn't possibly be that naive. What business was it of his, anyway? It wasn't as if she was threatening Tom in any way.

He wasn't a Moreland — well, perhaps that wasn't the case. Desiree rethought the matter. He could be related — a different last name didn't mean anything. His mother could be a Moreland or perhaps he was another illegitimate child. It gave her a faintly queasy feeling to think that there might be a chance he was related to her, even distantly. She'd been *attracted* to the man.

It was humiliating to think how very much she had been attracted to him. She'd initiated a conversation with him, flirted with him, made it obvious that she was interested in him. That was something she never did. There had been other men whose smiles had beckoned her or whose faces and forms drew her eye. She wouldn't deny that she had flirted with men now and again. After all, what fun was life if one went through it like a wooden statue?

But she never made the first move. In all things, just as in the games, Desiree played her hand coolly. She took her time and never betrayed her interest. Her head ruled her senses and emotions. Perhaps, as Brock said, she was too daring for her own good, but she was not that way when it came to men. She had her mother as an example of what not to do with her life.

But when she saw Tom, all that careful reason had vanished. Something about him had lit her up inside. She'd let him know; she'd made it clear. She'd been a perfect mark. And Tom had played his part perfectly. The way he had talked to her, the way he had looked at her, the way he had moved closer, his head bending toward her.

How could she have been so mistaken? Knowing people was her specialty, for pity's sake! It was infuriating.

In her bedroom, Desiree quickly divested herself of her clothes and pulled on the garments she had worn to enter Quick's office. Over that, she threw on her cloak and put on her flat, flexible slippers. Going down the back steps, she slipped out into the alley behind the elegant houses.

A row of mews sat across from the houses. She walked past the one directly behind their house, where their own carriage and horses were kept, going farther down to one that had once belonged to another house. Brock had bought it from the family, who had given up keeping a town carriage, and he'd had it outfitted for Desiree and Wells.

Unlocking the door, Desiree stepped inside and closed the door after her. The interior of the former mews had been stripped and rebuilt. Where horses and carriage had once been, now there was a single large empty room. Arrangements of bars and ropes were placed around the room, and one wall was inset with various outcroppings and handholds to facilitate climbing. A ladder led to a rope stretched between two poles, and next to the tightrope were other stands where trapezes hung. In the center, a climbing rope dangled from the ceiling.

Brock had dubbed it Desiree's and Wells's playroom. Here, she knew, she could get rid of her anger and ease her mind; it never failed her. Taking off her cloak, she stretched, loosening her muscles, then ran through a few cartwheels and flips before beginning the more difficult tasks of climbing the wall and the rope and swinging from bar to bar.

After a while, the door opened and Wells

came in. "I thought you must be here."

Desiree smiled, pausing to give him a wave as she climbed the ladder to the tightrope. Wells stretched below her, but Desiree withdrew her attention from everything but the rope in front of her. Intently focused, attuned to nothing else, she crossed the rope and returned.

Her mind was clear and calm now, the turmoil of emotions around Tom Quick pushed aside. She stepped over to the trapeze side of the ladder and took hold of the bar. Stepping onto it, she began to swing.

She'd made no plans, had not even thought about it for the past few minutes, but now Desiree knew what she was going to do. She would find more substantial proof that her father had been a Moreland. Sid Upton might not know who Stella's lover had been, but there could be other information in his head — small, extraneous facts that could lead her to identify the man.

"Want company?" Wells called to her. He had climbed the ladder across from her and was tugging the opposite trapeze toward him.

"Of course." She sat down on the bar, then pulled her hands away, hanging by her knees, as her brother began his swing, synchronizing his with hers.

There was a net below them, but she knew she and Wells wouldn't need it. She was completely focused, her mind serene. Tomorrow she would get Sid Upton's address from Brock, and she would go see him. But right now . . .

Wells said her name, and at her highest peak, Desiree launched herself forward through the air, hands outstretched to clasp Wells's arms.

Right now she would let herself fly.

CHAPTER NINE

Tom strode down the street, seething. That woman was worse than he'd thought. Not just an employee of Falk's — God knows, he could understand that — and not just a thief — again, he was one who could cast no stones there — but now she was after the Morelands! There was no way he was going to let her damage that family. She could take her schemes somewhere else.

Now he had a last name for her; the butler had called her Miss Malone. He could look up her birth certificate. He couldn't be sure of the year, but he could get somewhere in the range. She was too confident, too assured to be really young, but the light of day revealed a loveliness without lines.

And good Lord, had she been lovely. He had seen her without her mask last night, but that had been in the dim light of an East End street. He had thought she was as intriguing as she had been at the casino.

But today, in the light streaming in the windows, he knew he hadn't realized the full attraction of her. Her hair was a lighter, even more luscious shade of caramel than it had appeared last night, the color of her eyes an unusual gray-green.

But it was far more than those physical characteristics that caused that traitorous blow to his chest and the sudden heating of his blood. It was the light in those large eyes, the glow to her face — even if those had been caused by anger. It was the graceful way she moved, the way she talked with her hands, her entire body expressing what she felt. It was the confidence in her face and posture, the intelligence in her eyes, the freedom in her speech.

And it was something else, some indefinable quality that was simply *her* that reached out and grabbed him and made it nearly impossible to look away from her. Impossible to quell that lick of desire that ran through him even in the midst of his anger.

He shouldn't want her. He shouldn't have been flooded with relief when Brock had called Desiree his sister, not his wife or his mistress. It was distinctly annoying that it mattered to him. It wasn't as if he would come near this woman again, much less court her.

Tom pulled his mind away. Thoughts of Desiree Malone would get him nowhere. He needed to get started on proving her lies. The place to start was the Register Office, and it was there he directed the hack he hailed.

Estimating her age as somewhere between twenty-five and thirty, he started in the middle at the year 1865. He found no Desiree Malone there, so went down a year, then up a year. He found it in 1864.

No wonder he hadn't known her at Falk's. She'd been born only two years before he left. She was several years younger than he was, though Tom couldn't have said exactly how many, not knowing the date of his own birth.

Reed had estimated him as seven or eight at the time he put Tom in the duchess's orphanage. There was no point in looking up his own birth certificate in any year, since Quick was merely a name Falk had bestowed on him for his skills. Nevertheless, Tom had tried once, looking in several possible years, but if there was any record of his birth, there had been none of Thomas Quick.

He ran his eyes down the facts before him. Desiree Elaine Malone. May 29. There was a time written beside the date, which Tom knew from former searches meant a multi-ple birth, so he went further and found Wells Henry Malone. She had a twin brother. The man he had met today was named Brock, and Tom was certain he was older than Desiree, anyway. So there was another brother around, the same age as Desiree — no, five minutes younger, he saw on the certificate. Interesting, but not really useful.

The useful information would have been on the space for the father's name, but that was left blank, the sign of an illegitimate birth. So she and her brother were some man's by-blows, but that was no proof of who that man was. Her mother's name was Stella Malone, and she had also been the person who reported the birth to the register office. The birth certificate had provided him with nothing — though the twin broth-er's second name had given Tom a mo-ment's pause. Henry was the first name of the Duke of Broughton.

It seemed likely a woman could have given her illegitimate child his father's first name since she could not take his last. But Henry was a popular name, and the idea of the duke ever straying from his Emmeline was ludicrous. It could perhaps be the other way around: Desiree had learned that the duke's name was the same as her twin's middle name, so she had chosen to target him because of that bit of "proof." That seemed very convoluted. Either way, in all likelihood, the name was nothing but happenstance.

When he left the Register Office, he went to the Blue Lion public house. It had been a long time since the roll he'd had for breakfast and he was hungry, but his choice of the pub had a motive other than simply satisfying his hunger.

As he walked through the door of the place, a woman standing behind the bar called out, "Tommy, me lad! Come here and give us a kiss!"

Tom had known Jessie Smith as long as he could remember. As ignorant of her parentage as Tom was, she, too, had worked under Falk, though neither her fingers nor her feet were fast enough to be one of his prime pickpockets. A few years older than Tom, she had spent more of her time cooking food and seeing to the other children's welfare than she had stealing.

She had had a fondness for Tom, slipping him an extra bit of food or sharing her blanket with him. They had lost track of each other for a few years after Tom had gone to the duchess's orphanage, but they had run into each other after Tom left the orphanage and started working for the Morelands.

Jessie was at that time working in a pub, one of the few of Falk's children who had managed to get out of the criminal life. She had been determined to make something more out of herself and, like Tom, did her best to save her pennies. Eventually she'd managed to buy the pub where she worked. Tom had loaned her the money he had been squirreling away for years, and he had never regretted it. She'd made a success of the place and paid him back with interest.

Jessie gave Tom a buss on the cheek, then motioned to an employee to take her place. "Come back to the snug with me, luv, and have something to eat."

She led Tom back into the snug just off the bar. A barmaid brought them each a pint and a plate of food, and they settled down to eat. After they finished their meal, Jessie leaned back in her chair and looked at him shrewdly. "Well, now, Tom, what brings you around today?"

"Isn't seeing you enough?" He grinned, and she rolled her eyes. "Truth is, I wanted to ask you about somebody who used to work for Falk. She says she was one of his kids, but I don't remember her. She's younger than me, though. Her name is Desiree Malone."

"The Magnificent Malones?" Jessie laughed. "That's what they used to call themselves." She shook her head reminiscently. "Aye, what a pair they were."

"A pair?" Had the twin brother died? "I thought there were three of them. Brock, Desiree and Wells?"

"No, just Wells and Dezzy. I didn't know any Brock. Twins they were and looked like little angels — blond and blue eyed. They were there after you left, mostly. At first they came round sometimes just to make a bit of coin, but they lived with their mam. They lived with us later, after their mam died."

"Their mother died?"

"Aye, 'twas a terrible thing. There was a fire at the circus, you see, and she was killed. Can't remember her name."

"Stella?"

Jessie wrinkled her forehead. "I don't know — could be, I guess, but it don't sound right. It was something odd, like the others. Even odder." She shrugged. "Well, I never knew her, you see. Falk brought 'em in to live after that. He knew they were moneymakers, right enough."

"They didn't have a father?"

She shrugged. "I don't know. They was

part of her act — the Magnificent Malones, you see. But I guess there weren't much of a show after their mam died."

"They toured the country?" Tom supposed it didn't really matter, but he was interested.

"I suppose. But they were at the music halls, as well. Golden Palace and such."

"I see. So Falk turned them into pickpockets."

"No. They might have been good at that, too, but what he did was have 'em put on street shows. Like I said, they looked like little angels. I don't think they were more than four or five, but they could do all these flips and tricks." She shook her head. "They were something to watch, they were. Keep a crowd looking while the other kids nabbed their watches and wallets."

"Ah." Tom nodded. "Do you know what happened to them? Do they still work for Falk?"

"They were there when I left — that must have been, what, three or four years after you did." She shrugged. "I didn't keep up with Falk and his lot, though. No, wait — I lied — I *do* remember. There *was* another brother. One day he showed up and took 'em away from Falk. It was a big ado. I didn't see it, but everybody was talking about it."

"He came from Australia?" That was another dangling thread. His contact had said the man came from Australia with a fortune, but Brock had certainly spoken like an Englishman today.

"I don't know about that. Just recall he took 'em from Falk and Falk was furious."

"Did they run swindles for Falk?"

"Swindles? Like tricking folks out of their money?"

"Yes. Pretending to be someone they aren't or getting someone to put money in a phony business or such."

She shrugged. "I don't know. About the time I left, he'd started them doing second-story work. They fit in places nobody else could, and they could climb like little monkeys."

Tom nodded. He was well aware of that.

"I never saw the like of them," Jessie went on. "But they could have done the swindles, too. They were smart as whips. I don't know. Like I said, I didn't keep up with Falk much. Too glad to be rid of him."

"I understand."

"Sorry, luv, that's all I know about the Malones."

They continued to talk for a few minutes, roaming over all sorts of things besides the pub or the Malones. There was a certain ease in talking to Jessie that came from a shared past, and as the conversation went along, Tom found himself slipping now and then back into his old speech patterns.

He thought of the way Desiree had spoken — not quite the tone of the upper crust, but not that of the streets, either. It was, he realized, much the way he talked. He'd spent years learning his grammar, losing his accent, but he'd never perfectly matched that tone that came naturally to the Morelands and others. Obviously Desiree had done the same thing. And like him, she didn't belong in either place.

He left the Blue Lion and headed for the Golden Palace. He knew one of the dancers in an act there; he'd had a brief relationship with her that had turned into a sort of friendship after their ardor had cooled. As he remembered, she often rehearsed in the afternoons.

Matilda was happy to see him, but when he asked if she knew anything about the Magnificent Malones, she looked at him, puzzled, and said, "Malones? You mean the bloke that owns this place? He never had an act. He's, you know, some sort of gentleman."

"Brock Malone owns the Golden Palace?"

At her nod, he went on, "No, not him. These were children and long before your time. But I thought you might have heard of them or know some older performer who might."

"Oh, sure. Talk to Maisie. Come on, I'll take you to her."

It turned out Maisie had no memory of the act, either, but she in turn referred him to a graying magician at another music hall, who nodded and said, "Ah, yes, I remember them — Bruna the Italian Angel and the Magnificent Malones." He named the act in the manner of an announcer, sweeping one arm out in a grandiose gesture.

"Bruna?" The name on Desiree's birth certificate had been Stella. "Was that her stage name?"

The man shrugged. "I don't know. It's what everyone called her. She really was from Italy. She came here with a show, but after she met Sid, she stayed."

"Sid?" Tom's instincts went on alert at the mention of a male name, someone who could possibly be Desiree's real father.

"Trapeze artist. We used to lift a pint or two. But then I tried my luck in the States. I met him again over there, in fact. Odd, that. After Bruna died, their circus decided to tour America — get rid of the bad luck, I suppose. 'Course, the Malones weren't still with him then. He joined a different act . . . I'm not sure what the name was."

"He left the children here?"

The other man nodded. "Well, they weren't his, were they?"

That dashed Tom's rising hope that he had a name for Desiree's actual father. And he didn't understand the change in names from Stella to Bruna. "They were just Bruna's, then?"

Having been born in Italy would negate Desiree's claim almost as effectively as this fellow Sid's paternity. But that wouldn't match with birth certificate he'd found.

"Oh, well, they weren't hers, either. I don't know who their mother was or what happened to her, but Sid and Bruna took them in when the little ones were just babies."

"The twins."

"Yes." The magician opened his watch and glanced at it. "Sorry. I need to practice before I go on. That's all I know about the Malones anyway."

"Just one more thing. What happened to Sid? Is he still in the United States?"

"No, that circus came back, and I think he joined another one. Circus folk move around a good deal."

130

"Do you know where he is now?"

"No. Haven't heard anything of him in years. He was never the star of the show, you see. Without Bruna and children, he wasn't as popular."

"What was his last name?"

"Upton. Sid Upton."

"I appreciate it. Thanks for your trouble." Tom pressed a bill into his hand and turned to leave.

He had barely reached the hallway, however, when the other man hurried after him. "No, wait. I just remembered something that might help you, if you're wanting to find Sid."

"What?" The money had apparently jogged the magician's memory; Tom hoped his information was real and not something made up in a bid for more money.

"I heard that a few years back Sid was working at the Golden Palace. Not onstage — he would have been too old, but backstage or at the door. That sort of thing."

This new information meant a return to the Golden Palace, but, after a persistent inquiry (and another bill placed in the stage manager's hand), Tom learned that Sid Upton had indeed once worked there. He no longer did so, but the stage manager knew his address.

Tom returned to his home, buoyed that he had untangled at least some of the mystery around Desiree Malone. And the next morning, when he interviewed Sid Upton, he just might be able to put the threat to the Morelands to rest.

Desiree set out the next morning to see Sid Upton, their cook's plum cake in hand. Sid lived in a village on the outskirts of London, where Brock had bought him a small retirement cottage. She was oddly nervous. If the ring and the Moreland name didn't call up some other memory in Sid, she didn't know how she would discover who her father was.

Unlike the disagreeable Mr. Quick, she was not a detective. Years ago, she had gone to the Register's Office and found that hers and Wells's birth certificates listed no name for their father. And she knew of no one other than Bruna or Sid who would have known her father's identity . . . apart from the members of the Moreland family, of course.

Brock was doubtless right in saying the Morelands would turn her away. Tom Quick would make sure of it. She wished she hadn't blurted out her parentage to him yesterday. She had been so mad at him for his arrogant attitude — as if he had any

132

right to judge what she did or who she had worked for — that she'd said the first thing she could think of to shake him up.

It had certainly worked in that regard. Just not in a good way. Apparently even more than he disliked Falk, Quick loved the Morelands. She felt her irritation rising as she thought of Tom Quick, so she pushed him out of her mind. She was less than happy, therefore, when the door to Sid's cottage was opened by Quick himself.

Desiree scowled. "What are you doing here?"

"Trying to find out who your real father was," he replied. It lifted Desiree's spirits a bit to see that he looked thoroughly frustrated. "But Mr. Upton refuses to answer any questions."

"Does he, now?" Desiree smiled.

An old, stooped man came up behind Tom, his cane thumping against the floor, and Sid Upton appeared behind Tom. Since Tom filled the small doorway, he gave Quick a sharp jab in the ribs. Tom stepped aside, scowling, and Sid moved into the doorway to peer at Desiree.

"Hello, Sid. It's me."

"Dezzy?" He adjusted his spectacles, and his sour expression changed to a grin. "Why, so it is! Come in, come in, lass. You're a sight for sore eyes. Unlike some." He gave Tom a glare. "That 'un's been digging for dirt on your ma."

"I was not —" Tom began, then sighed and threw up his hands. "What's the point? If you've come to tell him to keep his mouth shut, Miss Malone, there is no need."

"I haven't done any such thing. I brought Sid a plum cake." She held it up, and Sid broke into a grin. Seeing his delight, Desiree thought guiltily that she should have visited him more often since his retirement.

"Did you, now? You always were a sweet girl."

Desiree didn't bother to look at Tom to see how he reacted to that statement. She was sure she already knew. She came inside, closing the door behind her. The next few minutes were spent unpacking the cake and making tea to go with it. Feeling gratifyingly generous, she even cut a slice for Tom Quick, who obviously intended to stay.

Let him. If he learned who her father was, it would only help her.

Sid spent some time complimenting the cake and inquiring about her brothers, and then they settled into reminiscences about the old days and questions about former friends and acquaintances. Desiree could feel Tom's impatience, but to give him credit, he didn't interrupt or try to push them along.

Finally, a break fell in the conversation, and Tom said, "Mr. Upton, I understand that you and your wife took in the Malone children when they were quite young."

"Aye, we did." Sid crossed his arms and gazed back at him, offering nothing more.

"Why was that? What happened?"

The old man regarded him stonily for a moment, then looked toward Desiree.

"It's all right, Sid," Desiree told him. "Go ahead. I want to know, too. Brock was too young to remember much of anything about my mother leaving."

"Aye, well . . ." He sighed and cast his eyes up toward the ceiling, as if his answers might lie there. "You were just a baby, Dezzy, you and Wells. Brock must have been, oh, five or six. And, well, your ma left. She went off one day with her man, and she didn't come back. After a few days, that woman, the housekeeper, got tired of looking after you, and she remembered about Bruna coming to visit, so she came to her and told her about Stella not coming home. Well, Bruna couldn't just leave Stella's children there, now could she? The housekeeper wasn't going to keep on taking care of them. And Bruna was right fond of babies . . . we couldn't have any ourselves."

"It was a very generous thing for her to do," Tom said.

"She was a good woman, Bruna." Sid's eyes turned a little watery. "I've missed her every day. The heart just went out of me when she passed on."

Desiree reached out and curled her hand around his wrist. It was bony, almost fragile, and it made Desiree's heart hurt a little. She remembered how he once was, the strength in his arms and hands. She remembered the first time he had latched his hands around her forearms and she had left her trapeze, swinging suspended in the air. She remembered the rush of excitement, the security of his hold.

"She was a good woman," Desiree told him in a soft voice. "I miss her, too."

Tom said nothing, and Desiree was glad he didn't spoil the small moment of shared grief. Desiree patted Sid's wrist and leaned back, turning to Tom. He took the glance to be a signal he could start again, as she had meant it to be. It was a little annoying, really, that he understood her, that they connected so easily.

"Did you think that Stella Malone might be coming back?" Tom asked. "That maybe keeping the children was only temporary?"

"No. There was a letter. That's when the housekeeper came to us. Stella said she'd gone to America with his lordship." The twist of his mouth as he said the words indicated little liking for the lord in question.

"A letter?" Desiree leaned forward. "I never heard there was a letter."

"Aye, well, I guess we never talked about it. No reason to."

"Did you keep the letter?"

"No. Bruna couldn't read, and I can't do that elegant kind. The housekeeper told us what it said."

"What did it say?" Desiree asked, hungry to hear her mother's words.

Sid shrugged. "I don't remember exactly. Bunch of romantic nonsense. They couldn't bear to be apart and whatnot."

"She didn't say anything about us?" Even as she asked the question, Desiree knew the answer from the uncomfortable expression on Sid's face. She struggled to keep her face smooth; she didn't want Quick to see the disappointment that swept her.

"I don't remember," Sid said. Desiree was certain it was a lie to ease her hurt, and Sid confirmed that with his next words. "I'm sorry, Dez."

Tom jumped into the silence. "What was

his lordship's name?'"

"Ah, well, that I don't know."

"Surely you saw him. Stella Malone must have mentioned him."

"I didn't go over there much. Bruna went to see her sometimes, but in the afternoon when *he* wasn't there — it would have been awkward, running into him."

"Not even early on? He didn't come to see her perform?" Tom pressed.

"I don't know about that. I guess he could have. Must have, to begin with. But he wasn't one of the ones who hung around the stage door all the time, trying to court her. Just all of a sudden, Stella left her act and moved into that house."

"Your wife was her very good friend," Tom said. "Wouldn't Stella have told her his name?"

"Aye. But Bruna promised she'd never tell anyone, and she didn't. She was a woman that kept her word, my Bruna was."

"She kept it hidden even from you?" Skepticism colored Quick's tone.

"Please, Sid." Desiree leaned forward again, laying her hand on his arm. "Don't worry it might hurt me or make my mother look bad or anything. I want to know who my father is, no matter what."

"I know." Sid patted her hand. "I'd tell

138

you if I could. But Bruna didn't say, and I wasn't going to ask her to break her word. I'm sorry."

"Could his name have been Moreland?" Desiree asked. "Do you remember ever hearing Stella say that name?" Desiree dug into her reticule and pulled out Brock's ring, holding it out to Sid. "He gave Brock this ring. Do you remember seeing him wearing it? I believe it's a family ring."

Sid took the ring and brought it up close to his eyes, examining it. With a sigh, he handed it back to Desiree. "No. I don't remember that name. Or the ring. I doubt I saw the fellow more than once at a distance. Like I said, it would have been awkward. We're not the sort he'd be chatting with."

"What about friends? Did anyone visit them? A friend of his lordship?"

"I'm sorry," he repeated. "I don't know of any."

There seemed little to ask after that, and Desiree took her leave not long afterward. Tom followed her out the door. She glanced over at him. The sun glinted off his blond hair, and she couldn't help but gaze at his eyes, that striking combination of blue fractured by ice very noticeable in the light. Desiree wished she was indifferent to his looks, that she hadn't stolen glances at him all through the interview with Sid.

Tom gazed back at her, and for a moment she thought he was going to say something, but he did not. Silence stretched awkwardly between them, and Desiree turned away, walking to her carriage. Tom started off down the street. Desiree stared after him, her brain whirring, then climbed into her carriage. The driver turned the vehicle and started back in the direction they'd come from. As they reached Tom, Desiree told the coachman to stop.

"Mr. Quick," she called, and he turned. "Are you taking the train?"

"Yes." His expression was faintly wary.

"Why don't you ride with me back into the city? It will be faster than the train." She opened the door in invitation.

The wariness in his gaze deepened into suspicion, but he came to the door, looking into the carriage. "Why would you offer me a ride?"

"Why wouldn't I?" She raised her brows, then smiled archly and said, "I don't bite."

"I'm not too sure about that." But he swung up into the carriage.

Theirs was a small town carriage, meant for only two people, so Tom had no place to sit but next to her. Desiree was intensely aware of how close he was, only inches separating them. Her heart beat a little faster.

"What do you want?" Tom asked as the carriage once again rolled forward.

"Must I want something from you?"

"Yes," he answered bluntly. "You're the kind who always has a hidden purpose."

"It's not hidden." She ignored the judgment in his statement and kept her voice businesslike. "I have a proposition for you."

He said nothing, just raised his brows in an irritating way.

Desiree took a breath and plunged forward. "I suggest that you and I work together."

CHAPTER TEN

Tom stared back at her. He wasn't sure what he had expected her to say, but it certainly had not been this. "I beg your pardon?"

"Work together. You and I," she said with emphasis — like he was a bleedin' idiot. "We can pool our resources, share our thoughts."

"So you can learn everything I find out, you mean. You must be daft."

"I assure you, I am not," Desiree said crisply. "I am simply practical. It makes perfect sense — we are looking for the same thing."

"No. *I* am looking for the truth," Tom said.

"And you think I'm not?" Desiree's eyes flashed and color flared along her cheekbones.

She looked beautiful in her anger — he had to admit that, and it galled him. It would be a great deal easier maintaining his dislike of her if he didn't have this urge to kiss her. When he opened Upton's door this morning and saw her standing on the doorstep, his chest had suddenly lightened, and he'd wanted to smile. He'd had to frown to keep from doing so.

Desiree's presence had distracted him throughout the interview; he feared he would later remember some important question he had forgotten to ask or a point he had missed because he'd been too occupied watching her. He hated that even knowing what chicanery she was trying to pull on the Morelands, he was still drawn to her.

He had warmed to the glint of laughter in her eyes, even when she was taking a jab at him; he had enjoyed hearing her laugh; he had wanted to see her smile. It had touched him to see her comfort the old man. The disappointment in her voice when she realized her mother had not given a thought to her children in her farewell letter made him want to help her. He'd jumped in with a question to move the conversation off that obviously painful topic.

All of that made it a very bad idea to be in her company. He should not have even accepted her invitation to ride in the carriage. She was too close: he could smell the subtle hint of her perfume and see the perfection of her skin, the softness of her lips. Tom had the completely unreasonable desire to reach out and trace the delicate curve of her eyebrows, a brown that was a shade or two darker than her hair.

"You apparently think I want to bilk your beloved Morelands. I fail to understand why you are so extremely devoted to a family of aristocrats who no doubt look upon you as little more than a servant, but that doesn't matter. I can assure you that I don't want their money. I want to know who my father is. That's all."

"You want to find out he's a Moreland," Tom corrected.

"No. I think he *is* a Moreland. There's a difference. It isn't a matter of desire. It's a matter of proof. The Moreland connection seems likely, but if you should find out that my father was someone else, I won't be upset. I want to learn who he is. I want the truth."

"And I will be happy to tell you when I find out. There's no reason for us to work together."

"Don't be absurd. It's obviously an advantage to have two minds working on the same subject. We can talk, we can present theories or break them down. We will come at the issue from different perspectives. You have a partner — surely you understand the value of two people working together."

"You will impede my investigation."

"I will not. Look at the interview you just had with Sid. You were getting nowhere with him until I came along and helped."

That was certainly true enough, but Tom wasn't about to admit it. He crossed his arms and gazed stonily back at her. Her mouth tightened, her eyes blazing brighter. Tom knew he was irritating her, and that fact gave him a certain satisfaction, though he wasn't sure why.

"We have different abilities to bring to the case," Desiree pointed out. "Different assets. It will be more effective if we combine them."

"I don't plan to break into any houses or scale any walls, so I don't think your skills will be of much use to me."

"I don't understand," she snapped. "I could help you. There are people who won't talk to you unless I'm there. And you don't know what skills you might need. You're just being stubborn. Why won't you let me work with you?"

"Maybe because you broke into my office? Because you work for Falk? Because you lie?" He'd started out in a light sarcastic manner, but his voice turned flat and harsh as he said, "I can't trust you."

Desiree twisted around so that she was facing him, her body taut with anger. "I don't work for Falk. I told him I wouldn't do anything else for him. And I didn't lie to you. I never told you I didn't break in or that it wasn't a job for Falk. You didn't ask. You're the one who was sneaking around, following me, spying on me, putting on that pretense at the club. All I want is the truth. How can you be so positive I'm lying? So sure that I'm untrustworthy? You don't know me."

"I do know you." Tom's voice was low and fierce. "I know you right down to the bone. Because you're the same as me. You grew up just like I did in that same hellhole of lies, thievery and deceit. I picked pockets for Falk just like all the ones who did it while you distracted the marks with flips and cartwheels. I stole and I lied and I did whatever it took to survive to live another day, and so did you. That's who we are. That's how I know I can't trust you."

They gazed at each other for a moment in a charged silence, then Tom turned his head sharply away, appalled at the way he'd lashed out at her and embarrassed by how much of himself he had revealed. "Stop the carriage. This is impossible."

He reached for the door handle, but Desiree clamped her hand down on his arm, stopping him. He turned to her. He was faintly relieved to see that it wasn't hurt that shone in her eyes, but fury.

"I don't care what you think of me." Her fingers dug into his arm. "All I care about is finding out who my father is. If you won't help me to do that, then I have no choice but to ask the Morelands about him."

Any regret Tom had had over the harshness of his answer vanished. "So you're adding extortion to your array of skills?"

"Call it whatever you want." Desiree's hand fell away, and she sat back, folding her arms. "I will do whatever it takes to get my answers."

Tom wanted to storm at her, to tell her that he would make sure she couldn't talk to the Morelands. But he'd spoken the truth when he said he did what it took to survive. And surviving this thing meant maintaining control over the search. And over himself. He had let emotion rule him too much already. He needed to be coldly practical.

The fact was he couldn't keep her from talking to one of the Morelands. There were a lot of them, and they were a freewheeling group. The only thing he could do was warn the butlers, but he couldn't possibly stop Desiree from approaching one of the Morelands outside the house, and he couldn't imagine any of them haughtily refusing to talk to a stranger. And if Tom warned the Morelands about her, he would himself be bringing them into the thing.

On the other hand, if he was working with her, Tom could exercise some control over what she did. At the very least, he'd *know* what she was doing. She was right in saying she would be able to provide him an entrée to people who wouldn't say anything to him otherwise. She knew the background, the people involved. Yes, no doubt she would lead him to people who would answer the way she wanted them to, but at least he would be able to question them and perhaps worm some real answers out of them, as well. Desiree could plant evidence, of course, but she could do that anyway, and this way he could keep a close eye on her.

"Very well." Tom leaned back. "Then let's use one of your 'assets' now. I want to talk to your brother."

"Brock? I already asked him, and he didn't remember much."

"I want to talk to him myself."

"Of course." Her eyes twinkled unexpectedly. "He may not be too eager to talk to

148

you, given your last conversation with him, but I'll ask him when he could see you."

"No. I want to see him now." He wasn't about to give the two of them time to plan Brock's answers. No doubt they had a story in place, but the man might slip up somewhere if Tom caught him unawares.

"Then we'll talk to him now," Desiree replied. "I imagine he's already gone to his office."

Tom felt somewhat disgruntled by her acquiescence. He would have liked to have something to continue to argue about. It might have eased his disgust at having been outmaneuvered by Desiree once more. Yes, it was more practical for him to work with her. But it still felt like a defeat.

She got the best of him at every turn. It wasn't something Tom was accustomed to. Obviously, he didn't always win; he didn't solve every case; he didn't come out on top in every argument — he probably never did with Con, who could outtalk anyone. But at least he usually didn't make one mistake after another, didn't feel so frustrated and lacking in control.

Desiree Malone disturbed him. Somehow, with her, his feelings were never far beneath the surface. She intrigued him as much as she aggravated him. She sparked his anger even as she ignited his desire. Just this morning, she'd irritated him, stirred his sympathy, aroused his desire and confirmed his low opinion of her character by extorting his cooperation.

Desiree was as silent as he was as the carriage rolled through the streets of London, speaking only to direct the coachman to the Farrington Club. There was no one there this early in the afternoon besides one employee. It felt strange to Tom to walk through the empty room, footsteps ringing on the marble floor. In the daylight, without the people and the noise, the casino seemed somehow smaller.

She led him through an open set of doors into a hall, where all show of glamour disappeared, replaced by a businesslike practicality. Desiree knocked at a closed door, then stepped inside at the answering "Come in."

The man Tom had seen the day before at the Malone house sat behind a desk as plain and functional as everything else in the room. His jacket was hung over the back of his chair, his sleeves unfastened and rolled up, as he entered numbers in a ledger. He looked up as they entered, and his eyes hardened when they fell on Tom. He rose to his feet. "What's he doing here?"

"Mr. Quick and I have settled our differences," Desiree told him breezily. "He has agreed to help me discover my father's identity."

Brock narrowed his eyes. "Has he, now? Why?"

"It seemed the obvious thing to do," Tom replied, deciding he needed to take control of the conversation. "As Miss Malone pointed out to me, she has more access to people with information about the matter. And, naturally, she has no desire to bother the Moreland family unnecessarily."

The other man let out a short huff of disbelief. "Yes, our Desiree is known for her reticence." He gestured toward the chairs facing his desk as he sat down again. "Then let's do it. I have work to do."

"Desiree said you had told her what you remembered about that time, but it would help me to hear it myself."

"Naturally. I never knew the man's name," Brock related in a dispassionate voice. "I don't remember that he was ever called anything but 'my lord' or 'sir' or some endearment by my mother. He seemed tall — but since I was only six, I don't know how accurate that is. His hair was dark. Our mother left on a trip with him one afternoon and never came back."

"Mr. Upton said there was a housekeeper there."

Brock nodded. "Nan. Yes, she kept us for a couple of weeks and then Bruna came and took us. I'm sorry, but I don't recall Nan's last name. I'm not sure I ever knew it."

"Do you have any idea where Nan lives now? Where she went afterward?"

"No. We went with Bruna and Sid, and I never saw her again." Brock turned toward his sister. "I did remember one other thing, Desiree. Well, one very small thing, not very helpful, I'm afraid. That other man who was sometimes at the house, your father's friend? His name popped into my head this morning — they called him Pax or maybe Pack."

"Pax?" Tom repeated. "Was that a first name or a last?"

"I don't know." Brock shrugged. "Sorry. I told you it wasn't very helpful."

"Sid told us there was a letter," Desiree said. "Stella sent a letter saying she wasn't coming back. Do you remember that?"

Brock's eyebrows rose. "No. What did it say?"

Desiree repeated what Upton had told them, adding, "Sid couldn't remember exactly. He and Bruna couldn't read. Did you know that?"

"No. Although, now that I think about it,

it was Gordie who taught us numbers and letters."

"Gordie?" Tom interjected. "Who's he?"

"Nobody who'd know anything about this. He was someone in the circus."

Tom went on. "Did your mother have any other friends who visited? Perhaps a neighbor?"

"Not that I remember. To be blunt, she was a kept woman. I'm not sure that any neighbor would have socialized with her. It was a nice area."

"What area? Where was it?"

"I've no idea. A child doesn't think about things like that. At least, I didn't. The houses were well made and attractive, not extravagant, but quite pleasant. Wide streets. Not too far away were grander houses. I remember walking past them on the way to a large park — actually a square. We only went there once in a while. There was a smaller park that was closer, and we went there often. I called it the Pie Park. Because of the way it was shaped — a triangle, like a piece of pie."

"What about the house where you lived? Do you remember the street? How it looked?"

"I've no idea the name of the street. It was one of a row of houses . . . they were all alike. Stone. We were number five." Brock smiled faintly, his gaze far away. "There was a gold five above the door, and Mum told me that was how old I was." He straightened, the memory falling away. "That was when we moved in. I was six by the time we left."

"What about across the street from you? Were they terraced houses, too?"

"They were different. They were attached, too, but the houses weren't all the same. Different colors, different materials, different styles. The one right across from our door was brown brick. And one of them up the street had a red door."

"That's good. This is pretty specific."

"If you're hoping to locate it, I have to remind you that was twenty-eight years ago. I doubt it looks the same."

"No. But I know an architect. He's pretty good at things like this." Tom thought for a moment. What they had was very little to go on, even with Alex's help. Finally, he said, "Do you remember anything else about the area? Places you went?"

Brock frowned, thinking. "There was a church nearby. And there was an odd intersection, where several streets came together." He paused. "Oh! And trains. Sometimes we'd walk over and look at the trains that went by. Those were farther away. I suppose there might have been a station somewhere around, but I don't recall it."

"Any street names? Or, I don't know, shops or monuments or anything else memorable?"

"No."

"Did anyone else work in the house besides the housekeeper? A maid or nanny?"

"There was the midwife when the twins were born. But I never even saw her, let alone knew her name. There was no nanny, but there were maids. I don't remember the last one's name. The one before her was Judy? Julie? Something like that, I think. She had red hair and freckles." Again there was that faint smile, as if at pleasant memories. "I liked her, but she had to leave. There was a big ado. She stole a pair of earrings. Something like that. Maybe it was more. I think that was why Stella put things away in that hiding place."

"Hiding place?" Tom and Desiree chorused, leaning forward.

"Yes. There were a couple of bricks that could be pulled out next to the fireplace in the parlor. I saw Stella down there one night, putting a necklace in it. I tried to get in it after that, but it was too high to reach. It was up on the left side, higher than the mantel."

Tom and Desiree looked at each other. He could see the same light glowing in her eyes that he was sure was in his own. "We have to find that house."

CHAPTER ELEVEN

Tom left soon afterward, clearly eager to talk to his architectural friend, and Desiree turned to her brother. "What do you think about Mr. Quick?"

Brock said carefully, "He seems to me to be . . . of value to you. As to whether he's good or honest or anything else, I don't know. What I can tell is limited. That's more your area. Do you think he's trustworthy?"

"I'm not entirely sure." How much was her judgment colored by her immediate, strong attraction to him? How much of that attraction was purely physical, just a response to those clear blue eyes or the wheat-colored hair that made her fingers itch to touch it? Or that firm, muscled form? She didn't usually have to separate such things from her instincts about a person. Never before had she felt that instantaneous connection. But Desiree wasn't about to get into any of that with her brother. "Mr.

Quick is annoying, and I resent the way he insists on believing I am dishonest. However, I don't get the sense that he's lying. Whether he's right or not, I think he believes what he says. I think I can trust him . . . at least after he's given his word."

"I think I remember him."

"You do?"

Brock nodded. "When you first said his name, I thought it sounded familiar. And the last couple of days, thinking about the past so much, I remembered that Falk had a boy who worked for him that was named Quick. The name made an impression on me because it sounded like such an excellent name to have. Someone told me the boy didn't know his last name, that he'd been given it by Falk because he was so fast and nimble fingered. I was very struck by the idea that someone could know so little about himself that he didn't even know his own name."

"Really? I couldn't remember him."

"You would have been too young, I imagine. He was older than you, closer to my age, I think. It was hard to tell. Falk's children always had an old look. This was back when Bruna first began to let you work for Falk." Brock's face hardened a little at the memory. Brock had always argued against Bruna letting Falk use her and Wells when the family needed the money. "I don't remember him being there later on. I guess I assumed he got nabbed by the bobbies."

"What was he like?" Desiree was always a curious person, but she found herself even more interested in everything to do with Tom Quick.

Brock shrugged. "I don't know. That's about all I knew about him. He had blond hair and a cocky grin. And everyone said he was slippery as the devil. I don't think I ever talked to him. I was never part of that group."

Desiree nodded. Brock hadn't worked with them. He wasn't nimble enough for picking pockets or distracting the marks with acrobatics. His good sense and hard work, his loyalty and protectiveness had no value for Falk.

"It's sad, isn't it?" Desiree said. "Not knowing who you are, not having a family. Whatever happened, I always had you and Wells. I might not have had a mother, but at least I knew who she was. To be so adrift . . . it must have been terribly lonely."

"I'm sure it was." Brock paused, then said, "Desiree . . . a sad life doesn't make one a good person. A man raised without love is bound to have a hard time loving anyone."

"I know." Desiree flashed him a teasing smile. "I'm interested in finding a father, not a husband."

"Mm." Brock made a noncommittal sound. "You may not be interested in him, but he's interested in you."

Desiree shook her head. "No. Maybe he was at first — although I suspect even that was a pretense to gain my trust. But now he's certain I'm a thoroughly wicked woman. A thief, a swindler, a liar, an extortionist."

"What an array." Brock chuckled.

"Yes, he's pretty sanctimonious for someone who used to be a hook for Falk."

"If he's so certain you're wicked, why does he want to help you?"

"He doesn't. I more or less forced him to," Desiree admitted. "I threatened to ask the Morelands about my father, to show them the ring. Quick *is* capable of love — he obviously loves that family."

"He's been working for them for over fifteen years." At Desiree's surprised look, Brock said, "I did some investigating of my own."

"What did you find out?"

"That he's considered a good detective, that he's clever and tough and he is respected by people on both sides of the law,

160

apparently."

"Well, that's not much." Desiree had hoped for more personal details. Like whether he was courting someone.

"It's enough for me to not object to you being around him. And it's enough to tell me he's loyal to his employers. He might very well be grateful to them for giving him a job, considering his background."

"Do you really think they knew his background? He wouldn't have told *them* he was a former pickpocket."

"No. But perhaps he's grateful anyway."

"I wonder why he left Falk's. And what happened to him after that? I wish I knew more about him."

Desiree had skirted the truth a bit when she told Brock she wasn't interested in finding a husband. That much was true. Several years ago, she had realized that marriage was probably not in her future. She met a lot of men at the club; some of them had stirred a feeling in her — a liking, an enjoyment of their company, even sometimes a little thrill of desire. But gentlemen weren't interested in marrying her. They wanted her, but as a mistress, not as a wife. And she was determined not to follow the path her mother had taken.

But while she was not interested in a

husband, she *was* interested in Tom Quick. She might hide that fact from her brother, but she wasn't going to hide it from herself. It was useless, of course, given Tom's opinion of her, but she couldn't keep from thinking about him. If they hadn't been at the opposite ends of this matter, could there have been something between them? Had he desired her, as he had seemed to, before he realized who she was? Would they have followed that path that opened to them that night at the club, moving into passion, maybe even into love? It was a heady thought, a beckoning question — and one that she would never know the answer to.

Somewhat more prosaically, she wondered whether Quick would adhere to his promise and include her in his investigation. She was well aware that he might well not venture near her again. It was a disheartening thought, but one she had to consider. What would she do if he ignored her? Would she actually go to the Morelands and tell them her story? She had never been one to let fear stop her, but she wasn't sure even she had the nerve to face some icy-eyed aristocrat and tell them she was the bastard child of one of them.

Such thoughts continued to occupy her mind the rest of the day. Her play at the club was not up to her usual standards. Desiree kept watching the door, wondering if Tom would show up. When he did not, she wasn't sure whether to be relieved or disappointed. She didn't want him hounding her, of course; she would rather not start another argument, especially here. But she realized that she had foolishly harbored some hope that he was interested in her, as Brock had said, that he would be intrigued enough that he would be drawn to the club. Nor could she help but wish that he could see her again in her element, glamorous and in control, sought after by other men.

As a result of her inattention, she barely broke even, and she left the Farrington earlier than usual, somewhat dispirited. Desiree could not hold back the gloomy intuition that Tom had no intention of letting her be a part of his investigation. He would doubtless ignore her, making her confront him time and again. Thinking such thoughts, her resentment grew until by the time the carriage reached her house, she was quite annoyed with Mr. Quick.

Desiree stepped down from the carriage in front of her home and waved a goodbye to the driver. As she turned toward the house, a little frisson of alarm ran through her chest. Something was wrong. She whirled around and scanned the street. Two houses down, on the opposite side of the street, sat a dark carriage, almost hidden in the shadows. But this was more than just the normal darkness of night or shadows. This was the kind of black void she sensed when something was wrong — dangerous or deceptive. Was Tom spying on her again? The brief moment of alarm was replaced by anger. What did he think she was going to do — sneak out and plant some evidence that would prove she was a Moreland?

Turning abruptly, she started across the street, angling toward the vehicle. Her pace increased at the same rate as the burgeoning indignation inside her until she was almost running. Before she reached the carriage, the driver snapped the reins over the team's backs, and the vehicle started forward. Desiree ran toward it, cursing her encumbering evening attire of corset and full skirts. "Stop!"

The carriage sped up, swerving out into the middle of the street, passing so close to her that Desiree had to jump aside. She stumbled and went down on her backside. Furious, she sprang back up, grabbing one of her slippers that had fallen off and hurling it after the departing carriage.

The shoe fell far short, of course, but the

action relieved a bit of her frustration. How dare he? Of all the suspicious, sanctimonious, infuriating . . . *prigs*! Accusing her of being sneaking and untrustworthy when Tom was the one lurking about spying on her.

She stalked over to retrieve her shoe and stepped on a pebble, exacerbating her ill temper. Shoving her foot back into the slipper, she limped into the house, making a list of all the things she was going to say to Tom Quick the next morning.

There was a spring to Tom's steps as he walked up to the door of the Malone house the next morning. He chose to believe it was excitement over the possibility of moving the case forward that prompted his eagerness, rather than the possibility of seeing Desiree Malone again.

He had spoken to Alex yesterday afternoon, and though the man had given him an odd look, he had refrained from asking questions, just as Con had the other day. Tom suspected that before long their inveterate curiosity would get the better of the pair and the Greats would want to know what Tom was up to.

Fortunately, Tom's question about the location of the house from Brock's memory was exactly the sort of thing Alex enjoyed untangling, and this morning he had handed Tom a list of areas he thought might be possibilities.

Tom caught a hackney to the Malone house immediately. He hoped Desiree was awake and ready to get started; her late nights probably made her a late riser, but he was too eager to wait. If she wanted to join him on the search, she was going to have to put up with some inconvenience. But the butler who opened the door to Tom's knock led him immediately down a corridor to a small dining area.

Desiree was at the table, already dressed, though her hair was down, a silken waterfall that was decidedly distracting. A man stood nearby, dressed casually in only trousers and shirt, the sleeves rolled up and the collar unbuttoned.

Was this her twin brother? His coloring certainly suggested that. He was slender, with golden-brown hair, blue eyes and the sort of face women swooned over. He watched Tom walk into the room, his expression one of haughty indolence that Tom had seen on many a gentleman's face. It immediately raised Tom's hackles.

"Mr. Quick, Miss Malone," the butler intoned.

Desiree, whose back was to Tom, whipped around in her chair and glared at Tom with such ferocity that it took him aback. "You!"

The greeting Tom had been about to give her died in his mouth. The other man said lazily, "So this is your Mr. Quick, Dez." He ran a gaze down Tom that managed to be assessing, dismissive and vaguely amused.

"How dare you spy on me!" Desiree ignored the man's comment, advancing on Tom with a furious light in her eyes.

"What?" Tom looked at her blankly. "Spy? I haven't been sp—"

"Oh? You mean it was someone else who was sitting outside our house last night when I came home? Someone else who almost ran me down?"

"Ran you down!" Tom gaped. "What are you talking about?"

The other man set down his cup with a rattle, turning to Desiree with a sharp focus that was at odds with his earlier stance. "You didn't tell me someone tried to hit you!"

"For goodness' sake, Wells, you just came downstairs. I haven't exactly had time," Desiree said to him before she swung back to Tom. "What I'm talking about is you sitting in a carriage across the street, watching this house."

"I wasn't!" Tom protested.

"When I went over to confront you, you took off and drove right at me, and I had to jump back to keep from being run over. I got mud on the back of my dress and broke a heel off one of my slippers," she added indignantly.

"Blast your slippers," Wells said with a grimace. "Are you all right?"

"Of course I am. I don't even have a bruise." She scowled at Tom. "No thanks to you."

"It wasn't me!" Tom insisted. "Desiree, I swear to you." He moved toward her. "I was not here last night. I wasn't spying on you. And I most certainly did not try to run you down."

She narrowed her eyes at him, studying him. "Honestly?"

"Yes, honestly. I'm telling you the truth. Why would I sit outside your house? You were at the club, weren't you?"

"Yes. You could have come to break in."

"That's more in your line," Tom retorted, and Wells let out a short laugh that he quickly turned into a cough.

"Sorry," Wells said when Desiree turned to focus her glare on him. "But he does have you there, Dez."

Tom decided her brother was less irritating than he had thought.

"I could be like some and presume that everything you say is a lie," Desiree told Tom with heavy significance. She swiped her hand through the air. "However, I choose to believe you. This time."

Her brother looked at her with an odd intensity, saying, "You're sure?"

"Yes, he's telling the truth." She turned back toward Tom and gestured toward the table. "Sit down and have some breakfast. This is my brother Wells, by the way."

Tom nodded to Wells in greeting. "Thank you. I already ate. I want to talk about this carriage."

"As do I." Wells poured a cup of coffee and handed it to Tom.

Tom took a sip and sat down across from Desiree. "Why did you assume it was me?"

"It seemed the logical choice," Desiree replied. "Given that you did the same thing the other night."

"What did they do? What did the carriage look like?" Tom asked.

"It was just sitting there, in the darkest spot of the street, and when I started toward it, it left." She shrugged. "Perhaps it didn't have anything to do with me," she said, but her tone lacked conviction.

"You didn't get a look at who was inside?"

Wells asked, sitting down beside his sister.

"No. The curtains were drawn, and the driver was blocking the front window." Desiree stopped, her brow creasing.

"What? You've remembered something." Tom leaned forward, sensing something important.

Desiree nodded slowly. "Yes. The carriage was . . . a little odd. I didn't really think about it at the time. It just seemed somehow off, but looking back on it, I realize that the driver wasn't sitting up on a high seat. He was right in front of the passenger. So it gave it a . . . a low look. It's not a huge difference, but I don't think I've ever seen a coach exactly like that." Using the saltcellar and jam pots, she demonstrated the two different silhouettes.

Tom frowned, trying to envision the vehicle. "I'm not sure I've seen one, either."

"I have," Wells said. "In America."

"America?"

"Yes. I saw a number of them when I was in New York City. They're quite popular in the States."

"So it was an American spying on her?" Tom's voice rose skeptically.

"Only if they brought their carriage with them," Wells replied. "Seems a bit excessive, doesn't it?"

"Is it any less likely that an Englishman imported a carriage from the United States?" Desiree countered.

"Maybe there's a company here that copied the design," Tom suggested.

"True. Or maybe a company on the Continent makes them," Desiree added. "They'd be easier to import from there than hauling one all the way across the ocean."

"Yes. I need to see if I can track down a company that makes them," Tom said. "If the thing is rare, it might be easy to find who owns it."

"Why would you want to find the carriage?" she asked.

"What do you mean *why*? Because they tried to hit you," Tom shot back. A little belatedly, he added, "It might have something to do with our search."

"What search?" Wells asked.

"Brock described the house where you and I were born," Desiree told him. "Mr. Quick thought a friend of his could identify it."

"From a description?" Wells cocked an eyebrow. "Seems unlikely."

"Actually, that's why I came over here this morning." Tom pulled a piece of paper out of his pocket and held it up before Desiree. "You ready to go hunting?"

CHAPTER TWELVE

"You found the house?" Desiree's voice rose in excitement.

"No," Tom admitted. "But I have a list of possibilities. It's a start."

"It's more than we had before. Your friend must be awfully good," Desiree said.

"He is. Of course, these are only general areas, and he's not sure they have every single one of the requirements."

"What are the requirements?" Wells asked as Desiree snatched the list from Tom's hand and began to read it.

"The right size and quality of houses." Tom began to tick them off on his fingers. "Terraced stone houses. Close enough to walk to grander homes, as well as a church, larger parks or squares, and a smaller triangular park. Oh, and an odd intersection of multiple streets."

"Upper Chelsea . . . Kensington . . ." Desiree murmured and glanced up at Tom.

172

"Those aren't terribly far from here."

Tom nodded. "I thought we could start with the Upper Chelsea first, since it's close. We'll have to take a cab to the others."

Desiree jumped up, her face alight with excitement. "Give me ten minutes. I need to change and grab a hat, and I'll be ready."

Without waiting for a reply, she ran out of the room, leaving Tom alone in an awkward silence with her brother. Tom sipped at his coffee, trying to think of something to say, as the other man studied him. After a time, Wells said, "Desiree has her heart set on finding her father. I hope you aren't planning to . . . . mislead her in any way."

"No. Of course not." Tom bristled.

"I'm rather fond of her," he drawled in that careless upper-crust way. Wells, Tom noticed, was pitch-perfect in his tone and speech, unlike his siblings. "I wouldn't take kindly to anyone using her or leading her astray."

"Are you threatening me?" There was more surprise than alarm in Tom's voice. He had little doubt he could hold his own with this man. Still, despite his languid air, there was something in Wells's gaze that was cold and a trifle unnerving.

"My dear chap, of course not." Wells's eyebrows rose lazily. "Merely stating a fact."

Tom wasn't sure what he was supposed to make of that, so he said nothing. It seemed to Tom it took a good bit of gall for Wells to warn Tom not to mislead Desiree when she was the one trying to pull off a swindle. Tom wondered what her brothers' roles were in this scheme. Was Wells warning him not to interfere in their plan? Or were his words meant to convince him that Desiree really believed what she'd told him?

Desiree came downstairs several minutes later than the ten minutes she had promised. She'd apparently taken the time to sweep her hair up and pin it, which was a disappointment. But Tom had to admit that she looked very fetching beneath a large hat with a feather that curled down enticingly to her cheek. Of course, he hadn't seen her in anything that didn't look fetching on her.

It was her face and form that made the clothes, not the other way around. He wasn't sure what was so appealing about her face. She wasn't beautiful in the way that Kyria Moreland was, so perfect in face and form that an artist might have made her. But then, Tom had always found Kyria a trifle overwhelming in her beauty.

Desiree's face was simply intriguing, the sort that made one keep looking at her, as if to find out why she drew him so. Perhaps it was the sparkle in her eyes, the sense of energy and laughter just waiting to bubble out. Or that delectably plump lower lip or creamy skin that looked so soft it was difficult not to reach out and touch her cheek.

Sternly, Tom pulled his thoughts back from their wayward direction as they left the house and started along the street. "Alex —"

"Who?"

"My friend the architect. He added a caveat about this list. His opinions are based on the city today, and he's not sure they're exactly the same as they were twenty-some-odd years ago. So it may no longer be exactly the way your brother described it."

"I know." Desiree's smile was sunny. "But I think we'll find it even so."

"He gave me a number of other areas, as well, but they're all farther out. It makes sense that the man in question would have wanted a place for your mother that was fairly nearby, so it wouldn't have been a long drive from where he lived."

"And his home would have been in one of the richer places, like Mayfair or Grosvenor Square or Belgravia."

"Exactly." Here he was talking as if Desiree's story was real, letting her suck him into her pretense.

For all he knew, Brock's words yesterday could have been a complete fairy tale designed to add verisimilitude to Desiree's story. Perhaps the incomplete description had been intended to lead Tom to a house that the Malones had already set up. A house that had a hiding spot where they'd planted some "proof" that they were Morelands. The proof would be more convincing if Tom discovered it than if they simply handed it to him.

But that seemed a very elaborate ruse, as well as a rather iffy way of leading him to it. What if Tom had found Brock's description too vague to pursue it? Or if Tom hadn't had a clever architect to ask? It also would be quite time-consuming. Perhaps if Tom had not come up with the list of areas, they would have "found" some further proof to steer him in the right direction or Desiree would nudge him toward the house they wanted.

He looked down at her face, so bright and eager. Could she really be this good at dissembling? Wasn't it possible Desiree believed what she'd told him? Maybe the house they were looking for had existed and Stella Malone had lived there with her children.

And maybe he was just as gullible, as eager

to believe a bewitching woman as any other mark. She was a thief, a card sharp.

"How do you win all the time?" he asked abruptly.

"What?" Desiree glanced at him, startled. "Oh." She shrugged. "It's not luck." Her eyes narrowed. "And it's not cheating, if that's what you're asking."

"You win game after game, and when you don't win, you fold early. It looks as if you know what's in everyone else's hands."

"Well, I don't." Her face, so happy before, was now sharp with anger. "I'm good at what I do, and that's why I win. I'm not a sharp, but I'm not a flat, either. I don't rely on luck and I don't play games that depend solely on luck. I don't play with emotion."

"And . . . ?"

Desiree heaved a sigh. "Well, you probably won't believe this any more than you'll believe I'm not an adventuress." She hesitated a moment, then said, "I don't read their cards, but I read the cardplayer."

"What does that mean?"

"It means that I look at the other players and I get a sense of what they'll do."

"Mind reading?" Tom asked skeptically.

"No. I can't tell what anyone is thinking. I read the emotions in their faces — if they're excited or disappointed in their hand. If

177

they have that mad gambling fever light in their eyes. Probably other people can tell what one is feeling in the same way." She hesitated, sending Tom a wary look, then said in a rush, "But I can sense when they're hiding something or lying. It makes me good at recognizing bluffs." She shrugged. "That's how I knew you were telling the truth this morning about that carriage."

"You know whether someone is lying?"

"Not always. It's harder if the person is someone who lies all the time because then he's acting in alignment with his true personality. And it's not exactly as if I see truth or lie stamped on one's face. But if they say things that have integrity, my inner eye will see them as particularly sharp and bright. Standing out from their surroundings, almost emitting their own light. I can see inside them in a way, see the essence of them."

"Their soul?" Tom asked. Surely she was making this up.

"I suppose you could call it that. To me, it's just their real selves, the core of their being. And when something is wrong or they're lying, there's another, darker outline, shifted slightly from that one. Rather like one of those photographs where you can see another image beneath it that doesn't quite line up. Their inner reality is slightly different from their appearance. It's a sign of disturbance. Discordance." She glanced up at him. "This morning, you were clear, very much in harmony with yourself. I was sure you were telling the truth."

"Do you always know what everyone around you is feeling?" That thought took him aback.

"No, thank goodness. That would be terrible. I have to concentrate on it, unless it's so strong it just bursts out of them. That happens most often with anger." She glanced over at him and smiled a little ruefully. "So do you think I'm insane or lying?"

"Neither. I believe that some people have abilities that others don't have." The Morelands certainly had enough peculiar skills. Was it possible that this odd ability of Desiree's meant she actually was a Moreland? "Do you dream?"

She gave him a strange look. "Of course I dream. Everyone does."

"I don't mean ordinary dreams like being in a crowd and suddenly realizing you have no clothes on."

Desiree chuckled. "That's what you dream?"

He ignored her. "The kind of dreams I'm asking about are important dreams. Like ones about the future or people you don't know or something like that."

"No." She looked at him as if she thought he was crazy. "Do *you* have dreams like that?"

"No. But sometimes people do."

"If you say so." They walked on in silence for a moment, then Desiree said, "Falk believed me. I hated it."

"Believed what? That you could read people?"

"That I could tell if they were lying. He'd call me in and ask me if somebody who worked for him was lying, and I didn't want to do it. I was glad if they'd managed to hold back something from him or lied to him."

"Why didn't you just tell him they weren't lying?"

"I did sometimes. But others told such obvious lies that I think he knew before I told him. And some people . . . well, I was happy if he tossed them out. If I hid too much from him, he wouldn't believe me when I said someone was innocent."

"So you had to decide who to let go and when?" Tom felt a pang in his chest. "That's a terrible thing to put on a child."

"I suppose. I didn't know any different, though. I had to stay on his good side. To protect Wells and me, to have better food and a warmer place to sleep, to not get a kick or a cuff to the ear. You know."

"Yeah, I know." He knew the life all too well.

"Look! There's one of those intersections!" Desiree pointed ahead of them, where four streets ran into one another at odd angles, creating a sort of misshapen star.

"Excellent. We need to walk a large square all around this place, looking for a white stone row." Tom paused and glanced around, then turned and started back the way they had come. "Let's begin a couple of streets up."

"How shall we do it? Divide it into quadrants?" Desiree asked.

"Yes, that's good."

Tom saw a man in the next block striding toward them, but the man suddenly stopped, then whipped around and began to walk the other way. Just as Desiree and Tom were doing.

They were being followed.

CHAPTER THIRTEEN

"Let's turn right here," Tom said when they reached the first cross street.

"Why? I thought you wanted to go to the next one," Desiree said, but she matched her movements to his.

"I did. But I'm running a test on someone I saw."

"A test?" She was silent for a moment, then said, "You think someone is following us?" Clearly, her mind ran along the same lines as his.

"That's what I'd like to find out. It might have been pure chance." Tom slowed his steps a bit.

"I'm not a great believer in chance," Desiree responded. She took his arm and looked up at him, smiling as if they were in pleasant conversation. It was nice to have someone who quickly understood and fell in well with his pretense. It was also a trifle disturbing that she took so easily to the nefarious and the deceptive.

"Neither am I," Tom responded and turned his face toward hers, glancing behind them. "Blast. If he followed us, he's too far back for me to see him without being obvious."

"Look. I see a square ahead. There are probably benches where we could sit."

"And see who turns up?" Once again, her thoughts meshed with his. "Would you care to rest for a while?"

"That sounds like an excellent idea."

They continued to stroll along. Desiree was much closer to him now that she had taken his arm, her body almost but not quite touching him. Her posture had changed, subtly turning in toward him and becoming somehow more pliant.

"You're damnably good at this."

She laughed, looking up at him in a way that probably appeared flirtatious, but Tom clearly saw the mischief dancing in her eyes. "Well, after all, it's best to seem innocent when one is scouting a place before a job." When he made no reply, she squeezed his arm. "Come, Mr. Quick, have you really grown so sanctimonious you've forgotten your past?"

"Of course I remember it. I know exactly what I did. It's helpful in my line of work to be able to think like a criminal." Tom knew he sounded like a terrible prig. He gave in, and the corner of his mouth twitched up. "And before you ask, yes, sometimes it was fun."

Desiree's smile was pleased rather than gloating. "There's good and bad in all of us, isn't there?"

"Some of us are better than others, however."

"Your beloved Morelands?" Her voice hardened. "They, I take it, are saints."

"Of course not. But they're good people. You'd understand if you knew them."

"I'd like to know them," Desiree pointed out.

They had reached the benches in the square, and they sat down, Tom angling toward her. Not looking at her but keeping his eyes trained on the street behind them, he said, "The Morelands are the closest thing I have to a family."

"You really don't have *any* family?"

"No. You have the better of me . . . at least you knew your mother." Tom meant to say it lightly, but somehow the words didn't come out that way. He shrugged. The last thing he wanted was pity. "The Morelands saved me. Reed plucked me out of that life and put me in an orphanage the duchess founded, where they fed us and educated us. And when Falk snatched me back a year later, Reed came and got me and thrashed Falk in the bargain."

Desiree stiffened, her eyes widening, and stared at him for a long moment. "Oh, my God! You're the Apple Boy."

"The what?"

"Brock said he remembered you, and I thought I didn't. But I *do*. I was little, but I remember this — once Falk had a boy tied to something."

Tom stared at her, astonished. "It was that great, heavy table."

"And I knew he was hungry, so I gave him the apple I'd swiped off the vendor's cart when Falk wasn't looking."

"I remember." And he did. "You had blond curls, and I thought you looked like an angel."

Desiree laughed. "Looks can be deceiving."

"I didn't recognize you when I saw you again."

She shrugged. "I was only four or so. My hair darkened as I grew older, and unfortunately most of the curl left, too."

Tom had not, would not, ever forget that moment. He had never been closer to despair — taken from the comfort and security of the orphanage, without any idea that anyone would come to rescue him. He'd been viciously hungry, made all the worse by being tied to the table where others were eating. Then the little girl had come up and gazed into his face for a long moment. She'd reached into her pocket and, after a quick glance around, slipped the apple into Tom's bound hands.

"You turned back around and stood so that you blocked me from sight," he said.

"There wouldn't have been any point in giving it to you if the others could see you eat it. They'd have grabbed it in a second. I knew to keep my extras for when I got home."

"Home? That was before you lived with Falk?" Tom grabbed the diversion. He felt such a strange mix of emotions; he had to shove it aside. He'd think about it later, when he was alone. When she wasn't watching him with that same unwavering gaze.

"Yes. We were still with Bruna and Sid then. We only worked for Falk when our act didn't have a job." She paused, then said, "We got one after that, so I wasn't there for a while. Then I never saw you again. Is that when you ran away?"

"That was the second time I left Falk. The first time, I tried to hook Reed Moreland's watch — that's one of the duke's sons — and he caught me."

Desiree drew in her breath sharply, and Tom saw in her eyes the knowledge of what happened to those who were caught.

He shook his head. "He didn't call a peeler on me. He took me back to their house and gave me food and clothes, made me take a bath. I thought he was right barmy. And he talked to me. I didn't know what to think. I was scared and cynical and mouthy. I knew there must be some trick in it. I thought maybe he was one of those men that would pay Falk for a boy, you know, but I wasn't pretty enough for that."

Beside him, Desiree shivered. "Yes, some of them wanted Wells. Me, too, sometimes. But we were too valuable to Falk for him to do it."

"That's good."

"So what happened with this Moreland man?"

"He took me to an orphanage, one his mother funded. I learned to read, and I had three good meals a day and milk and biscuits before bed." Tom smiled faintly, remembering his astonishment. "At first I'd steal a roll or two at dinner to hide away for later. Finally I realized I didn't need to. I got to like it there. The food and the beds.

And the books . . . the books were grand. But I did hate the rules."

Desiree chuckled. "Of course."

"I'd sneak out sometimes. Maybe I was testing them, seeing if they'd catch me. Or keeping my hand in, just in case it all went away. I'd steal a wallet or grab something from a food vendor and run. I always liked the running. Getting away. Outwitting someone." He looked at her. "You understand."

"Yes." Desiree smiled. "I do."

"Anyway, one day I went too far away from the orphanage, and one of Falk's men saw me and nabbed me. That's the time that you gave me the apple." He looked down, picking at a loose thread on his jacket. "I thought I was done. But then Reed showed up. The people at the orphanage told him I'd left and he tracked me down. I couldn't believe it. Reed took Falk down, beat the hell out of him. And he hauled me back to the orphanage. I got smart enough after that to stop sneaking out."

"That's why you're so beholden to the Morelands."

"It's not just that. They — blast! I forgot what I was doing. Bloody, blinkin' hell." Tom looked up, his gaze roaming up and down the street. "There he is." He relaxed.

What was wrong with him? Telling Desiree all that. Paying no attention to his surroundings.

"Where?" Desiree asked.

"Turn to look across the street. Toward that yellowish stone house. He's standing on the corner, looking uncomfortable." She did as he suggested, and Tom asked, "Do you know him?"

"No. Why would I know him? Oh." Her gaze cleared. "You think it's just me he's interested in. That maybe he was the one in the carriage last night."

"It would certainly be a possibility. But, actually, I was thinking he might work for your brother."

"Brock?" Her voice slid upward in disbelief.

Tom shrugged. "Protective older brother who's concerned about his sister traipsing around town alone with a man. Especially after someone was lurking outside their house last night."

Desiree tilted her head. "I suppose that would make some sense, though he'd know I'd be mad as a wet cat if he interfered. Brock is a bit protective. But I don't see how it's possible. I didn't tell him about that carriage last night. I haven't even seen him this morning. He left the house early.

And how would he know I went for a stroll with you? I didn't know it myself until you showed up this morning."

"Wells could have let him know."

"He got word to Brock and Brock sent a man after us in time to follow us?"

"Wells knew in general where we were going. We mentioned Upper Chelsea. But you're right . . . it does seem unlikely. What about Wells? He was the one issuing a warning to me."

"It wasn't Wells. He wouldn't have sent someone — he'd have done it himself. And we wouldn't have spotted Wells. He's very good at being inconspicuous."

"Which leaves us with Falk as our main suspect."

"Why Falk? I mean, he's certainly capable of it, but why would he want to follow us?"

"Because he's involved with all this. He's been involved from the first. He hired you to steal something from the office."

"But that had nothing to do with my father or me," she protested. "He wanted me to find some envelope, that's all."

"An envelope?" Tom repeated skeptically.

"Yes, an envelope," she replied in an exasperated voice. "Why would I lie to you about that?"

"I don't know."

"So just on general principle, you assume I'm lying."

"No." Tom looked at her, torn. He wanted to believe her. Her generous gift to him as a child warmed him in a way he couldn't describe. But a kind gesture from a child didn't prove that she was innocent now. "But it doesn't make sense. I have no idea how Falk fits into it."

"Because he doesn't," she said with some exasperation. "Falk wanted me to do the job for him, and he knew I wouldn't work with him unless he offered something really important. So he promised he would tell me who my father was if I took this envelope from your office."

"Why would he know who your father was?"

Desiree shrugged. "I've no idea. But I felt he was telling me the truth."

"Because of your ability to detect a lie."

"Because I can pick up on certain signals," Desiree corrected. "I saw no indication Falk was lying. What I sensed was a sort of glee, really, as if he *wanted* me to find out who my father was. There was this evil glint in his eye. Though I'm not sure why he would care."

"He'd always be happy to do something against the Morelands. He hates them — or at least he hates Reed. When he took me back, Reed humiliated Falk in front of his people, and Falk's not the sort to forget that."

"There is a certain . . . irony, I suppose, in having me search the Moreland office, knowing who my father was. That's the sort of twist of the knife that Falk enjoys."

"What envelope did he want?"

"Falk said it was a large envelope sent by an attorney named Blackstock. He didn't say who it was addressed to. I'm not sure he even knew that. He was rather vague about the whole thing. He thought it would be a large envelope or perhaps even a file. And it would be at your office."

"It still makes no sense." Tom sighed and stood up. "But we'd probably better continue or our friend will grow suspicious."

He politely reached down a hand to help her up. There was no reason to, of course — it was obvious the woman was anything but weak — but Tom couldn't resist the chance to touch her.

Desiree took it, saying, "Are we going to lose our spy?"

"I think I'd rather keep him," Tom said, and they started across the square.

Desiree nodded. "I agree. What's he going to learn from tramping all over the place after us?" She sent Tom that twinkling grin that did peculiar things to his insides. "And I wouldn't mind making him a little foot-sore."

"I'd rather not let him know we're onto him, at least not yet." Tom was silent for a moment, then said, "What if Falk thinks you have what he wanted you to find? That you lied to him about not finding it. And he's trying to get it back?"

"That's a possibility," Desiree agreed after a moment of thought. "He might think I had realized its value, whatever that is, and decided to keep it for myself."

"Did you?"

"No! I don't understand why you are so convinced I'm a cheat." Her eyes lit with anger; it was annoying that it made her even more attractive. "It isn't as if your past is spotless. I would think you could under-stand that a person might give up that life. Or that they can have a sense of honor even though they've broken the law."

"I'm suspicious by nature," Tom said. "And experience. I learned early on that it's the best way to get by."

"So you trust no one? You must have very few friends."

"Of course I have friends," Tom protested. As soon as he said it, he wondered if that was true. He had dozens of acquaintances. But were they really what one would call friends? There were Alex and Con, of course. They were close; he'd known them since they were children. He'd trust them with his life, and they knew he'd have their backs. But they weren't mates that one raised a pint or two with at the pub. They weren't the sort of friends you told your secrets to. Nobody was. Tom kept his secrets to himself.

They continued to walk, dissecting the area as they had planned, searching for the house they wanted. They came across a church — two, in fact — as well as trains and even a small triangular piece of grass that could perhaps be called a park. But there was no sign of a row of white stone houses such as Brock had described. After completing the outer square, they criss-crossed the inside of it.

"I think we're going to have to accept that this area is not the one we want," Desiree said. "Why don't we return to the house for tea and start again tomorrow?"

Tom agreed, and they started back. After a few minutes, Tom said, "Could you drop your handkerchief?"

"What?"

"Or glove or anything. I want an excuse

to look for our pursuer."

"Of course." Desiree let go of the handle of her parasol, and it fell to the ground behind her, tumbling down the road. Tom went chasing after it, and Desiree stopped and turned to watch him, her eyes scanning the street.

Tom grabbed the parasol and came back to her, grinning. Desiree was as clever as they came; the bouncing, rolling parasol had given him ample opportunity to unobtrusively scour the street. She stood there waiting for him in a perfect pose of fluttery feminine distress, leavened with just the right touch of flirtation. She looked utterly charming, and no doubt she had scouted for their pursuer, as well. Even knowing it was all an act, Tom wanted to pull her to him and kiss her.

Which was not at all the way to be thinking.

"Did you see him?" he asked as he handed her the parasol.

"Across the street, about fifty feet back?"

Tom nodded, and they started forward, still at a casual stroll. He considered the route back to the Malone house, searching his memory for just the right spot for the plan brewing in his head. At the next intersection they would turn right, and just beyond that intersection there lay a church with a small courtyard, partially separated from the street by the remains of an old wall.

They turned the corner. The church wall was beside them, as he had remembered. Tom cast a quick glance over his shoulder to make sure their pursuer was still out of sight around the corner. Then he snaked his arm around Desiree's waist and whisked her into the church courtyard.

CHAPTER FOURTEEN

"Tom! What —" Desiree said as Tom pulled her behind the old stone wall, out of view of the street.

He raised a finger to his lips, and Desiree went still. They waited in a silence broken only by the sound of their breathing. His arm was still around her, her body almost flush against his, as he turned his head, watching the sidewalk beyond the wall.

It occurred to Desiree that this was the third time she had been in Tom's arms, and none had been a romantic embrace. The other times Desiree's thoughts had been on nothing but escape, but here and now she was supremely aware of Tom's body against hers — his heat, his strength, the sound of his breath in her ear. And she felt no desire to leave. Swallowing, Desiree reminded herself that there were more important matters to deal with.

After a moment, the man who had been

following them walked past their spot and stopped, looking up and down the street in confusion. Tom released Desiree and jumped out to grab the man's arm and yank him back into the courtyard with them. The man let out a grunt of surprise and swung at Tom. Desiree moved closer, her parasol at the ready, but her help wasn't necessary. Tom neatly sidestepped the man and grabbed his arm, twisting it up behind his back. He slammed his opponent into the wall.

"Who are you? Why the hell are you following us?" Tom pressed his full weight into the man. "Answer me!"

"I'm not following you! I'm not! I swear. I was just walking along and you jumped me."

"Maybe you ought to call for the police, then. You can tell them your story. Who do you think they'll believe?"

The man just grunted.

"Tell me what you're after. Did someone hire you?" Tom twisted his arm higher.

The man made a pained noise, but said nothing.

"Listen to me," Tom growled, leaning into him harder. "If I see you following me or this lady again, if you lurk outside her house, I will take you apart limb by limb," Tom growled. "Do you understand?"

"Yes."

Tom released him and stepped back. The man took off, shoving past Desiree. Desiree swung on Tom. "What are you doing? Why did you let him go? You barely asked him any questions."

"He wasn't going to tell me anything." Tom took her hand and pulled her out onto the street with him. "And I want to follow him."

Their former pursuer had broken into a run, and they hurried after him, keeping a good distance behind him. The man soon slowed down and stopped to catch his breath, then started walking again.

After a few minutes of trailing him, Desiree said, "He's going back toward my house. Why? Do you think he's going to take up watching the house again?"

"He's not too bright if he does. But then, he wasn't very bright about following us, either."

Their quarry reached Desiree's house, but he walked past it and turned at the next street. Tom and Desiree continued to follow him.

As they rounded the corner, they saw their target stop beside a carriage. Bending down, he unhooked the weight that keep the horses in place.

"That's the carriage!" Desiree broke into a run, Tom beside her.

The man whirled and saw them. He jumped up into the driver's seat and took off, leaving Tom and Desiree standing in the street, staring after him.

Tom cursed and Desiree let out a long sigh, sagging. She'd left this morning with such high hopes, but after all they'd done, here they were at the same place.

"Come." She touched Tom's arm. "Let's sit down and take stock. It's teatime, and I, for one, am starving."

They returned to her house, and after consuming a few little cakes and dainty sandwiches and a great deal of tea, Desiree's spirits began to pick up. "At least we found out that the man following us was the one spying on the house last night. I'm certain that was the same carriage."

"We've got a bit more than that." Tom seemed surprisingly cheerful. With a grin, he stuck his hand into his pocket and pulled out a jumble of objects, which he dumped on the low table before him.

Desiree's eyes widened. "You picked his pocket!"

"I haven't lost *all* my skills."

She laughed. "No wonder you didn't try to question him more."

"I thought it was easier than beating him to a pulp in front of a church. And I doubt I would have learned anything anyway." Tom spread out the objects. "Let's see — a used ticket from Stepney."

"Perhaps he lives there. But that doesn't seem likely when he's got a carriage." Desiree moved over to sit beside Tom and examine the contents of the other man's pockets. Her arm brushed against his, and even though the material of his jacket lay between his flesh and hers, her skin tingled with awareness. She thought of that moment when they were hiding behind the wall and Tom's arms had been around her, his body close to hers.

"I suppose he could have hired the carriage," Tom said. "Or maybe he's working for someone."

"Like Falk, you mean," Desiree said.

Tom nodded. "I must say, though, one would think Falk would have sent someone better at the job."

"He *was* very clumsy about it," Desiree agreed. "That's not like Falk. I didn't recognize him as one of Falk's men, but that doesn't mean much. I haven't been around them for over a decade."

"A pouch of tobacco and cigarette papers," Tom went on, pushing them to one

201

side. "A folding knife." He opened it. "Long enough to be lethal. Sharp, too. A handkerchief. None of this is very helpful."

"What's in here? This looks like a coin purse." Desiree picked up a leather pouch that was bound with a drawstring and pulled it open, tipping the contents out on the table. Several coins of various denominations rolled out, as well as a set of gold cuff links, inlaid with a dark green stone. She picked one up to study the face of it. "These are very nice."

"Is that jade?" Tom reached down to get the other one.

"I think it's aventurine," Desiree replied.

"Naturally you know your gems."

Desiree shot him a glare. "It's not because I'm a thief, if that's what you're suggesting. I just see a lot of men wearing it in one form or another. Gamblers consider it a lucky stone."

"Desiree . . ." Tom said in an odd voice. "Look at the back side of it."

The cuff link was hinged, with an oval of the same size and shape on the other end. Usually the back side was plain, unlike the more ornate front, but this one was engraved. Curlicues were etched around the edge, and in the center it was engraved with three letters: *PAX.*

"Pax?" Desiree's voice rose in excitement as she turned to look at Tom. "The man Brock said was a friend of my father's?"

"Seems more likely than someone engraving *peace* in Latin on their lucky cuff links."

"But why would — do you think that was actually him? Oh, I wish we'd caught him!"

"He didn't strike me as the sort who'd be the friend of a duke's relative." Tom frowned. "But his hair was graying . . . I'd say he was probably old enough. He was dressed like an ordinary chap, but I suppose that could have been a disguise."

"But why would an old friend of my father's follow me around?"

"I don't know." Tom jumped to his feet and began to roam around the room, rubbing the cuff link between his thumb and fingers. "But it defies belief that a different man with the same name would pop up in the middle of this." He paced a bit more, then said, "We can't dismiss the gambling aspect. You said it was a gambling good luck piece." He gestured toward her. "Like the club token you wear."

Desiree's hand went instinctively to the token, once again on a chain and hidden beneath her dress. "We can't be sure that he's a gambler. After all, aventurine is used in other jewelry, as well."

"Very well, but let's go with the odds. This could have nothing to do with your parentage. Or with that bloody envelope, whatever that's about. Say this fellow's a gambler. He comes to your club frequently."

"I didn't recognize him."

"Well, that's because he's a lurker, isn't it? He doesn't go to your table — he watches you from afar. He admires you. He wants to see what's beneath your mask, wants to have you for himself."

"Tom, you're frightening me." A shiver ran down her spine.

"Maybe you should be frightened."

Desiree gazed at him for a moment, her chest tight. "No." She rose to her feet, crossing her arms defensively. "That is simply too much. This fantasy admirer would also have to have the same name as my father's old friend. An unusual name. And if he was someone who frequented the Farrington, Brock would have noticed that name."

"He knows the name of everyone who comes there?"

"If it's someone who goes there frequently, yes. My brother is not the sort to leave things to chance. He knows everything that goes on in that place. He circulates throughout the room, greeting people, chatting. Brock makes it his business to know his patrons, as well as his employees. He makes sure there are no arguments, and when he sees some young fool throwing away a fortune, he puts a stop to it. He wants the fool to come back. He wants the fool's friends and family to know that it's an excellent place to play. Trust me, he would notice someone who was dangerous."

Tom quirked his eyebrow at her. "He 'reads' people like you do?"

"No." *Not exactly.* "But he has a lot of experience, and he pays close attention. He would have recognized that name, and he would not have allowed anyone dangerous in the club — at least not more than once. I don't think it's connected to the club."

"Very well. Let's say the man following you is the man who was a friend of your parents." Tom took another turn around the room. "Why, after all these years, would this man decide to start following you? He's had ample opportunities to find you before this. He would know your names. You have been living in this house, working at that club, for some time."

"Yes, years."

"Then why — leaving aside the issue of why he wouldn't simply call on you — why would this man suddenly feel the need to hunt you up and watch your house? Why dog your footsteps?"

"Because I didn't start looking for my father until now," Desiree replied. "I mean, I'd always wanted to know. I wondered about it. I even looked up my birth certificate. But I have never made a concerted effort to find him. I didn't hire a detective."

"You didn't exactly hire one now, if you'll remember," Tom commented dryly. He paused, frowning, then said, "Come to think of it, if you wanted so much to learn who your father was, why *haven't* you hired a detective to find out before now?"

Desiree's stomach quivered. She hated the look of suspicion in his eyes, the iron in his voice. But how could she tell him the truth? Tom already thought she was a liar, and even though he had been surprisingly open to her explanation of her skill at "reading" people, she felt sure a full revelation of her powers would convince him that she was either mad or a fraud. Or both. "I hired you now because the opportunity arose. I found that ring in your office. I finally had some idea of who he was."

"Even before you found the ring, you wanted to know who he was badly enough you agreed to work for a man you say you despise, to put yourself in jeopardy by going back to thieving, because you wanted to find out his name. Then you threw in your lot with another man you disliked." He jerked his thumb toward his own chest. "All because you wanted so much to find your father."

"Yes. What does that matter?"

"What's your goal? You know his name, so you've satisfied your curiosity. You already knew that he ran off with your mother years ago. It seems unlikely to believe that you will have some happy reunion with the man. And you maintain that you aren't trying to squeeze money from his family. You just 'want to know.' You're hiding something. I can 'read' people well enough to tell that. What is it that you want to know? And why now? Why is it so incredibly, urgently important now?"

"Because something is wrong!" Desiree shot back, feeling pushed to the brink.

Tom stared at her blankly. "What do you mean? What's wrong? What does it have to do with your father?"

"I don't know! If I knew, maybe I'd know what to do." Desiree glared balefully back at him. "You won't believe me any more than you believe anything else I say."

"Try me."

"I've been having this feeling." How was she to explain this? How could she make him understand?

"This feeling." His voice rang with skepticism. "What, like the thing you sense with people, that they have integrity or not?"

"A bit. But I don't *see* anything. This is something inside of me, so it's not visible, even to my inner eye. It is more abstract, but somehow also stronger, more urgent than the warnings that the light and dark images give me." It was as if an alarm went off inside her that said that something was about to rip apart her internal life. Destroy her emotions. Corrupt her own constancy and solidity. But just the idea of saying all that to someone as calm and logical as Tom made Desiree want to run and hide. "Have you ever walked into a room and before you could even pinpoint what was missing, you knew something was different?"

"Of course," Tom answered. "Like when you broke into the office and I was sure something was wrong in the building, but couldn't say why."

"Exactly. But it's much stronger — I can feel little fissures in my inner world, as though the 'wrongness' is inside me, squirming in my stomach like an eel. A week or two ago, I began feeling twitchy and anxious, as if there was something I should be doing. I kept thinking about my parents, my father, and I knew that uneasy feeling was connected to him. I didn't know what to make of it or what I could do. Then Falk offered to tell me my father's name. And I knew it was meant to be. That I was supposed to find him. That it was important."

"What do you think is going to happen if you discover his name? What are you going to do?"

"I don't know! I just know that I need to find out! There's danger waiting."

"How can you be so sure? Have you ever had this feeling before? Did it come true?"

"Yes!" Desiree cried out. "The last time I felt like this was right before Bruna Upton burned to death!"

CHAPTER FIFTEEN

Tom's stomach dropped, an atavistic feeling of dread filling him. Was Desiree in danger? "Are you serious? You're sure it's the same?"

"Do you believe me?" Desiree looked surprised.

"I'm . . . not sure." Tom had seen too many things with the Morelands over the years to discount premonitions of danger. Which also raised the question, again, of whether this portent of doom was proof Desiree really was a Moreland. But that was something he would worry about later. Right now, there were more immediate concerns. "I think we'd be foolish not to consider the possibility. That's the only time it's happened?"

"They tell me that I was upset before Brock fell from a rope and injured his leg, but I was only two, and I don't remember it. I have — well, Brock calls it a gift, but I'm not sure what it is. I can sense when something is wrong. Dangerous or damaged or odd. It was helpful when Wells and I were thieving. I could tell if, say, there was a dog or a guard that we hadn't expected or if something was wrong with our equipment. I felt it last night when I saw that carriage. Sometimes I can see a deep darkness, a sort of void, where there's danger. Other times, it's just a little shock of awareness inside. Like goose bumps. Or the way you feel when music hits a discordant note."

"And you're feeling that same thing about finding your father?"

"No. This isn't just a bit of prickling or tingling. It's a knot in my chest, a nervous, restless feeling. A compulsion to *do* something. But I don't know what to do." Desiree threw her hands up in frustration. "It's not a premonition, just a vague, pervasive feeling. It's how I felt before Bruna died. I was young, only six, and I had no idea what it meant. I just felt frightened. Then one day a lantern turned over and the tent caught fire, and the only mother I'd known was dead. I realized that was the reason I had felt that way. I should have told someone. Warned Bruna."

Something in Tom's chest twisted at the sorrow on her face. "You couldn't have known. You're not a seer. That's far too heavy a burden to place on a child. Even an adult wouldn't have known what was going to happen."

"Yes, but . . ." Desiree set her jaw, her eyes bright. "I know now. And I'm not going to make that mistake this time. I have to act."

He nodded. There was going to be no holding Desiree back.

"It's been growing for a month now," Desiree went on. "I hardly noticed it at first. I thought I was just bored. But it grew stronger, and then when Falk offered me that job, I *knew*. I can't explain why, but I was certain that the urgency in me was to find my father, to learn who I really was. I'd always wanted to know about the rest of our family, but it wasn't the same sort of compelling need."

"Do you feel it more at certain times, certain places? Certain people? Was it stronger when you were talking to Falk?"

"No. At least, I haven't noticed that. But it grows more urgent all the time. I'm more certain that finding my father is important. But . . ." She broke off and looked away.

"But what?"

Finally, grudgingly, Desiree said, "It's not as strong when you're around." She added hastily, "I think perhaps it's because I'm actually doing something about it. Not just sitting around worrying."

Tom nodded. He had no idea what to say about her statement or why her words had warmed him. "Are you going to the club tonight?"

"Yes, I suppose so. Why?" Desiree looked over at him in surprise at his change of subject.

"Because I don't think you should go there alone. I'll go with you."

Desiree frowned. "I didn't mean that you needed to be with me all the time. It isn't as if that feeling is overwhelming."

"No, I know you didn't intend that. And I'm not talking about haunting your presence. Just escorting you to and from the club. That's when that carriage was lurking there."

"Our coachman takes me and carries me home."

That was true, but Tom didn't find it very satisfactory. "Your driver is watching the road. He's standing about chatting with the other coachmen while he waits. He's not going to look at things in the same way I will."

Desiree looked at him shrewdly for a moment. Then, to Tom's surprise, she shrugged her shoulders and acquiesced. "Very well.

Why don't you stay, have supper with us before we go?"

Something in him wanted to do just that. They could talk over their day, plan for tomorrow. But Tom shook his head. He needed to think, and that was harder to do around Desiree. His thoughts kept creeping toward completely inconsequential matters, like the exact color of her gray-green eyes or the wispy strand of hair that escaped her pins and curled along her neck or the way her laughter made him want to say something to make her laugh again.

"Thank you, but no," he said a bit stiffly. "I should get back to the office. I have to change into my 'gentleman's togs' for this evening."

Desiree didn't urge him to stay — and there was no reason he should feel disappointed by that. The last thing he needed was her meddling in his life, arranging his schedule and pulling his attention from the things he should be thinking about.

When he reached the office, however, he found that the change of location had done little to order his thoughts. He felt uncertain, which was not like him. He didn't know how he felt about Desiree Malone. He couldn't tell if she was telling the truth. And, frankly, he wasn't at all sure what he was doing or why. Was he trying to protect the Morelands? Prove she was wrong? Was he helping her because she'd coerced him into it . . . or because he enjoyed being with her?

Tom couldn't deny that he had enjoyed the day he'd just spent with Desiree. She drew him, not just physically, but in many ways. She was clever, she was different, she was irrepressible. There was an ease in being with her that he had never felt with anyone else. He knew her, and she him, because they were molded in the same fires. She understood without explanation things that no one else could. She'd lived, as he had, in two separate worlds.

But he didn't really trust her. And that, at least in part, was for exactly the same reason. He understood her and her life too well.

Still . . . she was the child who had reached out to help him long ago. There was a bond between them that he hadn't known existed until today. It was more than the fact that she had been kind or that he had been grateful. He could not help but feel that they were tied together, that they were somehow meant to meet again.

Tom would have said that he didn't believe in fate or destiny. Life was more like a throw of the dice, and sometimes you were lucky, sometimes not. But still . . . there had been so many places along the way where his life could have gone in a drastically different direction. If Reed hadn't been there that day or Falk hadn't urged Tom to pick the man's pocket. If Reed hadn't been the sort of man he was or the duchess hadn't set up an orphanage wherein children were treated humanely. If Olivia hadn't started this detective agency or he'd gone to work somewhere else.

Desiree had traveled an equally varied and even more unusual road, both of them moving far away from Falk and their old life. And now here they were again, brought together by Falk, their meeting once more ruled by a series of events that seemed pure happenstance — him waking up when Desiree broke in, her dropping that gambling chip.

It would be easy to read into that a design, lives arcing around and coming back to touch again. Perhaps he had been fated to help her as she had once helped him. Fated that he and she were tied to the Morelands.

Could it be that she really was a Moreland? Tom had been certain she was not. It had shaken his certainty a bit when she explained her ability to "read" people, but after some thought, he'd dismissed that. After all, many people relied on intuition or instinct, whether it was real or not, and Desiree had not claimed to have significant dreams or other, stranger abilities. But this foreknowledge of danger? That spoke of a more serious power.

Granted, it wasn't something as unusual as seeing ghosts or pulling information from objects or a long-dead witch jumping into one's dreams, which were all things the Morelands had done, but not all the Moreland skills were either strong or constant. Kyria, for instance, had responded only to that particular ancient relic, and Reed's and Theo's otherworldly experiences consisted of no more than dreams. Desiree's feeling of impending danger seemed to fit in with the Moreland propensity to live at the edge of reality.

On the other hand, this story was so bizarre, so full of twists and turns and co-incidences that it seemed something Dickens or Eliot might write. Or a long inventive fraud set up by a family of swindlers.

He felt, as he had from the beginning, that he was being pulled into something he ought to avoid, that one misstep could land him in a quagmire, entangle him in such a way that he could not find his way out. Tom liked to have his feet on the ground. He wanted to trust in his pragmatic, realistic, even slightly cynical view of the world.

He had set up a life for himself. Tom knew where he stood and what he wanted. He had been saving money for years so that he could buy a house. Nothing large, nothing grand. Just something that was *his*. Though they were rather vague in his envisioning, there would also be a wife and children in that home.

For all the risks he'd taken in his life and his often cocksure attitude, for all his involvement in the frequently bizarre activities of the Morelands, when it came down to it, at the core of him, Tom desired certainty and solidity. He didn't want this twitchy feeling that danced in his nerves when Desiree was around. He didn't like the emotions that clashed in his chest — the thought that she was in danger and the urge to protect her, the suspicion that she was playing him like a mark, even as he wanted to believe what she told him.

None of those feelings, of course, kept him from showing up at her house that evening to escort her to the club. She was wearing green tonight, her eyes bright behind the mask, and it was, he thought, a crime how much that mask made a man want to kiss the lips below it. You'd think he'd grow accustomed to her scent, as well, that seductive, subtle fragrance that conjured up thoughts of moonlight and tangled bedsheets, but every time it laid him low all over again.

He imagined nuzzling her neck, burying himself in that scent, kissing the thin skin over the pulse in her neck. Which didn't exactly put him in a decent condition or help him watch for an enemy. Distracting. That was the word that described Desiree.

Tom did, however, manage to keep an eye out as they walked out to the carriage and as they left it at the club, glancing up and down the street for any sign of the man who had been following them. Neither the man nor the odd carriage was there. After Desiree sat down at her table, Tom strolled through the place, checking out every face, a practice he repeated at various times throughout the evening.

In between those times, his eyes went back to Desiree. He heard her laugh, and it was like fingers up his spine. He watched her enchanting expression that gave nothing away. He saw the admiration, even hunger, in the men around her, and he felt a rather smug satisfaction that he was the one who would be leaving with her tonight.

Now and then, Tom would stroll outside the club, stopping to chat with the guards and keeping a watchful eye on the street. Once or twice, he walked up and down the surrounding streets, searching for the distinctive carriage.

There had been no sign of the man by the time they left the club and climbed into the waiting carriage. Desiree settled down in the seat beside Tom. She was warm, the faintest sheen of perspiration on her face as she removed the mask. Desiree leaned back against the seat, closing her eyes, and let out a sigh.

"Tired?" Tom asked.

"A bit." She opened her eyes, rolling her shoulders. "It gets cramped sitting there for so long. I quit early tonight. Today was rather wearing."

He grinned. "You could say that." He paused. "You want to do it again tomorrow?"

"Of course." She flashed him a grin. "You don't think I'm going to quit after one day, do you?"

"No." He smiled back. "But I thought you might want to wait a day or two."

"No. If it gets too taxing doing that and going to the club in the evening, I'll skip the games. It's not as if I have to do them."

"We might do the Marylebone districts tomorrow. I think the one near Percy Circus may be more likely than the area in Kensington."

"Very well." They pulled up in front of the Malone house as Desiree spoke.

Tom exited first, looking up and down the street before giving her his hand to climb down. "I'll walk around a bit after you go in, make sure he's not parked farther up the street."

"Let's both walk," Desiree suggested, and when Tom hesitated, she went on, "You know I'm not fragile or a liability. I'd like to walk after all that sitting tonight."

His hesitation had not been from fear she wouldn't be able to handle herself if they discovered their pursuer. It was the thought of being with her alone in the warm darkness that gave him pause. It wasn't wise. But he said, "Of course."

Desiree took his arm as they strolled. "What did you think about the club this evening?"

"I think it has good security, a high-level clientele, and it probably rakes in a lot of money. Your brother is, as you said, very visible and active in the club." Tom stopped in the shadows of a tree, turning toward her. "And you had the whole table in the palm of your hand."

She arched her brow. "Now you're going to say how that tells you I'm wicked?"

"No. It makes you talented. It makes you intriguing." His eyes glinted as a grin flashed and was gone. "And maybe it makes you a little dangerous." Tom curved his hand against her cheek. "I like you, Desiree. I can't seem to keep myself from it."

"But that doesn't mean you trust me."

"No. More than that, it means I don't trust myself around you." He bent and touched his lips to hers.

Desiree's arms slid around his waist, and when Tom started to draw his head back, she followed his kiss. Hunger rolled down through him. He'd been wanting to kiss her from the first moment he saw her in the club. Now something broke inside him, and he allowed himself the pleasure. He followed his instincts instead of his head.

The result shook him. He was lost in the moment, heat surging through him, pulsing at his restraints. He had no thought for the man they sought, for the street around them or the danger that might lurk there. His world had narrowed to Desiree's lips beneath his, her soft body against him, the desire thrumming through his veins. He could feel the heat rising in her, too, and she molded her body to his in a move that sent his hunger spiraling even higher.

There was, moreover, a heady pleasure in knowing that Desiree did exactly as she wanted, that anything she gave, she gave freely. There was no need to consider whether she was trying to please or placate or tempt him. No reason to worry that she might regret this kiss or that he was taking advantage of her vulnerability. Desiree Malone didn't regret, and nobody took advantage of her.

When at last their lips parted, he gazed down into her face, his chest rising and falling rapidly, his skin tingling as heat flooded him. Desiree didn't look away, her eyes intent on his.

"You're making this very complicated for me," he murmured.

"No." Even here in the shadow, he could see the twinkle in her eyes. "*You're* making it complicated. For me, it's quite simple."

"You have no concerns, no doubts, no worries about what will happen?"

"I didn't say that. But my desire is to let it all play out. That's part of the fun, isn't it, discovering what you don't know?"

Tom couldn't deny that. The desire to know her in every way was hammering in him right now. He kissed her again, wrapping his arms tightly around her and pressing her into his body. Their kiss was long and deep, and when Tom finally raised his head, they were both flushed and breathing hard, the heat between them palpable.

"I think . . ." Tom said, taking in a calming breath. "Perhaps right now we ought to tend to business."

"Of course," Desiree replied and stepped back, curling her hand around his arm once more and turning to walk forward. "After all, there's always tomorrow."

CHAPTER SIXTEEN

After their kiss, Desiree had trouble going to sleep. She hadn't expected it, which had only added to the pleasure. However irritating Tom Quick was, he stirred her. She spent an inordinate time remembering the moment, remembering, in fact, every encounter with the man, and as a result sleep eluded her for hours. Despite that, she popped awake earlier than usual the next morning, surging with energy. She dressed and went downstairs to eat alone, both her brothers still sleeping.

Afterward, she ordered the carriage brought around. They needed transportation to Percy Circle, so it made more sense for her to pick up Tom at his office than to wait for him to come to her. Besides, she had a certain fondness for that office. It had been a challenging exit. She'd like to see it in the daylight. And there was even the possibility that she might get a look at the

Moreland of Moreland & Quick.

Today Desiree entered the building in a more conventional way, going in the front door and up the stairs. As she reached the top of the stairs and turned down the hallway, she heard the sound of male voices and a laugh. One voice belonged to Tom; she knew that immediately. The other voices puzzled her; there seemed to be two of them, but they sounded almost the same.

She understood when she stopped in the doorway and saw Tom talking with two men who looked exactly alike. All three glanced over at her — the two dark-haired men with mild inquiry and Tom with alarm.

They were twins. Like her and Wells. Desiree's heart picked up a beat. Tom hadn't mentioned that there were twins in the Moreland family. For these must be Morelands; one of the men was sitting behind the desk farthest from the door, suit jacket off and looking very much as if he belonged here. His brother lounged against that blasted squeaky-doored cabinet.

"Desiree!" Tom jumped to his feet. "I — um, I didn't know you were coming here this morning."

"We're going to the Percy Circus area, aren't we?"

"Well, yes. I just thought . . ."

"That I would wait like a good little girl for you to fetch me?" Her eyes twinkled. "Surely you know me better than that."

"I do," Tom replied in a grim voice.

"Percy Circus. You're the one who wanted to know about that house?" This remark came from the twin who was standing.

"Yes." Desiree turned to him. "Are you the architect who's a friend of Mr. Quick's?"

"I am, indeed." He had laughing eyes. So did his brother. It felt very strange to be looking at people who might be her . . . what, brothers, cousins? Did she feel a connection? She couldn't see a resemblance to her. Their eyes were green, but a different shade. Their hair was black as midnight and they were tall, both things unlike her. The man went on, "I'm Alex Moreland."

"I'm sorry," Tom inserted quickly. "Miss Malone, allow me to introduce you to my business partner, Con Moreland, and his brother Alex. Gentlemen, Miss Desiree Malone."

Desiree had the distinct feeling Tom wanted to ward off any attempt by Desiree to tell the men who she was. She had a very strong urge to do just that. But Tom clearly didn't want her to, and while it shouldn't matter to her what he thought, the truth was that it did. Also, she had implied that she wouldn't confront the Morelands if Tom agreed to help her find her father, even though she hadn't actually said those words. So she would not, even if she was so conveniently (and through no fault of her own) meeting them.

Con had already risen from his chair, curiosity bright in his gaze. "Tom's helping you locate a house?"

Desiree nodded, not sure what to say.

"Yes," Tom inserted quickly. "It's where her brother lived when he was young."

"It's an interesting puzzle," Alex explained. "There were certain parameters — the location of a triangular park and an intersection of multiple streets, as well as some other things."

"That sounds like Percy Circus, right enough," Con agreed. "What's the story?"

Desiree hesitated and glanced again at Tom. He looked pained.

"I'm sorry," Con said. "No doubt it's a private matter."

Tom muttered something under his breath, let out a sigh and said, "The thing is, Miss Malone is looking for her father."

"Ah, a missing persons case."

"Not exactly. Miss Malone believes, well —"

"I'm the person who broke into your office," Desiree announced.

Both the Morelands gaped at her. Tom began to laugh. "Well, there's an accomplishment. You've rendered the Greats speechless."

"I couldn't think of any subtle way to say it," Desiree told him. She turned back to the brothers. "I didn't take anything." She explained about her search for the envelope from the attorney named Blackstock, ending with, "I couldn't find any envelope like that."

"No doubt because it wasn't here." Con seemed more confused than upset as he looked over at Tom. "Was it?"

"Not that I ever saw," Tom replied.

Con went on, "I don't know any lawyer named Blackstock. Do you, Alex?"

Alex shook his head. "Peculiar thing to steal."

"But the envelope isn't the important thing." Desiree pulled the conversation back to her subject.

"It seems rather pertinent to me," Con replied mildly. "But go on. What is important?"

"What I *did* find while I was searching was . . . a ring with the Moreland coat of arms."

"Con's ring?" Alex asked. "I don't understand."

"Neither do I," Con replied cheerfully. "But it's all very intriguing. Go on, Miss Malone. I assume there's more. Did you take it?"

"No." She dug into her reticule and her fingers closed around Brock's ring. Nerves danced in her stomach. "But I recognized it." She held it out in her open palm. "My brother has one just like it."

"Good Lord." Con plucked the ring from her hand and examined it. "It is just like it." He handed the ring to Alex. Then his eyes narrowed and he said, "Wait. Is this a joke?" He looked suspiciously at Tom, then his brother. "Did you pinch my ring to run a game on me?"

"No, I swear it's not a joke," Tom told him.

Alex raised his hands. "Not me."

Con was already back at his desk, reaching into the top drawer. "It's still here." He returned to the others and held up his ring against the one in Alex's hand. "Alex, do you swear that's not *your* ring?"

"No. Mine's back at the house in Somerset. I never wear it now." Alex waggled his left ring finger, encircled by a wedding band.

"Then how —" Con looked up at Desiree. "Are you saying that you're a Moreland?" He handed back her ring. "But whose child are you? We've never met, have we?"

"No. I don't know who my father is. I never knew him. I was, as they say, born on the wrong side of the blanket."

"I see. Well." Con cleared his throat. "I apologize. Everyone will tell you, I often open my mouth before I open my mind. I didn't mean to embarrass you."

"I'm not embarrassed," Desiree assured him even though that wasn't completely true. She never let anyone see a weakness in her, and it was especially true for these two. They seemed pleasant enough, but she suspected that their friendly attitude would soon change. "I'm not the one who did anything wrong."

"True." Con smiled. He had a very winning smile.

"Miss Malone believes that her father must have been a Moreland," Tom explained. "Because of the ring. But she has no proof."

Desiree glared at Tom. Con nodded and said, "Yes, you'll probably need something more than that to be sure."

"Let's see if we can figure this out." Alex pulled over a chair for Desiree, then perched himself on the edge of Tom's desk. Con brought over his desk chair, and Tom took up a place next to Alex.

Desiree sat down, prepared for an interrogation. But Con said, "Now . . . who are the possibilities? Not our father, of course."

Alex let out a laugh and said to Desiree, "I'm sure you'd be an excellent sister, but the duke simply isn't a possibility. He's thoroughly devoted to Mother."

"Nor Uncle Bellard," Con added, and all three men grinned at that suggestion.

"No. Unless your mother has an exceedingly extensive library, Uncle Bellard would never have met her," Alex assured her, adding, "He's also a bit old, I would think."

"Who else is there?" Tom asked, apparently resigned to the investigation.

"Not Cousin Albert, surely," Alex said.

"God, no," Con agreed. "I don't think he'd be the right age, either. It would have to be someone in the duke's generation, wouldn't it? There's Uncle Richard. I suppose he might be a possibility. He has a couple of children, so he must not be off chasing butterflies *all* the time."

Chasing butterflies? Desiree glanced over at Tom and he shrugged.

"There are all those cousins," Alex commented.

"Cousin Castor. And his brother." Con

began to list them on his fingers. "I can't remember his name, except that thank God they didn't name him Pollux."

Pollux? What did that mean?

"There's the one up in Scotland," Alex added.

"The fellow with the cannons?"

Alex nodded and said to Desiree, "You wouldn't want to be related to him, really."

Desiree was beginning to wonder if these two were playing a joke on *her.*

"Con . . . you do realize that she could be making up the whole thing, don't you?" Tom pointed out.

"Well, of course." Con looked at Desiree. "I don't mean to be impolite, but one has to consider all sides. It's possible as well that you might be mistaken, that your brother has the ring for some entirely different reason."

Alex took up the next part of the conversation, so smoothly that Desiree suspected the twins often spoke this way. "The thing is, you have to settle on who it is before you can prove or disprove it."

"That's what Mr. Quick and I are trying to do. We thought if we could locate the house, we might be able to find someone who had knowledge of the past residents." She thought it would be better if she left

233

out the part about planning to break into it. As pleasant and odd as the twins seemed, most people took a dim view of illegal entry.

"Do you know absolutely nothing about your father?" Con asked.

She shook her head. "My mother left not long after Wells and I were born. We didn't know either of them. Brock, our older brother, was only six or so."

"Your mother left?" Con looked astounded. Clearly this was an idea that didn't fit into his world. "You mean she, well . . ." He stopped, obviously groping for a polite way to say what he wanted to.

"I mean, she ran away. With my father."

"He absconded?" Alex and his brother exchanged confused glances. "I've never heard of any Moreland who ran off."

"Who raised you? Mightn't they know something? Surely your father must have sent them money for your keep," Con said.

"No. We never had anything from him. From anyone."

It was clear both men were surprised, even shocked. "That doesn't sound like — he would have had to be the black sheep of the family," Con told her.

Alex nodded. "I think perhaps you are wrong about it being a Moreland. Even if one of them was that irresponsible, surely someone would have stepped in."

"Maybe the family didn't know about the children," Con suggested.

Desiree thought they were touchingly naive to think gentlemen provided for their by-blows. They were young, but Desiree didn't think she'd ever been young enough to have such a rosy vision of life.

"How did you live, then?" Alex asked. "Were you with a relative, an aunt or someone?"

"A friend of their mother's took them in," Tom said, and a faint smile touched his lips as he looked at Con and said, "Miss Malone and her brothers were raised in a circus."

Desiree was hurt that Tom looked so amused and expectant as he revealed something that would make the Morelands recoil from her. She had to tell them eventually, of course, but couldn't he have waited a bit? And he needn't have looked *gleeful* about it.

"The circus!" Con's eyes widened, and delight flooded his expressive face. He looked over at his brother, and the two of them grinned like little boys. "Really?" He turned to Tom. "I cannot believe you didn't tell me about all this."

The dimple in Tom's cheek popped in as he grinned at the other two. Was *this* the reaction he'd been expecting? Something in Desiree's chest warmed as she watched him. It wasn't just relief that he had meant no cruelty to her. It was the way he looked, so open and at ease, the affection in his eyes. They really were almost like family to him. She better understood his desire to protect them — though they certainly didn't seem to need any protection.

"What was it like?" Alex leaned forward. "Did you travel from town to town? What did she do? The woman who raised you, I mean."

"Yes, we traveled sometimes, but a lot of the time we were here in London." Desiree felt much more comfortable now. "We were acrobats — Bruna the Italian Angel and the Magnificent Malones."

"The Magnificent Malones!" Con exclaimed, a wide grin on his face. "That's grand."

"You, too?" Alex asked. "The children?"

Desiree launched into the tale of her life in the circus. She enjoyed their eagerness, the friendly atmosphere. She was sure it couldn't be true of the whole family, of course, but she liked the twins. She said less about their time with Falk, though Con and Alex were interested in that, too — asking her questions about climbing houses and picking locks, even, astonishingly, launching into a comparison of various locks and the ease in opening them.

"You know how to pick a lock?" Desiree asked.

"Oh, yes," Alex answered. "Tom taught us. Con's better at it than I, though. He's had more experience."

Desiree sent Tom a startled look. "*You* taught them?"

He shrugged. "It was the only skill I had. Well, besides hooking watches, and I didn't think they'd have much use for that."

"Oh, we used that a time or two, as well." Con sent his brother a laughing glance.

Desiree was no longer surprised when the two were intrigued by her current life, as well. After she finished, the Morelands were silent for a moment, digesting the spate of information.

Con said, "Still, interesting as all that is, we haven't come up with a name for this alleged Moreland. Unfortunately, there are a number of Morelands — cousins and second cousins and so on . . . and some whose connection I sincerely doubt," Con said. "Alex and I are in the wrong generation to know any of the gossip about your father. What we really need is someone who knows all the Morelands and their history."

Alex nodded. "You're right. We should talk to Uncle Bellard."

Tom groaned and dropped his head into his hands. "I was afraid you'd say that."

CHAPTER SEVENTEEN

Desiree gazed up at the huge stone mansion, her stomach tight with nerves. She had been anxious the whole ride to Broughton House, alternately excited and scared, and, underneath it all, disbelieving of what was unfolding around her. Con's casual assurance that it would "be fine, although the duchess might kick up a bit of a fuss" had not helped ease her fears.

Now, taking in the sight of the largest mansion she had ever seen, she couldn't help but feel out of her depth. Swallowing hard, she glanced at Tom; however much he disapproved of her, he was the closest thing to support she had here. His expression was somewhat gloomy, but at least he didn't look scared or hesitant. Desiree would have liked to take his hand for comfort, but, of course, she could not.

A footman greeted the twins with a bow when they walked inside the door. As they handed over their hats, Alex asked for Uncle Bellard.

"In the Sultan Room, sir, with the duchess, having a light luncheon," the footman responded.

Oh, Lord, she would have no choice but to face the duchess, as well. Desiree pictured a woman vaguely resembling the queen, a white cap atop her iron-gray hair, her mouth set in a thin line as she looked down her nose at Desiree. Desiree stiffened her back. She was not about to back down from some aristocratic harridan.

Still, she was grateful that Tom took her arm as they walked across the marble-floored entry hall and down a wide corridor. Desiree stopped in the doorway and stared. The entire room was done in red, from the textured wallpaper to the velvet couches to swags of draped material that fell from the center of the ceiling to the walls, giving the appearance of a tent's interior. Desiree could see why they called it the Sultan Room, though it looked to her more like a bordello parlor. But there was also something warm and comfortable about the space once one became accustomed to its exotic grandiosity.

"Hallo, Mother." The twins went to the woman sitting behind the tea cart, pouring.

"Con, Alex, my loves." She set down the teapot and stood up, offering her cheek to each of her sons for a kiss. She was nothing like the picture Desiree had imagined, but she was just as intimidating in her own way.

The duchess was tall and striking, with red hair liberally streaked with gray and a face that retained its beauty even as it aged. Her eyes were bright with intelligence, and she carried herself with the air of a woman sure of herself and her place in the world. It would take a great deal to daunt this woman. Desiree didn't look forward to presenting her with unpleasant news.

The duchess smiled at her sons with affection, then turned her warmth on Tom and Desiree. "Hello, Tom, I haven't seen you in quite a while." She held out her hand to him. "I must thank you for helping that poor couple reclaim their home."

"Thank you, ma'am. It was no trouble." A faint line of red stained Tom's cheekbones, and he smiled at the duchess almost shyly. "It wasn't hard to prove he'd cheated them out of it." As the duchess turned her gaze to Desiree, he went on hastily, "Allow me to introduce Miss Desiree Malone to you, ma'am."

"Good afternoon, Miss Malone. Welcome to our home."

"It's a pleasure to meet you, ma'am." Desiree had the uneasy feeling that the duchess's blue gaze could see everything inside her. For one of the few times she could remember, Desiree was thankful Brock had insisted on sending her to a finishing school, for she was able to make a proper curtsy to the older woman.

"Alex, ring for Smeggars, there's a dear. We need more tea and sandwiches. Come sit down with us. Let me introduce you to Uncle Bellard."

She led Desiree to one of the sofas where a small old man sat, studying her with great interest. His eyes were bright, his nose prominent, and his white hair was wildly disordered. A pair of spectacles was pushed up to the top of his head.

He sprang to his feet with an agility at odds with his years. "Miss Malone, eh?" He patted around his head and found his glasses, pulling them down to peer at Desiree. "I don't suppose you're related to Dennis Malone the entomologist, are you?"

"No, sir, I'm afraid not."

"Quite all right." He smiled at her benignly. "Come, sit down." He gestured toward the sofa. As Desiree took a seat, she saw that one of his shoes was black, the other brown.

"I'm afraid the girls have gone shopping," the duchess told her sons. "Sabrina wanted more yarn."

"More?" Alex smiled. "She must have ten blankets already."

"Oh, well, these are for the coming baby, not yours."

"Lilah went out?" Con's expression turned worried.

"Yes, dear, women do that, even when they are expecting," his mother said, a twinkle in her eye.

"But the air is thick today. And it's rather hot."

"She took a parasol with her. And the air is always thick. Do sit down, Con, and stop fidgeting. What brings you here today? Happy as I am for you to join us, I suspect you have some motive other than the pleasure of our company."

"You know me well." Con gave in to his mother's request. "We came to talk to Uncle Bellard, actually. About family history."

The old man beside her perked up. "Indeed? What's the question, dear boy?"

"Well, um . . ." Con stopped, his gaze going to Desiree. "I'm sorry, Miss Malone. Perhaps you'd rather not?"

"Go on. It's all right." Desiree had little desire to air her history in the duchess's presence, but this was what she'd been searching for a long time.

"Miss Malone is trying to find her father. She thinks he may have been a Moreland."

"A Moreland?" Bellard looked at her in surprise, adjusting his spectacles. "But who —"

"That's what we're trying to find out. That's why we came to you. She doesn't know who her father is. He was . . ." Con paused again, obviously searching for a polite way to tell the story.

"I am illegitimate," Desiree told Bellard.

"Oh. Well. I see." But the old man still looked a bit confused.

"You don't know who he is? You mean he abandoned you and your mother?" The duchess's voice rose in shock and indignation. "A Moreland? Bellard, do you know who it is?"

"No, my dear, I've never heard anything about it." He turned back to Desiree. "Are you sure he was a Moreland, child?"

Desiree pulled out Brock's ring and handed it to him. As he took it from her, she saw that the old man wore a ring like it.

"Well! My goodness." He pushed his spectacles back onto the top of his head and brought the ring close to his eyes. "Yes, it certainly looks like one." He handed it to

Desiree and sat back, looking thoughtful.

Desiree told him what she knew about her parents, reluctant to look at the duchess. When she finished, though, it was the duchess who spoke first. "It's unconscionable! Men have their way and then casually walk off, leaving the mother to bear all the burden. For them to live in poverty. I'm appalled that a Moreland would do such a thing!"

"Do such a what, dear?" A man strolled into the room. He gave everyone a vague smile as he went straight to the duchess to kiss her on the cheek and sit down beside her. The man, whom Desiree assumed was the Duke of Broughton, glanced around the room. "Why, hello, Con. Alex. I didn't realize you were here. And Tom." He paused when his eyes reached Desiree. "I'm sorry, do I know you? I'm a bit poor at remembering names."

This remark drew a hastily covered snort from Con, and Alex said, "No, Papa, this is Miss Malone. Con and I met her this morning."

"Ah, Miss Malone. Are you related to that American antiquarian?"

"No, sir."

"That's good." He nodded. "The man doesn't know a Theban knife from a Roman gladius." His eyes fell on the tea cart. "I say, is it time for tea already? I'm sorry, I didn't realize I'd been in the workroom so long."

"No, dear. Uncle Bellard and I were just taking a light luncheon. I was feeling a mite peckish."

"What she means, Hal, is that I forgot breakfast again," Bellard said with a smile at the duchess. "I'm sorry, Emmeline, but I was lost among the Plantagenets this morning."

Desiree sneaked a glance at Tom to see if he was as at sea as she was. He again gave a little shrug, a smile teasing at his lips.

"Ah, excellent." The duke nodded as if Bellard's statement made perfect sense, and he turned back to his wife. Taking her hand in his and patting it, he said, "Now, love, what has you in such a pet?"

"This young woman has an all-too-familiar story of a man having an affair and then abandoning his child and her mother."

"Who? A Moreland? She thinks it's one of us?"

Emmeline smiled fondly at him. "No, no, Henry, not one of *our* Morelands, of course. But there are quite a number of others."

"True." The duke reached out to take the cup of tea she poured for him and took a meditative sip. "Rather too many of them, really."

"The thing is, Papa, we think it would probably be someone in your generation, so we came to ask Uncle Bellard," Alex explained.

"Well, I wouldn't think it was Richard," the duke said. "He and Valinda get along rather well, I think — though that may be because he's so often gone on his butterfly hunts. My other brother Nicky died young." Sorrow touched his face for a moment. "What do you think, Uncle?"

"I've never heard any gossip like that. Though one of the girls would know better — my sisters have all the gossip about everyone."

Desiree hid a smile as she realized that the "girls" he referred to were women his age. She supposed sisters always remained "girls" to their brothers.

"Now, my generation had more boys in it," Bellard went on. "And they had sons who would be the right age. Let me see . . ." He began to list male names, finishing, "I think that's all . . . well, there was Alistair, too — Conrad's son, but he moved to America a long time ago."

Desiree stiffened. "America?" She glanced at Tom, who looked equally alert.

"Lord Moreland, do you remember when that was?" Tom asked.

"Oh, goodness, years and years ago, must be close to thirty years." He looked over at the duke and duchess.

There followed a good deal of discussion between the three older members of the family concerning the dates of various exhibitions, discoveries, treatises and social reform legislation, as well as a couple of births and a wedding in the family before they agreed.

"1864," Bellard said firmly. "Yes, the autumn of 1864. That's when he left."

Desiree felt as if her stomach had dropped to her toes. Tom said sharply, "1864? Are you sure?"

"I'm almost certain." Bellard nodded. "Though Wilhemina would know better, I'm sure. She was his age, and they were rather close. Well, as close as he was with anyone. He was always a bit shy."

The duchess, watching Desiree, said, "I take it that year is significant?"

Desiree nodded. "That's the year I was born. And the year our mother ran away."

CHAPTER EIGHTEEN

"I see," Emmeline said gravely.

"It wouldn't be terribly surprising if Alistair had an affair. His was not a happy marriage," Bellard said.

"True. A woman as straitlaced as Tabitha should never have married a Moreland."

Bellard nodded. "They were not compatible. The dowager duchess and Alistair's mother pushed him into marrying her. Tabitha's family was quite old, and, as I remember, Cornelia thought it would be an advantageous marriage."

"No doubt she felt it would make up for Henry being so wayward as to marry me." The duchess cast a decidedly flirtatious smile at her husband. In response, he raised her hand and kissed it.

"No doubt that played a part," Bellard agreed. "I believe he was engaged to Tabitha, then balked, and of course it would have been a scandal if he'd jilted her. I'm sure Cornelia and Agatha — that's Alistair's mother," Bellard explained in an aside to Desiree and Tom, "were at him day and night to 'do his duty' and not damage the family's name. I had the feeling there was something more, some worse scandal, that forced his hand, but I don't know what it was."

"Alistair always was a bit of weak reed," Henry said. "He couldn't have stood up against Mother. As I remember, Aunt Agatha was equally ironfisted." The duke added, with breath-taking irony, "Alistair was an odd chap. He was a poetical sort, wasn't he? And isn't he the one who collected carriages?"

"Yes, he did," Uncle Bellard agreed. "I think it was something of a bond between Alistair and his father. My brother Conrad had a large collection of them at their country estate. He kept the family's coronation coach from, oh, must have been the second Charles's coronation."

"Didn't Conrad find a tumbril from the French Revolution?" the duke asked.

"Well, that's certainly gruesome," the duchess commented.

"Yes, Conrad had an unusual sense of humor," Uncle Bellard agreed. "After his death, Alistair continued collecting them.

His were more normal. I remember he had a lovely phaeton made by Davies. A tilbury. And that carriage from America."

"America!" Desiree stiffened and cast a glance at Tom.

"Yes, everyone thought it was foolish to import one, but Alistair saw them when he went to New York and fell in love with them. That was the one he drove the most."

"Sir, what did that carriage look like?" Tom asked, leaning forward.

Bellard's eyebrows rose slightly at Tom's intense tone. "Ah, I'm not sure I ever saw it, actually. I — there was something odd about it, as I recall."

"The driver's seat was low?" Tom asked. "Right in front of the passengers?"

"Yes, that may be it. Why?"

"I think I might have seen it," Desiree said.

"Oh, I wouldn't think so." Bellard shook his head. "That was years ago. Alistair's the only one who liked it. I imagine it's been sitting in that barn on the estate with all the others since he left."

"It doesn't seem the sort of thing Tabitha would use," the duchess agreed. "I've never met anyone less likely to step out of bounds than that woman."

"I don't remember any of these people," Alex said, looking puzzled.

"No, you wouldn't, dear," his mother told him. "The older children might, but Alistair was gone by the time you and Con were born. And his wife didn't associate with us much after he left. She thought the Morelands were far too scandalous."

"I would think Alistair leaving her would have been more of a scandal than anything we've done," Con pointed out.

"Well, yes, but, you see, *he* was a Moreland, so that was the fault of the family, too," Emmeline explained. "I confess I could never really like Tabitha. She was always concerned with such trivial matters. She hadn't the first idea about social reforms or the world at large. But I did feel sorry for her after Alistair ran off. It wasn't only that it was scandalous and humiliating for her, but she was apparently madly in love with him. Wilhemina said Tabitha took to her bed and cried for days after she found his note. It must have been terrible to love someone that much and know it's not returned."

Desiree felt an unreasonable stab of guilt at the pain her father had caused. Her parents had carelessly left a trail of broken lives in their pursuit of love.

"Tabitha was the woman who came to see me the other day," the duke told Alex.

"Didn't you see her?"

"No." Alex shook his head.

"That's right. You were still at breakfast." The duke turned to Tom. "She's the woman you met."

"Why did Tabitha call on you, dear?" Emmeline asked.

"Oh, something about Gregory. She's always worried that Gregory isn't getting his proper share of the money or that he's been overlooked or he's being slighted." He paused. "Well, to be fair, sometimes it's about her being overlooked and slighted."

"As if I slight her," Emmeline said indignantly. "I invite her to every large family gathering even though I know she isn't going to come."

"Gregory? Cousin Gregory?" Con asked. He said to his brother, "You remember Cousin Gregory's mother. We called her Aunt Cat."

"I remember her." Alex nodded. "I'd forgotten her real name. But that fits, of course. Tabby. Cat."

Con turned to Desiree. "I'm afraid Cousin Gregory will be a disappointment as a brother, Miss Malone. He was always a prig. Still is, last time I saw him."

Alex nodded. "Terribly rigid. He was, what, only five or six years older than us, but he was already an old man. 'One mustn't do this, one mustn't say that. Building a mud fort would ruin his clothes.' "

"And do you remember him asking what was the point in getting onto the roof of the barn?" Con and Alex both shook their heads at that peculiarity.

"To be fair, boys," Emmeline said, "you two played a number of tricks on the poor lad."

"Because he was so stuffy," Alex protested. "And I did *not* throw a frog at him like his mother said. I'd never do that to a frog. I just handed it to him to hold because Con and I had to go look for Augustus. His mother let out a shriek like I'd offered to stab him, and she slapped me."

"She what?" The duchess's eyes took on a dangerous light. "She actually laid a hand on you?"

Alex shrugged. "I ducked. I should have said she *tried* to slap me — she only grazed the top of my head. But it was most unfair because it was Con who'd let Augustus out, and that was the reason I had the frog in my hand." He turned to look pointedly at his brother as he made this remark.

"Yes, but you were the one who told her she'd better hold on to that little dog of hers since the boa constrictor was loose," Con retorted.

"You have to admit, it was sound advice."

At that moment, there was the sound of footsteps in an odd rhythm, and a moment later a little girl came galloping into the room. She stopped with a whinny in front of the duke and duchess.

"Athena!" Henry said with delight. "Are you a horse now?" She nodded, and he went on, "Well, that's a very fine thing to be."

She leaned against his leg, abandoning her animal act, and the duke lifted her onto his lap. "Where is your sister?"

"Brigid's slow," Athena told him.

At that moment a smaller girl came into the room in a crouched stance, holding her hands like claws and swiping them through the air. "I'm a tiger." She followed her sentence with a roar.

There were a few minutes of confusion as the girls made their rounds of the room, giving kisses and collecting sweets. A couple strolled into the room in the midst of it. The man was very tall and broad shouldered, with black hair beginning to gray at the temples. He was immediately recognizable as a close relative of Con and Alex. The woman with him was small and dressed in a trim skirt and jacket of blue, which Desiree admired. Her cinnamon hair was

255

done up in a simple bun, and her reddish-brown eyes twinkled.

"Theo, love. And Megan dear." The duchess rose to greet them. "Come and sit down. You must meet Miss Malone. We think she's a new member of the family." She turned to Desiree.

Desiree's heart skipped a beat at the older woman's words. Had she really accepted her so easily? With no protest or suspicion? Desiree thought she herself would have been slower to accept the sudden arrival of a hitherto unknown relative.

"Theo and his sister are my older set of twins," the duchess explained to Desiree. "And this is his lovely wife, Megan."

More twins?

"A new Moreland? How is that?" Theo looked as intrigued as Con and Alex had. His wife, on the other hand, had a certain wariness in her eyes. Here was the suspicion that Desiree had expected.

"We think she may be Alistair Moreland's daughter," Emmeline said. When Theo raised his brows in mute inquiry, his mother added, "Cousin Gregory's father."

"You don't say." Theo's green eyes went back to Desiree thoughtfully. "Does Cousin Gregory know this?"

"No, I've never spoken to him," Desiree

said. "Until the past few minutes, I'd no idea who Alistair Moreland was."

"I shall hold a dinner," Emmeline said decisively. "To introduce you to the family."

"Mother, I don't understand," Theo began.

"Of course you don't. We have just now had the opportunity to meet this lovely young woman, whose father callously abandoned her and her brother, not only not acknowledging them but not providing for them. Leaving them in the poverty and crime of the East End. It was a monstrous thing to do. And for a Moreland to do such a thing!"

Desiree watched in fascination as the Duchess of Broughton held forth, her voice growing more impassioned, her eyes fierier as she expounded on her subject. Desiree's gaze went to the mild-mannered duke sitting beside Emmeline, admiration glowing in his eyes as he watched his duchess. Desiree glanced around the room at the other occupants. Bellard was cheerfully munching his cake and nodding at the duchess's words; Megan was frowning; and the duchess's three sons had similar expressions of amused resignation.

"Mother," Theo said when Emmeline paused for breath. "I'm not at all sure that a dinner with all the family would be a good thing. Cousin Gregory . . ."

"No, no, dear, of course not him and Tabitha, nor the whole outlying family. Just us." She waved her hand vaguely toward the rest of them. "Henry's and my children and their spouses. Olivia and Stephen are in town now. They're staying with Kyria and Rafe. It's a pity Reed and Anna are at Winterset, but all the rest of you children are in London." She turned to Desiree. "Do say you and your brothers will come. Did you say you had two of them?"

"Yes, but my oldest brother, Brock, is our half brother. He has a different father." Desiree felt a blush creeping into her cheeks. It made it sound as if her mother was a doxy, not caring whom she slept with. But this seemed not to faze the duchess in the least.

"We would love to meet him, too. He's part of your family, after all."

Desiree beamed. "You're very kind. Yes, I would love to meet the rest of your family, and I'll give my brothers your invitation."

"But, Duchess," Tom spoke up. "We cannot be certain that Alistair Moreland was Miss Malone's father. Let me investigate this a bit further first."

It hurt that Tom still refused to believe

that Desiree was telling the truth. After that kiss, she would have thought he'd feel more kindly toward her. But it was foolish to expect that; all he had said was that he desired her, not that he held any regard for her. Besides, that was all she felt for him, as well. Wasn't it?

"Dear Tom." Emmeline smiled at Tom benignly. "You are so good to want to shield us. But what harm is there in a little social gathering? We can't be certain, of course, that Miss Malone is our relative, but she is an interesting young woman, and no doubt her brothers are, as well. I'm sure everyone in the family will enjoy meeting them. Besides, Smeggars will be so happy to have a social occasion to plan."

This latter point seemed to settle the matter. Desiree wondered who Smeggars was that his happiness was so important. She discovered that a moment later when the butler entered the room, carrying a large silver tray of more tea and sandwiches. When the duchess told him of her plans, his eyes lit up with an almost religious zeal, and he bustled out of the room with great purpose.

As more tea was served and food passed about, Megan sat down, taking her youngest daughter onto her lap, and saying,

"Duchess, I still don't understand exactly what has happened."

The older woman launched forth upon the tale of Desiree's birth and background, aided now and then by comments and further explanations from the other Morelands. It seemed to Desiree that her story sounded much more dramatic and compelling in the Morelands' retelling.

"I see." Megan nodded, her bright eyes going to Desiree. Desiree suspected that the duchess's daughter-in-law wasn't about to accept the story whole cloth. That was all right; Desiree sensed in Megan an independent, tough-minded, realistic woman not unlike herself. As with Tom, there was in Megan a fierce protectiveness of the Moreland family. Desiree wondered what it would be like to engender such devotion in others.

"The person you need to talk to is my cousin Wilhemina," the duke told Desiree.

"Yes, she and Alistair were close," Uncle Bellard agreed. "They were much the same age, and their families didn't live far apart."

"You should call on her." The duchess nodded. "The woman knows all the gossip of about half of London, let alone all the Morelands."

"Better take someone with you, though,"

Theo advised. "She can be a bit prickly."

Desiree and Tom turned toward the twins, but Con began to laugh, and Alex said, "Not either of us. She's never been too fond of us since that time with Wellie."

Theo let out a hoot. "It wasn't just the parrot — there was an incident with insects, I believe. Or maybe it was the snake." He turned to his wife. "You best go with them, love."

"She thinks I'm an upstart American," Megan protested.

"Take Sabrina and Lilah with you," Con suggested. "Aunt Wilhemina's surprisingly fond of Alex's wife and mine."

"No doubt she pities them, being married to you two," Theo jibed.

"Probably true," Con admitted agreeably.

"You might want to ask your wives first before you volunteer them," Megan said.

Con shrugged. "Lilah doesn't mind Aunt Wilhemina. Well, if you'd met Lilah's aunts, Aunt Willie probably wouldn't seem that bad."

"Besides, Sabrina and Lilah will be furious they missed this whole thing," Alex put in. "They'll jump at the chance to meet Desiree."

Desiree wondered if that was really true or if the men's spouses, like Theo's wife, might have a warier view of her. Whether or not Alex was right, Megan and Desiree arranged to meet, with the understanding that their plans could change because of the other two women.

Tom had apparently had enough of the camaraderie. A few minutes later, he reminded Desiree that they still had business to attend to and must leave. There was a round of friendly farewells. The duke called Desiree Miss Miller as he smiled pleasantly; Uncle Bellard patted her hand and told Tom that he must bring her around sometime to see his collection of battles; the duchess squeezed Desiree's hand warmly; and the little girls tugged her down to plant sticky kisses on her cheek.

Desiree's throat closed at the girls' sweetness, and she had to blink away the moisture that suddenly threatened to fill her eyes. She took Tom's arm and left the room, resisting the urge to look back to make sure it was really there. As the front door closed behind them, Desiree released his arm to spin around, arms upraised, in a joyous gesture.

"Oh, Tom!" It was all she could do not to hug him in her exuberance. "They were so wonderful. And he has a name! Alistair. That's a nice name, don't you think? And the duchess!" She shook her head, unable to describe what she thought of the woman.

"She's one of a kind." Tom watched her, a faint smile playing at his lips. "I told you they were different."

"Oh, but no one could describe how different they are!" She laughed. "I wouldn't have believed you if you had tried."

She climbed into her carriage and turned to Tom, continuing to chatter. "Those little girls kissed my cheek! Did you see?"

"They're charmers," he agreed.

"I didn't know what to do," she went on candidly. "I've never been around children . . . well, I mean since I *was* one. And I don't think any of us were like them."

"You don't really have do anything with those two. Though I've found giving them lemon drops strengthens their friendship."

"And Uncle Bellard was such a sweet little man, though I had no idea what he was talking about sometimes. What are Plantagenets?"

He shrugged. "I've no idea. Sound like flowers to me, but given Uncle Bellard, they're likely some kind of historical thing. He sets ups little re-creations of different battles, with little tin soldiers and cavalry and all. Don't worry. He doesn't expect people to know what he's talking about — no one else is as smart as him. Well, except maybe the duke, but the things the duke talks about are all two thousand years old and in foreign places."

Desiree settled back in the seat. "I never thought I'd find them. Not really. I used to make up all kinds of stories about my family, and I wondered about them, wished I knew who they were. But I didn't really believe someday I'd meet them."

"Desiree . . ." Tom said carefully. "It seems like you might be related to them, but there's no real proof."

The little sting of hurt that had pricked Desiree earlier now blossomed in her chest, and she turned in her seat to face him. "Why are you so unwilling to accept me? Why do you not want me to belong to them, to be one of them?" Tears sprang into her eyes, surprising her, and Desiree jerked her gaze away, staring out blindly at the street.

"No, that's all wrong," Tom protested. "It's not that I don't *want* you to have a family or to be a Moreland. All I ever wanted in this was to keep the Morelands from being taken advantage of — worse, from being hurt if they discovered that you'd lied to them."

"I'm not lying!"

"I know. I believe you. It's clear how much you want this to be true, how much you'd like to be connected to the Morelands, not for money but simply for your own happiness."

Surprised, Desiree looked at him. Tom was watching her with sympathy in his eyes, and the pain in her chest receded somewhat. "Then why —"

"Because you're building up a whole pile of hopes on what isn't much evidence."

"Brock's ring," she protested. "And Alistair ran off to America the same year our mother did. And what about that carriage? That must be the carriage that man was driving yesterday. You heard what Lord Moreland said — a carriage from New York. That's what Wells told us."

"There could be other carriages like that."

"Following me?" Desiree cocked an eyebrow. "That seems most unlikely."

"Yes, but why? Why would someone in Alistair's old carriage be watching your house? Following you? What would it have to do with them running off years ago?"

"I don't know, but . . . what if it was Alistair himself? What if my parents have come back from the United States?"

"Desiree . . ."

She saw the pity in Tom's eyes, and she flared. "Why not? It wouldn't be impossible. They could have returned. They could want to see us." Her throat closed up, and she stopped talking, not wanting him to hear the pain in her voice.

Tom took her hand. "It's not impossible . . . you're right. But it seems more likely to me that it was this Pax fellow, whose cuff links were in the man's pocket. It wouldn't be too surprising if he bought his friend's carriage, knowing that it was special to Alistair. I'm afraid you're getting your hopes up about something that's not real. I don't want you to be disappointed if it turns out not to be true. I don't want you to be hurt."

"I know it's unlikely that it was my father in that carriage. I know I could be wrong and he isn't even my father. And I will be disappointed if it turns out that way. I'll be sad," Desiree admitted. "But you can't hold back from happiness just because it might change. What is the point in protecting yourself by limiting yourself?" She looked into his eyes. "Would you take back that kiss last night? Just because it might not be there again tomorrow?"

"No." His voice was husky, and he shifted his hand to interlace his fingers with hers. "I'd like to keep that." Tom's eyes gleamed, and the dimple flashed in his cheek. "And maybe add a few more."

"Well, you're not doing a very good job of achieving that at the moment," she teased.

"I'm not going to trade the truth for kisses, even for an exceptional kiss like that."

"Was it exceptional?" She smiled at him, all thoughts of the Morelands or hurt melting away in the face of this topic.

"You know it was."

Desiree could see the spark that lit his eyes, feel it in the surge of warmth in his hand.

"Perfect, do you think?"

"I don't know. I think we might do better yet." He leaned closer.

"Then perhaps we ought to try again." Desiree twined her arms around his neck and kissed him.

CHAPTER NINETEEN

Desiree had thought it might be different in the day, that moonlight and darkness might have woven a sheen of magic into their kisses. But it was that same hot flood of sensation, the same breathless need rising in her. No, perhaps Tom was right, and it was even better.

Tom pulled her closer to him, his lips sinking into hers. Her hand drifted over the bare skin of his neck, and she felt the answering surge of heat in him. Her fingers moved up into his hair, fingertips pressing against his scalp. He made a noise deep in his throat and dragged her over onto his lap, his arm supporting her back as he continued to explore her mouth. One of his hands went to her waist, his fingers digging in a little.

Desiree touched his cheek, his neck, his ear, her hand gliding over him. She wanted to hold him tighter and slide her hands over his chest and back. She wanted . . . oh, God, she *wanted.* Tom's hand went up into her hair, knocking her hat askew, and his lips moved from her mouth across her face to take the lobe of her ear gently between his teeth and worry at it. Desiree pressed her legs together at the quiver that ran through her, bursting into heat low in her abdomen.

Tom's mouth moved down onto her neck, and she tilted her head to give his lips more access. His hand smoothed across her stomach, stroking her, then upward until he cupped her breast. Pleasure rocketed through her.

The sway of the carriage stopped as the horses came to a halt. Tom's body tensed, and he lifted his head. The coachman's voice floated in through the window. "Miss Malone? We're here."

Tom muttered an oath and set Desiree aside. He raked his hands through his hair as Desiree tried to gather her scattered thoughts. She started to speak, but her voice came out a croak. Clearing her throat, she said, "Yes, thank you, Merriwell."

Desiree had been so lost she had forgotten they were in a carriage, forgotten the driver, forgotten everything. Hastily she tried to straighten her hat and tuck a stray curl back into place beneath it. Desiree was sure her face was flushed, and she must look as if . . . well, as if she had been doing what she'd just been doing for the last few minutes.

Tom had enough presence of mind to tell the driver to continue to the end of the block to let them out. Desiree turned to him, and his gaze went immediately to her mouth. Then he pulled his eyes upward. He settled her hat a bit differently on her head, his fingertips brushing the side of her face as he pulled them back, and the touch of them made her shiver.

Tom took a breath and turned to look out the narrow rear window. The last few minutes, they could have had half a dozen men following them, and they wouldn't have noticed.

When the carriage stopped again, Tom sprang out as if he'd been shot out of a cannon. He gazed up and down the street so thoroughly he didn't glance at her once. Desiree stepped down from the carriage. She rather missed him lifting a hand to help her. It was, she decided, a very pleasant courtesy.

Her spirits remained high even though they found no more success this afternoon than they had the day before. There were still other possibilities to visit, and, frankly, Desiree found herself looking forward to spending more days in Tom's company. Besides, her visit with the Morelands overwhelmed any failure in their search.

She was brimming with her news when she reached home, but to her disappointment she found that both her brothers were out. Brock was at work and would return late this evening, but Wells had apparently left the city and would not return until the following day. Such sudden departures without explanations were nothing new with Wells. She hoped he would come back when he said he would — which was not always the case — because she wanted to talk to both her brothers about the Moreland family at the same time.

Desiree had told Tom she wasn't going to the club this evening. She was too restless to settle down and concentrate as she needed to during a game; her thoughts were occupied with the Morelands and her search for her father. Her mind was equally busy thinking about Tom Quick.

She wasn't sure what Tom felt for her. Indeed, she wasn't all that certain what she felt for him, either. They'd been antagonists from the beginning, but their relationship had changed to a wary partnership as they worked together, then became . . . well, whatever their relationship was today.

Desiree was drawn to him, had been from the first moment she saw him, before she knew who he was or what he wanted. She had felt as if a light had sprung to life inside her. She had wanted him in an immediate, visceral way that she had never felt with any other man. If he had not come over to her, she would have gone to him.

It wasn't just the light gleaming on his blond hair or those compelling blue eyes or the long dimple that popped into his cheek when he smiled. It wasn't simply the way he walked across the room or the lean, tensile strength in him or the sound of his voice, though admittedly all those things made her want to touch him, to feel his lips on her.

Desiree liked him. She couldn't help but like him. More than that, she trusted him — and Desiree was not one to give her trust easily. There was a sense of understanding between them, a mutual knowledge and way of thinking that sprang, she supposed, from their common pasts. Though she had known him for only a short amount of time, Desiree knew his life because it had been her life, too.

Tom felt that connection, too. However rude and antagonistic he had been when he'd said it, he had said truthfully that he knew her. Nor was he immune to the physical attraction between them. Desiree wasn't mistaken about the way he had looked at her that night in the club; the heat between them had not been all on her side. And this afternoon in the carriage! Desiree's lips curved up. Tom was anything but indifferent to her.

She had no idea what would happen tomorrow, what Tom would say or do. Whether he would pull back or come closer. But Desiree looked forward to finding out.

Tom left the office early the next morning. He'd spent much of the night tossing and turning, thinking about Desiree, and he was glad when the sun came up and he could start doing something. Anything. He was tired of thinking. Tired of feeling, as well.

He was no longer sure what he thought or felt. Yesterday, watching Desiree with the Morelands, with a curiously hollow feeling, he had seen clearly how well she fit with the family. It wasn't just that they easily accepted her, which had been his worry all along, but that it was so easy to believe she was one of them.

Her manner and accent weren't as aristocratic as theirs — for no matter how egalitarian the Morelands were, their heritage and upbringing always shone through — and she didn't resemble them in coloring, but her spirit, her boldness, her confidence and lack of concern for the opinions of others were so like theirs that he imagined any stranger entering the room would have thought that she was a member of the family. What was it Megan liked to say the Morelands had? *Joie de vivre,* that was it. And despite all the hard knocks in her past, Desiree had that.

In more practical terms, the way Desiree had reacted to them, the happiness and eagerness with which she gazed at the Morelands, simply did not look like someone scheming to hurt them. She had not pressed her claims; it had been the Morelands who had provided the fact that the duke's cousin matched Desiree's story.

Her brother's possession of the ring and the timing of Alistair Moreland's disappearance were not, as Tom had pointed out, actual proof that Alistair was Desiree's father. It wouldn't satisfy a court of law. But in pragmatic terms, those things certainly hinted strongly at it.

Tom thought of the way Desiree had spun around, arms thrown up in glee, and her face glowing with such joy that it made his heart hurt. Try as he might to hold on to his skepticism, he could not. He had told her the truth when he said he believed her. He did believe she wanted only her father's identity. And he believed Desiree thought Alistair was her father.

But the fact that she believed it didn't mean that it was fact. Tom wanted it to be true for her sake. He didn't want her to be hurt or disappointed. His search was becoming a quest to prove she was right, and that was the worst way to conduct an investigation. Looking at something with a desired end in mind was a sure way to go astray.

He must not let himself tilt the evidence to please Desiree. That was the danger in getting involved with a client, and Tom had never had that problem before. He might like or dislike a person for whom he worked, but he had never *desired* one.

And he desired Desiree. Her name was all too apt. Yesterday, caught up in her beauty and excitement, he'd ignored everything from propriety to ethics to safety and kissed her. In a carriage, curtains not drawn, only a few feet from her coachmen. And paying absolutely no attention to whether they were being followed. Followed, hell — the man who'd been after them could have come up and peered in the window and Tom wouldn't have noticed.

The woman was absolutely devastating to his senses. Far less of his thinking last night had been about the foolishness of what they'd done than about how pleasurable it had been. How much he would have liked to continue. How he could maneuver it so that they were again somewhere private and alone.

Any way one looked at it, it was a foolish infatuation. Desiree was a client. Good Lord, she might very well be a Moreland! And even if she was not, Desiree wasn't the sort to live a quiet life in a modest house, the wife of an ordinary working man.

Not, of course, that he actually wanted to marry someone like Desiree, who would be a constant source of worry and aggravation. Tom had enough excitement in his life from his investigations without having to worry about a wife scampering across rooftops.

What he wanted was to sleep with her. He wanted that a great deal. Ordinarily he would have thought an affair might be something they could indulge in. She was a woman of the world, someone who'd grown up in the stews of the East End and lived a sophisticated life, not a sheltered flower of a lady.

But an affair with Desiree was all too

likely to turn into something bigger. To make him hunger for more. And affairs were all too easily broken off. What would happen to him if Desiree grew bored or realized she wanted someone else, needed something more than Tom could give her?

His thoughts made him too restless to get any work done. All his focus was on Desiree's case, anyway. They had planned for Desiree to once again come to the office and go to Marylebone from there, but, unwilling to sit still any longer, Tom took a hackney to Desiree's house.

She looked up and smiled when the butler ushered him into the dining room, and Tom's breath caught in his throat. What would it be like to be greeted by that smile at breakfast every day? To see the light in her eyes, the luscious curve of her lips?

"Tom! Sit down. Have breakfast with me." She gestured at the empty table. "As you can see, my meal is solitary. My brothers are always late to bed and to rise."

Tom couldn't resist the invitation since it was exactly what he'd been envisioning. Sitting down, he watched as Desiree poured him a cup of tea, and that was almost as nice as seeing her smile.

"I am surprised to see you here," Desiree went on, ringing for a servant. "I thought I was going to fetch you from your office."

"You were, but I wanted to change our plans. Instead of the other location in Marylebone, let's try the Pimlico area."

"Very well. Why?"

"Because last night I researched Alistair Moreland's wife and learned where she lives. I assume it is the same address, as it's been in his name since before you were born. He lived in Belgravia."

"Not a long drive to Pimlico." Desiree clearly understood the import of his words immediately.

"Exactly."

"Megan Moreland wrote me. Apparently the twins — what did you call them?"

"The Greats."

"Well, their wives think it will be a lovely idea to visit Aunt Wilhemina, so day after tomorrow we will be going to see her. You'll come with us, won't you?" An unaccustomed look of uncertainty flitted over her features. "I'd rather not be alone with so many aristocratic ladies."

"Yes, I'll go, too." It warmed him to think she wanted him there, that perhaps she needed him. "But you'll like Sabrina and Lilah. They're very easy to be around — well, they're married to Alex and Con, so they'd have to be."

"I liked Alex and Con."

"Most people do. Bit harder, I imagine, to live with them." Tom grinned.

They continued to chat lightly through the meal, then drove to the area in Pimlico that Alex had circled. The driver let them down at the small triangular park. Tom cast a careful eye all around them to check for anyone following them. Reassured they were alone, they began to stroll, moving away from the park in a methodical path.

It was an hour later that they turned a corner and Desiree grabbed Tom's arm. "Look!"

"I see it." His gaze was focused on the next block and a row of white stone houses. They started forward in a rapid walk.

When they reached the row, they paused, looking all around them. The scene was just as Brock had described: a row of white stone terraced houses on one side of the street and across from it another row of terraced houses in differing materials and styles. They moved farther down the street, hardly daring to believe what they saw, and stopped in front of a door with a number five in gold above it.

"This is it." Desiree's voice was barely above a whisper. "We found it."

"Do you know that — I mean, does your

talent tell you that?"

"I'm not sure. Sometimes it's difficult to separate what I think rationally from what my instinct tells me. Perhaps it's both." Desiree tilted her head and squinted. "Either way, it certainly fits Brock's description."

"Yes. Let's walk," Tom said, starting forward again. "We don't want to be too obvious." As they strolled, he said, "You want to break in, don't you?"

"Of course. Don't you? It'll be dead easy — all we have to do is take the service steps down to the trade door, and then we're hidden from sight while we break in."

"It's still theft."

"It's not theft. The things in the hiding place belong to my family," Desiree argued.

Tom couldn't help but laugh. "Try telling that to a bobby."

"The bobbies don't matter. We won't get caught," she tossed back. She bumped her shoulder against his arm lightly. "Come on. You know you want to see what's hidden beside the mantel."

Tom grinned at her. "You're right. Let's walk back and take another look."

So it was that at one o'clock that night, Tom and Desiree stood in the same place, looking at the front of number five. There were no lights inside; the same was true of every house around them. It was a quiet street of early risers. A streetlamp cast its light directly in front of the house, but luckily they would only have to cross the short distance to the service steps down to the sublevel. Once down the stairs, they would be invisible to the street. The entrance stood in a pool of shadow at the base of the stairs.

Tom looked over at Desiree. She wasn't dressed in her thief's costume, which he thought a pity, but in the same simple dark dress she had worn the night Tom had followed her. "Ready?"

She nodded, and they slipped quietly from the shadows to the almost hidden staircase. Desiree carried the lantern, which was shielded into darkness, and when they reached the bottom of the stairs, she lifted the shield a narrow slit and held it over the lock. Tom pulled out his picks and inserted them. She immediately lowered the cover. The rest of the job was more by feel than by sight.

Tension built in Tom's chest as he worked, a familiar mingling of excitement and fear. He smiled as he heard the telltale click, and he eased the door open. They were in the kitchen. There was enough light coming through the high windows that lay above-ground for them to make out the general bulk of objects around the room and make their way into the servants' hall.

Here was where the most danger of discovery lay, where the servants lived and might be awakened. Desiree stopped and expanded her awareness, focusing on the possibility of danger. No dart of alarm arrowed through her chest; there was only a sense of emptiness.

Desiree opened the lantern a sliver, and they crept down the dark hallway and up the narrow servants' stairs to the floor above. This should be the safest area, with the owners' bedrooms on the floors above. It was a narrow house and thus easy to find the front parlor.

As they started across the hall beside the main staircase, there was the sound of a cough from the floor above. Desiree and Tom stopped and melted back into the shadows beneath the staircase. Desiree immediately covered the lantern, holding it behind her skirts. They stood in complete silence for several long minutes, but there was no further sound from upstairs and no light appeared.

They slipped out and crossed to the parlor, casting a wary glance up at the stairs. Inside the parlor, they didn't close the door behind them — the squeak of the cabinet door that had awakened Tom fresh in their minds — but went immediately to the fireplace.

The fireplace was set into bricks, as Brock had described, confirming their theory that this was indeed the house he remembered. Setting down the lantern at their feet, they began a swift search of the bricks to the left of the fireplace, tugging and pushing to no avail. They turned to look at each other. Desiree frowned in consternation.

"What if someone who lived here later sealed it up?" Desiree whispered.

Tom thought it was better not to suggest that it had never been here and Brock was mistaken, or they were in the wrong house. Instead, he pointed to the other side of the fireplace. "Maybe he didn't remember correctly. It's been almost thirty years."

They moved to the other side of the fireplace. Desiree took the strip beside the hearth and Tom concentrated on the higher areas that she could not reach. Nothing moved. As Desiree turned away, Tom shifted aside, bracing his hand against the mantel. There was, he realized, a small circle of wood that protruded a little on the underside of the mantel. He brushed his thumb over it, following the contour, then, acting on instinct, he pressed it. The circle of wood went up into the mantel, and on the other side of the fireplace there was a scraping sound, brick against brick.

Desiree whirled and hurried toward to the opposite side. There, two joined bricks now stuck out an inch from the others. Even in the dim light, Tom could see the gleam in Desiree's eyes, and his own breath came faster. Desiree pulled out the set of bricks and handed it to Tom before raising the lantern to peer into the hole that had been revealed.

Her hand trembled as she reached in and pulled out a rectangular wooden box.

CHAPTER TWENTY

Desiree's heart thudded wildly in her chest. She'd hoped, but she hadn't dared to really believe they would find anything. She clutched the box in both hands, emotions whirling through her, paralyzing her in an uncharacteristic way.

Tom slid the brick back in place and picked up the lantern, then took her arm and started toward the door. Desiree went with him, happy to let him take the lead. Tom peered out the long, narrow window beside the door, looking up and down the street, then quietly unlocked the door and opened it. He followed Desiree out, easing the door closed behind him.

Desiree had recovered her senses enough that she was already hurrying down the steps. It had made sense for Tom to choose to go out the front door even though they would be in the light of the streetlamp for a moment; that bit of exposure to an empty street was less dangerous than traveling back down through the servants' hall, where someone might wake up and see them. But it was prudent to move out of the circle of lamplight as quickly as she could.

Tom was right on her heels, both of them stopping to cast a look all around after they stepped beyond the light. Desiree had a vague sense of uneasiness, but she could see no movement on the street in either direction. She was just jumpy from the storm of excitement, hope and fear that the sight of the box had engendered in her.

They started up the street. Desiree clutched the box tightly to her chest, her arms wrapped around it as if it were a baby. Neither of them spoke as they crossed the road and turned right onto Sussex Street. They were moving in the direction of Victoria Station, where they were more likely to find a cab even at this time of night. They crossed George Road, as darkly silent as the other streets they passed.

Suddenly a shock of alarm ran through Desiree, a dark tangle of tension knotting her stomach. She whirled around, just as a dark shape hurtled out of the night, straight at her. Tom jumped to the side, pulling her with him, but the man grabbed the box from Desiree's grasp and charged past them down the street.

"No!" Desiree shrieked and ran after him, but Tom quickly passed her, gaining on the man. His quarry threw an anxious glance behind him and turned toward Warwick Square. Tom ran across the street at an angle that cut off more of the man's lead, recklessly ignoring the carriage rolling toward him. He caught the thief as he reached Warwick Square, leaping forward to take him down to the ground. The box flew out of the man's hand and skidded into the street.

As the two men grappled on the ground, Desiree ran for the box. It didn't break as it tumbled across the pavement, and she grabbed it up, coming back to Tom, who had hauled the other man to his feet.

"Who are you?" Tom shook him. "Who sent you?"

"Let go of me." The man wobbled but said defiantly, "I don't have to tell you nothing."

"You bloody well will." Tom drew back his fist, but Desiree laid a hand on his arm, stopping him.

"There's no need," she said. "I recognize him. He's one of Falk's men. I saw him there the other day." She turned to him. "Tell Falk I don't have his blasted envelope. I didn't find it. This isn't an envelope!"

Desiree held up the box, shaking it. "I'm not looking for the envelope. I have no idea where it is, and I don't care. Falk is wasting his time having you follow us around."

The other man sneered, jerking out of Tom's hold, which had relaxed. Tom grabbed him by the lapels and pulled him forward, his voice cold and hard. "Stay away from us. I'm letting you go now so you can give Falk Miss Malone's message. But if I catch sight of you anywhere near her, I promise you, you won't be walking again anytime soon." He shoved him back. "Now get out of here. Tell Falk that if he doesn't stop, it's him I'll be coming after."

The man backed up sullenly, wiping the blood from his nose. "Big talk."

Tom's eyes lit up and he started forward. Falk's man turned and ran. Tom muttered an oath and turned back to Desiree. "Are you hurt?"

"I'm fine. I didn't fall. I'm afraid the box isn't in as good a condition." She ran a finger ruefully over the scratch. "But at least it didn't break."

The rest of their walk was without incident, and they managed to hail a hackney when they reached Vauxhall Bridge Road. "At least we know now who was having us followed," Tom said as they settled into their seats. "Obviously this chap was better than the one the other day. I didn't spot him — which is something of a blow to my pride, even if he was a professional."

"I didn't see him, either. He's no brighter than the other man if he mistook this for an envelope." Desiree once again cradled the box against her chest. "But . . . what about the cuff links you took off the other man? The ones that said *Pax*?"

Tom shrugged. "I've no idea. Nothing about this case makes sense. If Pax is one of Falk's men, I can't see how it could be the gentleman Brock remembers being a friend of your father's."

"He was clumsy, though, as one would expect a gentleman to be," Desiree replied.

"True. It seems bizarre, but I'm beginning to wonder if we might have two different sets of people following us — this Pax person, who was obvious, and Falk's man, who was skillful."

"That would require a good deal of coincidence," Desiree pointed out. "Falk looking for this envelope and this other fellow, Pax, looking for . . . what?"

"It wouldn't be such a coincidence if they both want whatever's in this envelope. Maybe the envelope has to do with your past. With your father."

She looked at him doubtfully. "Such as?"

"Such as . . ." He thought for a moment. "Proof of some sort that you're Alistair Moreland's daughter?"

"Why would Pax care about my parentage? Or Falk, either, for that matter?"

"What if this lawyer chap found out about you and *he* wants to extort money from the Morelands?"

"And Falk found that out and is trying to do the same thing?" Desiree straightened. "Now, that would make sense. Let's say that Blackstock discovered our parentage, so he sent proof to the Morelands, and whatever it was, Falk found out, as well. Falk wants this letter so he can be the one to swindle the Morelands. But what about Pax?"

"He found out, too."

"I must say, this doesn't seem a very well-kept secret," Desiree said. "But let's say that's so. Why would Pax want the letter? He's a gentleman, not a crook. And Alistair was his friend."

"I have to point out that a gentleman can be every bit as much a crook as a lawyer or a kidsman. However, let's say our Pax is the loyal friend and gentleman. Maybe he wants to get this proof so that he can destroy it and save his friend's reputation."

Excitement fizzed in Desiree's chest. "Falk

could have learned my father's identity from servants' gossip. He buys information as well as stolen jewelry from servants. It's invaluable for breaking into people's houses. This Blackstock fellow or maybe Pax let it slip in front of his valet or maid or whoever, and they sold it to Falk."

"Falk would notice anything that had to do with the Morelands. He'd be glad to do them a disservice. Especially if it would bring you back to the fold."

Desiree gazed at him intently. "I wouldn't have done anything to hurt the Morelands. Even before I met them."

"I know."

Warmth spread through Desiree's chest at his belief in her. She smoothed her hands over the wood. "I wonder what's inside."

"Open it and see."

She shook her head. "It's locked. We'll have to break it." She sighed. "I hate to damage it, but I suppose it doesn't matter with that scratch already there."

Tom picked it up and studied the tiny keyhole. "I can probably pick it with a hairpin. This is the sort of box the Greats were always wanting to open. Diaries and keepsake boxes."

"Of their sisters, no doubt. And you helped them!"

Tom cast her a grin. "You should try withstanding their pestering. Besides, they didn't really care what was inside — they just wanted to figure out how it worked. In my defense, I'm only a few years older than them."

"How many years?"

Tom shrugged. "I don't know. No idea when I was born."

Desiree put her hand on his arm. "I'm sorry."

"It's all right. Just a fact of life. I don't know anything before I was at Falk's. I don't even know when I wound up with him."

Desiree's chest ached for him. No wonder Tom was a suspicious man. Growing up in Falk's world without anyone to call your own would make you raise impenetrable barriers. "Have you ever tried to find out? I could help you."

"I wouldn't know where to start. Falk tried to bribe me with information about my mother when he wanted me to steal from the Morelands, but I'm not going to do anything for him, and there's no way he'd tell me something for free. Besides, I wouldn't trust anything he said. He could just pluck a name out of the air, and I wouldn't know any different."

Desiree wanted to say something to make

it better, but she could think of nothing.

Tom smiled at her and reached over to take her chin between his thumb and forefinger. "Don't look so sad." Tom leaned in and kissed her lips softly. He lifted his head, gazing into her eyes, and for a moment she thought that he would kiss her again. Everything in her rose in anticipation. But then he sighed and sat back, his hand dropping from her chin. "I'm my own man — no one to curse and no one to thank."

It seemed a lonely way to live. No one else might own you, but you didn't belong to anyone, either. She wondered if Tom truly believed it or if he was trying to convince himself.

The carriage pulled up in front of the Moreland & Quick office building, and the conversation ended. Tom unlocked the building and ushered her inside, turning up the gaslights. As they climbed the stairs, he said, "I could use a cup of tea. Or something stronger. Would you like some?"

"Please." Alcohol was something Desiree had never had much of a taste for; she remembered too well the gin-soaked, vacant-eyed women of the rookeries, escaping their hellish lives in a bottle of blue ruin. But her nerves were jittering about so tonight that she thought it might be wise to calm them a little.

Tom nodded and started up the next flight of stairs. When he opened the door upstairs, though, he halted and looked at her in some uncertainty. "I'm sorry. I didn't think — this is my flat. Perhaps you wouldn't want to be — that is, I could bring it down to the office if you'd rather."

Desiree cast him a teasing smile and walked past him into the room. "Are you planning to ravish me, Mr. Quick?"

"Of course not." The light he turned on showed the tinge of pink along his cheekbones.

"Then I see no problem. Don't worry. I'm not the sort of woman who has to maintain a spotless reputation."

As Tom walked over to a small cabinet and pulled out a bottle, Desiree surveyed the room. It was tidy and rather Spartan in appearance, which didn't surprise Desiree. The only thing except the most necessary of furniture was an overflowing bookcase. Books were stacked on the floor in front of it, and another pile stood beside a comfortable-looking chair with a standing lamp next to it.

Desiree's eyes went to the other end of room and the neatly made bed, and despite her cool words a moment earlier, her breath hitched a little and she quickly turned away. "You like to read?"

"Yes." Tom glanced over at her, pausing in the midst of pouring whiskey into two glasses. "Surprised?"

"You said you liked the books at the orphanage, but still, you seem more a man of action."

"I'm not sure I'd ever seen a book before the orphanage. I certainly couldn't read one. But once I learned how, I couldn't stop. I wanted to know . . . well, everything outside the world I'd lived in, which was a great deal. Fortunately, Reed let me borrow books from the Moreland library. Which is about three times larger than this entire flat."

"They seem a very generous family."

"They are. And they have a love for learning. All you have to do is want to read a book, and Uncle Bellard is your friend for life. He stumbled across me down in the kitchen reading one time, and he gave me three books." Tom crossed the room to hand her the drink. He took a sip from his own glass and reached out to stroke his forefinger down the spine of a gilt-edged, leather-bound book, a fond smile on his face. "*Vanity Fair. Great Expectations. Last of the Mohicans.* Those are the three he gave me."

"I never heard of that last one."

"James Fenimore Cooper. He's an American. Derring-do in the wilderness — very exciting stuff for me."

"Why were you reading in the kitchen?"

"I went there to read whenever I borrowed books from the Morelands. For one thing, Cook would give me tea and biscuits. And I felt . . . more comfortable there. The library at Broughton House is a trifle imposing."

Desiree smiled. "I can imagine."

He turned back toward the small table and the two stools beside it. "Shall we open your prize? Or would you like me to make a spot of tea, as well? I can heat up a kettle."

"This is fine." Desiree pulled in a shaky breath and held the box out to him. As he examined the lock, she pulled a hairpin from her hair and handed that to him, as well. Tom put the box on the table and sat down in front of it, working the hairpin delicately into keyhole.

Desiree took a sip of her drink and watched him, too restless to sit down. The whiskey burned like fire down her throat, reminding her why she didn't care for it, but in a moment she felt a smooth warmth stealing through her. Finishing it off as if it were medicine, she went to the table and sat down across from Tom.

296

"Ha!" Tom said and looked up at her triumphantly. He swiveled the box around so that it faced Desiree. "Care to open it?"

"I would." But she hesitated, her hand hovering over the lid.

"Want me to do it?"

"No. I will. It's just . . . a bit frightening." Taking a breath, she ran a finger along the scratch, then lifted the lid.

The box was lined with dark maroon satin. In it sat a velvet pouch, a stack of folded papers tied with a narrow satin ribbon, and a large lump of something wrapped in velvet. Desiree pulled out the velvet pouch and opened it, pouring its contents onto the table. Small pieces of jewelry fell out: a pair of sparkling diamond earrings, a ring mounted with rubies in the shape of a flower, a heart-shaped brooch of pavé diamonds, another ring set with an emerald, a ruby and a sapphire in a row, and several narrow bangle bracelets of pavé diamonds, emeralds and rubies.

"Look at all this!" Desiree picked up one of the rings and examined it. "These look like real gems. I'd have nabbed them in an instant."

"Yes. I'd have a jeweler appraise them, but they look real enough."

"To think of this sitting behind those

bricks all these years . . ." Desiree turned to the object wrapped in velvet and lifted it, realizing that it wasn't a single object. "Sapphires," Desiree breathed when she folded back the velvet. She set it down on the table and separated the pieces of jewelry. "Earrings, necklace, bracelet, a tiara." Desiree picked up the narrow tiara and settled it onto her head.

"Beautiful," Tom said, his eyes on her face, not the jewels.

She felt her cheeks flush, and she turned her attention back to the jewelry on the table. "They're a set. See how they match?"

"It's called a parure, I think." When Desiree looked up at him with a quizzical expression, he explained. "I had to find one that was missing a couple of years ago. Turned out her husband gave them to his mistress."

Desiree's eyes widened. "You don't suppose that this . . ." She looked down at the pile of jewelry as if it were a snake.

Tom shook his head. "I wouldn't think so. The Morelands don't pinch pennies. I suspect these were all things he bought specifically for her."

"Why would she leave them behind?" Desiree wondered.

"I suppose it's possible they aren't jewels

he gave her. Maybe they were from Brock's father instead, and they would have made him jealous."

Desiree rubbed a dangling earring between her fingers. "I can't help but think how much we could have used the money these would have brought."

"I don't want to speak ill of your mother, but she could have left you better provided for, even without your father's support."

"Yes. It's always haunted Brock, the way she tossed us away." Carefully, she wrapped up the set of jewels again and laid them aside.

She had put off looking at the item she was most curious about, her eagerness threaded with a fear that the stack of what looked to be saved letters would turn out to dash her budding hopes. Taking a quick breath, she picked up the bundle and untied the ribbon. She unfolded the top one.

Beloved,
Words cannot express how much I miss the sight of your face, the sound of your voice. I wish that I could be with you this very moment. It is a source of constant sorrow to me that I am bound by honor and duty to remain in this charade.

I bitterly regret the prison to which I committed myself long ago, and even more I regret the pain that it has cost you. Please believe that if I could change what I have done, I would. Every day of emptiness is an atonement for the wrong I did you.

The moments of joy we steal are precious to me, jewels of time that I hold to comfort myself in the days we are apart.

I remain yours always,

A

Desiree lifted her head, her eyes brimming with tears as she handed the letter over to Tom. "It's from him. And he truly loved her."

CHAPTER TWENTY-ONE

Tom took the letter. The fellow sounded exceptionally dramatic to him. And the scrawled *A* scarcely provided actual proof that it was Alistair Moreland who had written it. But Tom wasn't about to say either of those things to Desiree, who was opening the letters and scanning them. Not just because he wasn't about to pop the bubble of her excitement, but also because he thought the letters *were* a strong indication that Desiree's father was Alistair Moreland. It sounded just like the sort of letter a "poetical sort" — as the duke had described him — would write, and really, how many *A*s were involved in this case?

He knew logically that the whole thing could be an elaborate setup, the letters planted there by the Malones to be discovered and provide proof of their story. But that intricate a plot sounded far more unlikely than the story of a feckless aristocrat running away with his mistress, leaving his children behind like so much unnecessary baggage.

Picking up another one or two of the letters Desiree discarded, he found that they contained much the same sort of thing: avowals of undying love, regrets and descriptions of his loneliness. One talked of his desire to be with his "little family." It seemed to him that the chap could have left his wife without taking off to another continent. Or, if he had to flee, at least he could have taken that "little family" with them.

It didn't seem at all the sort of thing a Moreland would do. But then, the man hadn't been one of "Tom's" Morelands. And Tom remembered meeting the dowager, Cornelia, who had badgered Alistair into an unwanted marriage; she'd been enough to turn any man's knees to water.

"Oh, Tom!" Desiree jumped to her feet, the letters scattered across the table, and Tom rose to face her. Her voice was tight with tears. "He was so in love with her, and . . . this proves it, doesn't it? Alistair really is our father!"

Tom nodded. "It seems the likeliest explanation." He reached out to take her hands, but Desiree threw her arms around his neck instead, hugging him tightly.

"Thank you! Thank you! I'm so happy!"

"I didn't really —" He didn't finish his sentence, for she took his face between her hands and kissed him.

After that, he was lost, fire spreading through him like a spark to kindling, invading every part of him and sweeping away all reason or thought. There was nothing but heat and feeling, his skin suddenly so sensitive he felt the rub of his shirt against his skin, his senses wide-open to the taste and scent of Desiree, the sound of her little moan deep in her throat.

Tom murmured her name, laying feather-soft kisses across her face and jaw and down onto the tender skin of her throat. Desiree tilted her head, exposing her bare throat to his kisses, and he took what she offered, tasting her with lips and tongue.

Desiree's body was pliant beneath his hand, her simple dress not underpinned by the armor of a corset. Her flesh was firm and lithe, making the pillowy softness of her breast a delight of contrasts. His thumb dragged across her nipple, teasing it into hardness, then his hand glided down over her ribs and waist onto the swell of her hips.

Desiree sank her hands into his hair, the little tug against his scalp accenting the pleasure of her fingers upon him. She slid her hand down to curl around the back of his neck, sending a frisson along his spine. Her fingers stroked his neck, and desire stabbed straight through him. Tom let out a groan, and his mouth returned to hers, his fingers grasping her hips and pressing her body into his. She moved against him, turning him even harder.

He thought of his bed, so temptingly close. He wanted to sweep her up and carry her there, to undress her with slow care, caressing every inch of her body. He was stiff as a board, throbbing, and he ached to sink into her. Desiree pulled her mouth from his and was on tiptoe, kissing his neck and cheek. The feel of her soft, plump lips against his evening stubble made him shudder.

His hands groped across her back — how the devil did this thing fasten? He tugged on the bow of her sash and discovered exactly how simple her dress was. The front wrapped around her and tied in the back, so that now it loosened and sagged open, allowing him to slide his hand inside onto her stomach, covered only by the cotton of her chemise.

It was heavenly, and the way her fingers dug into his shoulders told him that Desiree felt the same. He kissed her, caressing her through the thin cloth that was more an enticement than an impediment. Then his fingertips were beneath the ruffled top of the chemise, dipping down to take her breast in his hand. It filled his palm perfectly, the nipple pressing into his skin. He ached to feel it in his mouth, to tease and stroke and arouse them both to a peak of passion.

Desiree's fingers went to his waistcoat, unbuttoning it to slide her hands inside it. Tom shuddered under her caress, imagining her hands on his skin. Her mouth on his skin. Then, letting out a noise of frustration, Desiree jerked away. "No."

Her voice was low, her breath coming in pants. Her face was flushed, her eyes bright with desire, as Tom knew his were. Her lips were full and softened by passion, swollen from their kisses. It was all he could do not to drag her back to him and kiss her again. He curled his fingers into his palms and waited, struggling to control his breathing, to dampen the fire surging through him. He ought to say something, but he could not, his mind too inflamed, too dazed to form a coherent thought.

"We can't — I'm not my mother." Desiree drew a shaky breath, dragging her dress around her and retying the sash. "I won't let myself be." She cast him a regretful look.

"Of course." Tom found his tongue at last. He nodded, sweeping his hands back through his hair to restore some sort of order to it . . . and to his thoughts. "I shouldn't have brought you here. I should have thought."

He turned away, going to the table to carry the glasses and bottle of whiskey over to the cabinet. He shouldn't have given her whiskey, either. "I hope you know I didn't intend this." He turned back to her. "I didn't bring you here with the idea of seducing you. I didn't mean to ply you with liquor or — I know it must look as if I had ulterior motives, but I swear I did not."

"I believe you." She smiled at him. "I didn't think you did. I was the one who threw myself at you, after all." She took a step closer to him, saying earnestly, "I won't deny that I would like to go on. I enjoyed kissing you. I wanted to do more than that."

Tom ran his sweating palms down his jacket. "You're not helping here."

Desiree gave a rueful chuckle. "I know. But I want you to know that I don't think ill of you or blame you. It was . . ." She let out a little shuddery sigh. "It was quite lovely. But I made a vow long ago that I

306

wouldn't do what my mother did. I won't fall into any man's hands like a ripe fruit or give my life over to him."

"I know. I would not ask you to."

"Good." She smiled. "But perhaps it is time I went home."

"Of course." He watched as she gathered up the letters and tied them together, putting everything back into the box. He understood her. But he needed a bit of time to shove all his own hunger back.

They left the building a few minutes later and once again had difficulty finding a hackney. It was almost three when they pulled up in front of Desiree's house, and Tom was surprised to see that there were lights shining in several windows downstairs. As he walked with Desiree to the front door, it opened, and Brock limped out.

"Oh, dear," Desiree said under her breath. "And his leg's hurting him tonight."

Right behind Brock came the other brother, and even his normally indolent expression was now creased into a frown. Tom had intended to leave as soon as Desiree went in, but he thought perhaps he ought to stay beside her.

"Brock! Wells! I have something so exciting to tell you." Desiree had obviously decided to take the offensive.

"Where the hell have you been?" Brock was just as clearly not led away by her diversion. "Templeton says you left the house late this evening."

"Templeton is certainly turning into quite the spy for you," Desiree shot back. "I thought we'd reached an agreement on this."

"In normal circumstances, of course," Brock replied, and eyed Tom with disfavor. "But you have been absent from the club two evenings in a row, and you've been running all over with this fellow."

"You didn't tell anyone where you were going," Wells added mildly.

"That's because I didn't want a bunch of nosy parkers knowing what I was doing." Desiree took Tom's arm and pulled him with her past the other two men and into the house. Desiree went into the parlor and turned around to face her brothers.

Brock followed, saying, "I'm not trying to find out your secrets. I was worried because you're stirring things up. You could be putting yourself in danger."

"I'm not in danger."

"You told me you were followed the other day," Wells pointed out.

She shot Wells a glare as Brock thundered, "Followed! You didn't tell me that."

"I would have, but I've been busy. Besides, it wasn't dangerous. He merely followed us around and we got rid of him."

Wells eyed the box in her hand. "You've been out pilfering things again, haven't you?"

Desiree snorted. "You should talk."

All three looked ready to embark on another round of arguments, so Tom said in a moderate tone, "Why don't we all sit down, and Desiree can catch you up on what we've found out the past few days?"

The siblings glowered at Tom in unison, but Desiree sat down, followed by Brock after he heaved a sigh, and Wells went to stand by a bookcase, hooking his elbow on one of the shelves. Tom seated himself in a chair some distance from Brock and Desiree. The less he inserted himself into this, the better; it was clear that neither of Desiree's brothers trusted him.

"I've found our relatives," Desiree said.

"What?" Brock's eyebrows shot up, and even Wells straightened.

"We are Morelands, and our father was named Alistair. I met them, Brock." Desiree's eyes shone, her voice reclaiming its former excitement. "I talked to them, and they're very nice."

"Nice?" Brock looked skeptical.

Desiree launched into the tale of talking to Alex and Con, then going to Broughton House and meeting the others. Her brothers said nothing, just listened, somewhat slack jawed, as Desiree described the Morelands and the conversation they'd had. When she finished, there was a long moment of deafening silence.

Finally, Brock said, "They gave you that box?"

"No. We found the house, Brock. The one you described. That's where we got the box. We went in tonight and found the hiding place you told us about, and it was in there."

"You broke in? Desiree, you promised you were going to stop thieving."

"I wasn't thieving," she answered indignantly. "It belongs to us."

"I'm not sure the people who live there now would take such a sanguine view of it," Brock retorted, but he spoke without heat and his eyes strayed back to the box.

"Do you recognize it, Brock?" Desiree asked.

"I'm not sure." It was the first glimpse of uncertainty Tom had seen on the man's face. Brock picked up the box and set it on his lap. He smoothed a hand across the top.

"I'm sorry about the scratch. I, um, dropped it," Desiree said, and Tom knew

310

she didn't want to tell her brother about the man attempting to steal it from them. "But we managed to pick the lock instead of breaking it."

Brock opened it and took out the wrapped jewelry, unfolding the cloth to reveal the sapphire splendor. Brock's face didn't change, but Tom heard the hitch of his breath. "I remember these." He brushed his fingertips across the gems. "She looked like a princess."

He rewrapped the jewelry quickly and stuck it back in the box, his movements efficient and businesslike. Opening the pouch, he poured the contents into his palm, picking through them. "These, too. They're your mother's." Brock set the pouch back and held the box toward Desiree. "You should have them, Desiree."

"They belong to all of us," Desiree protested. "But that's not the important thing. It's the letters." She pulled one of them from the stack and held it out to Brock. "Read it. See the signature?"

He grimaced as his eyes skimmed down the note to the bottom. "It's an *A*. Desiree, that's no proof." He handed the letter back to her.

"I don't know why you're being so stubborn." Desiree plucked the note from his hand. "Of course it's Alistair — the More-land ring, the Moreland who left the country at the same time as our mother, the letter *A* on the letters? It's plain as can be, but we're going to find out more. The Morelands are taking us to see an aunt who knew him better."

"Why would these people try to help you?" Brock almost growled.

"Because they are kind and —"

"You cannot trust the aristocracy," Brock snapped. "I don't know what they hope to achieve, but they aren't trying to help you. They aren't going to take you into their family like the prodigal son returned home. You don't know them, Desiree."

"I do! I met them. They weren't like other aristocrats. They're, well, they're a bit eccentric, but very open-minded."

"They're known as the Mad Morelands," Wells offered. Tom glanced at him; he'd almost forgotten the other man was there. Desiree was right; her twin was very good at making himself unnoticed. "I asked around about them. The duchess is some sort of social reformer, and the duke's a bit dotty."

"He's not dotty," Desiree protested. "He's sweet and still madly in love with the duchess. You can see it."

Brock rolled his eyes. "What does that have to do with the matter?" He threw a contemptuous hand toward the letters. "Love notes from a lord to his mistress are easy. It would have been more to the point to have provided for you and Wells in some way. To take you with them. As for this exemplary family, where were they all the time you were growing up? Why did they never offer a bit of help or acknowledge you in any way?"

"They didn't know about us!" When Brock snorted, Desiree went on. "I know them better than you do. I've met them. But you can meet them, too. You can decide for yourself."

"I'm not trotting over to the duke's house, hat in hand."

"The duchess invited us to dinner. To meet the family. You can talk to them."

"I'm not going to dinner with the Morelands." Brock's voice was flat and unbending. "You can mingle with the aristocracy all you want. Wells, too. I'm not going. They're your family, not mine."

"That doesn't matter," Desiree protested. "The duchess invited you, too. They want you to come."

"No." Brock grabbed his cane and surged to his feet. "I'm not going." He turned and walked out, leaning on his cane.

"Brock, wait . . ." Desiree rose to her feet and started after him.

"No. Let him go," Tom said, going to her.

"But he's being so stubborn! If he'd just meet them, he'd understand. They'd accept him, too. Wouldn't they?"

"I imagine so," Tom agreed. "It's not the Morelands, Desiree. It's your brother. He's right . . . they're not his family."

"But —"

"When you don't have something, it can hurt more to see what you're missing than it does to not have it at all."

Desiree looked up at him, her eyes widening as she took in his meaning. "Oh. Yes, I see." She laid a gentle hand on Tom's arm, looking up at him. "I'm sorry."

She might have been talking about her brother, but Tom was certain that she was offering her compassion to him, too, for his own childhood. The look in her eyes warmed him, and he bent a little toward her. When she edged in a little closer, he thought she was about to kiss him, and suddenly his heart started to pound.

But then she paused and glanced back at Wells. Giving his arm a little squeeze instead, she took a step back. "Thank you."

Her brother pushed away from the bookcase he'd been leaning against. "I think he's right, Dizzy. Brock feels it sometimes, you know. That as much as he loves us, he's not the same."

Desiree's eyes filled with tears. "I'm sorry. I never meant to hurt him."

"You didn't," Wells assured her. "It's not anything to do with us. It's Brock."

"Don't worry." Tom smiled at her. "I'm sure he'll come around. The Morelands will wear him down. No one can hold out against the duchess for long. That's why government officials flee the moment they see her."

"I'm sure they do." Desiree chuckled and turned toward her brother. "You'll see." She added a little anxiously, "You *will* go to the dinner with me, won't you, Wells?"

"Of course. How could I pass up the opportunity to meet this woman? I know an official who's absolutely terrified of her." He paused. "Do you really think they're our family?"

"I do. It fits, Wells, I promise you."

"And it all seems —" he flicked a glance at Tom "— *right* to you?"

"You can say it. Tom knows about my intuition," Desiree said. "And he hasn't yet told me I'm insane." She flashed a smile at Tom before going on. "Wells, there's no way

315

I can tell if all these clues are real. That's not the way it works. But I don't think there's anything false about the Morelands I met yesterday. They are unusual, but then, so are we."

A half smile touched Wells's lips. "That's true enough."

"Read the letters Alistair wrote to our mother," Desiree urged him. "I think he really loved her. And I felt — I don't know. It made both of them seem more real to me. As if I knew them a bit."

"How are these Morelands you met related to us?"

"They're cousins of some sort, I guess. Alistair is the duke's cousin." She cast a glance toward Tom for confirmation, and he nodded.

Wells turned cool gray eyes on Tom. "What exactly is your role in all this?"

"He's helping me, Wells, I told you," Desiree said with some exasperation.

"I'd like to hear it from him," Wells said mildly, crossing his arms and continuing to gaze at Tom.

Tom straightened a little, his eyes turning as flat and cool as those of the man across from him, his jaw setting. The skin along his spine tingled, making him think of a dog's hair rising up down his back. "I'm looking to find the truth."

"Ah. Like Demosthenes. Or was it Diogenes?" His indolent drawl was underlaid by a taunting tone. He employed the uppercrust pose well, Tom thought, using that careless hauteur to intimidate. Tom was certain it was an act, though he wasn't sure exactly why Wells used it. But he wasn't about to let the other man think he could be pushed about.

"I wouldn't know about any of those Greeks. You'll have to ask your cousin the duke about them." Tom's smile was more a baring of teeth, at odds with the lightness of his tone. "I'm just a man of the streets, myself." He shrugged. "Of course, I can understand why you're concerned I might take advantage of Desiree. You want to protect your sister. Shelter her, keep her safe, what with her not being able to do it herself. I'm sure Desiree understands that, too."

Wells's eyes widened fractionally as he realized what Tom had just done. Out of the corner of his eye, Tom could see Desiree drawing up, her gaze taking on an unholy light, and she said in a viciously sweet tone, "Yes, Wells, why don't you explain why I need looking after like a child? I'm sure I'd like to hear it."

Tom's eyes danced. Wells shot a rueful glance at him, the ghost of a smile touching his lips, and he murmured, "Well played, Mr. Quick."

Tom decided that this was an excellent time to leave. Nodding to Wells and Desiree, he bade them goodbye and started toward the door.

"Wait." This time it was Desiree who stopped Tom. "Tomorrow . . ." She stopped, and Tom suspected the realization had hit her, just as it had that moment occurred to him. "Oh. I don't suppose there's anything we need to do tomorrow. I, um, I shall see you when we go to visit Aunt Wilhemina, then?"

He nodded, disappointed. The next day seemed devoid of interest now. "I — you still should have someone with you when you go to the club. If you're planning to keep up your games."

"Yes, I am. Though I rather think Falk will have received the message after tonight."

"Perhaps. Well . . ." Tom was very aware of her brother still lurking in the background. "I shall see you tomorrow evening, then. Good night."

Tom went to the front door and opened it, but couldn't resist turning and casting a last glance back at her. It was gratifying to see that Desiree had trailed after him and was watching him from the door of the parlor. It was even better to see her smile at him. And that would have to do for this evening.

He trotted down the steps and started off, casting a quick glance up and down the street for the carriage that had lain in wait for Desiree the other day. There was no sign of it, but that didn't mean anything. It was very late. And even if Falk had gotten the message tonight, there was the possibility that the man who had stalked them the other day was not working for Falk.

It was, therefore, perfectly reasonable to escort Desiree to the club and back. It wasn't merely an excuse to see Desiree again.

Tom snorted. Who was he trying to fool? It was exactly that. And he'd spend tomorrow just waiting for the moment he could be with her. He was as sure of that as he was of the fact that he'd spend the rest of tonight thinking about her.

He was in serious trouble.

CHAPTER TWENTY-TWO

Tom was sitting at his desk the next morning, trying to find something to do to make the time pass until this evening, when a well-dressed man stepped into the office. The visitor paused for a moment, casting an encompassing look around the office and landing on Tom. His hair was dark and his eyes gray, and his well-modeled face would have been handsome had it been less inexpressive. He stood straight as an arrow, his immaculate clothes clearly tailored to fit his slim figure, his cravat tied in a moderate fashion. Gold glinted discreetly at his cuffs, and a pearl stickpin nestled in the folds of his cravat. He was the picture of a gentleman, well dressed but understated, wealth and privilege in every line.

Tom took an instant dislike to him. He kept stubbornly to his seat, though normally he would have risen out of politeness; he was sure this fellow was all too accustomed to everyone popping up when he came into a room.

"Can I help you?" He remembered a second too late that "may" was correct, not "can," and it bothered him that he'd slipped in front of this man. It also bothered him that it bothered him.

"I am looking for Lord Moreland. I understood that this was where he could be found." He glanced back at the door as if he had mistaken the name.

"Yes, this is Moreland & Quick, but he's not in yet. Can I help you?" Tom deliberately repeated the mistake.

"I think not. It's Constantine to whom I must speak."

"You know Con?" Tom asked, a bit surprised that Con was close enough to someone of such perfection that he called him by name — even if it was a name Con never used.

The man's expression turned faintly disapproving at what he doubtlessly considered impertinence, but he answered. "Yes, I know him. He is my cousin."

Tom's brows shot up. Cousin? It wasn't their cousin Albert; Tom had met him. There were others, he knew, but his mind went straight to Gregory, Alistair Moreland's legitimate son. The man certainly fit the twins' description of their cousin. Could this man be Desiree's other half brother? If so, Tom supposed he had to be polite to him. "I see. Well, he's probably still at the house. I'll give him a message from you, if you'd like."

"No, I'll just —" At that moment, Alex appeared in the doorway, and the man turned. "Ah. Constantine. There you are." Obviously, he didn't know Con well enough to distinguish him from his twin. "Good morning."

"I'm Alex," Alex said, looking at him curiously.

"Oh. I beg your pardon." A line of red bloomed on the man's cheekbones, which did, now that Tom thought about it, have a resemblance to the Morelands' angular bone structure. "I, um . . ."

"Do I know you?" Alex asked, still studying their visitor. "You look familiar."

"I am your cousin," the other man said, irritation threading his voice. "Gregory."

"Cousin Gregory!" Alex glanced over at Tom, then back to Gregory. "Then I will beg *your* pardon," Alex said with an affable smile. "I should have recognized you. At least you knew it was one of us."

"Yes, well, you two are difficult to forget," Gregory said dryly.

Alex's lips twitched. "I'm sure we plagued you when we were younger. We did everyone. I'll beg your pardon for that, too. We have become more civilized. At least somewhat."

"It was no matter." Gregory waved away the apology, but did not offer up a smile.

"Con should be here soon," Alex said. "He was right behind me. He stopped at the apothecary for a moment."

"Is he sick?" Tom asked. It seemed unlikely, since Con was one of those annoying sorts who were always hale and hearty.

"No. No one is sick. Con's determined to find something to cure Lilah's morning sickness. I told him it would be gone in a couple of months, but you know Con," Alex said with all the authority of a man who had just become a father.

Gregory's mouth tightened. "Really, Cousin Alexander. Hardly a fit subject for conversation."

Tom could practically see Alex's brain spinning, trying to decide whether to be polite or say what he thought. Fortunately, Con appeared behind his brother, saying, "The blasted man didn't have anything. Why are you standing in the doorway, Alex?"

"You have a visitor." Alex moved aside so

Con could enter.

Con's eyes went to the man standing in his office. "Hullo." He, too, frowned in puzzlement, but then he said, "Cousin Gregory?"

"Yes. I'm surprised you recognized me."

"I didn't," Alex put in.

"Told you I had a better memory." Con added candidly. "It was only because we'd been talking about . . ." His voice trailed off. "That is to say, what can I do for you, Cousin?"

"You may give me the papers Blackstock sent you. I would have thought you would have done so already, frankly, since they pertain to my family."

"Blackstock?" Tom blurted.

"Yes," Gregory said shortly with a surprised glance at Tom before he turned back to Con.

"*You're* the one who's after that bloody envelope?" Con exclaimed. "You hired her?"

"Her? Hired who?" Gregory frowned. "I haven't the foggiest notion what you're talking about."

"Then you and I are in the same boat because I've no idea what you're talking about, either. Who is Blackstock? Why would he send me an envelope? What's in it?" Con retorted.

Gregory's frown deepened. "Are you serious or is this one of your silly jokes?"

"It's not a joke. I'm not ten years old anymore." Con folded his arms. "Look. You came to me. You appear to want my help in some way. If so, you're going to have to be a little less obscure."

Gregory's gaze flickered to Tom once again, then in a tight voice he said to Con, "This is family business."

"Oh, for pity's sake," Con began.

"Con, I can leave," Tom offered.

"No. This is absurd." Con faced his cousin. "Tom is my partner in this business, which this envelope of yours apparently involves, given that *someone* broke into our office trying to steal it."

"What?" Gregory gaped. "Steal it!"

"Yes, and since you're the one who's so bloody eager to get your hands on it, I can't help but suspect you are the one who hired the thief."

Gregory's nostrils flared. "Are you mad? Why would I steal my —" He stopped and drew a deep breath, pulling his expression back to its former composure, though a look in his eyes hinted of anger still bubbling below the surface. "Mr. Blackstock was my father's lawyer. Perhaps you are unaware of it, but my father . . ." The muscle of his jaw tightened. "My father deserted us many years ago, when I was a child. There has been no word from him since. It's clear he will not return. We have no way of knowing if he is even alive, but my mother has been reluctant to petition the court to have him declared dead. She has always hoped he would come back to her, though I cannot imagine why she should wish it." His voice turned bitter. "How she can continue to love a man who humiliated her by running away with his mist—" Gregory stopped, with another glance toward Tom.

"You knew about Stella! You knew about the children?" Con exclaimed.

"Stella. Who the devil is Stella? What children?"

"Never mind that," Alex said, shooting Con a look. "What does that have to do with this envelope?"

Gregory, who was still staring at Con with a puzzled look, said, "I need to assume my place as his heir. I'm about to be married. I need to get on with my life. So I informed my attorney that I wanted to petition to have Alistair Moreland declared dead."

"What if he isn't dead?" Alex asked.

"He is to me."

"Your lawyer is this Blackstock fellow?" Con asked.

"His son is my attorney. The elder Black-stock was my father's lawyer, and when he learned what I was doing, he sent some legal papers to you."

"To me?" Con stared at him. "Why send them to me? Why not to you? Or the duke?"

"Believe me, I have asked that many times," Gregory said sharply. "The man was on his deathbed, and, frankly, I think he'd gotten a bit dotty. Whatever the reason, he told his son he'd sent it to the Moreland business. I thought perhaps he meant your father's man of business, Cummings, but the younger Blackstock spoke to Cummings, and the man said he'd received nothing from either of the attorneys."

"I cannot imagine why he'd send anything here. Why doesn't Blackstock's son ask his father about it?"

"I told you, the man was on his deathbed, and now he is no longer conscious. Needless to say, my problem is not the most important thing on his son's mind right now. However, it's rather important to me. It may be nothing, just the product of an ill and confused mind, but it's possible it could be a more recent version of my father's will."

"I don't know what to tell you," Con said. "Nothing like that has come here. Trust me, we've scoured the office."

Gregory stood for a moment, studying Con. "Someone broke into your office? Are you sure they didn't get it?"

"Positive," Con replied.

Tom spoke up. "I chased off the thief. There was nothing in her hands."

"The thief was a woman?" Gregory asked dubiously. "Are you certain?"

Tom nodded but didn't elaborate.

"Why would anyone else want it?" Gregory seemed to be asking himself more than anyone else. He straightened and asked Con, "Will you tell me if you do receive it? Or if you hear any word of it?"

"Of course. It's your business, as you said."

Gregory nodded and started toward the door, but he stopped and turned. "You said — what did you mean when you asked if I knew about Stella?" He paused, then went on as if the words were pulled out of him. "Was that her name? His mistress? And how the devil do you know that?"

"Because I've met one of her children."

"Her children! You can't mean — my father's — there were no children."

"There very well may have been," Con replied. "They have a Moreland ring. Their mother ran away with her lover at the same time Alistair left."

328

Tom noticed that Gregory's thumb went to the bare ring finger on his right hand. "That's nonsense." Color surged in Gregory's face, and he took a step forward, his hands clenching. "It's no proof of anything. Anyone who told you that is lying. I have no idea who his mistress was. My mother and I were not privy to my father's secrets. But there weren't any children. It's impossible. If there had been, they would have taken them along."

"Not all parents are so caring about their children."

"I am well aware of that." Gregory's gray eyes were stormy now, everything about him so tightly clenched it was a wonder something didn't snap. "My father was weak and faithless and a fool, but he didn't do that. Someone is trying to take advantage of you. You may be gullible enough to believe them, and God knows you have no compunction about embarrassing the family, but I am not so foolish."

"You could meet them yourself," Con said. "Aren't you interested in seeing if you have any siblings? Mother is having a dinner for them. You could come and talk to them."

"Meet them? Sit down and chat? You really are mad if you think I'd want to do

329

that. I have no interest in talking to swindlers," Gregory retorted. "I have no siblings. And if you go running all over the city telling people that my father left a string of bastards in his wake, I will *kill* you. I will not allow you to humiliate my mother any more than the Moreland family already has. Do you hear me?"

"Yes. You're quite audible," Con snapped back. "I might have known you'd be too stiff-necked to consider anything but what you want to believe. I don't know why I even bothered to ask."

Gregory's jaw worked, and for an instant, Tom thought he was going to erupt, but he spun on his heel and left the room. The room was silent for a moment, the only sound Gregory's footsteps ringing through the hall and down the stairs, punctuated at the end by a slamming of the outside door.

"Well, you're as diplomatic as ever," Alex said wryly.

"And Gregory's just as rigid and self-absorbed," Con responded. He let out a sigh and plopped down in his chair. "I suppose now we have a new suspect for thievery."

"He certainly didn't appear to know anything about the break-in," Tom commented.

"No. And I wouldn't think our cousin is a

tremendous actor," Alex added. "I imagine he's right — it's a new will. I wonder what it says."

"*I* wonder why anyone would send it *here*," Con said.

"A lawyer giving a new will to anyone except the heir seems suspicious," Tom said. "Maybe he thought it would be safer at a detective agency."

"Yes, it would be easy for the heir to tear it up if it wasn't to his liking," Con agreed. "It doesn't seem likely, though, that Alistair would have cut out his only legitimate heir."

"Maybe Alistair left something for the Malones," Alex posited. "Or acknowledged them, at least. Gregory wouldn't like that getting out, obviously."

"Or maybe the will wasn't written long ago," Tom mused. "Alistair could have sent it to his lawyer from America or wherever they went. He and Stella could have had a whole other family that he wanted to leave money to. After all, there's nothing to say when Alistair died. In fact, he could still be alive. Alistair wouldn't even be as old as your father."

Tom's mind went to Desiree's wild theory that her father had returned to England, but he didn't say anything. It was exactly the sort of idea that would intrigue Con and

331

make him run with it, which Tom feared would only wind up hurting Desiree. And, as much as Tom liked Con, there was a selfish urge in him to keep the investigation to him and Desiree only.

Con nodded. "If that's true, it would certainly create a problem for Gregory's plan to have him declared dead. It didn't sound as though Gregory knew for sure there was a will in that envelope. It might be something else. Maybe proof that Alistair is alive."

"I should tell Desiree." Tom jumped to his feet and started toward the door.

He caught the look that Alex and Con shared as he left the room. He knew they were sure that he simply wanted to go see Desiree again. But that wasn't it. Well, only partly it. Desiree should know this latest development. Still, he couldn't deny the eagerness rising in his chest as his hack pulled up in front of the Malone house. Tom bounded out of the carriage and up the steps to the front door.

The butler admitted him, saying, "Miss Malone was about to leave, sir. I'll see if she is available."

Before Templeton could even turn, there was the sound of footsteps on the stairs, and Tom looked up. Desiree was coming toward him. And she was wearing her formfitting acrobatic costume.

Tom swallowed. Maybe this hadn't been such a good idea after all.

CHAPTER TWENTY-THREE

"Tom!" Desiree smiled, happiness surging in her chest when she saw him standing in the entry. "I didn't expect you this early."

"Yes, well . . ." His eyes ran down her form before he pulled his gaze back to her face. He yanked off his cap, holding it between his hands. "I, ah, something came up. I mean, I had a bit of news I thought I should tell you."

A warmth spread all through Desiree at the look on his face, a little stunned and wholly hungry. She suspected she was blushing. Her costume had only a short skirt, revealing her legs in the clinging outfit from her midthigh down. The bodice was equally fitted to her body. She had never worn the costume around anyone but her twin, as they'd always been alone together on their jobs.

Desiree was fully aware of how revealing the outfit was and what the look in Tom's eyes meant. She wasn't sure if the heat inside her was more from embarrassment or pleasure at having his gaze linger on her. Desiree took the cloak she was carrying over her arm and pulled it on as she continued down the stairs.

"I was about to practice. Would you like to come along? We could talk there."

"Of course."

Desiree led Tom through the house and down the alley to the converted mews where she practiced her skills. She kept her eyes on Tom's face as he followed her inside, and it filled her with delight that he gazed around the room in awe.

"This is amazing," he said. "It's like — well, I don't know what it's like because I've never seen anything like this."

"Brock renovated the mews for Wells and me so we could continue doing what we enjoyed. We were both terribly bored when Brock rescued us and we quit 'the life.' "

Tom walked around, looking at all the various ropes and bars and barriers. Desiree followed. "Would you like to try some of it? I could teach you a few things."

Tom threw a laughing glance at her. "I'm afraid I'm long past the age of learning how to tumble."

"Somersaults aren't terribly useful, but

you could climb." She pointed to the wall dotted with handholds, and to the center, where a rope hung from the ceiling. "That's quite useful."

"If I'm going to be around you, I suppose so."

"Take off your shoes and jacket. That waistcoat, too."

Desiree watched as Tom did as she suggested, something deep within her responding to the sight of him undressing. He rolled up the sleeves of his shirt and unbuttoned the top button, revealing a tempting V of his skin.

His shirt, though not clinging like her own bodice, showed more of his form than the multiple garments men usually wore. And his was a very nice form. Tom was not as tall as Brock or as wide shouldered, but he had a muscular build. His hands, which she had admired from the first, were long fingered and supple, and his forearms were equally attractive, firmly muscled and lightly dusted with blond hairs. Even the knobby bones of his wrists somehow stirred her. Desiree did her best not to stare — or, at least, not to let him see her stare.

She cleared her throat. "It's best to stretch before one starts."

Desiree began to demonstrate, and Tom

watched her. She could feel the blood pulsing through her veins, her abdomen turning molten under his gaze. "Come, do this with me."

"I can't do that." His voice was slightly rougher and lower than usual.

"Not as far as I," she agreed. "But you can do it a little."

He joined her, and Desiree soon understood why he enjoyed watching her. It made her heart beat faster, her breath turn unsteady as she watched his shirt stretch across his back and the muscles of his forearms clench and loosen.

Desiree went through a few of her warming-up exercises before they started climbing the wall. The next hour passed quickly, full of laughter and quips and the satisfaction of physical motion. They climbed the wall and the rope, swung from ring to ring — though Tom refused to try a turn on the trapeze — and she even persuaded him to walk the low beam.

She reached out to steady him once, her fingers curling around the firm muscle of his forearm, and a shiver shot straight down to her abdomen. It was all she could do not to let her hand slide up and down his arm. Tom's shirt began to cling to his chest and back, and his forearms glistened. Her gaze was again drawn to that V of skin at the top of his shirt, her mouth going dry as she watched a drop of sweat trickle down to nestle in the hollow of his throat.

Desiree thought of their kisses last night, of the heat and hunger. Was she being foolish not to grab at that pleasure? Their search would come to an end before long; she could think of nothing to do after they had visited Aunt Wilhemina. She'd have no reason to see Tom anymore.

Her heart contracted at the thought, but she had to be realistic. It never helped to pretend. They would go back to their lives. Even if they established that Alistair Moreland was her father, it wouldn't really change anything. She would know and be satisfied; hopefully the anxiety that nagged at her would go away. But beyond that, she would still live here and go to the club in the evenings. She would flirt with ineligible men, but her heart would stay whole and apart.

What were the odds that she would ever meet a man like Tom again? A man who knew her past and wasn't appalled by it? Who lived, as she did, in some shadow world between gentility and the slums? Who admired her skill and understood her? Perhaps this was her one chance, and she was letting her pride stand in the way.

Desiree pondered these things as she took to the trapeze while Tom lay back on one of the mats, recovering his breath and watching her. But she came to no decision, still torn between hunger and her lifelong determination not to fall into the trap her mother had.

Her concentration fractured, Desiree climbed down from the high bar and sat down with Tom, then lay back on the mat beside him. Even this, she thought, was fraught, lying only a foot or two apart, their bodies still heated and tingling.

"You came to tell me something," Desiree said, turning her face toward him.

Tom nodded and rolled onto his side, going up on one forearm. "Gregory Moreland visited the office today."

"Gre— Alistair's son?" Desiree's eyes widened. "What did he want?"

"He's looking for an envelope from a man named Blackstock, who was Alistair Moreland's lawyer."

"No! He's the one who wants it? What's in it?"

"That's the thing. No one knows exactly. It seems the lawyer is dying, and all Gregory knows is that Blackstock sent some legal papers to our office."

"Why would he have done that? Why send it to you and Con?"

Tom shrugged. "That's the question. One can only think that whatever is in that envelope is something the lawyer wanted to keep away from Alistair's heir."

"That's . . . very intriguing. Is Gregory the one who hired Falk? Is that why Falk knew who my father was?"

"Possibly, though Gregory seemed genuinely confused when Con asked him about it. He wasn't the man who followed us. I would have recognized him. But Gregory could have hired the man."

"But what about the cuff links you took from him? They said *Pax*."

He nodded. "I know. It's stretching belief to think that there might be two different parties after it. A third seems ludicrous."

"Perhaps Alistair's friend is helping Gregory?" Desiree suggested.

"That's possible."

After a moment Desiree asked softly, "What was he like? Alistair's son."

"He dresses well."

Desiree laughed. "That's all you can say about him?"

"No, not all," Tom protested. "But it seemed very much who he was. Expensive clothes and shoes, expert tailoring, but everything quite muted and understated. As if everyone knows he has wealth and power and it would be crass to flash it about."

"I know the attitude."

"Not haughty exactly, but very aware that he's at the top. Very correct and rigid, as if his butler starched and ironed him every day. Didn't fly into a temper with Con until the very end."

"Did he say anything — does he know about us? The Malones, I mean?"

Tom hesitated, and she said, "Tell me. I don't — I don't expect him to like us. I just wondered if he knew we existed."

"He didn't seem to. He disputed it quite vehemently when Con told him Alistair had other children."

Her eyes flew to his. "Con told him who we are?"

"No. Gregory obviously knew that his father ran off with his . . . with someone."

"You can say mistress, Tom. It's what she was."

"Very well. He knew Alistair ran away with her. He was clearly bitter about it and the insult to his mother."

"One would be," Desiree said.

"But Con called your mother Stella, and Gregory didn't seem to recognize the name. Of course, he wouldn't have been more than

341

a child — he looks to be my age or Brock's, and it's likely that no one brought it up with him later on. He was adamant that Alistair had no offspring. That was when he got mad at Con. He thinks you're lying. Trying to swindle him."

"Ah. The way you did." Desiree gave him an arch look.

"Yes, the way I did." Tom smiled. "Are you going to hold that against me the rest of our lives?"

The rest of our lives. Desiree's heart stumbled. Was he planning to continue to see her? Did he believe they would . . . what? Be lifelong friends? Marry? Have an affair? Or was it just a figure of speech? She kept her breath even as she replied lightly, "Only for a decade or two. Truth is, I don't blame you. I'd have distrusted me, too. Now that I've met the Morelands, I can understand why you wouldn't like anyone who might hurt them."

He reached out to cup her cheek in his hand. "It was never that I didn't like you. I liked you far too much. I was afraid I'd let it cloud my judgment. I didn't want to be your mark."

"You weren't. Ever." His touch sent shivers through her, melting her core. Was he about to kiss her? He was gazing at her so intently that it made her heart pound, her flesh heat. She wanted him to kiss her. She wanted to ignore all her earlier thoughtful decisions about men and relationships and act solely on instinct.

"Desiree . . ." Tom's fingers drifted over to stroke her hair, then slid slowly down her neck, making her breath catch in her throat. "We shouldn't be here like this. It's too tempting." But he made no effort to sit up or move away.

Neither did she. "I know."

For the only time in her life that Desiree could remember, she wanted to let a man make the decision for her. It would be so easy to let Tom seduce her, to not have to face the reality that she would be breaking her own principles. Just let his touch pull her into the vortex of passion.

Tom's hand slid farther down her arm and back up, and his eyes flamed as he looked at her body, at his hand gliding across the top of her chest, fingers tracing the line of her collarbone beneath the material of her costume. He trailed his forefinger over the hollow of her throat and down, following the bony path of her sternum until it ended.

Desiree waited, her flesh quivering, not knowing what she would do if he explored further. He laid his palm flat against her stomach and drifted upward, until it brushed against her breast. Tom leaned over, bracing himself with his arms on either side of her, and bent to touch his lips to hers. Once, twice, he brushed her mouth softly, until Desiree ached to reach up and sink her hands into his hair and pull him in for a proper kiss. But there was no need to do that, for then he kissed her.

Not a proper kiss, she thought. A most improper one that went on and on, claiming her mouth with his lips and teeth and tongue, and the whole time his hands remained against the mat, not touching her anywhere, using only his mouth to tease and inflame. Desiree dug her fingers into the front of his shirt, pulling, her body aching to feel him against her.

She felt his knee crook to cover her legs, his body beginning to roll over to cover her. And then, with a groan, he rolled away and sat up. Desiree swallowed a growl of frustration. Tom sat with his feet flat on the mat, arms braced on his upraised knees and both hands plunged deep into his hair. His back rose and fell in quick, hard breaths.

Desiree wanted to follow him, to press herself against his back and wrap her arms around him from behind. She wanted to press her lips to that spot at the nape of his neck just above his shirt. In fact, surprising herself a bit, she wanted to nip at that spot with her teeth. But all that would be unfair to him. Tom had managed to leash his hunger and do the right thing. She shouldn't try to make him slip his leash. So she stayed where she was, drinking in the sight of him, her body humming with the desire he'd awakened in her.

"I should go," Tom said finally, his voice low and hoarse.

Desiree wanted to protest, but she did not. He was right. They shouldn't have come here. She shouldn't have worn her costume with him around. They shouldn't have played and sweated or clasped hands to help each other up. She knew all that.

But what she said was "We could practice again sometime. If you wanted."

He let out a harsh little huff of air, half laugh and half groan. "Desiree, you'll be the death of me." He rose to his feet and rolled down his cuffs, not looking at her. "You know I want to." He swung his head toward her. "You know exactly what I want and how much I want it."

"I know." Desiree's voice was a trifle shaky. She did know. And she knew how much she wanted the same thing.

"But that's something you're going to

have to decide." He redressed, pulling on his vest and jacket, running his hand through his hair, trying to straighten out the mess he'd made of it. Desiree liked it better this way, tousled and silky and looking as if he'd just been pulled from his bed. "I'm not going to try to inveigle you into anything."

"I know," Desiree replied.

He put on his shoes last. As he knelt, tying them, Desiree said, suddenly a little alarmed, "But you don't mean — you're still going to escort me to the club, aren't you?"

Tom straightened and turned to her. "Oh, yes. You can't get rid of me that easily. I'll be here tonight at eight." Then he grinned and was gone.

CHAPTER TWENTY-FOUR

Desiree did not follow Tom out of the building. Instead, she went back to her exercises, funneling all her turmoil and frustration into the work. By the time she finished, she was exhausted, her muscles quivering and her lungs heaving. She dropped to the mat, lying back as she had with Tom. She had been successful in her efforts; she was now too tired to think. Turning over on her side, she closed her eyes, and after a moment she dozed off.

She jerked awake as a heavy weight hit her shoulder. Her eyes flew open, but she was already being flipped over onto her stomach, and a knee landed on her back, knocking the breath from her and pinning her down. A rough hand clamped over her cheek and mouth, and a point of cold metal touched her throat.

"Not so full of fight now, are you?" a voice growled. The assailant bent low, his voice oddly muffled. "No man to punch for you."

Desiree's mind raced. No point in screaming; she was too far from the house for anyone to hear. She was in a bad position to fight him, with no leverage to push off his heavy weight. But she could bargain. This must be the man who had followed them the other day or Falk's man from the night before. In either case, they wanted something from her.

"What do you want?" Desiree whispered, putting a tremor in her voice. It was always an advantage to appear weaker and more frightened than she was, giving her the element of surprise. She dared not turn her head lest the knife slice her, but she cut her eyes as far as she could to see the man. She could catch only a glimpse, but it wouldn't have mattered if she had seen his entire face. He wore a mask.

Her attacker grated out a laugh. "You know what I want. The bloody will."

"You can have the will. I don't want it. I was just after the money."

"Money? I don't know about any money."

"There was money, too. You can have it. I'll give you all of it, if you promise not to hurt me. But it's in the house. I put it in the safe. I have to get it."

"You think I'm stupid?" her assailant

asked. Desiree thought it better not to answer. "I'm not letting you go get it."

"Then how can I give it to you?"

"Oh, you'll give it to me. But I'm going with you." He jumped to his feet, yanking Desiree up with him.

He could not keep the knife at her throat as he pulled her up, and Desiree, instead of resisting or pulling away, went with his movement, pushing up with her own strong legs. She slammed into him, adding a sharp jab of her elbow into his midsection. The man staggered backward, and she pivoted, ripping her arm from his grasp, and ran. He came pounding after her, but with a leap, she grabbed the rope that hung from the ceiling, lifting herself up and twisting to kick out with her feet.

Her kick landed solidly against his chest, and her attacker staggered back and fell heavily. Desiree whirled and ran. Flinging open the door, she pelted out into the alleyway, shouting for help. Her voice echoed around the small alleyway, and, as she had hoped, doors along the row of mews opened and heads popped out in curiosity.

Merriwell, the Malones' coachman, gaped at her for an instant, but then his eyes went past her, and he shouted, "Oy! You!"

Merriwell shot past her, and Desiree

349

looked back to see her attacker dashing away from her, with Merriwell chasing him. Desiree stopped, breathing hard, watching as the two men ran out of sight. It occurred to her that she was standing there in only her formfitting costume in public view.

She hurried back to the studio to don her cloak and shoes. Desiree hadn't noticed it while she was running, but she could feel now that she had stepped on several pebbles in her flight down the alley. And there was blood trickling down her neck; his knife must have sliced her a bit as she lunged away.

As she left the building and locked the door, Merriwell came into view, breathing heavily. "He got away, miss. I'm sorry. Jumped in a hack before I could catch him."

"That's all right, Merriwell. I'm just glad you chased him off."

Desiree returned to the house, where a quick look in her mirror told her that the cut on her neck, while not deep, was long and obvious. Everyone would be sure to notice it. She wouldn't be able to hide it from her brothers, who would be bound to fuss about it, but perhaps it would be best not to go to the club this evening. A long red scratch across her throat would hardly complement her elegant low-necked evening gowns. She sent a note to Tom, canceling their visit to Farrington. She was a little surprised how disappointed she felt.

She was even more surprised when Tom Quick showed up at her door. "Tom?" She stood up, happiness rising in her chest. "What are you — did you not get my note?"

"Yes, I got it. What's wrong? Are you ill?" He stopped, his eyes going to her neck. "What the devil is that?"

He strode forward, reaching out to tilt up her chin and inspect her neck.

"It's a scratch," Desiree replied with a sigh.

"That's not a scratch, it's a cut." He frowned at her. "What happened? I knew there was something wrong about that note. Why didn't you tell me?"

"Oh, for heaven's sake, don't you start, too. Brock and Wells already harangued me about it. It's not as if I did it on purpose. Yes, I should have been more careful. Yes, I should have locked the door to the exercise room, and I will next time. It isn't normally a dangerous area. In any case, I handled it."

"Handled what?" Tom was looking grimmer by the moment.

Desiree told him about the attack. He continued to scowl, but when she described her escape from her assailant, he relaxed into a chuckle. "Trust you to damage him more than he did to you. I hope he has feet-sized bruises on his front."

She gave him a smile. "I rather enjoyed that part of it."

"Who was it? What did he want?"

"The will. No surprise there." She added irritably, "And I don't know who he was. I don't even know what he looks like. The blasted man had on a mask. I wish I'd torn it off."

"Don't worry about that. All that matters was you got away from him."

"It was either Falk's man or the fellow that followed us the other day, because he said something about you hitting him," Desiree went on.

"I should have hit him harder," Tom muttered. He thought for a moment. "Your message to Falk's man was pretty clear. Falk is distrusting but he also should know you well enough to know you told him the truth about not having the envelope."

It warmed Desiree to hear Tom's faith in her honesty, so different from his past attitude, but she said only, "Yes, and Falk never mentioned a will, only an envelope. I'm not sure he knew what was inside. Which would lead to the conclusion that it was the man with Pax's cuff links. I couldn't tell if it was the same voice."

"It still seems odd to me that Alistair's friend would be so interested in his will. My money is on Gregory Moreland being behind this. He's the one who was trying to find it yesterday morning. It's most suspicious that you were attacked the very afternoon after he learned that Con didn't have it."

"Yes, but you said he didn't know about us and Con didn't tell him our name. How would he know to come here?"

"There's nothing to say Gregory was telling the truth. I thought he seemed surprised, but maybe he's just good at lying. Maybe he's known who you were all along, but it didn't matter because this new will didn't surface until now. But when Con mentioned you, he decided you must have it."

"But if Gregory is the man who hired the man who followed us, who hired Falk?"

Tom sighed, rubbing the back of his neck. "I've no idea. It's as confusing as ever." He went to her. "The important thing is that nothing happened to you." He stroked a finger down her throat beside the scratch. "I hate to think of anyone hurting you. Promise me you'll be more careful in the future."

"I will." Desiree looked up into his eyes, and the air between them was suddenly electric.

Tom's fingers tightened on her arms, and he leaned closer. But then he dropped his hands and stepped back, clearing his throat. "I . . . ah, should leave."

"Tom." Desiree wanted to take Tom's hand and tell him to stay.

He stopped. "What?"

Desiree's fingers clenched at her sides, and she said, "Nothing. I will see you tomorrow."

Then he was gone, leaving Desiree standing in the parlor alone. She looked around her and sighed. It was better this way. Really.

All she had to do was convince herself.

Desiree met Tom the next morning at the office, and they drove to the Morelands' home. They were to meet the three wives of the Moreland siblings for a call on Aunt Wilhemina. Desiree was silent, stomach dancing, and she had to clasp her hands firmly together to keep them from fidgeting.

Tom glanced over at her once or twice. "Nervous?"

"A little." It continued to surprise her how easily she admitted her doubts and mistakes to Tom. All her life she had kept them a carefully guarded secret. If you admitted fear, if you let them know you had made a slip, people didn't let you do things. But somehow with Tom, it didn't bother her.

"About meeting Aunt Wilhemina?" Tom asked.

"Some. But more about meeting Con's and Alex's wives."

"Sabrina and Lilah?" He smiled. "Don't worry. You'll like them."

"It's not that. I'm worried whether *they* will like *me.* I think they're more apt to be like Megan than the others. I'm fairly certain she was suspicious of me."

He shrugged. "Megan doesn't give her trust as easily. You have to remember, though, that she's a reporter. Sabrina and Lilah aren't — and you have to be pretty open-minded to marry a Moreland. They'll give you a chance, even if they might be more protective of the family. The Morelands tend to have that effect on people close to them."

"I know." Desiree smiled, relaxing slightly. "Tell me about Sabrina and Lilah."

"Well, they were very good friends before they met the Greats, which makes for a happy situation. Sabrina is sweet and kind, and she just had a baby. Ooh and aah over the baby, and she'll like you. Lilah is more conventional in manner. She was raised by a very proper person. And she can be tarter than Sabrina. But underneath, she's . . . well, she married Con, which should give you some idea of how tolerant she is."

Desiree laughed. "Poor Con! Everyone picks on him!"

Tom joined in her laughter. "Don't feel sorry for him. Con enjoys being outrageous. But he'll be glad to know he has a champion in you."

Tom had chased away her nerves, and when they were ushered into the Sultan Room, Desiree was able to greet the occupants of the room with confidence. Sabrina was a small woman with black hair and blue eyes, and she held a baby in her arms. Lilah was taller, her eyes gray and her hair a striking red-gold color. Both of them had more reserve in their gazes than the duchess, who took Desiree's hands and greeted her warmly, but neither of them seemed haughty or antagonistic.

Desiree admired the baby, who was sound asleep and did indeed look like a perfect angel, as her mother described her.

"We had an intruder last night," Megan told them. "I'm not sure if it's related to the people who've been after you."

"Oh, no!" Desiree cried. "I'm so sorry to have brought any trouble to you."

The duchess gave a dismissive wave of her hand, as if such things were a minor annoyance. "No need to be alarmed. He came in through the kitchen, and the cook heard him. She threatened him with a meat cleaver, so he ran. Con was a bit irritated that she chased him off because he wanted to question the man, but really, one cannot expect the servants to capture intruders, as well. And Mrs. Hooper is getting up in years now."

Desiree could think of nothing to say to that. Tom said, "This chap was certainly busy yesterday."

"Why do you say that?" Megan asked. "Did they break in at the office again?"

Desiree related the attack on her, though she left out the part about the knife, not wanting to alarm them. That, however, proved to be wasted effort. The others applauded Desiree's escape; Lilah asked her if the scratch on her neck had come from a knife; and they all seemed more intrigued by Desiree's converted mews than alarmed by the attack.

"I wonder if we could build something like that here?" Megan mused. "There's ample room for another building in back. We could use it to practice some of those defenses Tom and Con have been teaching us. Theo would love to have a place to spar, as well."

"Con will be imploring you to teach him acrobatic tricks," Lilah put in.

By the end of the discussion, Desiree had invited the Morelands to visit her exercise room. Sabrina handed the child over to the duchess, and they left the house. In the carriage, they debated whether or not to reveal Desiree's identity to Aunt Wilhemina and her daughter Susan.

"She's a terrible gossip," Lilah said. "If we tell her who you are, it will be all over London soon. Would you rather keep it secret?"

"I wouldn't want to embarrass the family," Desiree assured them. She was surprised when the other three women laughed.

"The Morelands don't care what people think of them," Sabrina explained. "Well, Aunt Wilhemina might, because she's a bit stodgy. But really, I think she rather revels in the attention, whether it's good or bad, and since she would be the one spreading it, she would have only herself to blame. The duke and duchess and their children would not care at all. I promise."

"It might be hard to explain our interest in Alistair to her without revealing it," Tom pointed out.

"True. If Uncle Bellard is right about her being close to Alistair, she might not want to admit he did anything wrong," Megan said. "On the other hand, it might make her want to help."

In the end, they agreed that they would tell Aunt Wilhemina who Desiree was and that Lilah would take the lead, as she appeared to be the woman's favorite — or, as Lilah put it, the least disliked.

The carriage was too small for all five of them, so Desiree dismissed it, and they walked the short distance from the Morelands' home to Aunt Wilhemina's house. A footman answered the door and showed them into a large sitting room that looked much smaller than it was because it was stuffed with furniture and knickknacks. Antimacassars adorned all the chairs and couches, and lace runners and tablecloths covered the tops of every table. Vases of flowers and one full of peacock feathers were scattered around the room, and the shelves were filled with everything from ceramic statues to glass paperweights to a collection of thimbles. Needlepoint samplers and paintings occupied each empty area of wall. It seemed as though there was not a surface in the room that was left undecorated.

At the center of the room sat a rotund gray-haired woman in a lavender dress and a lace cap that bore a great deal of similarity to the doilies draped about the room. Her blue eyes were bright with interest. "Well, there you are," she greeted them. "Right on time. I like people who are punctual. Please excuse me for not getting up. My lumbago has laid me low today. Susan, don't just sit there. Go greet our guests."

This latter was directed to the rather colorless woman sitting in a chair near her. She was as thin as Aunt Wilhemina was round, and her face was set in a resigned expression. "Yes, Mother," she said and made her way through the various tables, chairs and ottomans to Desiree and her companions.

As the women sat down, Aunt Wilhemina launched a lengthy description of her various aches and pains, illnesses and resentments. Finally, she ground to a halt and peered at Desiree. "You must be that by-blow of Alistair's everyone's talking about."

Desiree's jaw dropped. This was what the Morelands considered stodgy?

"Mother . . ." Wilhemina's daughter sighed.

"Well, no point in ignoring it, is there?"

Wilhemina retorted. "My maid told me. If the servants know, then everyone else soon will, too." She directed an accusatory look at the Moreland women. "I would have thought one of you would have visited me as soon as Miss Malone turned up."

"You're absolutely right," Lilah replied. "We are terribly sorry. But you see, I wanted to accompany them, and I have been feeling a trifle under the weather lately." She laid a hand on her abdomen meaningfully.

"Yes. Of course. I remember how I was with Susan. Not a day went by when I didn't have to take to my bed." Wilhemina shook her head reminiscently, apparently mollified by Lilah's excuse. She followed this remark with a thorough interrogation of Lilah's symptoms, adding frequent comparisons to her own, apparently horrific, pregnancy, ending with, "You're a jewel, Lilah, and I don't know how that boy with the lizard ever managed to catch you."

"Con." Lilah supplied his name, a bit of steel slipping into her voice. "His name is Con."

"Yes, well, I never could tell the two of them apart."

"Lizard?" Desiree asked, puzzled. "I thought it was a parrot."

"Humph," Aunt Wilhemina retorted.

"Don't remind me about *that* squawking monster. I'll never forget the uproar that bird caused back when one of the girls got married — not the redhead, must have been Olivia. As I remember, that was the wedding where that foreign man was stabbed and then some ruffians disrupted everything by taking Emmeline hostage. It was a most disquieting visit."

Desiree pressed her lips together tightly and forced herself not to look at Tom, for she was certain she would break out laughing if she did. It was no wonder the Morelands were inured to scandal. Desiree was beginning to think that the Malones were too staid for the Morelands.

"Now." Wilhemina directed her gaze at Tom and said, "I can't imagine what you're doing here. Emmeline has always been far too lax with her servants."

Desiree opened her mouth to give a heated reply to Aunt Wilhemina's comment, but Tom caught her eye and shook his head, and Desiree, after an internal struggle, clamped her lips shut.

"Tom isn't a servant, Aunt Wilhemina. He's Con's business partner," Megan said.

Wilhemina turned to Desiree. "I imagine you're here today to find out about Alistair."

Desiree answered as politely as her irritation could allow. "Yes, ma'am, if you don't mind."

"I never mind talking about Alistair. Dear boy." Wilhemina dabbed at her eyes with her handkerchief. "We were close, you see. Almost like brother and sister. Our families lived near each other, and we often visited. Alistair and I were much the same age." She sighed ruefully. "But I don't know anything about your birth, I'm afraid. Of course, he wouldn't have talked to me about setting up a mistress."

Desiree sagged in disappointment. She had told herself she would likely learn nothing from her father's cousin, but she'd hoped for at least a scrap of information.

"I knew he was unhappy with Tabitha," the older woman went on. "Anyone could have seen that marriage was a mistake. Tabitha was horse-mad, like all the Darringtons — rode to the hounds and all that. She was always outdoors doing something — archery, lawn tennis, croquet. The woman was tiring to be around. And so dull. No sense of humor at all. Whereas Alistair was such a homebody and so witty and intelligent. The two of them couldn't have been less alike."

Wilhemina brought her handkerchief to her eyes again. "But Tabitha was obviously head over heels about him. She chased him from her first Season. It was quite tiresome, really. One could scarcely have a good chat with Alistair at a party without her showing up, making sheep eyes at him. I thought he shouldn't have proposed. I would have told him so if I'd known he was about to ask her. But Alistair was young and no doubt flattered by her adoration of him . . . I think perhaps he mistook that for love. And, of course, Grandmother and Aunt Agatha pushed him to offer for her."

"Why did they want so much for him to marry her?" Desiree asked.

"They liked the match. It had always chafed Grandmother that Henry had married a nobody — although, really, a Moreland can scarcely marry up, now, can they? So Alistair proposed to Tabitha. I think he realized almost from the start that it had been the wrong thing to do. Then he fell in love with someone else. I remember him saying to me that he hadn't known what love was before he met her."

"Did he tell you her name?" Desiree asked.

"No. I gathered that she was unsuitable. I knew the things he said about eloping with her to Scotland were all pipe dreams. After all, a gentleman couldn't break off an engagement. It would have been a terrible scandal, and not only would that affect the Moreland name, it's always worse for the jilted bride. Aside from the scandal, it would have devastated Tabitha, and Alistair was always so tenderhearted. Grandmother and Aunt Agatha positively hectored him to 'act honorably,' and heaven knows it was hard to stand up to either one of them, let alone both." She paused, then added in a confidential tone, "I think there was more — it was whispered that Alistair and Tabitha had been caught in a compromising situation . . . alone in a closed room . . . *in one another's arms.*"

"That hardly sounds like a man in love with someone else," Desiree said with disappointment. She was illegitimate, but at least she had believed she was born out of love.

"Oh, I wouldn't blame Alistair for that." Wilhemina shook her head. "I imagine it was more a case of Tabitha throwing herself at him and begging him not to leave her. I always found it a bit suspicious that someone happened to walk in at that exact moment. If word of that got out and he didn't marry her, Tabitha would have been ruined. In any event, Alistair went ahead and married her. Poor boy. I knew he was unhappy, but of course an affair was not the sort of thing he would have talked about with me."

"Did he tell you he was leaving the country?" Megan asked.

"No! And it wasn't at all the sort of thing Alistair would have done. He wouldn't have just abandoned his family without a word. If it hadn't been for the note he left Tabitha, I wouldn't have believed it. I was sure he would write me and explain everything. But I never heard from him." She dabbed at her eyes again, her voice thick with tears. Looking up, she said bitterly, "I'm sure that friend of his encouraged him. That Paxton boy. It was just the sort of harebrained thing he would do."

"Paxton!" Desiree barely kept herself from shooting up from her chair. She glanced at Tom, who was looking back at her with the same excitement. "You said my father had a friend named Paxton?"

"Why, yes." Wilhemina looked startled at Desiree's enthusiasm. "Lloyd Paxton. Though Alistair always called him something silly. Pax, I believe it was."

CHAPTER TWENTY-FIVE

"He was always a wild thing, a terrible influence on Alistair," Wilhemina went on. "Gambling and drinking and engaging in silly stunts. Anytime Alistair went astray, you could count on it being at the encouragement of Lloyd Paxton. But Alistair simply would not give him up. That was one thing Tabitha and I agreed upon — Alistair would have been better off without him. But if one said so, Alistair got very stubborn about it."

"Do you know where Mr. Paxton lives, ma'am?" Tom asked. "Is he still in London?"

"Goodness! I have no idea. I never kept up with the man." Wilhemina looked offended at the idea. "I suppose he's still alive. At least, no one has told me he died. I haven't heard much about him the last few years. He must not have stirred up any scandals. Perhaps he reformed."

Desiree had a difficult time sitting still and

politely chatting for the next few minutes, but eventually they had satisfied the demands of courtesy and were able to take their leave. Outside, they parted from the Moreland women, who walked back to the Moreland house while Tom flagged down a hack for him and Desiree.

Desiree could barely hold back her excitement until they were seated inside the vehicle. "This is what we needed. I know it. Mr. Paxton is the person most likely to know everything about my parents — not just whether Alistair was my father, but what they were like and what they said and did. He might have been privy to their plans!" Excitement swelled in her. "Perhaps he's even corresponded with them. I know Aunt Wilhemina believed Alistair would write her, but I think it's more likely he would have written his lifelong friend. Don't you?"

"Maybe. Desiree, you know, he may not —"

"Don't tell me not to get my hopes up," Desiree said. "I know quite well that life doesn't always turn out the way you wish, but I don't intend to give up. Surely we can find this man Paxton."

"We will. I'll start on it as soon as I get back to the office," Tom said. "I'll find him."

He leaned in and kissed her softly — and far too briefly. "I promise."

"Can I help?" she asked.

He shook his head. She thought — she hoped — she saw regret in his eyes. "I need to talk to some of my contacts. An extra person, let alone a female, would not be welcome." He paused. "Are you planning to visit the club tonight?"

"Yes." She looked at him in surprise. "Why wouldn't I?"

"Because someone attacked you yesterday?"

"I am not going to let some ruffian — some incompetent ruffian, at that — keep me from living my life," Desiree retorted, eyes flashing.

Tom chuckled. "Somehow I thought that was what you would say. Then I will see you tonight." He paused, then added, "Unless you don't want me."

A slow smile spread across Desiree's face. "Yes, I want you."

He had no idea how much.

"Miss Malone, Lady Moreland is here to see you."

Desiree looked up from the book she was reading — or, rather, trying to read, for she found her thoughts drifting off to Tom

Quick and the investigation far too much. Templeton stood in the door of the library, looking awed.

"Moreland?" Desiree stood up. What was a Moreland doing here?

"I seated her in the parlor."

"Thank you, Templeton." Desiree hurried to the parlor, but when she entered, Desiree found a woman she'd never seen before sitting in one of the chairs, her back straight as a board. The woman turned to look at her, her chin lifted in a haughty manner.

"Lady Moreland?"

"Yes." The woman rose to her feet. Her eyes were gray, as was the hair atop her head. Both were almost the same shade as her fashionable dress, giving her a uniformly colorless look. Diamonds sparkled at her earlobes, and on her fingers, matching the iciness of her gaze. "I am Lady Alistair Moreland."

Tabitha. A little shiver ran through Desiree, but there was no need to use her skills to see that this woman thoroughly disliked her. Tabitha's antipathy was written all over her face and even in her posture. Desiree went toward her, holding out her hand in greeting, determined to be polite. After all, it was understandable that a woman would resent the children who were the result of

370

her husband's affair. "Good afternoon. Allow me to introduce myself. I am Desiree Malone."

The other woman's nostrils flared slightly, and she ignored Desiree's outstretched hand. "I am well aware of your name."

"Please. Sit down." This close to Tabitha, Desiree caught a whiff of alcohol. Had the woman been drinking? In the middle of the afternoon? That would certainly explain the touch of disorder that Desiree felt from her.

"I did not come to sit and chat, Miss Malone." Tabitha remained standing. "I have heard about your monstrous claims. You must cease them at once. I don't know what you want — I presume it is money — but I will not allow you to slander my husband's name." She jabbed her forefinger at Desiree. "You will *not* create a scandal. I can assure you that you will not get any money, either."

"You walk into my home and accuse me of trying to take money from you?" Desiree's voice rose. It was one thing to be polite to the woman, but she wasn't about to meekly take an insult from her. "I have no need of your money, as you can see." Desiree swept her hand around her, indicating the elegantly furnished room.

"This?" Tabitha looked around the room

as if the Malones' fashionable and commodious house was a hovel. Her lip curled up in something that, if not a sneer, was certainly a close cousin to it.

"Yes! This!" Desiree had helped Brock choose this house and every piece of furniture in it. "I think it's time you leave this place that is so beneath you."

"Your slut of a mother —"

"What!" Desiree almost shrieked, fury shooting up in her.

The other woman ignored her, plowing ahead, "Your slut of a mother may have ensnared Alistair — all men are subject to lust — but I am his wife. He belonged to me."

"I can certainly understand why the man fled across the ocean to get away from you!"

"How dare you!" Tabitha slapped Desiree.

Desiree gaped at her, so astonished she hardly felt the sting in her cheek.

"You will get nothing from us. I will not let you stain my husband's name. You will not hurt my son!"

"I am not trying to hurt your son," Desiree shot back. "And you have no right to come here and insult my mother. To insult me. I'll —"

"Mother!" A man rushed into the room, followed by a protesting Templeton.

Desiree turned to the new arrival. He was tall, slender and dark, and although he did not resemble Tabitha, his stiff posture and cold expression were enough to tell Desiree that he was Tabitha's son. Gregory Moreland. Her half brother. Desiree felt not the slightest connection to him.

His gaze went from his mother to Desiree, and his eyes widened as he saw the red mark his mother's slap had left on Desiree's cheek. "I beg your pardon," he said in a tone that belied his words. "It's rude for me to barge in like this."

"Gregory!" Tabitha turned to him. "What are you doing here?"

"I came looking for you. You shouldn't be here, Mother. It will only upset you."

"This girl has been most impertinent." Tabitha waved her hand in Desiree's general direction. "She must apologize to me."

"What? I should apologize? *You're* the one who slapped *me*."

"I'm sure that's not necessary, Mother." Gregory sent Desiree a look of apology and embarrassment, mingled with dislike. "We should leave now."

"What is all this racket?" Wells stood in the doorway, frowning, his arms crossed.

There was a long moment of silence as Wells and Gregory stared at each other.

"I beg your pardon for disturbing you," Gregory told him coolly. "We are just about to leave."

Gregory wrapped a firm hand around his mother's arm and steered her out of the room. Wells watched them coolly as they passed him, then turned a questioning gaze on Desiree. She ignored him and followed the Morelands to the front door. Looking out through the sidelight at the front door, she watched Gregory hand his mother up into the coach. It was a shiny, elegant black town carriage that perfectly suited the man. Not an odd American-made coach.

Wells turned back to Desiree. "What, may I ask, was that?"

"*That* was our father's wife . . . and your half brother."

Wells cocked an eyebrow. "What delightful relatives."

"Are you serious?" Tom asked when Desiree told him that evening about her visit from Alistair's wife. "She slapped you?" Tom's eyes went to Desiree's cheek, fury rising in him.

"Yes, but she doesn't deliver much of a punch." Desiree shrugged. "I believe she'd been drinking."

"What did she say? Why did she come?

374

Just to slap you?"

"No. She did that when I said an unkind thing to her, which I shouldn't have. I was just so angry because she'd insulted my mother. She told me a number of things, primarily that she was not going to let me cause a scandal or get money. That she wouldn't allow me to hurt her son. But she didn't offer any explanation of how she intended to stop me. It was more along the lines of an aristocratic command, as if I would do what she said simply because of who she was. You know, that sort of air."

"Yes, I know." Tom had been on the receiving end of such remarks more than a few times himself. "She said she 'wouldn't let you' get money, not that she wouldn't pay you?"

Desiree nodded. "Yes. I noticed that, too. It didn't seem that she was worried about me blackmailing her. She seemed more afraid that I would bleed her son. She was very protective of him."

"Or she's worried about what's in that will. There's a reason someone is after it, and with wills, that reason is usually money."

"His son is surely his heir," Desiree said. "I can't imagine why anyone would think Alistair left his money to his illegitimate children."

"He wouldn't have to have left all of it. A small bequest or even a mention of you would be enough to create scandal," Tom pointed out.

"If the lawyer sent the will to Con, it's possible Gregory doesn't even know what's in it," Desiree mused. "He may just fear what it might contain."

"Sending his mother to harangue you substantiates the idea that Gregory is the most likely suspect for that attack on you."

"I don't think he sent her. I think it was more that he came running in to take her home and keep her from embarrassing herself. And him." She paused. "It was odd seeing him and Wells together. Their coloring is different, but there was a recognizable resemblance. Their build, the structure of their faces."

Tom tilted his head, considering. "I guess Wells does have the Moreland jaw."

"It was a trifle eerie. Wells said he couldn't see it, but I'm sure of it."

"What did you think of Gregory?"

"Very stiff and formal, as you said. It was so peculiar to think that he was my half brother, as closely related to me as Brock. I felt no connection to him whatever. I was more at home with the duke and duchess than with him. I thought he might have been the one who had us followed, but I looked at his carriage, and it was not the same one."

"Carriage aside, those cuff links would make one think the culprit has to be Pax. But Gregory has the motive. I can't figure out why Paxton would be following you." The corner of Tom's mouth quirked up. "I guess we'll have to ask him tomorrow when we pay him a call."

"Tom! You found him! That's wonderful!" Desiree's smile was so beautiful it was enough to stop his heart. She reached toward him, and Tom thought she was about to hug him, but then Desiree pulled her hands back.

Disappointment swelled in Tom's chest. It was stupid to feel that way, of course. Desiree was right to hold herself too valuable for casual entanglements. And what else could there be between them? He could offer her nothing but a flat above the agency and a nest egg for a future house. And even that future house wouldn't be a worthy setting for a woman like Desiree. She should have a man like . . . well, he wasn't sure who would be the right match for Desiree, who was so unusual, so lovely, so free and daring. But obviously it wasn't someone like him. She was a Moreland, and he didn't even know his last name.

Tom turned his head away and stared out the window as the carriage rumbled through the night.

Lloyd Paxton lived near Grosvenor Square. The house was an elegant one in the Queen Anne style, but up close it was obvious that it was suffering from neglect. Tom wondered if that was due to lack of interest or lack of money.

The servant who answered the door looked to be at least a hundred years old. It was a long wait for him to shuffle off and return, after which he led them at a snail's pace to the drawing room. The man seated there was middle-aged, his blond hair threaded with gray, a bit of a paunch developing around his midsection. He wore a casual smoking jacket over his white shirt, with no cravat, obviously at leisure.

He stood up as they entered the room, saying, "Mr. Quick? I don't believe —" His gaze went to Desiree standing beside Tom, and he stopped, a faint frown forming on his brow.

"I apologize for arriving without notice, Mr. Paxton," Tom said. "I am Tom Quick, of Moreland & Quick Agency."

"Moreland & Quick!" Paxton's eyes widened. His gaze flickered to Desiree and back. "Why are you here?"

"I would like to introduce you to Miss Desiree Malone." Tom turned toward Desiree.

The older man's face went blank. "Malone?" He turned to Desiree. "I say." He grabbed a pair of spectacles from the table beside him and settled them on his nose, peering at Desiree more closely. "Good Gad — are you —"

"I am Stella Malone's daughter," Desiree said.

"Good Gad," Paxton repeated, looking dazed. "You do have something of her in your look." He recovered from his astonishment. "I'm sorry. Come in. Sit down. My goodness, I never expected . . . Would you like some tea?"

He made a movement to ring for a servant. Tom, envisioning the ancient butler shuffling in and out, quickly said, "Thank you, but no. We only came to talk to you."

"I'm so glad you did." Paxton seemed genuinely pleased, taking his seat across from them and smiling. "I've wondered now and then what happened with the three of you."

"You didn't inquire about the children?"

Tom asked.

Paxton looked surprised at his question. "Me? No. I knew they were in good hands. That friend of Stella's took them, the foreign one, can't remember her name."

"Bruna Upton," Desiree supplied.

"Bruna! Yes. It was the best thing, of course. The little boy knew her, and Mrs. McGee couldn't continue to stay there taking care of them after Stella left."

"Mrs. McGee?" Tom jumped on the name. "Who was she?"

"The housekeeper. Can't remember her first name. Lord, I'm surprised I remember her last name. Probably wouldn't have if I'd had to think about it." He chuckled. "It's been twenty-five years ago or more."

"Do you know where Mrs. McGee went? Where she lives now?"

"Me? Goodness, no. She was just the housekeeper."

Tom gritted his teeth at the man's careless dismissal of a servant, but Desiree quickly took over the questioning. "Mr. Paxton, do you remember anyone else who visited the house at that time? Who knew my mother?"

He lifted his eyes toward the ceiling in a ruminating manner. "There was Bruna, of course. Falk sometimes."

380

"Falk!" Tom exclaimed. "What the devil was he doing there?"

"I can't imagine why Alistair let the fellow hang about," Paxton said in a confiding tone. "He wasn't there often — he was never *received,* naturally — but every once in a while, I'd see him lurking around the place." He shrugged. "Perhaps he was a friend of the housekeeper."

Tom contemplated the idea of Falk turning up once again, but Desiree had obviously been caught by something else Paxton had said. "You said 'Alistair.' Was Alistair Moreland our father?"

"Yes, of course." Paxton's brows shot up in surprise. "Didn't you know? Surely Bruna must have told you."

"No. She said my mother wanted to keep it a secret. Bruna had promised her not to say a word."

"Well, of course, Alistair didn't want it spread around. He was cousin to a duke, after all. And he didn't want his wife to find out. There would have been the very devil to pay with Tabitha, and, more than that, he didn't want to embarrass the woman. I found Tabitha a dead bore, and I suspect Alistair did as well, but she *was* his wife and the mother of his son."

"Could you tell me a bit about Alistair?"

Desiree smiled sweetly at the man.

Paxton apparently had as little ability to resist Desiree's smile as any other man, for he beamed and said, "Of course. I actually met your mother first, you know. Pursued her like mad, but she chose Alistair instead. I couldn't even be angry. Alistair was a splendid chap. We were friends since childhood. He was loyal. Honorable. A good man and a true friend." His eyes glistened, and he blinked, offering them a crooked smile. "He was a bit too bookish for me, of course."

"Did you know about their plans to run away?" Tom asked.

"No. I was completely surprised. I had just seen Alistair the night before, and he didn't say a word about it. We had plans to meet that evening at Stella's house, but when I went there, the housekeeper said they'd left. Of course, we thought they'd only gone to his cottage in Dorset and would be back in a few days. They'd visited there before. But I began to worry when they didn't return the next week. I couldn't believe that they left you children behind. Stella was so over-the-moon happy when you were born. She was devoted to her children. Alistair, too. He positively doted on you."

"Did you make inquiries when they didn't come back?" Tom asked.

"Well, it was a bit delicate, you see," Paxton said uncomfortably. "I couldn't reveal Alistair's secret. I could hardly ask Tabitha if she'd heard from him. But I was at the point of going to the cottage myself to inquire. Then I got Alistair's letter telling me they'd taken off to the States." He looked suddenly older, his affable expression falling away.

"Do you have the letter?" Desiree asked eagerly.

Paxton shook his head. "Goodness, no, child. Got rid of it years ago. After Alistair left, well, I went through a bad period. I was angry with him, you see, for leaving and not even telling me goodbye. A letter! As if I were a mere acquaintance or one of his relatives! Somewhere in there, I tossed the note. Regretted it after I settled down, but . . ." He shrugged, staring off into the distance for a moment. "Well, there you have it. I'm afraid that's all I know. If you don't have any other questions . . ." He started to stand up.

"I do have one other question," Tom told him, his gaze fixed on the other man's face. "I'm wondering why you've been watching Miss Malone's house. Why did you have us followed?"

"What?" Paxton looked at him blankly. "What are you talking about?" He glanced over at Desiree. "I had no idea you were even in London until today." His tone turned indignant. "I can't imagine why you would accuse me of such a thing."

"Because," Tom said, reaching into his pocket. He opened his hand and held it out, showing Paxton two gold cuff links engraved with *Pax*. "Your man left these behind."

CHAPTER TWENTY-SIX

Paxton's face was as astonished as Tom could have hoped. What he hadn't expected was that the older man's eyes would fill with tears. "My studs!"

Tom and Desiree glanced at each other as Paxton picked up the engraved jewelry and examined it more closely. Tom felt that he had somehow lost the advantage here, but he went on, "So you admit those are yours?"

"Yes, of course they're mine, though I don't understand how you came to have them."

"They were in the pocket of the man you had follow us."

"Yes, you said that, but that doesn't make it any clearer. I don't know what man you're talking about, and I've certainly never asked someone to follow you." Paxton looked at Tom as if Tom had lost his wits. "These weren't even in my possession. I haven't seen them in years and years."

"If you didn't have them, who did?"

"I lent them to Alistair one evening when one of his broke, and he forgot to give them back. This wasn't long, you see, before he and Stella left. After that, I never felt comfortable asking Tabitha to return them. Alistair's wife and I . . . well, we didn't have the best relationship. But I'm surprised she got rid of them. They say she kept everything of Alistair's. But I suppose his jewelry and such would be his son's now. Gregory might have sold the set when he saw it wasn't his father's. Though it does seem to me he might have had the decency to return these to me, since they had my name on it. I hope you don't mind if I keep them." His hand curled around the cuff links, rendering his question moot. "I'll pay you for them."

Tom looked over at Desiree, his brows lifting in question. She nodded slightly, and Tom knew she was signaling that Paxton was telling the truth. Tom's instinct was to keep them as evidence, but since he didn't see how they could be used against anyone other than Paxton, he shook his head. "No, they aren't ours. We didn't pay anything for them."

Paxton smiled faintly. "I'd say not, if you took them from somebody." He looked at

Desiree, frowning a little. "Why would anyone be following you?"

"That's what we're trying to discover," Tom replied.

"Hmm. Well. It seems very odd," Paxton went on. "I hope you will be careful, my dear." He paused. "Um . . . any other questions you have for me?"

Tom could think of nothing else to ask, and a glance at Desiree told him she couldn't, either. "No, sir. You've been most kind."

"Yes, thank you," Desiree said, rising.

"Think nothing of it," Paxton answered and stood up to take Desiree's hand again, his gaze lingering on her face. "Yes, I think there's quite a bit of Stella in you. Such a beautiful woman."

He sighed, his hand sliding from hers, and after an exchange of polite farewells, Tom and Desiree left the house.

"That was quite successful, don't you think?" Desiree bubbled, taking Tom's arm as they walked to the carriage. "We confirmed that Alistair was my father and that he wrote Paxton a farewell letter. And that my father had those cuff links, not Mr. Paxton."

"Are you sure he wasn't lying about the cuff links?" Tom asked, though he was already certain of the answer.

"Yes, reasonably sure. It's not a science. What I sense, really, is an underlying disturbance, a distortion or corruption in a person or an object — I can see that something's not right just under the surface. With people it looks like a dark-edged double image. Like staring at someone through a pane of blackened glass. It's easier to see with some people than others. The more free they are with their emotions or the more corrupt they are, the more I can actually see it. When it is faint, it's more a vague sense of something wrong, so it is difficult to separate it from just a . . ."

"Just normal intuition?" Tom supplied.

"Exactly. I had difficulty getting anything from Gregory yesterday because he's very . . . *insulated.* He's wrapped up tightly. Now, his mother was positively bursting with clashing emotions. When we first met Mr. Paxton, I felt a flash of disturbance, but it disappeared after he knew who we were. Perhaps it was just surprise, for after that he was quite open and relaxed. I don't think he lied to us, but still . . . I felt that there was something he wasn't telling us. He didn't have that bright, clear glow that people have when they are totally truthful and in harmony. But very few of us have that — most people are holding something back."

"Any idea what?"

She shook her head. "No. It might not have been related to any of this. Or something that isn't important. But I felt as if I just knew the right question to ask, I could find out more."

"Well, as you said, we've learned a good deal. It eliminates one of our suspects. It makes sense — there really wasn't any reason for Paxton to be spying on you. Gregory, on the other hand, has a great deal of motive. I wouldn't be surprised if he both hired Falk and set his own man on it, too."

"Tom, don't you see? I know you think my father's coach is not significant. But these cuff links, too? The carriage was his favorite. The cuff links were in Alistair's possession. Maybe it really *was* Alistair in that carriage. Maybe it was both of them."

"Why would your parents spy on you? Why not just come up to the door?"

"Because they're afraid of how we might react. I mean, they abandoned us. It wouldn't be all that surprising if we despised them. Brock does. Maybe they're trying to work up the courage to approach us. Or they just wanted to see what we look like, what we're doing. Make sure that we're all right."

Looking into her shining eyes, Tom didn't have the heart to try to dissuade her. "You could be right. I think it's more likely that Gregory is watching you. But obviously your father or both your parents could have returned to the country. It's not as if there's anything to stop them."

"But you hate for me to get my hopes up," Desiree said. "I know it's not likely that they would suddenly decide they wanted to see us after all these years. I'm not going to count on it. But it's not impossible, either." She sighed and settled back in the seat, and after a moment, she asked, "What do you make of Paxton saying he saw Falk at my mother's house?"

"I don't know." Tom shook his head. "I can't conceive of Falk being friends with Alistair. Or with anyone, really."

"The idea of Falk carrying on a romance with one of the servants seems equally unlikely."

They were silent for a moment, then Tom said quietly, "At least this is solid proof that Alistair was your father."

"Yes." Desiree smiled gently, her expression reflective. "And it was comforting to learn that his family didn't ignore us, that they just didn't know."

"That's certain." Tom smiled faintly. "The duchess would have been on it like a shot. I'm sorry they didn't know, that you grew up without the Morelands."

"I can't regret my life," Desiree told him. "I hated Falk, and I hated being hungry. But we were happy with Bruna and Sid, even if we were frequently short on money. I loved the circus and I loved the acrobatics. Bruna taught me so much. Even Falk found someone to train us more. The things that I can do make me happy. Wells and Brock and I love each other and know we can always count on the others. When Falk took Brock away from us and Brock told me he would come back and get us, I knew he would."

"I don't remember ever feeling that way when I was a child," Tom said honestly. "Certainly not before Reed helped me. When Falk had grabbed me back that time, I never had the hope that anyone would rescue me from him. It was a miracle that it had happened once, and truthfully, I had been expecting it to be taken away from me the whole time I was with the Morelands."

"But then Reed came for you."

"Yeah. After that, I hoped, I half believed Reed would help me, but it was years before

I really trusted it." He glanced at her, suddenly embarrassed. "I don't know why I'm telling you this."

"Because you know you can." She studied him for a moment. "What about you? Do you wish you'd lived a different life?"

"I don't know. I have trouble imagining anything else. But no, I don't think so. I wouldn't be who I am now, have what I have now, if my life had been different. I've wished I'd known my mother. But who's to say it wouldn't have been worse to have grown up with her? When you don't know who or what you are, when you don't have a place in life, you can be whatever you want. It's freeing."

"What is it that you want?"

"Oh . . ." Tom shrugged, aware of the familiar tug of discomfort, the desire to wrap a protective silence around himself. He thought of what Desiree had said about Gregory — he was insulated. He said, "Pretty much what everyone wants, I suppose. A place of my own." His voice came out almost fiercely on the last words, and he added, unable to hold it back, "Something that belongs to me. Somewhere I belong." He glanced away, then leaned forward and gave their driver an address.

"Where are we going?" Desiree asked.

"You'll see." Tom felt a flush rising up his neck. Why had he done that? But he would look even more foolish to tell Merriwell he'd changed his mind.

They drove back to Marylebone, and the carriage rolled to a stop on a quiet street.

"Where are we? Whose house is this?" Desiree leaned across to look out Tom's window. She was so close he could see each eyelash and the vein that beat in her throat. Her perfume wrapped around him, as intoxicating as it had been the night he met her.

"It's no one's," he replied, his voice gravelly. He cleared his throat. "It's for sale."

"Are you thinking of buying it?" Desiree turned her head to him, eyes bright with interest. She reached for the door handle. "Let's look at it properly."

"That's not necessary," Tom began, but Desiree was already opening the door and scrambling out. There was nothing he could do but follow her.

"It's charming." Desiree studied the narrow gray house, walking up and down in front of it. It was a modest home, set in a row of modest homes, but its red shutters and door set it apart, and it looked very cozy and snug. She turned to him. "Do you plan to buy it?"

Tom shook his head. Looking up at the house, the yearning he'd felt for it from the first rose in him again, but he did his best to keep his voice flat and pragmatic. "No. I haven't enough money for it yet. It's been tied up in probate court for a few months, but that won't last forever. It'll be at least two more years before I can afford it." He shrugged. "But this is the sort of place I'd like to have one day."

Desiree turned to gaze at him instead of the house. "You really want *this* one, though, don't you?"

He should have remembered Desiree's perceptiveness. Of course she would sense just how deep his longing for the house went. "It appeals to me, yes, but there will be others I could like just as much."

"Couldn't you borrow money from one of the Morelands? I'm sure they'd be happy to help you."

"No." He almost barked the word at her. He drew a breath. "Sorry. But I won't ask the Morelands for anything. They've already given me too much. Con handed over half the agency to me and he wouldn't take anything in return. Said I'd earned it working there so long. I'm sure they'd be the same way about a loan. I won't take advantage of them."

"Of course. I should have realized." Desiree took a last look. "It's a lovely house."

She was right. It was a lovely house. And Tom would have it one day. It seemed even more important now.

Brock still refused to attend the Morelands' dinner party. Desiree told him that Mr. Paxton had confirmed that Alistair Moreland was their father, but Brock merely growled, "He's not mine."

So it was only Wells and Desiree who arrived at Broughton House the following evening. Desiree's chest tightened with anxiety; however nice the Morelands she had met had been, she was afraid that there were some who would come only to find fault in the Malones. Wells, of course, seemed completely unaffected by nerves.

The butler ushered them into a large anteroom adjacent to the formal dining room. Despite the room's size, it seemed to be filled with people and noise. Desiree and Wells halted; she thought even Wells was a bit taken aback. Lilah turned and saw them and started toward them, smiling, and Desiree relaxed.

"Welcome to the family." Lilah reached out to take Desiree's hand. "Tom told us about your meeting with Mr. Paxton."

"Not really a surprise," Con added, coming up behind her. "I was sure you were a Moreland after talking to you the other day."

They exchanged polite greetings with Wells, and Lilah said, "Allow me to introduce you to everyone. I'm sorry it's such a madhouse. That's the children. Nurse will take them upstairs in a few minutes. But they were terribly eager to meet you."

Looking at the group again, Desiree could see that much of the noise came from a large number of children who seemed in perpetual motion. Seeing Desiree and Wells, the children converged on the pair, chattering eagerly. There was a dizzying array of them in all sizes, shapes and hair colors. There was even another set of twins, an adolescent boy and girl whom Con introduced as the Littles.

Desiree and her brother were pelted with questions from all sides. One young boy pulled a small green snake out of his pocket to show them, which set off a few shrieks as well as a cry or two of delight and caused the tallest girl to exclaim, "Jason, you didn't! Papa told you not to bring Pierpont."

Con swooped in to resolve the matter of the snake by handing it over to a resigned-looking footman, and a few minutes later, a middle-aged woman herded the children away. The volume in the room lowered dramatically, and Lilah began to make a circuit of the room, introducing the Malones to the adults of the family.

There were three of the duke's and duchess's brood whom Desiree had not met the other day, along with their spouses. Kyria was a tall, attractive redhead who greatly resembled the duchess, and her husband, Rafe, was an American with a lazy drawl and a great deal of charm.

"I hope my boy didn't frighten you with that little snake," he told Desiree, his bright blue eyes twinkling.

"I'm sure Emily took care of it," his wife added with some amusement. "She regards herself as the general of the group. What I want to know is, are you really going to teach Sabrina and Lilah acrobatics? I do hope you'll allow us older ones to join."

Beside her, Rafe groaned. "That's all I need — you learning cartwheels."

"Of course you may join us," Desiree replied, no longer surprised by the Morelands' statements. "I'm not sure what everyone wants to do."

"Thisbe." Kyria raised her voice and gestured at an equally tall, slender woman with coal-black hair. A striking swath of silver swept back from one temple. "Come here and listen to this."

Thisbe — some of the Morelands had the oddest names — joined them, followed by her husband, Desmond, a quiet, bespectacled man, and within moments, the youngest of the Moreland sisters, Olivia, and her husband, Stephen, entered the ever-widening circle.

There was little need to talk, for the Morelands swept the conversation along, and Desiree was able to study the others. Olivia was the only one of the Moreland women who wasn't tall, and her more subdued coloring and almost shy manner could lead one to assume she was more ordinary . . . until she began to talk about ghost hunting and the detective agency, which she had founded. Kyria was the most sparkling member of the family and the only one who seemed interested in clothes and parties. Thisbe was the most serious and was apt to embark on conversations about topics that only her husband understood.

But none of them were in the least aloof, and before supper even began, Desiree found herself not only adding all the women to the invitation to visit her studio but also agreeing to go shopping with Kyria and Sabrina, book hunting with Olivia and Lilah, and to attend a new exhibition at the British Museum with Thisbe.

As they talked, the men drifted away to form another group surrounding Wells. Desiree glanced over at him from time to time, but Wells was laughing with the others, so she decided he didn't need rescuing. It was a good thing, for the duchess soon pulled Desiree away to introduce her to a number of other women who were sitting with Aunt Wilhemina and her daughter Susan. They all appeared to be aunts and cousins of varying degrees.

The groups ebbed and flowed throughout the evening, breaking up and re-forming, filled with conversation ranging from the latest gossip to Mesopotamia to something called the Arrhenius equation. It was during this latter conversation that someone touched her arm and said, "Excuse me, could I steal Miss Malone from you for a moment?"

"Tom!" Desiree turned to him in relief and nodded to the others, so deep in their conversation that they barely glanced over when she left. Desiree took Tom's arm, whispering as they walked away, "Oh, thank you! They were talking about acids and bases and constants, and I hadn't the slightest idea what they were saying."

Tom chuckled. "That's often the case with

Thisbe and Desmond."

"I haven't seen you except across the room this evening," Desiree said. "Even at supper, you were far away."

"At least you were between Rafe and Stephen. I got stuck with Aunt Verity and her daughter-in-law, who have the distinction of being the only boring Morelands you can find . . . well, except for Cousin Albert."

"I kept hoping you would join me." The truth was Desiree had felt a trifle hurt that he had not.

"I didn't want to take up any of your time with the Morelands. But when I saw your eyes glazing over, I decided you wouldn't mind."

"No. Frankly, my head was spinning even before science came into it. I'll never remember half their names, and they must have talked about a hundred different things."

"Want a moment of peace?" he asked and tilted his head toward the door. "Come, I'll show you something."

Intrigued, she left the room with him. As he led her through the house, Desiree asked, "Where are we going?"

"You'll see. I don't want to spoil it." Tom went on, "I talked to Smeggars about Mrs. McGee when I arrived tonight."

"The butler? Did he know Mrs. McGee?" Desiree asked hopefully.

"No, but he said he'd make inquiries. If anyone can locate her, it's Smeggars. But it may take a day or two." Tom opened a door at the back of the house. "Here we are."

Desiree sucked in her breath as she stepped out onto a terrace. Before them lay the back of the Morelands' property, a wide expanse of green, unexpectedly large in the crowded city. A high wall ran all around the outer boundary. There were a couple of small buildings to the left of the house, as well as a neatly tended herb garden. Clusters of flowers and trees were scattered around the yard, and lights glowed here and there, softly illuminating the grounds.

"It's beautiful!" Desiree went to the low wall that marked the edge of the terrace and looked out. "It's their own personal park."

Tom took her hand and led her down the shallow steps to the lawn. They strolled beside the rose garden, the night heady with the flowers' perfume. There seemed something magical to Desiree about this place, hushed and walled, a hidden Eden amid the rush and noise of the city.

When Tom stopped beneath one of the spreading trees and turned to her, it seemed only natural to go into his arms. Their lips met.

And the world around them fell away.

Chapter Twenty-Seven

Their kiss was slow and sweet, savoring the moment. Hunger blossomed in Desiree, and she pressed against Tom, her kiss turning demanding. She felt his body tense and flare with heat, and his arms tightened around her.

Desiree slid her hands up his neck and into his hair, luxuriating in the feel of the silken strands sliding through her fingers. Everything in her was pounding, aching to have more of him. To feel more, taste more, do more. She trembled in her need, and in response Tom made a low noise in his throat and slid his hands down over her back, cupping and lifting her into him. Even through the barrier of their clothes, she knew the hard pressure of his flesh. Knew what it meant, knew what she wanted.

She moved her hips against him, sending desire soaring through them both. Tom kissed his way down her throat and across the expanse of her chest exposed by her evening gown's low neckline. It took only a nudge for him to move aside the flounce of lace and kiss the soft breast beneath.

"Desiree . . ." Tom breathed her name as his hand came up to cup her breast, caressing her through the cloth.

Hunger pooled low in her abdomen. "More," she whispered.

Her word shook him, and Tom slid his hand under her dress, pushing down the dress and chemise to reveal her breast. His mouth left a trail of fire across the soft skin, ending by circling her nipple with his tongue. The touch electrified her, and Desiree gasped as his mouth settled on her nipple, each tug sending ripples of pleasure through her. Desiree's fingers clenched in his hair, her breath coming hard and fast in her throat. She wanted this to last forever and at the same time craved to rush forward.

Tom groaned and pulled up his head, leaning back against the trunk of the tree. He let out a short expletive, his arms loosening around her. "We can't, Desiree." His breath came in short, hard pants. "Not here. Not now."

He was right, of course, but the passion thrumming through Desiree's veins didn't want to hear it. She wanted to protest, to snake her hands up his body and pull him back to her, to sink her lips into his and dare him to resist.

It took an effort of will for her to step back and turn aside. She busied the fingers that ached to caress him by straightening the bodice of her dress and smoothing her hair. It took some time for her breathing to slow and the heat in her to subside, and only then did she risk looking at Tom again.

He had combed through his hair with his fingers, restoring it to some order, and he'd moved farther away. "I'm sorry. I really didn't bring you out here to seduce you."

"You didn't?" Desiree's lips curved up, and she couldn't keep the flirtatious tone from her voice. "How disappointing."

Tom released a huff of a laugh. "You aren't making it easier."

"I know. Not for myself, either." Desiree smoothed her hands down her skirt and took another shaky breath. "Perhaps we should return to the party."

He thrust his hands into his pockets and looked around, then sighed. "I agree."

They turned and walked back to the house, keeping a careful distance apart. Neither the time nor the place, Desiree repeated to herself. But there would come a time. She was certain of that.

It took Smeggars a few days to come up with an address for a housekeeper named Nan McGee. Two days in which Desiree had all too much time to think. She had set out to find out who her father was, and that had been done. It could be said that she had no more reason to investigate. Yet her anxiety, even dread, was increasing every day. What was it that was so important?

There was this strange matter of the will. Perhaps they should look for that will. Given what had happened the other day in her studio, it seemed to present a danger to her. But her inner feeling, the thing that had set her on this whole search to begin with, told her it was tied to her parents. And anyway, how was she supposed to find this will? She knew nothing about it other than it supposedly was sent to Tom's office, and both Tom and Con had searched their office thoroughly.

There was nothing left to do in her search for her parents other than interview the housekeeper. Desiree was doubtful that Mrs. McGee — who Brock had agreed was his remembered 'Nan' — would be able to provide them with any more information than they already had. And after that, Desiree feared she would be left with an unabated sense of urgency . . . and no reason to see Tom Quick anymore.

And that prospect filled her with dismay. These days without Tom had been flat. In the evenings he had escorted her to the club and back, but that was very little time, no more than a few minutes of chatting, carefully avoiding the subject of their passionate kisses in the Morelands' garden.

Yet she found herself waiting with embarrassing eagerness for those moments to arrive. She wasted an inordinate amount of time trying (and failing) to come up with a reasonable excuse to go to his office. The remainder of her days she spent thinking about him and their kisses and worrying that soon she might never see him again. The prospect of her life, which had once been so comfortable, now seemed bleak without Tom Quick in it.

She had always been an independent woman, content and able on her own, but now she felt as if she was missing some essential part. Each evening when Tom arrived, that absent part slid back into place.

No other man had made her feel as she did when they kissed, so eager, so sizzling with heat and excitement. It had been easy in the past to let her head overrule her physical attraction, but now she realized that she had not really tested that control until

407

she kissed Tom Quick.

Desiree was determined not to give herself too easily, but she had never intended to spend her life celibate. One day she would meet someone to whom she could commit fully. Was Tom that someone? Was she brave enough to take that next step? Or would she be foolish to do so?

There was, she realized, no way of knowing if what she felt would last. She wasn't even sure if what she felt for him was love. It was more than passion; she desired his company as much as she desired him. But was that love or merely infatuation? Her head told her she had not known him long enough to fall in love. But did love follow the rules? Desiree certainly never had.

Then there was the issue of what Tom felt for her. Desire, yes, that was obvious. But what about love? There was a closed quality to Tom. She found him more difficult to read than most; it had been one of the things about him that had intrigued her from the start. He had traveled a long way from his initial anger and dislike to a present friendship. He was concerned about her safety. He respected her abilities. But did that add up to love? Perhaps all that would lead to love one day. Or it might not. Was Tom even capable of love, or had growing up as he had in Falk's unfeeling care, without parents or siblings, stunted any such emotion?

He yearned for that house. Desiree had seen that in his eyes, however much he had tried to gloss over it. One would think that his dream of a home would include a wife and family. Desiree suspected, however, that a woman like herself would not readily fit into that particular dream.

Such thoughts were running annoyingly through her head when the butler brought her a note from Tom saying that he had an address for Nan McGee. She jumped up and changed into something more attractive than the dress in which she had been lounging about the house, and called for the carriage.

Desiree couldn't hold back a wide smile when Tom got into the carriage. He looked equally happy to see her, which made her smile even brighter. Mrs. McGee — if indeed it was the same Mrs. McGee — was retired and living in a small flat in Lambeth.

They drove across the bridge and were soon there. Heart pounding in anticipation, Desiree walked up the stairs to the house-keeper's room. Tom rapped sharply on the door, and after a minute or two, the door opened the width of a hand, and a gray-haired woman looked out at them with narrowed eyes.

"Who are you?" she snapped.

"Mrs. McGee, we'd like to speak with you a few minutes, if you don't mind," Tom began.

"Well, I do mind." She started to close the door.

"No, wait!" Desiree put her hand against the door to stop her. "Please. I'm Desiree Malone. I need to speak to you."

Mrs. McGee frowned. "Malone? I don't know any —" She stopped abruptly, her eyes going to the folded ten-pound note Tom held up.

"My mother was Stella Malone. My father —"

"Good God! Lord Moreland's bastard?" There was surprise on the housekeeper's face, but no exclamation of happiness at seeing her old charge.

Tom stiffened beside Desiree, but she put a hand on his arm and said calmly, "Yes. I want to talk to you about him."

Mrs. McGee stepped back to let them enter, deftly snagging the folded bill from Tom's fingers as they went by. She sat down in the lone armchair in the room, leaving Tom to pull over the two straight chairs

410

from the table for him and Desiree.

"What do you want to know?"

"Did you work for my mother long?" Desiree matched the housekeeper's businesslike manner.

"A year and a half, two years. I think she'd just taken up with his lordship. Before that she was some sort of entertainer," Mrs. McGee said dismissively. "There was me and another maid and a pot-boy."

"You were there when my brother and I were born?"

She nodded. "Aye. The other boy was already with her. He was a quiet lad, that one. Always watching."

That was Brock, all right. But Desiree wasn't going to wander away from her goal. "Do you remember who came to visit? Besides Lord Moreland?"

"There was that other one that was mad for her," Mrs. McGee replied. "Don't remember his name."

"Lloyd Paxton?" Tom inserted.

"Aye, that was it. They called him Pack or Pax, some such thing. There was that other woman. Miss Malone used to work with her."

"Bruna Upton."

The housekeeper shrugged. "I guess. I don't remember much, except she was

411

French or something."

"Italian?" Desiree said.

"I suppose," the other woman agreed.

"What about Falk?" Tom asked.

"Falk!" Mrs. McGee scowled. "That kids-man — yes, he was there. Too often for my liking. The man was a scoundrel."

"He still is," Tom commented, and the housekeeper let out a short laugh.

"Was Falk in love with Stella also?" Given what the housekeeper had just said, Desiree couldn't believe Mr. Paxton's supposition that Falk was dallying with Mrs. McGee.

"Him?" Mrs. McGee's laugh was a hoot of derision. "That man never loved anyone but himself. No. He came to get the money. That's all."

"Money? From my mother? Why was she paying him?"

"No, not from her. It was Lord Moreland that was paying him. Blackmail, you understand. Falk knew about the affair, and his lordship paid Falk to keep him from telling Lady Moreland. Lord Moreland would leave it with your mother, and Falk would come by and pick it up every so often."

"Did you know what my mother and Lord Moreland were planning to do? Did she tell you?"

"No, not a word." The woman's tone

turned indignant. "*She* didn't know she was going until that morning. He sent her a note, didn't he? Told her they were going to hare off to his cottage by the sea for a few days. She was that excited, went running around, packing and all. Then that carriage of his pulled up and she went running out to it, like she was going to heaven. That was the last I saw of her. Left me here to take care of you lot. Didn't leave me any money, never sent me a note. Nothing. I didn't know if she was alive or dead till that Paxton fellow came over, claiming he'd got a letter from Moreland saying they were gone."

"He came over here before that, though, didn't he?" Tom asked. "Mr. Paxton? He came over the night they left, didn't he?"

"No, it was the day after they left. They went on a Monday afternoon, and then this Paxton showed up at the door the next day, saying they'd invited him for the evening. Typical. Not a lick of sense among the lot of them."

"Paxton came over the next day?" Tom asked. "Are you sure?"

"Of course I'm sure." She scowled at him. "She went running out one afternoon, and then the next day, in the evening, Mr. Paxton comes calling. Seemed put out, I thought, that they hadn't told him."

"Do you think they had planned to run away? Or did they decide to go to the United States on the spur of the moment?"

The housekeeper made a wordless noise of disgust. "I don't think *she* went anywhere at all."

Desiree blinked. "What? Why do you say that?"

"And leave you three behind?" Mrs. McGee shook her head firmly. "She was a flighty thing and mad as could be about that man, but she was a good mum. She loved you three to death. Why, she was still feeding you herself. I'm not saying she wouldn't have gone with him to the States or anywhere he wanted, for that matter. But not without her children. And what woman goes off to a foreign country with only one piece of luggage? Without taking all her jewelry? She left her jewelry box behind, and it was full. The only things missing were a few of the fancy pieces Moreland gave her." She looked at Desiree. "Wouldn't you take all your usual jewelry?"

"Yes." Desiree nodded.

"You seem well acquainted with Stella's jewels," Tom said dryly.

Mrs. McGee crossed her arms and glared at him. "I had to feed the children, didn't I? Pay the coalman and such."

414

"Yes, of course," Desiree said soothingly, casting an admonitory look toward Tom. This was scarcely the time to offend the woman by accusing her of theft — especially since it seemed to Desiree that everything she'd told them so far was the truth.

"Mrs. McGee, if you don't believe my mother ran away, then why didn't she come back? What do you think she did?"

"I don't think she did anything. Lord Moreland killed her."

415

CHAPTER TWENTY-EIGHT

Desiree gaped at her. "What? My father? You think he killed my mother?"

Mrs. McGee nodded. "Wouldn't be the first time that's happened."

"But why? Everyone says they were very much in love," Desiree protested.

"*She* was. Don't know about him — you never can tell with men. Maybe he got tired of her or she was pressing him to leave his wife. Or he was afraid his wife would find out. Maybe he just wanted to stop paying blackmail to Falk."

"But Lord Moreland disappeared, as well," Tom pointed out.

"Well, he ran away after he did it, I'd guess," the housekeeper replied. "Afraid he'd get his neck stretched for it."

"But the letter —" Desiree began, pulling up every ounce of her power to sense any deception on the part of the woman in front of her. But whether or not the housekeeper

416

was correct, she obviously believed that Desiree's father was a killer.

"Was written by him, now, wasn't it? Nobody got a word from her," Mrs. McGee pointed out triumphantly. "Mark my words, he murdered her. It's always the lover. Or the husband."

Desiree stared, too stunned to think of anything to say.

"Did you tell the police?" Tom asked. "Report your suspicions?"

The other woman let out a scornful laugh. "Me? Accuse a duke's kin of murder? I think not. They wouldn't do anything to a Moreland. And I couldn't prove anything. I wasn't getting involved with the police."

"I'd guess not, since you were pilfering her jewels," Tom retorted.

"I've had enough of you," Mrs. McGee shot back, glowering at Tom. "Coming into my own house and accusing me of thieving. I did you a favor and ans—"

"I *paid* you."

"Out!" Mrs. McGee jabbed a finger at the door.

"Tom, let's go." Desiree rose, starting for the door, and Tom followed.

They returned to the agency office, neither of them speaking. Desiree's head was still spinning. She could tell from Tom's frequent sidelong glances that he was worried about her. She wanted to reassure him that she was fine. But she wasn't sure she could. The housekeeper's words had set her reeling.

As soon as they were inside Tom's flat, Desiree whirled to face him, arms flung wide. "Now my father is a *murderer*?"

"We don't know that," Tom argued. "I am not at all sure we can trust that woman."

"She wasn't lying. I'm sure of it."

"All that means is that she believes what she says. That's her opinion, not a fact. Sit down, and I'll make us a pot of tea."

"I can't sit down," Desiree replied and began to pace. "I thought it couldn't be worse than my parents abandoning us, but now . . . my mother years dead, my father a killer!"

"Here now." Tom came up behind her, curling his arms around her and holding her close. "Don't fret so."

The feel of his arms around her, the warmth and strength of his body against hers calmed Desiree, and she leaned her head back against his chest. "The things she said made so much sense, Tom. It's hard to deny them. Leaving with only one case? Not taking her jewelry? And you and I know that Stella didn't take the expensive pieces, either, because they were stashed away in the secret place beside the fireplace. Who would set off on a long journey, much less a whole lifetime, with only a change of clothes and a hairbrush? Leave the letters that were so dear to her, the jewels she'd been given by the man she loved? I certainly wouldn't do that."

"They could have left on the spur of the moment," Tom reasoned. "They went to the cottage for a few days. When it came time to part, they simply couldn't, and they ran away right then and there."

"They were certainly a thoughtless pair if that's so. They could have come back here first. Packed their clothes and taken their children. How awful could it have been to spend one more week in London making preparations?"

"I don't know." Tom laid his cheek against her head, his hands sliding up and down her arms soothingly. "But I do know that Mrs. McGee's story doesn't entirely stand up, either."

With some reluctance, Desiree pulled out of his hold and turned to face him. "In what way?"

"For one thing, she didn't tell the police. She didn't have to tell them she thought Alistair murdered Stella. All she had to do was report her missing. It would have set an investigation in motion. But she didn't.

"And why would she have leaped to the idea that Alistair killed your mother? Everyone said they were madly in love. Even Mrs. McGee didn't deny that he appeared to be in love with Stella. If your brothers went off and didn't come back, would you assume one of them had killed the other? No, you'd worry that something had happened to both of them."

"She could have feared they would find out she'd been pilfering the jewelry."

"I know, but really, how would the police have known that? Only Stella would have recognized what pieces were missing, and if Mrs. McGee really believed Stella was dead, she would have thought Stella wasn't going to return to accuse her of theft. No, I think it's something she thought up later, making the facts conform to her theory."

The kettle whistled and he went to pour the water over the tea leaves. "There are inconsistencies in her story. For instance, she says they left in the afternoon the day *before* Mr. Paxton came over to find them gone. But *he* says Alistair was still in London the night before, which would mean that they would have left the *same* day Paxton showed up at the house."

Desiree lifted a shoulder. "One of them

420

doesn't remember it correctly. It was twenty-eight years ago, so that's hardly surprising."

"True. But there's an internal inconsistency, as well. She said on the one hand that she didn't tell anyone because the police wouldn't have charged a Moreland with murder, yet in the next breath she said that Alistair fled the country because he was afraid he'd get arrested. Those two things are opposites. I'm inclined to believe that she's right in saying the police would have been very reluctant to arrest a Moreland. So why would he have run away?"

"People often act impulsively when they're scared. They don't stop to think, they just run."

"Why did no one ever find your mother's body?" Tom asked.

"Maybe he buried her. Or hid her body somewhere else."

"If he was cool and calm enough to bury her, then why run?" Tom argued. "Hiding the body fits with returning home and brazening it out, not fleeing in a panic."

"I suppose. I don't know what to think." Desiree sighed.

"Desiree." Tom put two fingers beneath her chin to tilt her face up so that she looked into his eyes. "We don't know what happened. We may never know. But whatever your parents did or didn't do doesn't mean anything about *you.* You are what you have created. Your parents did nothing but give you possibilities. You are the one who turned those possibilities into the person you are today. You've lived through a wealth of bad things, but you came out of it strong and whole. You didn't let anyone defeat you, including Falk. I know that life, Desiree, and it's hard. Most of the people you grew up with are dead or in jail or living in a bottle of gin. But *you* are both tough and good. You're intelligent, you're brave, you're loving." He grinned. "And you can climb a building like a cat."

Desiree laughed and looped her arms loosely around his neck. "Thank you. You have a very nice way with words."

"I meant every bit of it." He stroked his hand across her hair, and down her neck, sending bright shivers all through her. "I didn't even mention how beautiful you are. How desirable. Whenever you smile at me, you turn me inside out."

Desiree drew in a little breath, passion rising in her. She laid a hand against his cheek. "I feel the same."

"Really?" His smile was lazily sensual, and his eyes heated. He brushed her cheek with his knuckles. "I like the sound of that."

"Do you? Yet you aren't doing anything about it." She reached up to trace his lips with her forefinger, and he caught it between his teeth, lightly nipping, then kissing it. Desiree melted inside. She slid her hands down his chest and under his jacket.

He made a noise, half chuckle, half groan. "Desiree . . . you're going to kill me here."

"That's not my intention." She moved closer, her eyes glowing up at him.

A tremor shook him and he wrapped his arms around her, pulling her into him. Desiree kissed him back, pressing her body up into him.

He lifted his head. "Desiree, we should stop."

"No." She shook her head, the need inside her a driving, pulsing force, matched by another, deeper hunger.

She felt his body flame beneath her hands, and his voice was a trifle shaky as he said, "Wait. Are you certain?"

Why in the world had she been dithering about this earlier? She wanted this man. On every level, heart, body and mind. And she wanted him forever.

"I'm certain."

There were few words after that, only a murmur of pleasure or a whispered name as they kissed and caressed, all the hunger of the past few days unleashed. And if Tom's fingers on her buttons were clumsy or her touch untutored, neither of them noticed or cared.

Pleasure rushed through Desiree as Tom kissed her, leaving her mouth to nip at her ear and explore her throat. All the while, he unfastened the long line of buttons down the back of her dress, and Desiree wished she had worn something less fashionable — and easier to discard — today. But at least the dress didn't require a corset; given the things that had been happening, she had taken to wearing something that would allow her more freedom of movement.

The dress sagged open, falling farther apart with each button, until finally it slid down over her petticoats to pool at her feet. Then his hand was on the bare skin of her upper back, her flesh tingling at the glide of his skin over hers. He slid his hands down over the thin cotton of her camisole and up beneath the hem of the garment, his fingertips hot and slightly rough against her skin.

Desiree trembled at his touch and pressed herself more tightly against him, her kiss deepening. But she ached to feel his body beneath her hands, so finally she pulled away, her fingers going to the buttons of his waistcoat. He helped her by shrugging out of his jacket and tossing it away, then working at the cuffs of his shirt.

His waistcoat open, she started on his shirt's buttons, wondering why men found it necessary to wear so many items of clothing. Then at last his shirt was open, exposing the bare strip of skin down the center of his chest, and her fingers went under the shirt, roaming his skin, exploring the hard ridges of his ribs and the firm muscles that padded his chest.

Tom hissed in his breath as she pressed her lips against his chest. Her mouth moved down the central line of his sternum. Desiree teased a pattern across his skin with her tongue, learning the faintly salty taste of him, and the faint moan she wrung from him increased her own pleasure.

She touched his flat masculine nipples, and, remembering the feel of his mouth on her breast, she twined her tongue around the small hard buds, first one, then the other. His body jerked in response, and he dug his fingers into her hair, sending hairpins flying and her thick hair tumbling down.

Desiree lifted her head. His eyes were bright blue, his face slack with passion. For a moment, he gazed down into her eyes, as if he could see straight to the center of her soul, then he bent to take her mouth in a fierce kiss, claiming and offering, taking and giving in a torrent of heat.

Pulling back, Tom swept Desiree up in his arms and carried her across the room to the bed. Setting her down beside it, he stepped back, toeing off his shoes and ripping his open shirt off his shoulders to drop it on the floor. Desiree, watching him, matched his movements, reaching down to the hem of her chemise and pulling it up and off over her head.

The sight of her stopped his movements. His eyes dropped to her breasts, hunger flooding his face. He covered her breasts with his hands, gently squeezing and caressing. He swept his hands down and back, linking his arms beneath her bottom and lifting her up to take one of her nipples in his mouth. He loved it long and attentively, and with every stroke of his tongue, desire coiled tighter in Desiree.

She stroked his shoulders, his arms, his hair, the ache deep inside her swelling. Digging her fingers into his shoulders, Desiree murmured his name in a broken voice, on the edge of simply shattering, wanting more and at the same time yearning for satisfaction.

Tom dropped her onto the bed, and Desiree bounced lightly, laughing up at him. He grinned, eyes glinting in a predatory way, and climbed onto the bed, straddling her legs. Desiree's breath caught in her throat, the familiar thrill of the chase permeated with sensuality. The throbbing between her legs turned hotter, fiercer, more demanding.

He went to the ties of her petticoats and underpants, impatiently snapping one when it knotted under his fingers. He bunched the waistbands in his hands and pulled them all down. Sucking in a breath, Tom sat back on his heels, his eyes blazing, and simply looked at her.

A flush touched Desiree's cheek, embarrassment mingling with a sensual satisfaction, the look in his eyes heating her blood, and she felt a wayward temptation to stretch beneath his gaze in a thoroughly wanton manner. So she did.

"Are you planning to just look?" she asked archly.

"No." His answer was low and husky. He reached out to trail a finger down the center line of her body from the hollow of her throat to the juncture of her legs. Moisture flooded between her legs. "I plan to do a great deal more than look." He planted his hands on the bed on either side of her, crawling slowly up her body. "I plan to touch." He curved one hand over her breasts and down her side. "And taste." He bent to kiss her mouth.

As they kissed, his body slid down from his crouch, so that he supported himself on his forearms and his legs were flush against hers. The fabric of his trousers upon her bare skin was somehow titillating, but as she stroked her hands over his back and down, she wanted to touch him without the cloth between them.

"Take off your clothes," she ordered huskily.

"Yes, ma'am." She felt the breath of his little laugh against her lips, and then his weight was off her. He stood up, unbuttoning and quickly shucking off the remainder of his clothing.

Desiree studied his naked body, her eyes widening a little at the sight of him. She had known what a naked man looked like. It had been impossible to grow up as she had in Falk's household without catching a glimpse now and then.

But she hadn't really known, she realized now, looking at Tom's sleekly muscled body. He was beautiful in a thoroughly masculine way, the lines of muscle and bone making her fingers itch to touch him. And if, in his heavily aroused state, he looked a bit dangerous also . . . Well, Desiree had never been one to shy away from danger. She held out her arms to him.

He returned, nudging her legs apart with his knees, and she opened to him. Desiree's hands went to the fleshy curve of his buttocks, caressing and clutching, then trailed down onto his thighs, delighting in the texture of his hair-roughened skin.

Tom kissed her, his hand caressing her breasts, her stomach, gliding down between her legs, finding the silken-soft flesh there, wet with the evidence of her desire. His mouth left hers, trailing down her body to devote his attention to her breasts, all the while his fingers still playing with her, stoking the fire within her.

"Tom . . ." Desiree moved her legs restlessly, her body knowing that only he could satisfy the ache that pulsed deep inside.

He murmured something unintelligible, his mouth drifting to the soft skin of her stomach as he slipped his finger inside her, hinting at the surcease she sought while increasing her need for it. Desiree dug her fingers into his shoulders, her nails biting into his skin. He groaned, a shiver running down his back, and he shifted, the head of his shaft teasing at her entrance.

Desiree widened her legs, pressing up against him, but he barely entered her, moving with relentless slowness as he sank into her, pulling back, then pushing forward. Her nails scored his back as Desiree wrapped her legs around him tightly, and he sank all the way into her, filling and fulfilling her need. She let out a soft moan, moving with him.

Passion built in her, coiling ever tighter, driving Desiree until she was trembling. At last, it exploded and an indescribable pleasure rolled through her. Tom let out a cry and shuddered, pouring himself into her, and they clung together, riding out the storm.

Tom collapsed against her, rolling to the side and taking her in his arms. His breathing was ragged as he murmured, "Stay with me."

CHAPTER TWENTY-NINE

"Of course."

That had been Desiree's answer this afternoon. Tom wasn't sure what she'd meant. Hell, he wasn't even sure what he had meant. Stay with me always? This afternoon? Weeks or months or years?

Standing here now, leaning against the wall of the casino and watching Desiree at work, he thought about this afternoon. What they'd said. What they'd done. Remembering the slow, languorous hours they had lain in his bed, kissing, talking, making love again, stirred up the embers of those flames.

That kind of thinking was asking for trouble. A few minutes of that, and he was hard as a rock, not really presentable, especially in a casino owned by Desiree's brother.

But thinking about what they'd said was perhaps even more dangerous. For a man who'd been steadily building a life for himself, laying a foundation for what he could become, the whirlwind of the present was a disturbing burst of pleasure and excitement, as alluring as it was exotic and just as likely to vanish as a morning fog in the sunny glare of daytime.

Desiree stirred him in more ways than he had ever imagined possible. She made him want to leap without looking, without even pausing to glance at what lay beneath or beyond. Caution had never been a hallmark of his character; he'd had to train himself to be steady, to work and plan instead of jumping at any momentarily appealing thing that came along.

It had taken him several years to accept that the Morelands weren't going to abandon him. It had taken even longer to realize that he could build some sort of structure that, however rickety, would support him in some semblance of the stability that other people, people with families and backgrounds of honor and honesty, possessed.

Yet here Desiree was: a thief like him, raised like him, possessing similar instincts and thoughts. Tempting. Enthralling. Offering him a dazzling prospect of joy. And he wanted to take that leap. God, he wanted to take it. Wanted it so much it scared him.

Desiree looked up from her cards, and her

eyes went to Tom. A sensual smile curved her lips, setting Tom's pulse pounding. He took out his watch and opened it. Another hour before the time she usually stopped playing. But as he watched, Desiree stood up, smiling at the other players and talking to them for a moment before she turned and walked toward him.

She was leaving early. Desiree's thoughts were clearly running along the same lines as his. He'd suspected that from the moment she'd dismissed Merriwell this evening, telling the driver that she and Tom would catch a hackney home. The knowledge that Desiree was as eager as he to be together again had kept his blood thrumming with fire the past two hours.

Desiree took his arm and they strolled out of the club. With a word of farewell to the guards at the door, they started down the shallow steps to the street below. Desiree paused and glanced around.

"What is it?" Tom asked.

"I don't know. I've just been on edge all evening. It's been harder to focus. But I think it's just . . . you know." Her eyes went to his mouth. "Us."

"I know." Heat pulsed in him at her words. But he tore his eyes away from her and looked carefully up and down the street. He couldn't allow his hunger to distract him from Desiree's safety.

A hack pulled away from the line of carriages and rolled to a stop in front of them. With a last glance around, Tom gave Desiree a hand up into the vehicle and climbed in himself, telling the driver his address. They started off at a fast pace.

Desiree turned to Tom and was immediately in his arms. They kissed as if they had been separated for weeks rather than a few hours. The temptation of watching Desiree all evening had built into a white-hot hunger.

Suddenly Desiree pulled from him. Her hand went to her chest. "Tom . . ."

"What is it?" His passion was shoved aside by alarm. "Danger?"

"I feel . . . uneasy. It's sharp."

"The way you felt before Falk's man took that box from us?"

"Yes." She slid away from him, her gaze going to the window as Tom did the same thing on the other side of the coach.

Tom let out a curse. "This isn't the way to my flat. Where the devil are we?" The street they were on was narrow and dark, with few streetlamps. The buildings were unfamiliar, overhangs creating deep shadows on the street below.

"The East End, I imagine," Desiree said as their vehicle rumbled onto cobblestones, the ride suddenly jarring.

"Stop!" Tom called to the driver, lunging forward to pound on the window between them.

There was no answer except for the hackney speeding up. The carriage was racketing along now, far too fast for the dark street. Trying to jump out would be sheer folly. They were bounced about and had to brace themselves against the walls and floor to keep from sliding off the seat.

"Damn!" Tom muttered. "I should have been paying attention."

"We were distracted," Desiree said wryly. "No point in berating yourself about it now. We're going to have to run, aren't we?"

"Yes. As soon as we stop."

"And I have on this blasted dress." To Tom's surprise, she turned her back to him. "Unbutton me."

His eyebrows went up, but he started doing as she said. "Desiree, what are you doing?"

"I'm getting rid of my corset," she replied. Fortunately, her low-necked evening gown had fewer buttons than the dress she had worn this afternoon, a wide sash securing it at the waist. He began untying her corset, and Desiree said, "Just cut them." Reaching into his pocket, he took out his penknife and sliced down the strings. The corset sagged open, and Desiree tossed it aside. He began to rebutton the dress but could manage only the very top ones, the waist now too tight.

While he worked, Desiree had turned up the skirt of her elegant dress and untied her petticoats. She shucked them off, adding them to the corset on the floor. "At least I wore low-heel slippers tonight."

Next she swept up her full skirts, twisting them and knotting them, then shoved the ends into her sash, with the result that her skirt now fell to her knees rather than her ankles. Desiree pulled out the glittering ornament she wore in her hair. Three prongs had secured the jeweled figure of a hummingbird to her upswept hair, and each of the metal prongs was wickedly sharp. She pinned the knot of skirts to the waistband with the ornament to ensure they would not come undone. The entire process had taken her about three minutes.

"That pin is lethal," Tom commented a little enviously. It looked a good deal more dangerous than his pocketknife, that was certain.

"Never hurts to have a weapon with you."

"*You* are a dangerous woman."

"I am," Desiree agreed, grinning at him.

"Sadly, I have nothing but this." Tom reached into his jacket and pulled a small derringer from his inside pocket. "It's only good at close range and has just one shot."

"Then you'd better make good use of it," Desiree responded. "We're slowing down."

Tom reached out and turned the door handle, peering out the window at the dark street. Four men stood in the shadows, waiting for them. Before the vehicle stopped completely, Tom flung open the door and jumped out, Desiree right behind him. There wasn't time to aim; he simply fired at the group, then turned and darted after Desiree. A shout of pain behind him told him he'd at least done some damage, and it gave them a few extra moments.

Amid the chorus of curses from the men, one voice rang out, "Get her!"

Glancing over his shoulder, Tom saw that the men had all dived for cover, including the one who was clutching his arm. Ahead of him Desiree was scanning the area around her, and he knew she was looking for something to climb. Heaven help him.

Suddenly she stopped, her head whipping around, and she ran back to the pub they'd just passed. A large barrel stood by the door, and Desiree climbed up on it, then jumped up to grab the bar of the sign above the door. Planting her foot on the top of the open door, she pushed up and scrambled onto a narrow ledge. Tom followed her, thrusting aside his doubt, and managed to get onto the ledge beside her. He gripped the bricks of the wall with his fingertips, unlike Desiree, who barely touched them.

Desiree was already sidling along the ledge and around the corner. When Tom edged around the corner after her, he found himself in an alleyway even darker that the street. It was rank with the smell of refuse and so narrow their bodies barely fit between the buildings. Apparently, Desiree had not only the eyes of a cat but the agility of one as well, for she continued moving along at a fast pace. She stopped when she reached the back of the building that abutted this one.

Tom could hear the running footsteps of their pursuers, then the sounds of the men attempting to copy Desiree's maneuver with the barrel and sign. That was followed by curses and a crash as the barrel turned over and rolled into the street. Tom couldn't help but smile to himself even though he and Desiree were stuck at a dead end.

He wondered if Desiree intended to cling

to the side of the building until the men gave up. Tom knew he could do some damage jumping down on them, but they were still outnumbered, and however courageous Desiree was, she was far smaller and slighter than any of the men.

The side of the building where they stopped was Tudor timbered, and Desiree began to scramble up the beams, somehow finding every divot or crack that she could use as a handhold. She crawled onto the roof. Tom followed less nimbly, tearing a fingernail and scraping his knuckles in the process. He swung his leg up and heaved himself over onto the flat roof.

"Good Lord, you're mad," he said, simply lying there for a moment. The cursing behind them continued as the men apparently tried to squeeze into the narrow alley.

"I'm good." Desiree grinned. "Now, just follow me."

She crossed the roof to the adjacent building. It was several feet higher than the one they were on, but the wall had enough chunks of mortar missing between the stones to make for easier handholds and footholds. They took off across the rooftops.

On the street below, their pursuers followed their path. There were only three of them now; the man he had shot had stayed behind. The men stopped once or twice to try to climb up a building after them but finally gave up and just kept up with Desiree and Tom from below. Eventually Desiree and Tom would have to climb back down.

They reached a cross street, and Desiree stopped, studying the street below and the building across from it. The lane was narrow, and the buildings on each side were in the same Elizabethan half-timber style, the upper floors extending out a few feet over the street. The gap between the two buildings was therefore narrower than the lane. Desiree began to back up.

"Wait." Tom took her arm. "You don't mean to jump across that street."

"We can jump it. It's only three feet."

"Three feet of empty space!"

"Don't worry. It's safe. We'll make it. I told you — my 'talent' came in quite handy for thieving."

Tom dropped his hand and watched, heart in his throat, as Desiree backed up, then ran forward at full speed and leaped across the strip of nothingness, landing on the balls of her feet and springing up. Tom moved back, reminding himself that it was a distance he could easily jump and that the height made no difference. He took a breath, then raced forward, jumping the gap and landing on the other roof with a good deal less grace than Desiree.

Desiree looked at the rooftops around her as Tom picked himself up, panting.

Her eyes gleamed as she said, "They made a mistake. This is *my* patch."

Once more she set off across the rooftops. The area was a warren of buildings, a hodgepodge of heights and styles. They had to crawl across the midpoint of a steeply pitched roof at one point and scramble up the less slanted side of another to reach a higher roof. The streets and buildings twisted and turned. Then, the street along which their pursuers ran came to a dead end, a warehouse blocking their way.

Desiree vaulted over the low parapet onto the roof of the warehouse and kept running, followed by Tom. At the other end of the warehouse was a large block and tackle, a rope running from the pulley to the lift platform. The rope had been tied off, holding the empty lift at the top. Desiree went to work on the knot, and Tom reached in to help. Tom played out the rope, letting the platform down to the ground, then retied it to keep the rope taut.

Using her skirts to protect her palms, Desiree grabbed the rope, wrapped her hands and legs around it, and slid down the rope to the street. Tom followed suit. They crossed the rough ground to the street on the other side of the warehouse. They were now on the street parallel to the one they had traveled earlier. The men, if they were persistent enough to follow them, would have to backtrack to the last cross street and come around, too, putting them a good distance behind them.

They trotted down the street, a little breathless from their exertion. Everything was silent around them, making it very noticeable when a few moments later their pursuers emerged onto the same street. One of the men let out a shout, and they charged after Desiree and Tom. Tom cursed. Desiree grabbed his hand, taking off across the street and through the door of a building.

Bolting up a set of stairs, they ran down a hallway and out onto a gallery on the back side of the building. Below them, Tom could hear the lap of water, and looking down, he saw that the river was below them. They rounded the wooden walkway and ran back toward the front of the building, where they climbed another set of stairs.

With anyone else, Tom would have questioned the strategy of running upward, but he trusted Desiree and stayed on her heels.

They came out on a higher gallery. Next to them was an obviously abandoned building. The roof had caved in, leaving only the walls. The front wall was the same height as the building on which they stood, and it stretched all the way to the next building.

Desiree swung her leg over the railing of the wooden gallery and Tom said, "Desiree, wait . . . you expect us to walk across that?"

"You can do it," Desiree told him encouragingly. "It's wider than the beam you walked on in our exercise room."

"Yes, but that was a foot off the floor, not thirty feet," Tom pointed out.

"Oh, I don't think it's more than twenty," Desiree replied. She gazed at him for a moment, then nodded. "Stay here. I'll go across and draw them off. You head back down the stairs and come out after they've passed."

"And leave you to face them alone? You really are insane if you think that." Tom sighed and gestured at the wall. "Lead on. I hope to hell this thing isn't about to fall in like the rest of it."

"It won't. Trust me. I can 'see' it, just like with people." Desiree smiled and leaned over to give him a soft kiss. Turning, she stepped onto the wall and walked across. Tom swung his leg over and stepped down onto the wall, his hand still clenched on the railing. He looked down and sucked in a breath. On the right lay the street two floors below. On the left lay the debris of the collapsed roof. He'd never thought of himself as being scared of heights, but there were heights and then there were *heights*.

"Don't look down," Desiree said. "Just walk to me."

Lifting his head, Tom set his feet straight on the wall — it *was* wider than he needed, but somehow that fact did little to reassure him. Heart pounding, he released his hold on the railing and extended his arms to either side, as she'd showed him the other day, and began to walk toward her. He wanted — so much — to cast his gaze down at the street below, but he refrained. One step and then another. *Don't go too slowly. Don't think about the ground. Just walk to Desiree.* It lasted an eternity, and he could feel the cold sweat trickling down the back of his neck.

But then he was there, taking her hand and jumping down to stand on the roof beside her. Desiree took his hand and said, "You'll like this — there's a ladder down from here."

"Thank God."

There was indeed a ladder at the other end of the roof, and even though it was just as long a drop to the ground as the wall had been, Tom had no qualms about climbing down it. All it took was strength, and that was an entirely different matter. The rungs ended a few feet above the ground and Tom jumped to the dirt below, then turned back to reach up and catch Desiree as she let go. He set her down beside him, and they leaned back against the building for a moment, panting.

"Where the devil are we? The docks?" he whispered.

She nodded. "But it's not terribly far from the Strand. If we can just make it there, we'll be able to grab a cab."

They edged over to the corner of the building and peered around. The street was empty in either direction. Slipping out from behind the building, they walked quickly and quietly down the street, staying in the shadows of the buildings. They passed a tavern, but neither of them felt like going into a dockside pub for help.

Turning onto another street — now Tom was beginning to recognize where they were, as well — they saw two men walking toward them. The men broke into a trot when they saw them. Desiree and Tom came to an abrupt stop.

"There are more of them?" Tom exclaimed

in disbelief.

Whirling, Tom and Desiree fled back up the street. Darting into a side street, they ran on, turning corners frequently. The maneuver lost their most recent pursuers, but just as they slowed to a walk, they heard a shout. "There she is!"

Tom looked over to see the original three men running toward them. Tom and Desiree took off again. Desiree scanned the buildings around them as they ran, looking, no doubt, for a way to scale one, but they were all warehouses — large buildings with flat brick walls, void of ornamental doors, stonework, trellises or porches. There were no wooden galleries or trees. Streetlamps were few, just enough to see where one was going, creating pools of shadows.

Tom could see that Desiree was flagging; hell, he was, too. However athletic and agile Desiree was, the running and climbing they had done was very taxing, and the burst of energy that their fear and excitement had released was beginning to wane. Before long, both of them would come crashing back to earth.

Too late, Tom realized that they had run into a dead end. A loading dock lay at the end of the street, with only the river ahead and warehouses lining the sides. They skidded to a halt and turned, but the three men were too near. There was nothing for it but to stand and fight.

CHAPTER THIRTY

Tom didn't need to look at Desiree to know what she wanted to do. Tom squeezed her hand, and the two of them rushed forward, taking the fight to their enemies. The men skidded to a stop in surprise. One of them slipped and fell to the ground. Tom swung his fist, hitting the largest man in the stomach, and the man doubled over. Tom followed up with a blow to his jaw.

Out of the corner of his eye, Tom saw Desiree go into a cartwheel, kicking the third man in the face as she went by. He let out a yowl and staggered backward. Desiree whirled as soon as her feet touched the ground and hurled herself at his back.

Tom's opponent staggered but came back. He was less agile than Tom, but his big fist packed a wallop. The third man, who had fallen at the beginning, jumped up, and Tom glimpsed a short metal bar in his hand. He rushed at Tom, swinging the bar. Tom grabbed his opponent's jacket and jerked him between Tom and the man with the weapon, so that the blow landed heavily on the other man's back. He fell against Tom, carrying Tom down with him. They rolled across the street, grappling. The fellow with the bar followed, swinging at Tom, but he wound up in the street instead as the combatants rolled first one way and then the next.

Tom slammed his opponent's head against the bricks of the street, stunning him, and jumped to his feet as the man with the bar swung at him again. Tom blocked the blow with a raised arm, sending a shock of pain through him up to his shoulder, and punched the man in the jaw with his other fist. The man staggered back, and Tom grabbed the bar, wrenching it away.

As he'd fought, Tom had seen Desiree out of the corner of his eye only as a blur of movement, dodging, kicking, whirling, ducking under the other man's wildly swinging fists. She was holding her own, but Tom knew he had to get to her and disable her opponent.

For the moment, the man he had been fighting first was out of the battle, rolling away and struggling to his feet. So Tom went after the second attacker, who had recovered his footing and was moving forward. Tom slammed the metal bar into the man's arm, following up the blow with a hard kick to the side of his knee. The other man cried out and crashed to the ground, his hands grabbing his knee.

Tom whirled in time to see Desiree scramble halfway up a lamppost and swing her feet out to clip her opponent in the jaw. Tom ran to her side, shoving her would-be attacker into the wall of the building behind her. Desiree jumped down from the lamppost, and they ran back up the street. Behind them their foes staggered to their feet and began to pursue them.

At that moment, the two newcomers they had seen earlier turned onto the street ahead of them. Spotting Desiree and Tom, they started forward at a run. Tom let out a curse and pushed Desiree into the nearest doorway. It was set far enough into the stone wall to provide a bit of an alcove, and Tom placed himself in front of her, bar raised. Desiree gave him a push to the side and came up beside him in the doorway. She yanked the sharp-pronged hair ornament from her waistband and took up a fighting stance.

Her hair had long since come undone and tumbled riotously around her shoulders, and her eyes were blazing, her face fierce. She looked utterly wild. And utterly beautiful. Tom knew he would kill if he must in order to protect her.

Raising the iron bar, he roared at the trio of original enemies, who came to a halt a few feet away. One of them was limping badly, and they looked warily at the weapon in Tom's hand. In the next instant the two newcomers arrived.

The two men launched themselves at Tom's and Desiree's enemies.

Tom and Desiree stared in astonishment at the melee. There were only two of the new arrivals and three of the others, but the attackers were fresh, and within only a few moments, the original three broke and ran. The two rescuers were hot on their heels.

"What in the world?" Desiree gazed uncomprehendingly after the fleeing men.

"I have no idea, but I suggest we take advantage of it."

Tom took her hand, and they walked swiftly down the street. Tom kept the metal rod with him, but no one else popped up to confront them, and within a few minutes the area around them began to improve, and eventually they emerged to the Strand.

At first they walked, leery of hailing a hackney after their previous experience, but both of them were exhausted. Finally, Tom raised his hand to hail a passing cab. The driver looked askance at the iron rod in Tom's hand and sped up.

"I think perhaps we look a mite disreputable," Desiree said.

Tom turned to her. Desiree's hair was down and thoroughly tangled, and her skirt was smeared with dirt and God knew what else. No doubt he looked substantially worse, with a cut beside his eye that had bled down his face, a large tear in his trousers, and a jacket pocket that had torn halfway off and hung flapping. The bar in his right hand probably hadn't added anything trustworthy to his appearance.

He began to laugh, and after a second, so did Desiree, until they were roaring hysterically. As their riotous laughter slowed to a halt, Tom dropped the iron bar and pulled Desiree into his arms, wrapping his arms around her, and squeezed her tightly to him. He bent his head to kiss her hair.

"I was so scared you were going to get hurt," he told her, his voice throbbing with emotion. "It makes me shake, just thinking about it."

"I know." Desiree buried her face in his chest, her arms locked around his waist. "I was, too. It's easier when you only have to be afraid for yourself."

They stood that way for a long time, unmoving, just holding on to each other. Finally, Tom stepped back and took out his handkerchief to wipe as much of the blood and dirt from his face as he could. Desiree managed to pull back her hair and wrap it in a loose knot at the nape of her neck, securing it with her hair ornament/weapon. They dusted off their clothes, and Tom simply tore off the hanging pocket on his jacket. He hailed the next hackney that passed.

This one stopped and they climbed in. Tom pulled Desiree onto his lap. All the frenzied energy of the chase had drained out of her, and she leaned against him, closing her eyes. Tom could feel her body begin to sag and knew she was drifting toward an exhausted sleep.

All Tom wanted to do was to take Desiree back to his flat, to care for her and cuddle her. To lie down with her and hold her as she slept. To know she was safe and secure.

But of course, that was impossible. Even though they had left the club early, it was now late, and Desiree's brothers would be alarmed that she hadn't come home. Tom could scarcely justify worrying them even more just because he didn't want to leave her. He had no right, no standing, to protect and care for Desiree, however much he ached to.

Tom gave the driver Desiree's address. When they pulled up in front of her house, Tom kissed Desiree on the forehead, murmuring, "We're here. I started to carry you to the door, but I thought that might cause some consternation."

Desiree smiled up at him tiredly. "Thank you. It would indeed. Though if I'm lucky, Brock won't be home yet."

They left the cab and walked into the house. Desiree's luck held, for Brock was still closing the club, but Wells saw them from his chair in the parlor, and he got up and crossed the room quickly.

"Desiree? What happened?" Wells's piercing blue eyes swept a comprehensive glance over the two of them. "You look as if you've been in a fight."

"That's only reasonable, since we have been." Desiree attempted a light tone, but her voice betrayed her weariness.

"What in the — No, never mind." Wells gave a dismissive wave of the hand. "You can tell me in the morning. You clearly need to go to sleep." He turned to Tom. "I must say, you look just as dead on your feet. Come on." Wells nodded toward the staircase. "You can sleep in the guest room. No need to haul yourself back home."

Tom wavered only a moment before giving in and following Wells upstairs.

When Tom awoke the next morning, he lay for a moment in confusion, uncertain why he was sleeping in a soft bed with luxurious sheets and a canopy over his head. Desiree. He was in Desiree's house. He sat up, raking his hands back through his hair and trying to bring his disordered thoughts into focus.

It felt extremely odd to be here. He wasn't entirely unaccustomed to being anywhere but his own bed — after all, he had to travel now and then on business and he'd even stayed in one of the Moreland houses on occasion — but this was where Desiree lived, and that made all the difference. It brought up a number of decidedly lustful thoughts, but at the same time there was something so natural, even *familial* about it that it was disconcerting.

Tom got out of bed, every ache in his body making itself known. The soles of his feet burned; his cheek throbbed; and there didn't seem to be a muscle in his body that hadn't been strained. He found his suit, cleaned, repaired and neatly pressed, on a stand, his cleaned and polished shoes beneath it. There was even a fresh, starched shirt folded on the dresser; he presumed it must belong to one of her brothers. An open door showed the tiled room beyond, which he had discovered last night was a small but modern water closet. It boasted all the necessities from a comb to a shaving razor.

Sometime later, he emerged from his room, clean, shaved and dressed. The upper hallway was quiet, so he went downstairs, where the sound of voices led him into the breakfast room.

All three of the Malones were sitting at the table, and they looked up as Tom came into the room. Desiree jumped up, smiling, and came to take his arm and lead him to the chair beside her. He had hardly sat down before their efficient butler was there, pouring him a cup of tea, then dishing out a variety of eggs, sausages and pastries onto the plate before him.

"Desiree was telling us about your adventures yesterday evening," Brock said. He seemed, Tom thought, somewhat friendlier than before — or, at least, less antagonistic. "It's very fortunate you were with her. Thank you."

"I think Desiree helped me more than I helped her." Tom grinned at her, realizing a shade too late that perhaps his look held more affection than was seemly. "I couldn't have escaped them if she hadn't been there."

"Took you across the rooftops, did she?" Wells grinned. "There's none better than Dezzy up there."

"Who were these men?" Brock asked.

"I don't know," Tom admitted. "I guess they must have been Falk's crew, though why he would be so violent about it, I don't know. Frankly, it seemed to me that they were more intent on harming us than trying to get something from us. More accurately, I think they wanted to harm Desiree. When they first attacked us, they yelled, 'Get *her,*' not 'get them.' And later, when they spotted us, they yelled, 'There *she* is.' I think it was Desiree they wanted, and I was just in their way."

Desiree's brothers turned frowning gazes on her. She grimaced at Tom. "You were in more danger than I. They just wanted to kidnap me and make me give them the will. They wouldn't have had any qualms about killing you."

"But why take you to the East End?" Wells pointed out. "Surely they didn't think you carried the thing around with you. It seems more reasonable to attack you here, as they did before."

"Well, they weren't very successful before, were they? They realized it would take more men, especially with Tom escorting me back and forth to the club. And three men attacking people is less likely to get noticed there than in Knightsbridge."

"That makes sense," Wells said thoughtfully. "Or they might have realized that if they held you hostage, Brock and I would give them the will."

"If we had it," Brock interjected dryly. "What I want to know is who in the world were the men who came to your rescue?"

"I have even less understanding of that," Tom told him. "I suppose they could have belonged to some rival gang, continual enemies who seized the opportunity to take them on."

"Falk certainly has plenty of enemies," Brock commented. "Still, it seems a bit of a coincidence."

"The only people who have evinced interest in this will are Falk, who hired Desiree, and Gregory Moreland," Wells said.

"Except we assumed that Gregory hired Falk to begin with. I can stretch my belief to say that perhaps Gregory was so eager to find it that he hired both Falk and another set of men," Desiree said. "But why would they try to stop Falk's gang, or vice versa?"

"But who else would have any interest in it?" Wells asked.

"The problem is, we can't find that out without knowing what's in the will," Tom said. "Alastair could have left a bequest to almost anyone, and that person could want the will to be probated."

"I suppose," Brock said. "Though it seems odd that some bequest would be so important. Of course, it seems odd, too, that Gregory is so insistent on finding it. After all, he's the legitimate heir. I can't imagine that Alistair would have left such a large bequest to anyone else that it would have much effect on Gregory's inheritance."

"What if he's not the legitimate heir?" Tom asked, and everyone turned to him. "What if Alistair married your mother in secret before he married Lady Tabitha? Making you and Desiree the legitimate heirs. That would certainly be enough reason for Gregory to want to destroy the will."

"Sounds like a novel," Wells said. "Besides, I don't see how that could be true. Gregory is older than we are, isn't he?"

"You're right," Tom agreed. "I looked him up when we first started on this, and Gregory is thirty-three years old."

"So just a year younger than I," Brock

said. "I was four or five when Lord More-land moved us into that house. Alistair would have already been married to Gregory's mother for a few years."

"Where the devil *is* this will?" Wells asked. "Why does everyone think you have it?"

"Because I lied to that man who attacked me. I told him I had it because I was trying to get him to move so I could run," Desiree explained.

"So it went astray somewhere?"

"Apparently. It hasn't shown up at the office or at Broughton House," Tom told them.

"Perhaps I ought to have a conversation with Falk," Wells said, his blue eyes icy.

"Trust me, that is exactly what I intend to do as soon as I leave here," Tom assured him grimly.

Wells regarded him for a moment, then nodded to Tom. "Very well."

Tom gave the other man a little nod in return, feeling as if he had been handed something significant, though he wasn't exactly sure what.

"I'm going with you," Desiree declared.

"Naturally you want to walk into the lion's den," Brock grumbled.

It was on the tip of Tom's tongue to tell Desiree it was too dangerous, but after one glance at the glower Desiree sent her older brother, Tom wisely held back the words. "Of course. We'll take care of Falk together."

CHAPTER THIRTY-ONE

In the hopes that they would better blend
into Falk's neighborhood, Desiree changed
into one of her simpler, looser garments and
sturdy walking boots and managed to dig
up some older, rougher clothes of Brock's
for Tom to wear. Tom was leery of taking an
elegant town carriage and matched pair of
grays into the Whitechapel area, but Desiree
pointed out that they would be unlikely to
find a hackney willing to take them there,
let alone hang about waiting for them to
return. Besides, their experience last night
had given Desiree a healthy distrust of any
conveyance but her own.

Merriwell let them out well before they
reached Falk's headquarters. The streets
were becoming too narrow to navigate suc-
cessfully and the vehicle was too tempting a
target. Desiree arranged to meet the carriage later, and she and Tom set off through
the crowded, twisting streets.

Finally, Desiree stopped and nodded at a building ahead of them, where a set of outside stairs curled up to the second floor. "That's where Falk's headquarters are now. See the man hanging about at the bottom of the stairs? That's one of Falk's men."

They walked up the street and turned toward the staircase. The man lounging beside it stepped in front of them. "Stop right there, mate. You can't —"

Tom grabbed the other man's arm, twisted it up behind his back and shoved the guard aside. He charged up the stairs, Desiree right after him. Below them, the big man bellowed. " 'Ere! You can't go in there!"

He ran up the stairs after them. Tom whirled and punched him in the mouth. The man fell and tumbled down several steps. Behind him, Desiree opened the door, and they darted inside. Desiree slammed the door and locked it behind them.

"Hey!" Falk jumped up from his chair behind the desk. "What the hell do you think you're doing?"

"This." Tom grabbed the other man by his lapels and slammed him back into the wall. "Stop sending men after Desiree! The next time your men show up, I'm going to meet them with a gun." He pulled Falk back slightly and slammed him into the wall again. "Then I'm coming after you! Am I clear?"

Tom released Falk and took a step back. Falk straightened his jacket with a jerk.

"Bloody hell! What is the matter with you?" Falk turned to Desiree. "I didn't send anybody to attack you! Why would I do that?" He shrugged, turning his hands palm up in a gesture of innocence.

"Are you trying to tell me that wasn't your man who tried to steal the box from us?" Desiree crossed her arms.

"Oh, that." Falk shrugged. "Bert's a fool. The envelope wouldn't have been in your mother's old house, now would it?"

"I don't have your stupid envelope!" Desiree exclaimed. "I told you. I didn't find it. I didn't steal it."

"Then who does?" Falk shot back.

"I don't know. But it isn't me."

"Well." Falk studied her. "Then what the hell are you looking for?"

"That is none of your business," Desiree retorted.

A loud banging began on the door, accompanied by loud shouts to open up.

"Look." Tom moved in closer, his face fierce. "I don't give a damn about this bloody envelope. I'm telling you — don't come near Desiree again. You hurt her, and

I will *end* you."

"Hurt her!" Falk widened his eyes innocently. "I wouldn't hurt my little Dezzy."

"No? Sending some ruffian with a knife isn't hurting her?" Tom snapped.

Falk gaped at him. "What? What knife?" He looked toward Desiree. "What's he talking about? I never did that."

"I guess you didn't kidnap us last night and chase us all over the docks, either."

"Chase you! Hell!" Falk snorted. "Those were my men that saved your hides last night!"

"You expect me to —" Tom started, but Desiree stepped forward, putting a hand on his arm.

"Wait." She stared intently at Falk. "That wasn't your man who attacked me in my studio?"

"I don't know what the devil you're talking about," Falk shot back. "Yes, I had you followed. I knew you two were up to something. And you ought to be glad I did, or my men wouldn't have been there last night. But I never sent a man to attack you. What would be the point in that?"

Tom glanced at Desiree and she gave him a nod.

"Really?" Tom asked her. "You believe him?"

"Yes, I think I do. Somebody did help us last night."

"Then who the devil is after you?" Tom asked Desiree. Ignoring the continued pounding on the door, he swung toward Falk. "Why are you looking for this will?"

"Somebody paid me, what d'you think? I didn't even know the bloody thing was a will." He addressed himself to Desiree and said, "I told you everything I know about it. A document from this lawyer, name of Blackstock, in the Moreland office. I don't know anything else."

"Who hired you?" Desiree asked.

"I can't go giving out names like that!" Falk protested. "I have a reputation!"

"The only reputation you have is for dirty dealings. Give me the name." Tom stared at him flatly. "I would welcome any opportunity to pay you back, so if I were you, I'd start talking."

Falk sighed theatrically. "Oh, very well. Lloyd Paxton hired me."

Falk's answer was so far from anything Desiree had expected that it took a moment for his words to sink in. "Paxton? What does Paxton have to do with it?"

"And why the hell would Lloyd Paxton come to you?" Tom added.

"Oh, old Pax and I go way back," Falk

said with a sly smile. "I knew 'em both, him and his *noble* friend. Your da was more of a stickler, Dez, but Pax always liked his fun. Hadn't seen the man in an age before this. They say Pax stopped his gambling and whoring." He shrugged. "More's the pity."

"Why does Paxton want Alistair More-land's will?" Tom asked.

Falk shrugged. "I don't ask my customers why. I just ask how much they're willing to pay to get it."

"Of course you do," Tom said in disgust.

Desiree studied Falk for a moment. "What are you not telling us?" He was a difficult man to read. Lies and subterfuge were so much a part of his reality that they didn't stand out; it was like finding something in the dark. Still, she was certain that he was concealing something; the glee he took in such things was palpable.

"I don't know what you're talking about."

"You know something else," Desiree insisted. "What is it?"

"I know lots of things," Falk said smugly. "But it takes money to find out."

"I don't know," Tom retorted, grasping the other man's shirt front in one hand, his other hand doubling into a fist. "I think it might just take a few bruises." He turned to Desiree. "What do you think?"

"He's not worth the effort," Desiree said. "I want to talk to Lloyd Paxton."

Outside the door, there was a sudden silence. Falk gave them a wicked smile. "One thing you didn't plan on — there's a spare key to the office. Don't worry, Desiree, like I said, I wouldn't hurt you." His malicious gaze went to Tom. "Now, Tom Quick is a different matter."

Desiree's senses were fully open, and she had already registered that the danger outside the door was growing. She cast her gaze all around the walls. There would be another way out; Falk always had one. And there it was — a thin line of light on the wall to their right. A door-shaped line of light. She ran to the low table that stood in front of it and yanked it back. As she suspected, it was fastened to the wall, and as she pulled the table, a section of the wall opened with it. As Falk stared at her with a stunned look on his face, Tom joined her. Desiree flashed her former boss a smile. "Surely you didn't think I wouldn't find your getaway door."

Desiree closed the slender section of wall after them just as the outer door crashed open. Tom had already lit a match, and they went down the stairs in its feeble light. At the bottom, a section of wooden wall opened beneath Tom's push and they emerged into an alleyway so narrow that Tom's shoulders brushed it on either side as they ran. The corridor ended at another lane, and they turned, walking quickly in the opposite direction from Falk's office.

Desiree took a complicated route back to their carriage, but they saw no sign of any pursuers. When Tom expressed surprise, Desiree said, "Falk might not even tell them where we went. I'm sure he doesn't want anyone to know his secret entrance."

Tom laughed. "How did *you* know it was there?"

"Falk always has a back door," she replied. "I could see that something about that wall was at odds with the rest of it. The wall looked smooth, but in reality, there was a crack there, a door-shaped crack. Its 'truth' didn't match its appearance. The truth looks sharp and bright to me. It was like a line of light outlined the door in my mind. It's very like the way I 'see' that a person's words aren't in line with reality."

"You actually saw the crack in the wall?"

"Not in the same way I'm seeing you. I see it in my mind. If I asked you to think of someone — the duchess, say — you could picture her in your head even though you couldn't physically see her. That's how I saw the hidden door."

"What about what you did last night? How did you know that the wall wouldn't collapse or where we should climb?"

How was she to explain her odd ability to Tom? He had accepted her skill at detecting lies and dangers from people. But communing with the world around her? She didn't understand it herself. "I cast out my senses, looking for the possibilities of escape, the places where an abnormality can help me or hurt me. If something is useful to me, a good possibility, I see light on it. That's what I got from that wall we walked across. But if it's a negative possibility, a danger, it's dark, not dark like the nighttime, but more like a void. When we jumped that street, I knew we could do it because I could see the line of light stretching across it."

To her relief, Tom didn't look unbelieving; he merely nodded thoughtfully, as if filing away the knowledge. He was quiet the rest of the way to their carriage at the arranged meeting place, but after they settled into their seats, Tom asked, "What is it that you think Falk knows?"

Desiree shook her head. "I'm not sure. But I am certain there was something he wasn't telling us. He's hoping we'll pay him to find out. He might know something important about my parents' leaving. Both Mrs. McGee and Pax said Falk hung around my mother's house a great deal. He could have overheard or seen something."

"Hopefully we'll get some answers out of Paxton," Tom said. "This puts him right back into the list of suspects."

"Yes. I didn't understand that flash of something being 'off' with him when we first met him, then changing so quickly. But I realize now that his reaction wasn't to me or my situation. It was when you introduced yourself. Your name, the agency's name, alarmed him. But that went away when he realized we were there about an entirely different matter."

"I'm not so sure that your father's name is a different matter. Paxton and Gregory are both looking for what is presumably a will written by your father. You're looking for him. Maybe you were right, and he *is* back in England."

"Writing wills and spying on me?"

"It makes no sense," Tom agreed. "But maybe that's what you're supposed to do. Make sense of it."

The carriage rolled up in front of Paxton's house, and as they disembarked, they saw Lloyd Paxton coming out his front door.

He stopped when he saw them, saying, "You again?"

"Yes, we have a few more questions. It shouldn't take long," Desiree told him.

Paxton hesitated for a moment, then let out a sigh and said, "Come in, then." He led them into the house but remained standing. "I can't stay long. I have an appointment later this morning."

"It will be quick if you tell us why you want Alistair Moreland's will."

Desiree saw the same panicked shift in Paxton that had been there briefly before, but this time it clung to him, blurring and darkening the edges of his being. "How could you — I don't know what you're talking about."

"We just talked to Falk," Tom told him. "So we know you hired him to break into our office to take that envelope. You needn't worry that you're going to be involved in a theft or any other scandal. We just want to understand why Miss Malone has been caught up in it."

"I say, young man, this is a damned impertinence. It's none of your business," Paxton blustered, but he could not maintain his belligerence, and he sagged, resignation in his face. "But I suppose it will be common news anyway if the will goes into probate. Alistair apparently wrote a new will before he went away, and he left it with his lawyer. I knew he had planned to, but I wasn't sure he'd gotten around to it before he took off."

"What was in it?" Desiree asked gently. There was such a look of defeat on his face that she could not help but feel some sympathy for the man.

"Alistair was supposed to leave me a piece of property. I was in something of a bind, you see. Gambling debts, so of course I had to pay — gentleman's honor and all that. Alistair bought some land from me because I needed the money. The place had been in my family for years, so it was a bit hard to let go of it, but I had nothing else that was worth enough money. Alistair was such a decent chap that he said he would leave the property to me when he died so that it would come back to my family."

"Why are you looking for the will now? Why not back when he disappeared?" Tom asked.

"Well, it wouldn't have been any use to me back then, would it? Alistair was alive. But now that his son means to have him declared dead, it's different. Besides, I didn't know it even existed until that Blackstock fellow wrote me."

"What did Blackstock's letter say? Did he tell you what was in the will?"

"No. Only said that he'd sent it to Moreland's business. Well, at first I thought he must have meant Alistair's man of business, but he knew nothing about it. Then I realized he must have meant your agency. Makes sense, when you think about it."

"Why?"

"There must have been something haveycavey going on, wouldn't you think? Otherwise, why not send the thing to Alistair's heir? Clearly, he was suspicious that something would happen to the will if he sent it to Gregory. He'd kept it secret all these years. There must have been something he didn't want out. And why else would the letter have all that about him dying and his guilt."

"Blackstock was feeling guilty? Of what?" Tom asked.

Paxton shrugged. "He was very vague about it all. And his writing was little more than a scrawl, deuced difficult to read. But he said he was dying and he wanted to clear his conscience. There was something about betraying his word to his client."

"Did you keep that letter?" Tom asked, remembering Paxton's behavior with Alistair's earlier letter.

"I did." Paxton gave him a smug look. He stood up and left the room, returning moments later with a folded note, which he handed to Desiree.

Desiree read through the single page, frowning, and finally said, "He's right. It is difficult to read. And that's just about all Blackstock says. He wants to make things right before he dies. He's sending it to the Moreland business. There's another word or two in there, but it's smeared so much I can't read it." She handed the note to Tom for him to scan it, as well. Turning to Mr. Paxton, she said, "You didn't have a man follow us a few days ago?"

"No. I'd never even seen you before you popped up at my door asking questions. And what good would it do to follow you? Why would you have the will?"

"Why, indeed," Desiree murmured.

Paxton stood up, holding out his hand for the letter. "And now, if you will excuse me, I must go."

"One last question," Tom said. "Something you said the other day has been nagging at me. You said you talked to Alistair one evening, and the next day you went over to the house, and the housekeeper told you they had left."

"That's correct," Paxton replied impatiently.

"But Mrs. McGee said that Stella and Alistair left the day *before* you came to the house."

"Then she's wrong. I'm certain I went there the day they left."

"How can you be so sure? As you said, it was many years ago."

"Because it was my birthday! Not something one's likely to forget. That's why I went to the house that day. We were going to celebrate my birthday. That's what Alistair and I were talking about the night before. He didn't say a word about going to the cottage. It was deuced peculiar. That's why I was a bit alarmed at first. But then I got his letter. I suppose in all the excitement of running off, Alistair just forgot." There was a wisp of hurt in his voice. He turned away and went to the door.

"Wait." The steady, low twist of anxiety inside Desiree's chest suddenly tightened. She hurried after Paxton. "The cottage."

"Yes?" Paxton opened the front door and turned to her, raising a brow.

Desiree ignored his obvious impatience. This sudden insistent tug in her chest was too important for politeness. "The cottage where they were supposedly going — do you

476

know where it is?"

"Oh, yes, Alistair and I went there sometimes after he married Tabitha. Alistair loved
it, but I found it boring. Nothing much to
do but sit up there on the cliff looking at
the ocean."

"Does his family still use it?"

"No, I think not. Tabitha despised it . . .
stands to reason since he used to take Stella
there. I don't know, but my guess is it's been
abandoned."

"Where is it exactly?"

Paxton gaped. "You want to go there? It's
not an inviting place."

"Still, I'd like to see it." Desiree gave him
her most winning smile. "Please tell me."

"It's on the Dorset coast. Um, its name
is . . . Sea View? No, odder than that — Sea
Gift. That's it. There's a little village close
by — I'm not sure, Red something, or
maybe it's something Red. Anyway, it's not
far from Abbotsbury. Sorry." Paxton
shrugged, looking faintly apologetic. "It's
been a long time. It was a dreadfully dull
little place."

"Thank you. You've been very helpful."

They left the house, and Paxton hurried
off down the street. Desiree turned to Tom.
"I want to go to that cottage."

"Why? What are you thinking?" Tom asked

as they got into the carriage. "We're not even sure they went there."

"I know, but I still want to see it. When he mentioned the cottage, I felt something." Desiree's hand tightened into a fist, and she tapped it against her chest. "Here. That cottage is calling to me."

CHAPTER THIRTY-TWO

"Calling to you?" Tom took her hand, seeing her obvious distress and wishing he could stop it. "What do you mean?"

"The feeling has been inside me for weeks, and it's been building."

"Your premonition."

"Yes, urgency, nerves, dread . . . whatever you want to call it. It's never gone away, only increased. It sits there in my chest, a constant hum underneath everything I feel. Like a banked fire. But this afternoon, it flared up when Paxton spoke of the cottage, and as I talked to him about it, that feeling burned hotter and brighter. It pulls at me." Desiree gazed intently into his eyes. "It's as if a hand has taken hold of my dress and is tugging at me, urging me to go with it."

"What does it want?"

"I wish I knew." Desiree sighed and slumped back against the cushions. "I've never felt anything quite like that before. I know none of this is logical or proof of anything, but I cannot help but feel it's important."

"Logical or not, I trust your instincts," Tom said. "Let's go back to the office and figure this out."

Returning to the office hadn't been what Tom had been anticipating doing with Desiree this afternoon. But he put aside the lustful visions that had teased at his brain all morning — they had all afternoon, after all — and when the carriage came to a stop in front of his building, they went to the agency office. It was much safer than his flat, with its nearby bed.

"I'm not sure going to the cottage will be of any help," Desiree began, sitting down in the chair by his desk. "If this is a premonition, I wish it would be a trifle more specific."

"That would be helpful." Tom smiled at her. "But the cottage plays a part in the story. There's something odd about your parents' leaving. Mrs. McGee seemed very certain of the day your mother left. But Paxton says they couldn't have gone that afternoon because he was with Alistair that evening."

"I believe Paxton," Desiree said. "He certainly was not lying, and though he

480

doesn't seem the most reliable man, a person does tend to remember his own birthday."

"I believe him, as well. So why the discrepancy? Why would Alistair still have been in the city after Mrs. McGee saw them leave?"

"They could have spent the night in London and left the next day," Desiree responded.

"Would you hang about in London an extra day if you're planning to flee the country? Or even if you're going to a cottage by the sea?" Tom said.

"Especially since you would run the risk of being seen by someone you know, like Paxton," Desiree agreed.

"Mrs. McGee didn't really see them leave," Tom pointed out after a moment's thought. "What she *saw* was your mother getting into Alistair's carriage. She only assumed Alistair was in it because Stella said she was leaving with him."

"Yes." Desiree perked up. "Alistair could have sent the carriage to take Stella to the cottage, and he went by train the next day."

"But why would Alistair invite his good friend Pax to Stella's house the next evening — for a birthday celebration, no less?"

A frown creased Desiree's forehead. "It makes me wonder even more whether Mrs.

McGee was right, that maybe Alistair did kill my mother. He could have planned to do away with Stella that night, and then the next evening arrive at the house when Paxton would be there and could attest to Alistair's surprise at not finding Stella at home."

"Then why didn't he show up? Why set up an elaborate scheme and not finish it?" Tom countered.

Desiree nodded thoughtfully. "And there would still be another problem — Mrs. McGee saw Stella leave in his carriage."

"And I'm not sure he would have had time to do all the running about that scheme would entail and still manage to get back to London to meet Pax at the appointed hour."

"Maybe that is what happened. He murdered her and afterward realized that he couldn't return in time to establish his alibi. So he ran," Desiree said.

"Either way, if Paxton is right and no one's been there since that time, it's possible we could find something at the cottage that would prove your parents were there. If they left from the cottage, there could even be a clue as to where they planned to go."

"There's another thing," Desiree said. "I know you don't believe that my father has returned and that he was in the carriage that night, watching the house."

"It's not that I don't believe you. I just think it's unlikely."

"I know. And you're probably right. No one has seen him. He hasn't tried to contact me or my brothers. But there's his carriage. And the cuff links. Maybe he's trying to hide from everyone. And where would be a more perfect place to hide than a cottage by the sea that no one ever goes to?"

"Why would he be hiding?"

"I don't know. Maybe he killed my mother, whether accidentally or on purpose, and he fled. Or they ran away, and she has now died, and he wanted to come back, but he doesn't want to have to face the mess he left behind. Or maybe the two of them wanted to return, but still want to live together in secret."

"It's certainly possible," Tom admitted. "If he returned, it might explain why there's suddenly a new will. Perhaps everyone has misunderstood that lawyer's letter, and it was Alistair himself that Blackstock sent the will to. It all sounds like something out of Dickens, but then, this entire thing has been rather outlandish."

"Maybe that's the goal of my premonition. To find them or to find out what happened or where they went."

"Then I'd say we need to investigate the cottage."

"Do you have a map?"

"Con does." Tom went to one of the cabinets and returned with a rolled-up map, which he spread out on his desk. "Here's Dorset. We know the cottage is on the coast."

"Near Abbotsbury," Desiree added.

"Right, here's Abbotsbury, near Weymouth. Where's a village named Red something, or something Red . . ."

"Ha!" Desiree stabbed the map with her forefinger. "Redham."

Tom grinned. "We can take the train to Weymouth, and from there we can hire a vehicle to drive the rest of the way." He frowned up at the clock on the wall. "If we hurry, we might be able to still catch a train." He stopped. "That is, I mean, if that is all right with you. We'd have to spend the night there."

"I don't mind spending the night there." Desiree moved closer, a slow smile curving her lips.

"Your brothers might take exception to it."

"My brothers have nothing to do with it." Desiree curled her arms loosely around his neck, her eyes warm on his face. "But I think I'm not in favor of rushing off to Weymouth right now."

"No?" Tom rested his hands on her waist.

"No. I have very different plans for this afternoon." Desiree went on tiptoe to brush her lips against his.

"Really." His hands slid around to her back, tugging her closer, and he returned her soft kiss. "What did you have in mind?"

"Oh . . . something that involved your bed." Her hands slid down his chest to the buttons of his waistcoat. "And nakedness."

"Mm. Sounds like an excellent plan." He kissed her again, his body instantly aflame. Tom sank back down into his chair, pulling Desiree into his lap, as they continued to kiss. With one arm around her back for support, his other hand was free to roam over her body. "Wait." He lifted his head and drew a shaky breath. "We can't — not here. Someone could walk in at any moment."

"Lock the door," she murmured, continuing her assault on his buttons.

"Con has a key."

"Blast." Desiree dropped her head to Tom's shoulder with a sigh, then stood up. "I suggest we repair to your flat. As quickly as possible."

"No argument here." Tom followed her out the door and up the stairs. They stopped midway up for another kiss. This time it was Desiree who pulled away and started up again. He followed, enjoying the view from behind her.

At the door, there was a bit of fumbling with the key, exacerbated by the fact that Desiree was distracting him by undoing the diagonal line of buttons that slashed across the front of her dress. But the key finally went in and turned, and they hurried into the room. Tom had enough presence of mind to pull the key from the door and close it, though he could not take his eyes off Desiree.

Desiree turned to face him as she finished the task of unbuttoning her dress. Reaching behind her, she pulled open the sash. It was another of those marvelous dresses that wrapped around her, secured in the back by her sash, so that now the front fell apart, its loosened folds revealing a center strip of frothy white underclothes.

Tom shoved the door closed and strode to her, ripping off his jacket and tossing it aside. He slid his hands beneath the sides of her dress, pushing the cloth apart as his hands roamed over her. Desiree's color was high, her eyes bright, and the signs of her passion stoked his own. His body throbbed with the need to be inside her, but Tom leashed that hunger, determined to take his time and enjoy every bit of pleasure possible.

He grasped the sides of her dress and pulled it down, letting it fall to the floor. The sight of her in the demure white underwear, edged with lace and held fast only by satin ribbons, stirred him beyond reason. Tom traced the circle of her nipples, thinly veiled by the cotton cloth, feeling them pebble beneath his fingers.

Desiree watched him, neither pulling away nor coming closer, her eyes darkening, her mouth turning heavy with desire, and he knew she enjoyed his eyes on her. She reached up and pulled the pins from her hair, letting the rich caramel strands fall one by one until her hair tumbled down over her shoulders and brushed against his fingers, sending a shiver through him. He had to fight back a primitive urge to rip the garment from her.

Instead, he took the end of the slick ribbon at the neck of her chemise and pulled the bow apart, feeling like a man opening a long-awaited present. Her chemise slipped down, revealing the top of her dark rose nipples and clinging to the hardened tips. Tom ran his fingers over the curve of one breast, and finally hooked his finger in the neckline and slowly slid the garment down, the material caressing her as it went.

Almost reverently, he cupped her breasts in his hands, his thumbs stroking lightly over her nipples. "Beautiful," he murmured, then pulled the garment lower, sliding it all the way down to her waist. He went next to the ties of her petticoat and underpants, undressing her bit by bit, his fingers lingering over the process as he feasted on her with his eyes, until at last there was nothing left but the last garments of her stockings and shoes.

Lust nearly choking him at the picture she presented, Tom went down on one knee to unfasten the ties of her half boots. She lifted her foot, putting her fingertips on his shoulder for balance, and he pulled off the boot, then rolled down the white stocking and removed it. He did the same with the other leg. He rose to his feet, his body aching from pent-up hunger.

But when he reached for her, Desiree put a halting hand on his chest and said, "Now it's my turn."

Tom swallowed. He hadn't thought he could be any harder, but he was learning new capacities for desire, his flesh straining against the cloth of his trousers. He swept his arms out to the sides in a gesture of invitation. Desiree smiled and began to undress him.

She started in reverse order, kneeling at his feet to remove his shoes and socks. Tom clung to the rapidly dissolving tethers of his control as he watched her. She went to work on his remaining clothes, taking what seemed to Tom to be an inordinately long time to do so. He shrugged off his waistcoat as she went to work on his shirt.

"No, no," she scolded in a teasing voice, pressing her lips to the bare skin that showed between the sides of his shirt. "Mustn't do that." She paused to look up at him, her eyes glinting. "This is all mine, remember?" She pushed his shirt back, exposing his whole chest, and kissed one nipple. "All mine." She kissed the other.

Slowly, delicately, she worked her way across his chest, kissing, licking, nipping. Her hands went to his waistband, but instead of releasing the flesh straining against the cloth, she ran her finger down the line of buttons, making him swell even more.

At last she began to undo the buttons, lingering on the process. Then, grasping the waistband, she pulled down his clothes and took him in her hands. Tom hissed as the spasms of pleasure went through him.

"Did I hurt you?" Desiree asked anxiously.

"No. God, no," Tom murmured, leaning his head against hers as his hands slid up and down her arms. "Your touch is . . . beyond pleasurable."

He tilted her face up and kissed her, his mouth telling her better than words the wild feelings that rippled through him. Finally, he broke from her, his voice hoarse. "Enough. I have to be inside you. Now."

Kicking off the garments that had fallen to his ankles, he lifted her up, and Desiree wrapped her legs around him, so that his pulsing member was pressed against the very place he most desired to be, slick and hot. Tom kissed her neck and shoulders as he walked almost blindly to the bed, and they fell onto it.

He pushed inside her at once, too far gone in his passion to tease either of them any longer, and Desiree responded with the same frenzied eagerness. Her nails raked his back as he began to move, his strokes deep and smooth, until at last his climax rolled over him like thunder. Tom cried out, feeling Desiree clamp tightly around him, her own release rippling through her.

Tom sank onto the bed, wrapping his arms around her and pulling her over onto him. He lay there panting, her head resting over his heart, her hair spreading over his chest and arm. And he knew, with his body as much as his mind, that he could not live without this woman.

CHAPTER THIRTY-THREE

Desiree awakened the following morning in a buoyant mood. She rose and put on the plain dark carriage dress she wore for traveling, and did up her hair in a simple style — her mind on tonight and the ease with which such a style could be undone.

She wanted, of course, to discover whatever she could about her parents at the cottage; the compelling pull inside her was impossible to ignore. But she could not help but look forward, as well, to the night before her, when she and Tom could be alone, free to be together the entire night without considerations of family or any other obligations. For precisely that opportunity, she had been sure to pack her laciest, most beguiling nightgown.

Downstairs, she was pleased to find Brock at the breakfast table. She had not seen him the night before, so she had yet to tell him the discoveries they had made. He listened, frowning, as she described what she and Tom had done the day before (leaving out, of course, the most personal details).

"Desiree, I'm not sure what you think you're going to find out," he said when she finished. "It all sounds most peculiar, I'll admit, but . . ."

"I know. I realize we may not discover anything that will help us, but I can't just sit here and do nothing. I would always wonder what we might have found."

"Yes, but traveling alone with Quick . . ." He scowled. "You do understand how it will look, don't you?"

Desiree cocked an eyebrow. "Yes. Scandalous. But when have I ever been anything but scandalous? I've spent my entire adult life being chaste, but you know good and well that everyone already assumes that I'm a scarlet woman. I'm sorry, but I'm not a lady, Brock, however much you wanted me to be one."

"Desiree, no," Brock said, taken aback. "I have never wanted you to be anything but exactly what you want. I didn't send you to finishing school because I wanted to mold you into a lady. I wanted to give you the opportunity to . . . to enter the world that you deserve, the one that should be yours by birth. You *are* a lady and my much-loved sister, and I would never regard you as anything but that. If you want Quick, then that is what I want for you. He doesn't deserve you, but I can't think of any man who would. I just don't want you to get hurt. I don't want you to be disappointed."

"I won't be disappointed," Desiree told him. "Do you honestly think I'm not capable of catching the man I set my cap for?"

Brock had to smile. "Well, no, not when you put it that way."

"That's why I'd like you to do something for me, if you would."

"What?" He looked wary.

"Nothing horrid." Desiree laughed. "Do you have a pencil and paper?" Her brother reached into an inside pocket and handed her a small notebook and a pencil stub, and Desiree opened it to the first blank page and began to write. "I want you to look at this for me. You know a good deal more about this sort of thing than I. I want it, but I'd like to make sure it's a good investment."

Brock looked at what she had written, and his brows sailed upward. "Are you serious?"

"Yes." She leaned forward. "I know, Brock. I know in here." Desiree tapped her closed fist over her heart. "He is the only man for me."

494

Her brother looked at her for a long moment, then said, "I told you I remember him from the days with Falk."

"Yes."

"What I didn't tell you was that I saw it — I knew he was important, valuable, somehow to you. I thought it was something that would happen back then, something immediate. But I saw it again the day you brought him here."

"Why didn't you tell me?" Desiree asked, puzzled.

"I didn't want to influence you. I didn't want you to think that this was preordained. I'm — it's easy to let what I see rule me. I'm not sure I can trust it."

"Even after all this time?"

Brock nodded. "Yes. And when it concerns you, I must be especially careful. I don't want to make a mistake."

"Well, this is no mistake," Desiree told him, putting her hand over his on the table. "I'm certain, Brock. I love him. And it's for life."

When Desiree arrived at Tom's office an hour later, he greeted her with a long, burning kiss.

"Well," Desiree said when at last he lifted his head. "That's quite a hello."

"Good morning," he offered and smiled, taking her hand. "I've been thinking about that since I woke up this morning."

"I'm glad. *I've* been thinking about to-night."

Light flared in his eyes. "That, too." He cleared his throat and stepped away. "I checked the schedule. There's a train to Weymouth at eleven. That gives us enough time to see Falk first."

"Falk? Why?"

"You said he knew something more than he told us. I'd really like to know what it is."

"Even if we have to pay him?" Desiree asked.

Tom grimaced. "Maybe. I was hopeful, though, that if we asked him some more specific things about your parents, like what day they left, whether they left together, or what he saw or overheard, you might be able to get some idea of what he's hiding. At least enough to know whether his information is valuable enough to pay the crook."

"It's worth a try," Desiree agreed.

As they rode to Falk's office, Desiree's stomach began to knot. She assumed her anxiety arose from her desire to find the cottage, but as they walked toward Falk's employee at the foot of the stairs, a sharp frisson of alarm shot through her, and it occurred to her that perhaps her dark feeling was about something else altogether.

"We need to see Falk," she told the guard abruptly.

The man was the one they had encountered yesterday, and he regarded her with a sour expression. "He's not in yet."

Desiree turned to Tom. "Something's wrong. Falk's always here early, taking in last night's receipts."

"You mean, you're having —" Tom began, but Desiree didn't answer. She was already running up the stairs to Falk's office. Tom followed her, and after a moment, the guard climbed after them. She grabbed the door handle, but it would not turn.

Dread was humming in Desiree now. She squatted down to peer through the keyhole. "I can't see. It's locked from the inside." She stood up and looked at the guard. "Did you knock?"

"Aye. I ain't stupid. That's how I knew he weren't here."

Tom banged loudly on the door. "Falk! Open up!"

"We need to get inside," Desiree said sharply.

Tom reached into his pocket and extracted his case of tools, then squatted down and

497

went to work. "There, knocked the key out." He peered through the hole. "But I can't see anything except the opposite wall." He went back to his picks.

"The boss isn't going to like this," their companion said, shifting on his feet and glancing around.

"Blame it on me," Tom told him and turned the handle. He opened the door and stepped inside, but he stopped abruptly, stretching out his arm to hold back Desiree.

It was too late for that. Over his arm she could clearly see Falk seated at the desk. He was slumped in his chair, his head hanging down, a black hole in his temple and blood streaking the side of his face. To her eyes, tendrils of darkness curled all around him. Desiree's stomach lurched. Behind her, Falk's guard let out an oath.

"He never shot himself, did he?" the man said in shocked tones.

"I seriously doubt it, though I think perhaps the killer may have hoped it would look that way if they locked the door from the inside." Tom moved forward and crouched down beside the chair. "Yes, here's a gun on the floor."

"But how they'd get out, then?" the guard asked, a frown creasing his forehead.

"Same way we did yesterday. He has —

had — another exit," Desiree replied, swallowing the gorge that rose in her throat. The scene in front of her was so dark and fractured that she felt dizzy. She made no move to go closer to Tom and the body.

Tom nodded. "It would have to be someone who knew about his secret entrance." He stood up and turned toward Falk's man. "You better go tell a bobby."

"A blue bottle?" The man stared, apparently as aghast at this idea as he was at Falk's death. "Are you cracked?" He hung there for a moment, then said in a relieved tone, "I'll go find Trotter."

After the man left, Tom looked over the desk, then opened drawers and rummaged around in them.

"What are you looking for?"

"Not sure. Some reason why he was shot," Tom replied.

"There are any number of reasons to shoot Falk," Desiree retorted, adding shakily, "but I think it was because of our search."

Tom nodded grimly. "Something about this information Falk was hiding would be my guess. He could have tried to sell it to someone who didn't want to pay the price. Or someone was afraid he'd sell it to us instead." Tom shut the last drawer and looked speculatively at the hidden door. "It would have to have been someone very close to him for him to reveal that escape hatch."

"I'm not sure Falk had anyone that close to him. But I figured out where it was. Others could have, too."

"Or he could have told someone who conducted business with him, someone who would be embarrassed to be seen coming in the front. A gentleman, say."

"Like Paxton," Desiree said.

"Or Gregory. We know Falk was into blackmail. Or perhaps Falk actually found that will and was withholding it for more money."

Desiree looked once more at Falk's lifeless body. "I don't even know what to feel. I've always hated the man. He was despicable. But it's so awful, seeing him there. I feel guilty for all the times I wished he was dead. It's not something I really meant."

"Of course not." Tom curled his arm around her shoulders, turning her away from the sight. "Even though his absence will only improve the world, no one had the right to kill him. But perhaps if we can figure this out, it might lead us to his murderer."

Desiree nodded. "You're right."

"We should go. We'll miss our train if we

have to stay and talk to the police. There's nothing we can tell them that they can't see for themselves, and we can always go to them when we get back. And if this Trotter fellow decides to do something besides call the police, it's just as well not to know about it."

"Yes, you're right." Desiree looked up at him, her hand going to her stomach. "It's urgent, Tom. We must get to that cottage. Now."

There was no possibility of getting there quickly, for the train rumbled along at its own speed, and it was teatime before they arrived in Weymouth. They had planned to spend the night here and go to the cottage the next morning, but Desiree could not wait. The urgency in her chest had been growing the entire trip, and now the pull from the cottage was too strong to resist.

"We have to get there as soon as possible," she told Tom.

He glanced at the sky. "It's summer. The days are long. It will be hours before complete darkness falls. Let's rent a trap and drive on to Redham."

The trap seemed impossibly slow, and the knot in Desiree's chest tightened with every mile. They had not yet reached Redham when they met a farmer driving his cart in the other direction, and they stopped to ask for directions to Alistair's cottage.

"Oh, aye, Sea Gift, that's Lord Moreland's place. It's 'fore you get to town. Only another mile or so. But there's nothing there to see. It's just been sitting there for years now, and it's a ruin."

"Yes, but we really need to go there," Tom told him, and with a shrug the man gave them detailed instructions of where to turn off the road, and Tom was able to follow them to a narrow lane that was rough and pocked with holes. A house came into view in the distance, sitting at the edge of the cliff. Every nerve in Desiree's body shivered to life.

As they drew closer, they could see that the farmer had not exaggerated the house's condition. Though the cottage had not collapsed, it had been worn by time and the salt air. It was small, and Desiree suspected that if it had been repaired and painted, it might have a certain cozy charm. As it was, it looked desolate, an impression that was not helped by the barren landscape around it. There were a few trees in front of the house, stunted and bent by the constant sea wind. Beyond the cliff was a gray expanse of ocean.

The house was gray and weathered, windows broken and shutters dangling or fallen. Two shallow steps led up to the cracked and weathered front door. Not far from one side of the house stood a rickety staircase leading down to the beach. A little farther along the cliff was a small shed, and attached to it was a wooden boxlike structure.

The entire scene was drenched in gloom, and Desiree's stomach knotted. She didn't want to be here, but she could not leave. This, she was certain, was where she was supposed to go.

"What is that?" Tom tied their horse to a stunted tree and walked over to the odd structure at the edge of the cliff. Desiree followed, grateful to put off entering the house for a moment.

The box seemed fastened to a set of rails, and it hung by a sturdy rope from the pulley above it. The rails were set all the way down the cliff, ending at the beach.

"It looks like a kind of lift to go down to the beach. Like a dumbwaiter," Desiree suggested.

"But inclined," Tom mused. "Like that funicular railway in Scarborough, only smaller and just one car." He gazed down at the rocky beach, where the sea surged and crashed around enormous rocks. "I wouldn't risk my life on it just to go down there."

"Mm. Not terribly inviting." She shivered, though it was not cold. "Nothing here is. This whole area reeks of something awful." She turned to face the house.

"You ready to go in?" Tom asked.

"No." Desiree stiffened her spine. "But I have to."

They walked toward the house, the urgency in Desiree growing with every step. Tom turned the rusty door handle, but he had to put his shoulder to the damp-warped door before it opened. They stepped inside. Sand had drifted in over all the floors and furniture. Both the front and side windows were broken out. There were stairs to the left, as well as a short hallway leading to what looked to be a kitchen and another room. The room where they stood ran the width of the house. A sturdy stone fireplace stood in the center of the outside wall. A caned-seat straight chair stood on one side of the fireplace. A small sofa and comfortable chair, along with a couple of small tables, were the only other furniture. In front of the fireplace was a large woven rug, its colors muted by the pervasive sand.

Despite the abandoned look of the place,

there was an eerie look to it, as if someone had just left. There were no dustcovers over the furniture, and the ragged curtains hung open. A teacup sat on a table by the sofa, and there was a hod half-full of coal beside the fireplace. A shiver ran down Desiree's spine.

Grit crunched beneath their feet as they walked through the room. Desiree went to the other window and looked out. The view it offered of the ocean and rocky beach was just as gray and grim as that in front of the house. "This hardly seems an ideal love nest."

"Presumably it looked more pleasant at the time." Tom went to the fireplace and picked up the poker. "Look, there are still ashes in the fireplace. I mean, obviously most of it's been blown about, but it's . . ." His voice trailed off as he shoved the ashes around.

"What?" Desiree joined him in front of the fireplace. The house was sad and cold, and the urgency inside her bubbled up, ever stronger. "What did you find?"

"I don't know. There are a couple of chunks of something. They're scorched but not completely burned." Tom dragged a blackened piece forward with the poker and bent to pick it up. He brushed away the ashes covering it. "It's metal. Looks like a clasp, perhaps?"

"A clasp?" Desiree's chest turned icy, and she had to force herself to breathe. "You mean, the sort that's on a portmanteau? Or a valise?"

Tom lifted his eyes to her, question mingling with trepidation. "Yes. Very like that." He stood up, holding out the object to her.

Desiree barely glanced at it, backing away from him. The alarm that had been growing in her all day was now clanging. Her words came in a whisper. "She was right. Mrs. McGee was right, wasn't she? Alistair killed my mother."

"We don't know that," Tom protested, pulling her close to him. "Here, now, you're trembling. That could have been attached to anything."

Desiree pulled back. "Such as? Someone just happened to burn something here twenty-eight years ago that looked remarkably like a clasp used on luggage?"

"You don't know when it was burned. The place has been abandoned for years. Vagrants could have camped here anytime. Twenty-eight years is a very long time for ashes to remain."

"You don't need to sugarcoat things for me, Tom. I'd rather know the truth, no matter how terrible it is. This is why I've been feeling this sense of disaster! That's why it's so strong. Don't you see?"

"Yes, I see. I just don't want you to . . ."

"Be hurt?"

"Yes," Tom admitted.

"I'm already hurt. I was hurt twenty-eight years ago when my mother was taken from me. I never got to know her. But at least now I know why. It fits, Tom — you have to agree it all fits. Why a woman who by all accounts loved her children left them without a word. Why a woman went away on a weekend trip with her lover and never returned. Why she didn't take her most precious jewels and keepsakes. Why she left with only a single piece of luggage. There was no letter from Stella saying that she had fled to America, only Alistair's note to his good chum Pax, a man who would of course believe him. My father murdered her."

"How can you be certain of that?" He took her shoulders, staring intently into her eyes. "Is it your brain talking or your inner sense?"

Desiree opened her mouth to speak, then stopped abruptly. "I'm not sure." She looked away, her hand going to her stomach. She didn't feel satisfied. There was no sense that it was over. The urgency still pulsed in her, tugging her away.

"Desiree? What is it? What's going on?"

"I'm not sure." She looked at him, her eyes wide. "I think there's more. I — I need to go somewhere else." Desiree started toward the door.

"Where?" Tom followed her, reaching out to pull the door open for her.

They froze, staring at the scene in front of them. Another carriage had pulled up beside theirs, an odd, low-seated vehicle. And a woman was striding from it toward them.

"Tabitha!"

"That's Lady Moreland to you." Tabitha stopped a few feet away from them. Her hair was in a neat bun beneath a small fashionable hat, and her gray suit with black trim was stylish. The only thing odd about her appearance was the wild light in her eyes. And the revolver she pointed at Desiree.

CHAPTER THIRTY-FOUR

"Lady Moreland." Desiree wasn't about to argue with a woman holding a gun.

"Lady *Alistair* Moreland." Tabitha's voice held a note of pride. "I am his *wife*! She was never anything but a whore to him. I was the one he married. I was the one who bore his heir, who carried his name."

"Yes. You are." Desiree curled her fingers into fists, but she kept her face and voice cool and calm. Tabitha's inner image was so dark and incongruous with her outer self that it was jarring; Desiree could barely stand to look at her. What was wrong with this woman? What could possibly be in that will that was so important she would chase them down, waving a gun?

"Good afternoon, Lady Moreland," Tom said politely from where he stood behind Desiree. His fingers curled around Desiree's arm, and she knew he intended to pull her aside. His other hand was still holding the door. In a pleasant, conversational tone, he went on, "I see your carriage. Where is your driver?"

"I don't need him. As if I can't handle the reins myself! I am an excellent horsewoman and an excellent driver. My papa taught me. Just as he taught me to shoot."

"You're the one who was watching my house?" Desiree asked, frankly puzzled, but also understanding that Tom wanted to spin the conversation out, make the woman relax before he made his move. "Why?"

"Of course. I had to. You were stirring it all up. Poking your nose into everything. Dragging the Morelands into this. They're fools, just as he was. All the Morelands are soft. Now you've turned them against me. Against Gregory."

"I haven't —"

"Don't lie to me, you little doxy. I know you're a thief. I know you stole Alistair's will. Falk told me you did."

"I don't have your blasted will!" Desiree shot back. "Falk's lying." *Was lying.* Desiree stumbled to a halt, her eyes widening. When had Tabitha spoken to Falk?

"Oh, I know he's always been a liar, but not about this." Tabitha smiled. "Having a gun aimed at a man tends to bring out the truth."

Tom's fingers bit into Desiree's arm. "*You* shot Falk?"

"That wretched little man!" Tabitha said bitterly. "He wanted more money! Can you imagine?"

"He was blackmailing you?"

"Yes, of course he was." Tabitha sounded impatient. "That's always what the little worm did, isn't it? He took Alistair's money for years." She snorted. "As if I didn't know about Alistair's harlot! *I* was the first person Falk came to, peddling his dirty information. After all, the scoundrel had been *my* family's footman."

"Falk used to be a servant?" Desiree said, astonishment momentarily distracting her.

"Until he stole our silver tea service." Tabitha sent her a look of scorn. "No doubt you're familiar with that sort of thing."

"But, my lady, why was Falk blackmailing *you*?" Tom asked, pulling Tabitha's attention back to him.

"That's none of your business," Tabitha snapped. She frowned. "Who *are* you, anyway?"

"I'm Tom Quick, Lady Moreland," Tom said. "We met not long ago at the duke's house. I work with Con Moreland."

"The man that fool Blackstock wrote to? Of course! You must have helped her take the will."

"We don't have the will." Desiree knew it was dangerous to antagonize Tabitha, whose hand and eye remained remarkably steady and cool despite her rambling, hysterical words, and it was clear Tabitha would not believe Desiree's denial. But Desiree saw a way to keep the woman talking . . . and maybe even get them out of this situation. She went on, sending a sly note into her voice, "But if we *did* have it, why in the world would we give it to you?"

"You insolent little whore! You *will* give it to me." Tabitha waggled the gun at Desiree, her face flooding with red.

"How do you intend to make me? If you kill me, you'll never get the will. It isn't as if I had it on my person." Desiree felt Tom squeeze her arm, and she tensed, readying to move. "If you kill me, you'll never know where the will is. When it will pop up. Or where. Now, perhaps we could talk about price."

"You think you can bargain with me?" Tabitha screamed and took a step forward, extending her gun hand.

Tom shoved Desiree away with one hand, and she went with it, diving into a somersault. With the other hand, Tom slammed the front door shut and threw himself after

512

Desiree. Tabitha fired, and he heard the bullet thwack into the door as Tom leaped to his feet and followed Desiree, who was already halfway across the room, running to the side window.

Desiree vaulted through it, and Tom swung his leg over the sill and jumped out after her just as Tabitha burst into the room. He hit the ground running, and Desiree heard another gunshot crash into the window frame behind them. Tom caught up with her, and they raced forward, zigzagging to throw off Tabitha's aim.

Tabitha and her revolver were between them and their vehicle, so they took off in the opposite direction, running along the edge of the cliff. It was a terrifyingly sheer drop to the beach far below, but they had to find a way down. Up here in this flat, open countryside, they were much too easy a target. As if to prove Desiree's point, there was another blast from the gun.

The beach at least offered big rocks to hide behind, and surely a middle-aged woman would not be able to pursue them quickly, especially given the rickety state of those stairs down to the sand. More than that, Desiree had a growing certainty that she must go to the ocean. The miasma of pain and fear lay all over the area, but it had not been centered in the house they had just left. A force was drawing her like a magnet, propelling her onward. Downward. She wasn't sure whether she was being called to danger or safety, but she knew she had to reach what beckoned her.

Ahead of them, Desiree saw a cleft in the land where the edge of the cliff had fallen in, cutting a V shape into the ground. Instead of running around the newly formed edge of the cliff, Desiree ran straight toward it and flung herself flat on the ground to peer over the rim. The cave-in had created a less sheer path down to the sand and pebbles. It would have to do.

Opening her senses to guide her, Desiree turned around and slithered backward over the edge. Above her, Tom let out a groan and dropped down to the ground to climb down after her. Desiree moved as quickly as she could, finding niches and outcroppings in the rock that shimmered in her mind, and guiding Tom from below as best as she could manage. Desiree slipped and slid down a few feet before she managed to grab a limb of a scrubby bush that had somehow survived the slide of rocks and dirt. Leaves and bark scraped her palm as her hand slipped down the branch, and the bush pulled partly out of the dirt, roots dangling.

But she dug in her toes and clung to the wall, and the shrub held.

She drew a shaky breath and looked up, redirecting Tom to the right. She edged over, finding an outcropping of rock, and continued down the cliff. Above her, Tom slipped but found his footing on a boulder, sending a shower of little stones and dirt down around her. Desiree ducked her head and continued her descent.

The incline became less steep as they approached the bottom of the cliff, until they were able to stand up and run the last few feet to the flat ground. To the right, a stretch of sand ran up to an enormous black boulder that jutted out to the water's edge, blocking their path. Tom glanced in the other direction, but Desiree grabbed his hand and pulled him toward the wall of rock. "No. This way."

"But she's on the cliff. She can't shoot that far." Tom looked at the lone dark figure standing at the cliff's edge.

"Trust me."

Tom did, turning and hurrying with Desiree toward the dark wall of rock. Behind them, there was a shout, then a loud grinding noise, and they looked back. Tabitha stood in the open wooden lift, holding on to a rope as the box slowly descended the cliff.

"She's utterly mad," Tom murmured.

With luck, the rickety structure would fail. But Desiree never depended on luck. She took off running. As they approached the large boulder, they could see that a narrow strip of sand lay between the rock and the ocean. Water was lapping closer with each wave; clearly the tide was coming in, crashing around the line of large, dark stones that lay farther out.

They slipped around the rock. A narrow inlet of water cut across their path and disappeared into a wide, dark hole in the cliff.

"A cave," Desiree breathed. "This is it." She started toward the opening in the cliff, drawn inexorably toward it. The premonition that had driven her for weeks swelled inside her, stretching into the cave, pulling her with it, seeking . . . she wasn't sure what.

"Desiree?" Tom followed her. "*What* is it?"

"Where I'm meant to be." Her steps hastened as the power pulling her grew stronger, more insistent.

"You think it's better to hide here?" Tom's tone was tinged with doubt.

"I don't know. I just know it's why I came." Desiree walked into the mouth of the cave, and Tom came up beside her.

The inlet of ocean ran into the cavern, and they walked along a narrow ledge of rock beside the water. A few yards inside, the backwash of ocean ended as the stone floor began to rise, flattening out as it joined their ledge. A few feet farther on was a small pool of water. Beyond that was only looming darkness.

Tom and Desiree stopped when they reached the pool, deep in the shadows. Desiree's heart pounded and her breaths came short and fast. The darkness seemed to pulse, reaching out to wrap its cold tendrils around her, push its way into her.

"I'm scared," she whispered.

"I know." Tom released her hand and wrapped his arm around her, pulling her close. "But I'm here with you. I love you, and I intend to marry you. I'm not about to let anything take you from me."

Warmth flooded Desiree at his words, pushing back the cold fingers tangling through her. Whatever awaited her, they would face it together. She smiled up at him. "I love you."

They clung together for a moment, then Tom stepped back and dug into his pocket. "Let's light a match. See what's here. Maybe we can get far enough back she won't find us." He struck the match and lifted it up to peer into the darkness.

As Desiree turned to look back at the mouth of the cave, she glanced into the pool beside them. "Tom!" Frozen, Desiree stared down into the shallow water.

At the bottom of the pool lay two skeletons, side by side.

Their clothes were mere tatters, their flesh rotted away. One skeleton was smaller than the other, and each had a rope around its chest, binding it to a large rock. Bits of gold glinted beside the smaller frame's skull and on its neck and wrist.

Tom, following her gaze, let out a startled curse.

"It's them," Desiree whispered. "My parents." The dark turmoil that had permeated Desiree for weeks drained out of her.

The flame of the match reached Tom's fingers, and he dropped it. Immediately he pulled out another. The little flare of light revealed the same scene.

"They're both — he didn't kill her." Emotions surged in Desiree — relief, sorrow, horror, anger — all too fast and intense to separate.

"No. Somebody —" Tom's voice cut off, and he and Desiree stared at each other.

"It was her. Tabitha killed them!" Desiree's voice rang out.

"Of course I did," Tabitha said.

Desiree and Tom jumped and whirled to face Tabitha. She stood at the mouth of the cave, once again pointing a gun at them.

"You killed my mother!" Desiree took a step forward, too filled with rage to consider the danger, but Tom grabbed her arm and held her in place.

"Well, at least you're braver than she was." Tabitha switched to a high, mocking tone. " 'Oh, please don't kill me. My babies! Yes, I'll do whatever you say. I'll go down to the beach with you. Just don't kill me.' Anyone with a grain of sense would have known she was never leaving this place." Her lips twisted in scorn.

"You heartless bitch!" Desiree's hands curled into fists, and it was all she could do not to fling herself at the other woman.

"She took *everything* away from me — even this place. It was *mine.* I loved it. Papa brought me here as a child. I knew every inch of that beach. That's why Papa made it part of my dowry. But she took even that from me. Persuaded Alistair to turn it into a love nest. *My* cottage!"

"You didn't have to kill her!" Desiree shot back. "You were his wife, the mother of his heir. She could never have taken that away from you."

"Oh, yes, that's what my mother kept telling me. 'A lady turns a blind eye to her husband's squalid little affairs. Alistair is only a man, and men are so easily led. You have his name, his position, his home, his prestige.' But I *didn't* have him!" Tabitha's voice rose, her eyes flashing. "I tried. I'm a Darrington. A Moreland. I did what was expected of a lady. I ignored his peccadilloes and told myself he would come to his senses. But he didn't! He was going to leave me. Trot off to live with his hussy and their bastards. He was going to humiliate me! I could not let that stand. When I saw his letter to that Jezebel, gushing like a schoolboy about *love* and how *happy* they and their brats would be living together, I knew what had to be done. And I did it."

"I understand that you had to kill Stella," Tom said, drawing Tabitha's attention to him as he slid forward a cautious step. At the same time, he tugged at Desiree's arm, pulling her back.

Desiree knew what he was doing. He intended to position himself in front of her, to shield her when Tabitha fired. He would doubtless make a suicidal rush at Tabitha in an attempt to overpower her while Desiree ran farther back into the darkness of the cave to hide.

But Desiree wasn't about to accept that. She wasn't going to run; she was going to attack. All nerves were gone now; she was filled with a steady, determined calm.

Of the two of them, she was the one better able to bring Tabitha down. Instead of rushing at Tabitha, which was bound to fail, Desiree could dive down into a roll and come up beneath Tabitha's arm, knocking the gun from her hand, but the distance between her and Tabitha was too great. She would have to move closer.

Desiree's inner sense told her that Tabitha would follow through on her threat to kill them, but she also knew the woman didn't intend to shoot them just yet. Tabitha was insane, but she wanted that will. They could keep the woman talking while Desiree moved incrementally closer to her. It was too bad her abilities didn't include moving as quietly and unobtrusively as Wells.

Tom released his hold; he trusted her, and that warmed her. He continued to talk, drawing Tabitha's attention. "What I don't understand is why you killed Alistair, too."

"I didn't want to!" The gun wavered under the force of her emotion. "Alistair wasn't supposed to know. I was so careful. I planned it perfectly. And then that fool Falk ran to Alistair and told him!"

"Falk helped you? That's why he was blackmailing you?"

"No," Tabitha replied scornfully. "I didn't need his help. I told you, this is *my* beach. I knew about this cave. All I had to do was get her down here, right by the entrance, before I fired the gun, and it would be easy to drag her inside. I wasn't stupid enough to trust Falk. But the blasted man saw me driving the carriage, and he figured it out. He ran to tell Alistair. The man never missed a chance to make a little money."

"Ah, I see," Tom went on as Desiree moved a fraction closer. "You must have disguised yourself in the coachman's coat and hat so Stella wouldn't notice anything amiss about the carriage. Clever."

"It was easy. The little tart never even glanced at me. Just jumped into the carriage, happy as could be."

"And Alistair came down here to save Stella," Tom said, his guess more a statement than a question.

"He came to save *me*!" Tabitha cried out. "He knew what a scandal it would be, how it would hurt my reputation."

"Then why did you kill him if all he wanted was to protect you?"

"He wasn't thinking! He was hysterical. I had to stop him. I never meant to hurt

Alistair. Ever. I loved him. If only he'd been a few minutes later, everything would have been fine. I would have had him here with me all these years. We would have had a beautiful life. But we couldn't. *She* took him away from me."

Desiree could not hold back a sound at that statement, and Tabitha's eyes turned back to her, narrowing. "Stop! Don't come any closer."

"But you were cool and calm enough to cover his death up, weren't you?" Tom said quickly, drawing Tabitha's attention back to him. "You wrote that note to Mr. Paxton. You were able to copy your husband's hand-writing."

"Well enough to fool Lloyd Paxton," Tabitha snorted. She waggled the gun at Desiree, now a foot closer to her. "Don't take another step. And no more wasting time. I want that will. If you don't —"

She broke off at the sound of a man's voice, calling, "Mother! Where are you?"

"Good God. Reinforcements," Tom muttered.

Desiree's heart sank. Disarming Tabitha would be hard enough. She had no chance against two of them. She and Tom were going to die. Right here next to her parents. Well, she wasn't going down without a fight.

Surprisingly, Tabitha didn't answer. A furtive look came over her face, and she whispered, "Hush. Don't move."

Desiree had barely taken in that peculiar statement when Gregory burst into the cave.

"Mother!" Gregory stopped, staring at his mother. His hair was wildly windblown, his chest heaving. "No! What are you doing?"

"Go away, Gregory. This isn't something you should see." Tabitha raised her weapon, sighting down it.

"This isn't something you should *do*!" Gregory's shout seemed to stay her hand for the moment. "Mother, you aren't feeling well. Let me take you home. You need to rest. I'll send for Dr. McIntyre," Gregory said in a cajoling voice, moving closer to his mother.

"Stop! I'll shoot her," Tabitha snapped, and her son halted. "Go away, Gregory. Right now."

"No. Mother, this is wrong. What does it matter who has the will? We don't even know what's in it. It's not important. Give me that gun. Please. I can't let you kill two people." He stretched out his hand to Tabitha, palm up, but she made no move to do as he asked.

"We aren't her first victims," Desiree told him. "She killed our father, too."

"What?" Gregory gaped.

Tabitha started turning to him, then jerked back as Desiree threw herself forward into a roll. Tabitha's gun roared, but Desiree was beneath her line of fire and the bullet went harmlessly into the depths of the cave. Desiree jumped to her feet, only inches from Tabitha, and slammed into Tabitha's arm.

The revolver fired, the noise reverberating around the cave. Tom charged forward as Desiree sprang, and he grabbed Tabitha's arm, wresting the gun away from her. Gregory moved at the same moment, wrapping his arms around his mother and pinning her arms to her side.

Tom stepped back, gun still in his hand, eyeing the pair uncertainly.

"Mother, stop! This is madness," Gregory exclaimed as Tabitha continued to struggle, twisting and kicking in a vain attempt to get free.

"No!" Tabitha shrieked like a wounded animal. Then suddenly she sagged against her son, bursting into sobs. "No . . ." Gregory eased his grip on her as she cried, raising her hands to cover her face.

Gregory turned to Desiree and Tom as he held his mother. "I, ah, I beg your pardon. I don't know what came over Mother. Her —

her nerves have been unsettled by this whole thing about the will. I hope you will not . . . I'm sure she . . ." He ground to a halt, his face sinking into despairing lines. "What you said . . ."

"That she killed your father?"

"That can't be true." His words were automatic, without conviction. "She adored him, however little he deserved it. She's kept his bedroom a veritable shrine. She loves him."

Desiree felt a rush of pity for the man. It was clear his world had just fallen apart. In a gentle voice, she said, "It was an unhealthy sort of love. I'm sorry, but it's true."

Tom, less delicately, said, "See for yourself." He gestured toward the pool beside them.

Gregory hesitated for an instant, then dropped his arms from his mother and walked with Tom and Desiree over to the pool. Tom struck another match, holding it out over the shallow water.

"My God," Gregory whispered, shoving a hand back into his hair and staring as if struck to stone. "That's him? My father?" He lifted his eyes to Desiree.

"Yes," she said gently. "Your mother . . . um . . ." She fumbled for words and looked toward Tom in entreaty.

"She confessed," Tom finished. "She brought Desiree's mother here to kill her, but Alistair found out and came after them. So she killed him, too."

Gregory's face was blank with shock as he gazed down at the pool. "I barely remember him," he murmured. "Just that he was big and smelled of tobacco and —" He stopped, sucking in a harsh breath, and swung back around, saying, "Mother —"

Tabitha was no longer there. For an instant, all three of them stood frozen. Then Gregory broke and ran from the cave, shouting to his mother. Desiree and Tom ran after him. The beach was deserted. They skirted the huge rock, splashing through the water that now covered the former strip of sand.

There was no sign of Tabitha on this side, either. They swung around, looking in all directions. Twilight was rapidly deepening, making it difficult to see. In eerie contrast, the moon was rising early, a globe of white on the horizon.

"There!" Tom pointed to a cluster of rocks several yards out in the ocean.

The rocks thrust up in a line, like a row of blunt black teeth, tight together. Tabitha, drenched, was clambering up out of the water onto the lowest rock. She climbed up onto to the adjacent rock, then the next, as the ocean crashed and swirled all around her.

Tabitha reached the last shelf of stone. It was the longest and largest, and the sea foamed around its base, water spraying up with each crashing wave. The small dark figure went up the incline in a sort of running half crawl until she reached the very tip.

"Mother! No!" Gregory ran toward the ocean, but Tom caught him at the water's edge.

"No," Tom told Gregory, holding him back. "You'd never reach her in time. You'd only kill yourself trying." Desiree joined them, taking Gregory's other arm in a firm grip.

But Gregory was no longer trying to pull out of Tom's grasp. He simply stood, staring in horror, and whispered, "Mother . . ."

Tabitha reached the top of the rock and stood poised there for a moment, arms spread, looking out across the dark gray water. She turned toward them, her arms still out wide, before she fell backward into the sea.

CHAPTER THIRTY-FIVE

For a long moment, they stood, staring out to where Tabitha had disappeared. Desiree turned to Gregory. His face was desolate, and he dropped suddenly to his knees, as if all energy had drained out of him.

"My God," he said quietly and rested back on his heels, his hands loosely on his thighs. For a moment, he simply sat, gazing out as darkness gathered around them.

Desiree looked from him to Tom, and Tom shrugged, clearly not knowing what to do any more than she did. Desiree knelt beside Gregory, putting her hand on his back. Gregory turned his head toward her, his gaze raw with pain. "She loved him more than anything else in the world. More than anyone."

It seemed a very sad statement from a son, but Desiree said only, "I'm sure she did."

"I can't believe she . . ." He trailed off.

Tom squatted down on Gregory's other

side. "Come on, mate, we have to go."

"Yes, of course." Gregory drew a deep breath and pulled his face back into an approximation of its usual reserved state. "You're right. I have to . . . there are things one must do."

Desiree took his arm, and Gregory glanced at her in surprise. She wasn't sure if he was startled by the gesture of support or had simply forgotten she was there. Or perhaps he was offended by the familiarity. She didn't know; he was related to her, but she had no idea who he really was. He'd saved them, though, and he was in obvious pain. And he was her brother.

They took the stairs to the top of the cliff, none of them interested in trying the ancient lift. The stairs were as bad as they appeared, but Gregory, having taken the stairs down to the beach, warned them of this broken step or that loose railing. On firm ground again, they walked to the horses. Gregory had simply dropped the reins when he arrived, but the horse hadn't wandered off and was grazing beside his mother's team.

Gregory picked up the dangling reins and stood looking at the carriage. "I don't know what to do with that blasted carriage. I'd like to leave it here to rot. She would never hear of getting a different one. Because

Alistair bought it in New York City on their honeymoon."

In the end, he decided to tie his horse to the back of the carriage, and they drove back to Weymouth in a gloomy procession. It seemed surreal to sign into the hotel room, such a mundane task, after all that had just happened. But Desiree felt too numb and exhausted to do anything else. Obviously, Gregory, signing in after them, felt the same way. The clerk looked askance at their bedraggled appearance and asked for his money up front, but he gave them rooms.

Gregory gave Tom and Desiree a nod and turned away. He had managed to recapture the controlled face of a proper English gentleman, but Desiree knew that inside him emotions were boiling, and he was simply hoping to get to his room before he broke down.

"Poor man," she murmured, watching him walk down the corridor. "His whole life has been turned upside down. His whole world, really."

Tom nodded as he opened the door to their room. "I'd not want to be him right now. I'd rather not know who my mother is than learn she was a murderer."

As he closed the door behind them, Desiree went into his arms. And here, alone, safe, everything that had happened crashed in on her. She began to cry, suddenly weak and trembling, and unable to stop. She wrapped her arms tightly around him, her hands clenching in his jacket.

Tom bent his head to hers, his arms curving around her, murmuring soft words of comfort. "It will be all right, love. I promise."

Her sobs quieted, but still she clung to him. "I know." She drew a shaky breath. "It's silly, really. I never knew them. But to see them lying there like that! I'm not even sure what I feel! All this time that I've been looking for them, angry and hurt that they abandoned us, they were dead, hidden in that cave. I've found them and lost them all at once. I hardly know whether to be happy or sad."

"I'm sure you're both." Tom's lips brushed her hair. "But you found what you needed to."

"Yes, that awful feeling is gone."

"Good."

Desiree continued to lean against him, content in his arms, soothed by his hand as he stroked her back. Sheltered in his love. Now a different emotion rose in her. Softly she asked, "Did you mean it?"

"Mean what?"

Desiree leaned back to look into his face. "When you said you loved me."

He looked startled. "Of course I meant it."

"I — I wasn't sure. I thought it might have been something you said in the heat of the moment. To make me feel better."

"I hope it made you feel better." Tom's lips curved up. "But I said it because it was true. I love you. I want to marry you. These days with you have been the happiest moments of my life."

"Even though we've been running from attackers half the time?" Desiree teased, warmth swelling in her chest.

"Yes. Even with the mad killers." Tom caressed her cheek. "I love you. I've never said that to anyone in my whole life. Maybe that's why I tried so hard to keep you away. I knew if I let you in, I wouldn't ever be able to let you go. That if you left, there'd be this hole inside me that nothing else could fill."

"I'm not going to leave." Desiree stood on tiptoe and kissed him softly. "I love you, and it's just as deep, just as strong. I know that you are the only man I'll ever love."

He kissed her again, his arms wrapping around her, and Desiree melted into him.

The sweet kiss turned into something much hotter, and Desiree pressed up into him, hunger flaring in her. She had thought that she was too tired and drained to do anything but immediately tumble into bed and go to sleep. But now, with Tom's mouth on hers, her weariness was gone. His love, his passion filled up all the empty spaces inside her, chasing away sorrow.

They undressed quickly, coming together in a storm of desire. Almost desperately, they kissed and caressed, fierce in their hunger. Desiree's nails dug into his back, and she whispered, "Now. Take me now."

Tom did as she asked, thrusting deep within her, each hard, deep stroke sending Desiree deeper and deeper into passion until the pleasure seemed almost too much to bear. With a cry, she crested, and he came with her, joined in fire.

Slowly, he relaxed against her, murmuring in her ear. "My love."

Desiree slid her hand over the slick skin of his back. The past didn't matter; she had all she needed here and now. Pressing her lips softly against his shoulder, she answered, "My love."

Tom and Desiree were in the public dining room the next morning, eating breakfast, when Gregory strode into the room. Seeing them, he came to a stop, then walked over to their table. Desiree had the feeling he'd had to force himself to do so.

Physically, Gregory looked like himself. His expression was cool and calm, with just a hint of hauteur. His cravat was perfectly tied, his black boots polished to a gleam. But up close, his eyes still carried the remains of the lost and grieving man from last night.

He greeted them politely, and when Desiree invited him to join them, he hesitated only a barely discernible instant before he sat down at their table. "I must beg your pardon again for last night," he said in a stilted voice. "I wanted as well to assure you that I had no part in it. I didn't know what Mother was doing. It was reprehensibly careless of me. I should have paid more attention. I . . . I assume that my father was indeed, um, that is, that we are related."

"Yes, I guess we are." Desiree wasn't sure what to say. She couldn't imagine that this model of an English nobleman across from her wanted to get to know his embarrassing half siblings, but she couldn't keep from trying to give him some comfort. "You needn't keep apologizing for Lady Moreland. It is good of you, and I believe you.

And, trust me, we are grateful that you came to our rescue."

"I'm glad I got there in time," Gregory responded. "I only wish I'd realized sooner . . ."

"How did you know to come here?" Tom asked.

"I had no idea what she was up to — it's been that way all my life, apparently. Mother has been acting strangely ever since I told her I was going to have my father declared dead. She was most upset. But I had to, you see. I am engaged now. We couldn't go on forever in this sort of limbo. But when our attorney told us that his father had sent off an envelope to the Moreland businessman, Mother became hysterical. I thought it was because of —" He glanced at Desiree. "Well, you know."

"Because she told you we were trying to cheat you."

Gregory nodded, a little shamefacedly. "That must have been a lie, too — telling me that Alistair wasn't your father."

"Yes. The body lying beside him is my mother."

"I . . ." He lowered his gaze. "I'm sorry. I don't know what to say."

"It's not your fault. Go on."

He nodded gratefully and said, "Last

night, Mother received some sort of note. She was furious, absolutely beside herself. I couldn't get her to tell me why. She went up to her room and refused to talk to me, so I went out. I had a commitment, you see, and I didn't realize . . ."

"You couldn't have known what would happen," Desiree said. Tom gave her a sardonic look, but she ignored him. Obviously, Gregory should have paid more attention to what his mother was doing. After all, he'd had to whisk the woman away the afternoon she accosted Desiree. But it must be hard for anyone, let alone a proud aristocrat, to accept that one's mother was stark staring mad.

Gregory continued, "This morning, right after I awoke, I looked out the window, and I saw Mother coming into the house. At that hour! So I dressed and went to talk to her, but she wasn't in her room. Nor was she downstairs. Then the coachman came to me and told me she had taken the carriage and was driving to Sea Gift. By herself. She enjoyed driving and often did so at the country house, but to drive all that way! It alarmed me, and I could see that the coachman was quite worried, so I questioned him further.

"He confessed everything to me. How she

would sit outside your house at night for hours. She even had him follow you one day. Then she'd hired some ruffians to 'scare you off.' The man was very loyal to her, you see, came with her when they married, but finally he became so concerned about her he had to tell me. He wasn't certain what she was about to do, but he knew it involved you and Sea Gift, and he knew she had her father's revolver with her." Gregory stopped and shrugged. "I could scarcely believe it. But I realized it was urgent, so I went after her."

"We're glad you did," Tom assured him. Another awkward silence fell. Tom cleared his throat and said, "We're returning to London this morning. Will you be going there, as well?"

Gregory shook his head. "I'll stay, at least a few days. I'm hiring some of the locals from Redham to sail out and see if they can find her. Then, of course, there's . . . that cave. I don't even know how to go about that. Um, I suppose the first thing I must do is go to the police. I can't imagine what people will say about Mother. God, what a nightmare." His voice roughened, and he suddenly seemed to take great interest in a small scar on the table. Sliding his thumbnail over it, he went on quietly, "I thought all my life that my father abandoned me."

Desiree reached out and covered his hand with hers, and he raised his head, surprised. She suspected he thought she was being terribly inappropriate. But Gregory would just have to deal with it. "I know. I understand exactly what you mean."

"Yes. I guess you do. I'm sorry. I must seem quite selfish and shallow, thinking about gossip at a time like this. It's just that Mother was always so afraid of scandal, so worried about her name." He let out a short, harsh laugh. "I guess she had every reason to be afraid, given what she'd done."

"We three are the only ones who know what happened yesterday," Desiree said significantly.

Tom added, "I have no reason to spread this story around. Nor will the Morelands."

"Nor the Malones," Desiree added.

Gregory stared. "But . . . I mean, after what she did . . ."

"Lady Moreland's dead. There's no one to charge," Tom said. "What good would it do?"

"I hate that she took my parents from me," Desiree told him. "I have no liking for her. But he was *my* father, too, and I don't want the Moreland name dragged through the mud. No one in either of our families would like that."

"The police will have to be told," Tom said. "I mean, you can't just leave them there."

"God, no," Gregory said in a horrified voice.

Desiree shuddered at the thought of the two bodies remaining in their watery grave. "But while you must tell them, I think this could all be dealt with quietly. My brother could help."

"The gambler?" Gregory's eyebrows shot up. "How?"

"Brock's not a gambler — he owns gambling clubs," Desiree corrected. "But I'm not talking about him. I mean my twin, Wells. You met him the day you were at my house."

A little to Desiree's surprise, she saw a twitch of amusement at the corner of Gregory's mouth. "That's a diplomatic way to describe it. I don't understand. How can he help?"

"He knows people who can have things handled quietly."

"You mean criminals?"

Desiree chuckled. "No. People who are with the government. Although perhaps the two aren't so different."

Gregory flushed. "I didn't mean, that is . . ."

Desiree took pity on his floundering. "Lord Moreland, I am aware that you don't know us and are inclined to think that the Malones are a bad lot and out to hurt you. It's true that we are illegitimate, and we come from the sort of people you would normally have nothing to do with. I'll admit that we appear odd to just about every layer of society. But we aren't sinister. And we have no desire to hurt you or the Moreland family."

"Again, I must beg your pardon," he replied stiffly. "I didn't mean to insult you. I just don't know — well, at the moment, I don't know much of anything. If your brother is willing to help, I would greatly appreciate it. Thank you." He started to rise, but Desiree tugged at the sleeve of his jacket.

"No. Sit down. I have something else to tell you."

"Very well." Gregory looked at her warily.

"I don't have this will that everyone has been talking about," Desiree told him.

"It never arrived at our office," Tom added. "Or anywhere else that we can find. We don't know where it is."

"But if it turns up someday, I will give it

to you," Desiree promised. "You needn't fear we're going to create trouble for you. We don't care about Alistair Moreland's estate. We have ample money. We have no interest in causing scandal. And we're quite happy to be merely Malones."

Gregory nodded and thanked her, sat for another awkward moment, then took his leave. Desiree, watching him walk off, said, "Do you think he believed me?"

"Who knows? It's hard to believe he's actually a Moreland."

"Well, you have to consider who his mother was," Desiree pointed out. "You and I know what it's like to not have a mother. But it might be even worse to have the *wrong* mother."

When Desiree and Tom arrived at the Moreland house that evening, they found not only all the Morelands awaiting them but also Desiree's brothers and Sid Upton. Desiree went immediately to Sid, taking his hand in hers and saying, "I'm so glad to see you here."

"Nothing could have stopped me," the old man said with a grin. "I've been waiting twenty-eight years to find out what happened."

"It's not a happy tale," Desiree said, sorrow in her voice.

"I thought as much. But, still, it's good to know."

Desiree turned to her brothers, standing beside Sid. "I'm surprised to see you here, Brock. Did Wells have to drag you?"

"As if he could," Brock retorted. "No. I came because I wanted to hear what happened."

"Plus, it's rather difficult to tell the duchess no," Wells added with a grin.

"She invited you in person?" Desiree asked.

Brock nodded. "She came right into the casino this morning. Said she'd always wanted to see the inside of one."

The duchess herself swept up to them at that point and demonstrated her persuasiveness by pulling Desiree and Tom to the center to tell their story.

Everyone knew how things began, having heard it the other night at dinner, so Desiree and Tom had only to relate the events of the day before. There was a moment of stunned silence when they finished.

"Well," the duchess said finally. "I never liked Tabitha, but I would never have thought she was a murderer."

"I understand why Tabitha killed Stella, then had to get rid of Alistair when he interfered," Con said. "Falk was blackmailing her, so she killed him, too. But I don't understand why she pretended that her husband had run off with his mistress. I mean, that created the sort of scandal she wanted to avoid."

"I don't think she intended to reveal all that at first," Tom told him. "She planned to make Stella disappear, and she figured no one would look for Stella, let alone suspect Tabitha. But when she had to kill Alistair as well, she had to somehow explain his absence. There weren't many options."

"However much she hated it, it would have been the best choice," Kyria put in. "The scandal of his infidelity kept people talking about *that* instead of wondering why Alistair had disappeared and where he'd gone. Plus, it gave Tabitha a reason not to report him missing to the police. People would have been reluctant to ask her direct questions about the details. Society gossiped about it, but everyone would have regarded her as the wounded party. They helped her keep it hushed up officially."

"Hide her secret inside another, less scandalous secret." Con nodded. "Makes sense."

"But what did this Pax chap have to do with anything?" Theo asked. "And why was Tabitha so intent on killing Desiree?"

"I don't think Pax had anything to do with Tabitha's schemes," Tom said. "He wanted the will, and that's all. His cuff links were with Alistair's jewelry, and I suppose Tabitha must have paid the coachman with them."

"I'm not sure Tabitha set out to kill me," Desiree said. "I think she wanted only to find that envelope. She was worried about what the will might reveal and what the lawyer said in the letter. She was afraid Alistair had given us money, I suppose, which would take something from her son. And she probably thought we were going to blackmail her. After all, Falk had been doing that for years. But then, when we kept digging, Tabitha must have begun to fear that we would discover what she'd done. Especially after we went to the cottage."

"What I wonder is how Tabitha was able to carry them to that cave," the duke said with unaccustomed practicality.

"From what she told us, she forced Desiree's mother to go down to the beach near the cave, and when Alistair tried to rescue Stella, Lady Tabitha shot him, too," Tom replied. "So she didn't have to drag the bodies far, and if the tide was in, she could have floated them on top of the water, perhaps. I think that would have made it easier."

"Tabitha wasn't small, and I imagine she was rather strong, given all that riding," the duchess said.

"Aunt Wilhemina said one of Tabitha's hobbies was archery," Lilah added.

At that moment, there was the sound of footsteps in the hall, and a man and woman Desiree didn't recognize walked briskly into the room. From the looks of the man, Desiree suspected he was another Moreland.

"Reed!" Emmeline stood up, beaming, and went to hug him, confirming Desiree's guess. She turned to hug the woman. "Anna, dearest. Welcome."

The duke shook his son's hand. "Reed, my boy, I didn't realize you were coming to visit." He looked at his wife. "Did I?"

"No, dearest, we hadn't the slightest idea."

"Anna had one of her misgivings yesterday," Reed said. "It was very vague, but she was sure it was something to do with the Morelands. And I needed to come to London anyway." He opened the valise he carried and pulled out a large envelope. "It's the most peculiar thing. Who in the world are the Malones?"

CHAPTER THIRTY-SIX

"You!" Tom exclaimed. "It was you. Of course! Why didn't I think of that? The Moreland businessman, isn't that what Gregory said?"

"Lord, yes." Con let out a laugh and came forward to shake his brother's hand. "Blackstock didn't mean our office — he meant the Moreland who handles the Moreland business affairs. Of course he'd send it to you. Everyone misunderstood."

"Well, I still don't understand," Reed said in a disgruntled tone. "I've had a few matters I've worked on with Mr. Blackstock about Alistair's interest in the Moreland estates — the man created quite a mess when he ran off. But I've never heard of these beneficiaries named Malone. It's very peculiar."

"So there was a new will," Tom said.

"No. Well, yes, there was a will written not long before Alistair left, but that's the standard sort of thing, all to Gregory, et cetera. Except for a clause about a piece of land returning to someone named Paxton. But it's the trust I'm talking about, the one for a woman and three children named Malone."

The entire group of Morelands turned to Desiree and her brothers. Reed followed their gazes. "Oh! I say, I'm terribly sorry. I didn't realize — pardon me for talking family business."

"Reed, these are the Malones," Tom said. "They're Alistair's . . . other family."

It was Reed's turn to be speechless. After a long silence, he said, "I see."

"I doubt that," Con laughed. "But let me introduce you to the Magnificent Malones — Miss Desiree Malone. Mr. Wells Malone. And Mr. Brock Malone."

Reed's brow cleared. "You own the Farrington Club. And one of the music halls."

"Yes," Brock agreed, still looking stunned. "Did you say three children?"

"Yes. Those are the given names. Alistair set up a trust for the three of you years ago — it must have been a few months before he left. Am I to assume that you didn't know about it?"

"No."

Reed frowned. "That was the impression I

received from Blackstock. I don't know why he concealed it. It was a terrible dereliction of duty on his part."

"What was?" Theo asked. "Good God, Reed, get to the point. We don't know what you're talking about."

"The trust," Reed replied. "The thing has been in effect for years and years, ever since Alistair signed it. But as best I can tell from his letter, Blackstock never told anyone about it. Never paid out anything. He invested the principal and let it sit there. His letter rambled on about not wanting to die with this sin on his conscience, which is certainly understandable. Apparently, after Alistair ran off, Blackstock didn't want to tell anyone about the trust because of the distress it would cause Lady Tabitha and Gregory."

"There you are." Uncle Bellard beamed. "I didn't think Alistair was that shallow a young man. He *did* provide for his children, or, well, he did his best to."

"It was for your care, entirely separate from Alistair's estate," Reed told the Malones. "It made — I mean, it would have made you and your mother independent."

Tears filled Desiree's eyes, and she turned to Tom, reaching out for his hand. "This is so . . ."

"I'm sorry." Reed looked taken aback. "I'm sure it must be distressing to hear of this miscarriage of duty. I shouldn't have sprung it on you in that way."

"No." Desiree smiled at him, blinking away her tears. "It's wonderful. It's the best thing we could have heard." She turned toward Brock. "You see. Our father did care for you."

"This can't be right," Brock insisted. He turned to Reed. "I'm not Alistair's child. Only Wells and Desiree are. I was born years before he met my mother."

"Well, um . . ." Reed shrugged. "That's not what the trust says. In the letter, Blackstock called all three of you Alistair's natural children. It says so in the trust agreement, as well." Reed pulled a document out of the envelope and handed it to Brock.

As Brock studied it, Uncle Bellard said, "It wouldn't be impossible, you know. Alistair wanted to marry a young woman, but had to marry Tabitha instead to avoid the scandal. Perhaps that young woman was Stella Malone. And perhaps she bore him a son. There's nothing to say Alistair didn't go back to the same woman years later. When were you born?"

"December of 1858," Brock answered, looking up from the document in his hand.

"There you are. Alistair was married in . . ." Bellard cast his eyes upward, seeming to search some list in his head. "Yes, definitely 1858. I believe the wedding was May or June. So he was married to Tabitha after March, which would, um, be the pertinent date regarding your birth." Bellard blushed.

"But . . . I . . . ." Brock turned to his siblings. "Why wouldn't they have told me if that was the case?"

"I don't know. Perhaps because our mother had already told you that polite fiction about your 'heroic' father who died. Maybe she wanted to wait until you were older so you'd understand," Desiree suggested.

"I don't think you can deny it, Brock," Wells put in, grinning. "Look around you — you look more like these people than either Desiree or I. That's why our father gave you his ring. It wasn't to hold for me. It was because *you* were Alistair's son. His first son."

Sometime during the hubbub that followed, Desiree took Tom's hand and pulled him aside. "I very much like my new family, but right now, I think I'd enjoy a bit of peace and quiet."

He smiled and they slipped out of the room and walked through the house to the terrace in the rear. Desiree leaned against Tom, and he slid his arm around her shoulders and for a long moment they simply stood, gazing out at the lovely grounds and drinking in the tranquility of the place.

"It's hard to believe it's all over," Tom said.

"Yes. I can't imagine what we'll do now," Desiree replied lightly. She cut her eyes over at Tom, a suggestive smile playing on her lips. "Although I can think of a few things we could do to occupy our time."

Tom's pulse quickened, and he turned toward her, his voice thickening with desire. "Miss Malone! What an indelicate thing to say."

Desiree widened her eyes. "Why, Mr. Quick, your mind goes to the most shocking places. I meant planning our wedding."

Tom tightened all over, and his hand slid from her. "Desiree . . ."

"What? Don't tell me you plan to jilt me." Her eyes danced. "You should remember I have two brothers."

"Of course not. But we cannot — Desiree, I can't ask you to marry me *now*." He reminded himself that he had to be practical. Desiree, of course, would charge ahead, ignoring any problems.

"If you are planning to bring up that nonsense about me being a Moreland, I shall scream."

"No. It's not that. I meant we have to wait . . . if you're willing, that is. I'm not yet in a position — I haven't saved enough for a house for us. I can't ask you to live in my flat above the agency."

"I rather like your flat. I have very pleasant memories of it." Desiree put her hands on his arms, moving closer, and went up on tiptoe to brush her lips against his.

Everything in him quivered. "Desiree, you're trying to distract me."

"Am I succeeding?"

"Yes." He bent his head to kiss her more thoroughly, one hand curving around the nape of her neck. When at last they broke their kiss, he leaned his forehead against Desiree's, unable to keep his thumb and fingers from moving up and down her neck in a slow, rhythmic caress. "But it doesn't change the facts."

"I would live quite happily with you above the agency . . . though I fear we would go hungry, as I have little knowledge of saucepans." Desiree took a half step back to smile up into his face.

"That could be a problem, since I don't, either." Tom had to smile even as he shook his head. His insides were in a turmoil, torn between love and regret, desire and pride. "Desiree, I love you more than life itself, and I know it's wrong of me to ask you to wait. But —"

"Then it's fortunate, is it not, that I happen to be buying a house?"

"What?"

"A narrow gray house with red shutters."

He gaped at her. "But — Desiree, I am *not* going to live on your brother's largesse."

"Oh, for pity's sake. Of all the pigheaded, antiquated notions!" She took a step back, planting her fists on her hips and glaring. "It is *my* house. Brock isn't buying it. I asked Brock to inquire about it for me because he knows real estate far better than I. But *I* am the one who's going to buy it. I told you — I have my own money. I earned it myself with years of playing at Farrington Club. And if you are going to tell me that you cannot accept the idea of a woman contributing to a marriage, of a wife working and being an equal partner, then . . . then I will tell the duchess!"

Tom began to laugh, relief and joy sweeping through him, along with the realization that he was being enormously foolish. "You're right. I am pigheaded, and the duchess would ring a peal over my head for it." He moved forward, smiling down into her face. "I'm being an idiot."

"You certainly are." But to his relief, Desiree gave up her pugnacious pose and closed the remaining gap between them. "But for some reason, I love you anyway."

"I think —" Tom paused, this admission taking some effort. "I'm scared, Desiree. You're all that I could want and more. And I'm afraid of grabbing for everything I've dreamed of and finding only air."

"Oh, Tom . . . my love." Desiree reached up to cup his face in her hands. "I'm scared, too. Believe me, I know the fear of reaching out and finding only air. What you have to do is trust your partner. I trust you. Do you trust me?"

"With my life." Tom kissed her, and Desiree flung her arms around him, holding on with all her strength. After a very long time, he raised his head and looked down at her quizzically. "Did you really buy my house?"

"I'm in the process. I knew I would work you around to seeing it my way sooner or later."

He shook his head in mock chagrin. "I'm never going to win an argument with you, am I?"

"No." Desiree grinned. "Thinking of changing your mind?"

"No." He kissed her lightly. "As long as I'm with you, even the losses are wins."

ABOUT THE AUTHOR

Candace Camp is a *New York Times* best-selling author of over sixty novels of contemporary and historical romance. She grew up in Texas in a newspaper family, which explains her love of writing, but she earned a law degree and practiced law before making the decision to write full-time. She has received several writing awards, including the RT Book Reviews Lifetime Achievement Award for Western Romances. Visit her at www.candace-camp.com.